Praise for
GRANDMOTHER SPIDER
and other CHARLIE MOON mysteries

"Doss' best yet, smoothly weaving the folkways of shaman Daisy Perika with the world-wise know-how of her nephew, Southern Ute Acting Chief of Police Charlie Moon . . . an amusing web with a pattern we can't discern until the very end. Ya gotta love Charlie . . . Doss has a ton of fun revealing the truth, and so will the reader."

Denver Rocky Mountain News

"Doss' knowledge of Ute mysticism and sense of humor play a big role in this story, and readers will find themselves propelled by fast-paced action and intriguing characters. The end of the book is especially interesting."

Indianapolis Star

"Definitely the best. With economy of words, Doss brings the new reader into his series and up to speed. Then he proceeds to tangle him in a carefully constructed web . . . GRANDMOTHER SPIDER is crafted like a fine 24-jewel Swiss timepiece."

Santa Fe New Mexican

"James D. Doss could be accused of poaching in Tony Hillerman territory . . . But Doss mixes mysticism and murder with his own unmistakable touch."

Orlando Sentinel

The Shaman Mysteries by
James D. Doss

THE SHAMAN'S GAME
THE SHAMAN SINGS
THE SHAMAN LAUGHS
THE SHAMAN'S BONES
THE NIGHT VISITOR
GRANDMOTHER SPIDER
WHITE SHELL WOMAN

JAMES D. DOSS

A CHARLIE MOON MYSTERY
GRANDMOTHER SPIDER

AVON BOOKS
An Imprint of HarperCollinsPublishers

This is a work of fiction. Names, characters, places, and incidents are products of the author's imagination or are used fictitiously and are not to be construed as real. Any resemblance to actual events, locales, organizations, or persons, living or dead, is entirely coincidental.

AVON BOOKS
An Imprint of HarperCollins*Publishers*
10 East 53rd Street
New York, New York 10022-5299

Copyright © 2001 by James D. Doss
ISBN: 0-380-80394-1
www.avonbooks.com

First Avon Books paperback printing: December 2001
First William Morrow hardcover printing: January 2001

Avon Trademark Reg. U.S. Pat. Off. and in Other Countries, Marca Registrada, Hecho en U.S.A.
HarperCollins ® is a trademark of HarperCollins Publishers Inc.

Printed in the U.S.A.

10 9 8 7 6

For

Fr. Richard Godbold
Fr. Colin Kelly
Louise Weiss

. . .

At Trinity-on-the-Hill, Los Alamos

Little Miss Muffet
Sat on a tuffet,
Eating some curds and whey.
Along came a spider,
And sat down beside her,
And frightened Miss Muffet away.

—"Little Miss Muffet"

1

TO THE EAST, an iridescent rainbow arches shimmeringly over misted mountains. In the west, the crimson sun descends through opalescent clouds. Far above—unbound by the fetters of this world—a lone hawk floats serenely. Having gathered perfume, the evening breeze whispers sweetly of blushing flowers. How glorious, these hours.

But wait.

The translucent mask of day slips away. At twilight's cue, the bright masquerade ends . . . the darkling's dance begins. In the black heavens are fiery omens. On the flinty field, sheep of the flock are scattered in terror. And where the icy water drips . . . living flesh is cleaved from bone.

In this wilderness of windswept sandstone mesas and deep, cool canyons, dusk approaches with tremulous sighs and elusive whispers. As the sun blushes scarlet, a misty breath of twilight is exhaled from the mouth of *Cañon del Espíritu*. A triad of shadowy fingers reach out from Three Sisters Mesa, slipping stealthily along the piñon-studded ridge toward the isolated home. As if to grasp and crush the Ute elder's modest dwelling.

Were it not for the child and her black cat—and the wandering ghosts who have not found that elusive exit from Middle World—the old woman would be quite lonely. But loneliness is banished by activity. So, from long habit, she keeps busy. In her small kitchen, Daisy Perika fusses about the propane stove, preparing supper for two. She stirs a bubbling pot of green chili stew. Moreover, strong coffee is brewing. And trouble.

The girl sits cross-legged on the kitchen floor with a tattered schoolbook in her lap. Sarah Frank's frown reflects the student's painful concentration and the child's instinctive distaste for the subject at hand. Her assignment is to study the structure of arachnids, of the order Araneae. These terrifying, alien creatures are the stuff of nightmares. Eight hooked legs, a pair of poison fangs, bulging black eyes. Some spin a sticky web to ensnare poor butterfly. Other members of this sinister clan hide in a dark pit under a cunningly crafted trapdoor, waiting to leap out and snatch pretty ladybug. How perfectly horrible.

At this very moment, across the cracked linoleum . . . *along came a spider*. And sat down. Besider.

Poor, unfortunate, arachnid (of the order Araneae). His spongy brain could have rested comfortably on the tip of a sharp pin. Life is hard enough for all God's creatures. It is particularly difficult for those who are unwilling—or unable—to think.

Sarah spied the ugly thing within a handbreadth of her leg. The benefits of a modern education were not lost on her. Without an instant's hesitation, she smacked the creature with the schoolbook.

Daisy Perika—though mildly startled by this sudden noise—did not bother to look over her shoulder. "What was that?"

Sarah recalled the Ute elder's warning about killing spiders. "Just a bug," she muttered.

"Oh." The old woman gave the thick brown broth a double stir, then touched the spoon to her tongue. Needed just another dab of salt . . . half a smidgen of black pepper.

The child smiled at the memory of the last time she had killed one of these awful creatures. It had been a long time ago—on one of their walks in *Cañon del Espíritu*. Daisy had warned her that if you murder a spider, members of its family—the Spider People—would come that very night, climb into your bed—and bite you! The impressionable little girl, only six at the time, had been terrified by this threat. But the shaman, as usual, had a solution. At Daisy's instruction, Sarah had used a stick to draw a circle in the dust around the dead spider. And the Ute-Papago child had said these words to the spider's spirit:

"A Navajo killed you. Send your family to bite the Navajos."

Sure enough, the falsehood worked. The vengeful eight-legged creatures had stayed away from her bed. But had the spider's family searched out an innocent Navajo girl—and bit her a thousand times? The child had never managed to dismiss this troubling image from her mind.

Now Sarah is nine years old. And very grown-up. Moreover, she is well educated. She knows that spiders do not have hateful spirits or avenging families. So she does not bother to draw an imaginary circle on the cracked linoleum around the corpse of the reprehensible creature, or to verbally direct the terrible vengeance of the Spider People on the Navajo nation . . . which has troubles enough.

The old woman did not look away from her duties at the propane stove. Her mouth wrinkled into a wry smile. "So, after all my warnings—you killed another spider?"

As if Daisy Perika had an eye in the back of her head, Sarah nodded.

The old woman—as if she could see the doleful nod—shook her head wearily. She turned down the burner under the bubbling stew. "Shouldn't have done that."

Sarah—though she did not believe half the old woman's warnings—was a cautious little soul. And was already considering cheap repentance. "I could draw the circle around it—and say the words."

Daisy snorted. "Too late."

The child shrugged.

"Tonight," the old woman muttered darkly, "she'll be on the prowl. And have her revenge."

Sarah tended to stutter when she was anxious. "Wh-wh-who . . . ?"

Daisy cupped her hand by her ear. "What was that? Did I hear a hoot owl?"

The child licked her lips and tried again. "Who'll be on the prowl?"

The Ute elder turned, fixed the little girl with a stern look. "*Kagu-ci Mukwa-pi.* Now that you've killed *two* of her clan, she'll *have* to come out and bite somebody."

"What's a kagu . . ."

"Grandmother Spider," Daisy said with a shudder. "She's head honcho of all the Spider People. She makes a web of fine blue silk. Each strand is as fine as a hair on your head, but old Grandmother can tie up a full-grown horse so tight that it can't flick a whisker while she puts the bite on him."

This is just another of the old woman's silly stories. Sarah attempted a knowing smirk, but her mouth felt oddly stiff. Furthermore, she could not deny her curiosity. "Is there a Grandfather Spider too?"

Daisy was pleased with this astute question. "Used to be there was a *Kunuu-ci Mikwa-pi*," the Ute elder said with an air of regret. "Until one time about a thousand or so years ago. My great-uncle Cecil Kiawot told me that . . ." She hesitated. "But I don't think you're old enough to hear such a scary story."

This was maddening. "What happened?"

The Ute elder allowed an appropriate silence to pass before she began. "Uncle Cecil, he said Grandpa got crosswise of old Grandmother. One morning—it was during the Moon of Dead Leaves Falling, not long after the first hard frost. They was having a big argument over who'd killed the most Navajo that past summer. The old fella should've known better than to argue with his wife. Grandmother Spider don't never like to hear no sassy back talk, 'specially when she's not feelin' well. And it was her bad time of the month—she had the belly cramps and a throbbin' headache that made all six of her eyes feel like they'd pop right outta her head. But her husband, he just kept at it. Swore he'd fanged at least 'leven dozen Navajo, and claimed she hadn't killed half as many. She finally got bone tired of hearin' his tongue flappin'. She'd had enough." Daisy paused.

Sarah really didn't want to know. "So what'd she do?"

"What a spider-woman always does. First, she bit her husband's head off. Then she fanged him and sucked all the spider-juices outta his body."

The child was shocked into silence.

Daisy was on a roll. "Next morning, she dusted Grandfather Spider with flour, fried him in bear grease, and had him for breakfast." Daisy licked her lips. "Mmmmm."

Sarah made an awful face. "She *ate* him?"

The old woman ladled stew from the blackened saucepan into a crockery bowl. "That's the way of the Spider People. One of their women gobbles up her husband like you'd eat an apple, then she goes out and looks for another fella." Daisy stole a quick glance at the child, who was looking queasy. "Sure as it rains in April, old *Kagu-ci Mukwa-pi* will come outta her home tonight."

"What kind of home? Does she have a big web in some—"

"She's always lived in a deep, dark cave."

"If it's dark, how does she *see*?"

"Old Grandma, she has fire in her mouth. When she needs some light, she just yawns."

The child thought this doubtful. "Fire in her mouth . . . but that'd *hurt*."

Daisy nodded. "I expect it does hurt some, but Grandmother Spider don't much care. She's tough as boiled jackrabbit."

"Where is her cave?"

"Not too far from here." Daisy pointed the dripping ladle southward. "It goes way back under a big sandstone bluff; used to open up right on the banks of the San Juan. Then the *matukach* dammed the river to make Navajo Lake. Well, they say old Grandmother was set in her ways—she decided not to move. Ever since then, the door to her home has been under the waters." Daisy got a carton of milk from the refrigerator. "Yes, I've got a feelin' she'll come out tonight. And she won't go back till she's tasted blood!"

Sarah's hands and feet began to tingle unpleasantly, just like when she stood near the edge of the cliff on Three Sisters Mesa and thought about how scary it would be to fall to the very bottom of *Cañon del Espíritu*. She tried to sound nonchalant. "*Whose* blood?"

The crafty old woman shrugged. "When *Kagu-ci Mukwa-pi* is on the prowl, you can never tell who'll feel the sting of her fangs. You remember my cousin, Gorman Sweetwater?"

Sarah nodded. Gorman—who drove a rickety old pickup—occasionally dropped by Daisy's home at mealtime and helped himself to whatever food was on the table. He was always on his way to tend to his white-faced cattle in the Canyon of the Spirits. And half the time, he was silly-drunk.

Daisy Perika lowered her voice as if someone might overhear their conversation. "Just nineteen years ago last October, Grandmother Spider stole one of Gorman's Hereford steers right outta the canyon—not half a mile from my house. A deer hunter found the animal way up a pine tree. Wedged up real tight between the limbs."

Sarah frowned at this unlikely tale. "In a tree?"

"Sure. When she's out on a prowl, that's where Grandmother Spider stashes her kills—up in a tree where the coyotes can't get at 'em. Later on, after she gets real hungry, old Grandma will climb up the tree and eat 'em—bones and everything—right on the spot. Or if she's not so hungry, she carries 'em home for a late-night snack. Why, if she was determined to, I expect she could carry eight steers—one under each arm."

The child smirked. "Then how would she walk?"

"Slow."

Aunt Daisy is making this up. "Did you ever *see* the big spider?"

"Not me. And I don't want to."

"Then how do you know it was a spider that put that cow up in a tree?"

" 'Cause its head was bit off." Daisy snapped her teeth with a ghastly click. "And there was two bloody holes in his side where she fanged him." The old woman made a dreadful biting motion with two fingers. "Great big holes you could poke your fist into. It was awful; the poor animal was drained of his blood." The missing blood was not part of the legend. But a nice touch, she thought.

The girl didn't want to believe a word of this. "I don't see how a spider could bite off a cow's head."

"Wasn't a cow—it was a steer. Anyway, Grandmother Spider is lots bigger'n any ordinary spider—and then some. So she sure wouldn't have no trouble biting a head off a pint-sized little girl . . . but I wouldn't want to *scare* you." The old woman turned away to enjoy a secret smile. Having a child around was such a blessing.

Sarah felt an unpleasant sourness in her stomach. But she knew the old woman got some small pleasure from frightening her. She had learned that it annoyed Daisy if you didn't pay her stories any attention. Besides, if you thought about bad things right before bedtime, you would have scary dreams. Like awful, fuzzy tarantulas crawling under the covers on your legs . . . up your belly . . . along your neck . . . onto your face . . . where they would bite your eyeballs and you'd go blind. For this very sensible reason, the child was determined to dismiss the shaman's terrifying tale from her mind. She would read her book.

She tried.

So very hard she tried.

The more diligently she worked at this scholarly pursuit, the more the two-dimensional spider-corpse on the linoleum pulled at the corner of her eye. Maybe he did have a family, sort of. She imagined his saddened brothers and sisters, wailing at the news of his untimely death . . . his mourning parents, weeping shiny spider tears. And worst of all . . . his horrible grandmother—her bulbous body, big as a house. Eight legs the size of trees . . . with horrible pointy knees. Bloodsucking fangs, great jaws that could snap a cow's head right off. What if the frightful old spider-woman really was out and about tonight . . . thirsting for blood? No, she assured herself firmly, that was too silly. And besides, it was best not to imagine such things. Making up pictures of horrid things in your head could make them take on form and substance . . . become real.

TEN MINUTES LATER,
THE NORTHERN SHORE OF NAVAJO LAKE

The truck was parked on a small peninsula. Lake water lapped against the rocky bank. It was a pleasant, peaceful sound. The lone occupant seemed quite ordinary; hardly worth a passing glance—a middle-aged man sitting in the cab of a GMC pickup. Except for oddly protruding ears, there was nothing memorable about his appearance. The oval face was crowned with thinning brown hair, the weak chin squared by a neatly clipped beard. Rimless spectacles were fixed over slitted gray eyes that seemed to squint perpetually, even in the twilight. There were broad shoulders under the cotton shirt, and a deep chest. Pizinski had once been lean, almost athletic. Now—after seven years' desk duty, endless meetings, heavy dinners, too many beers, not enough sleep—he was becoming sedentary. Showing signs of going soft around the middle. Puffy bags were forming under his eyes. He'd recently taken up the can-

cer sticks again. Now he couldn't run a hundred yards
without collapsing into a coughing fit.

But these were ordinary enough problems and he
was—or seemed to be—a quite ordinary man. A fellow
who had paused here for a few minutes to sit alone in
his pickup, staring at the lake. He might have been a
fisherman. It was not uncommon to see hopeful anglers
casting cunningly crafted lures from this sandy spit of
land. Anyone who saw the man in the truck might not
have given him a second glance.

If there had been anyone to see him . . . if they had
bothered to take notice.

There was.

They had.

William Pizinski, distracted by the cares of this life,
was unaware that he was being watched. He was thinking. Like a beagle frantically chasing its tail, his
thoughts ran in a tight circle around the past two
decades of his life. He'd been married to Margaret for
most of those years. And to his work. Mostly the work.
Margie's boorish brother owned the firm. And Kenny
Bright didn't give a hot damn what RMAFS, Inc., was
up to as long as the fat U.S. Air Force contracts continued to roll in.

Margie was somewhere in France now, on a bicycle
tour. Shedding ten pounds. And, she'd said: "Getting
my head together"—"Finding out who I am." Pizinski
grinned crookedly. *I know who you are, kid. Ask me,
I'll tell you.*

There was a distant rumble of thunder over the lake.

Pizinski pulled a Coors from a cooler, popped the steel
tab, took a long drink. He closed his eyes and dreamed
of a simpler life. Imagined himself independent. Living
close to nature. Like old What's-his-name who built
himself a cabin by that pond in New England. Sure. An

isolated fishing shack somewhere along the lakeshore. Free of all cares. In a moment, he was imagining himself out on the lake. In a houseboat. Fishing seven days a week. Frying trout in a crusty iron skillet. Broiling porterhouse steaks in a propane oven. Growing a *serious* beard. Sleeping late. *Passing gas whenever I feel like it*.

An unexpected sound interrupted this blissful reverie. He looked upward through the windshield. A few drops splattered fatly on the glass. The clouds grumbled among themselves—the beginning of a rumble up there. But he'd heard something much closer than the hint of a thunderstorm. The sound of an engine.

The big vehicle, its lights off, was easing slowly along the rocky shore. Toward him. Someone had mounted a pair of steer horns on the hood. A tasteless thing to do, Pizinski thought. The Ford flatbed pulled up beside him; the driver was barely a yard away from his left elbow. Pizinski glared under bushy eyebrows at the unwelcome visitor.

The driver of the flatbed grinned. "Hey."

Pizinski grunted a response. No telling what kind of nut you'd meet in a place like this.

The dark-skinned man stared at the frosty can in Pizinski's hand. "You got another beer?"

"What if I do?"

"Thought maybe you'd let me have a cold one."

Pizinski turned his face away, spat out the window. "Why should I give you a beer?"

" 'Cause I'm thirsty."

"Think of a better reason."

The man thought about this for some moments. "Well, you're parked on my land." It wasn't exactly true. It was, in fact, a deliberate falsehood.

Pizinski gathered his eyebrows in a bunch and glared at the stranger. "You tellin' me you own this place?"

Without shutting off the Ford's engine, the driver of the flatbed got out and walked around to the passenger side of the GMC pickup. His shiny cowboy boots—purchased in a Durango thrift shop—flopped loosely on his feet. He waved his arm in a sweeping gesture. "This here's the Southern Ute Reservation." The lakeshore was actually state park land, but the *matukach* wouldn't know that. He had New Mexico plates.

"Let me guess—you're chief of the whole outfit."

"No. But I'm an enrolled member of the tribe." A spicing of truth made a lie easier to swallow.

Pizinski figured he'd pulled the short straw. "Get in, then."

The Ute opened the cab door and slid onto the seat. "Name's Tommy Tonompicket."

The *matukach* stuck out a hairy right hand, which was accepted. "I'm Bill Pizinski."

The Indian got a closer look at the bearded white man. Nothing out of the ordinary. Except one thing. The fellow had big ears that stuck straight out from the sides of his head. But Tonompicket was not one to be put off by a man's appearance. Other things were more important. Like beer. He took a hard look at the can in the *matukach*'s pale hand. And licked his lips.

Pizinski kicked a scuffed boot against the Styrofoam cooler. "Help yourself to a brew."

Tonompicket stuck his hand under the slush of icy water. "So . . . you a fisherman?"

"I sometimes wet a line. But not today; been driving a long ways. Just stopped to rest a while. And think."

White people did way too much thinking. And a lot of trouble had come of it. The Ute downed a drink from the frigid can. "Whatta you do for a livin'?"

Pizinski was mildly annoyed with the grilling. But the

Indian wanted to talk. "Aeronautics engineer. Work for a firm in Albuquerque."

"I'm a truck driver," the Ute said. "I work for myself."

Pizinski glanced sideways at the flatbed. "You own that rig?"

Tommy Tonompicket shrugged. "Yeah. I haul all kindsa stuff. Right now I got a contract with Ozzie Corporation."

"And what do they do?" *As if I care.*

"They own a chain of restaurants—Ozzie's Fine Seafood. They serve up everything from fried catfish to that raw stuff."

"Sushi."

"Yeah." The Ute grimaced.

"So. You haul fish?" *Somebody's got to do it.*

"Nah. I'd need a refrigerated rig for that."

Pizinski realized he'd asked a dumb question.

"I mainly move hardware for 'em. Commercial appliances, mostly. Like stoves and refrigeration units. Cash registers. Tables and chairs. Stuff like that. Whatever needs hauling."

"Sounds interesting." *Like watching grass grow.*

"It pays for the groceries. So what kinda stuff do you engineer?"

His work was classified. "Oh . . . this and that."

The Ute grinned. "Sounds interesting."

Despite himself, the engineer smiled. "Yeah." He sought to find some common ground with his guest. "And I'm kind of a truck driver too."

The professional trucker's mouth curled into a snide grin. "Is that right?"

"Sure." Pizinski was mildly offended by the condescending tone.

"So whatta you haul?"

You'd be surprised, bub. "Technical apparatus. Systems . . . components."

"Components, huh? Sounds like somethin' you could send by FedEx."

Pizinski ignored the sarcasm. "Sometimes when I need to visit our manufacturing plant in Colorado Springs, I move some pretty heavy stuff. Hundreds of pounds."

The Ute suppressed a snicker. "Well, whatever the load—truckin' is still truckin'."

Pizinski gratefully accepted the small praise.

And so they sat in the GMC pickup. Guzzled cold beer. Talked. About women. Politics. Fishing. The weather. Women. And drank some more. As the alcohol soaked into their brains, the unlikely pair gradually felt the beginnings of a warm mutual fondness. And absurd notions took on the air of brilliant insights.

"I got an idea," Pizinski said with a wag of his bearded face. "Why don't you and me change places?"

The Ute belched sourly. "You want to sit on this side?"

"No. What I mean is—why don't I move onto the reservation and become an Indian? You could take my place." He laughed drunkenly and jabbed a thumb to his chest. "Become *me*."

Tonompicket was not completely drunk. "Why'd I want to do *that*?"

"I got a nice house down in Bosque Farms. On two and a half acres."

"I already got me a house. On fifteen acres."

"I've got a good job too—make big bucks. You'd be welcome to it." He snickered foolishly. The white man, in spite of the alcohol short-circuiting the wiring in his brain, did not tell the Indian that he'd get a nagging wife in the bargain. No point in queering the deal right up front.

A high-paying job? Tonompicket scratched his belly. "Would I hafta haul . . . *components*?"

Pizinski slapped his palm on the dashboard. "Nossir! Not if you didn't want to."

"This house down in New Mexico . . . it worth a lot of money?"

The engineer raised his arms to support an imaginary load. "A bushel." *Once you pay off the four-hundred-thousand-dollar mortgage.*

The Ute reached over to stroke the steering wheel. "Along with your house, would I get this truck?"

The white man thought about this. A man might give up his wife, his job, even the roof over his head. But his pickup? "Only if I get me a choice piece of the reservation." His bleary eyes stared over the rippling surface of the steel-blue waters. "I'd want a lakefront lot. At least a thousand feet of shoreline."

The Ute, who was feeling the mellow warmth of several beers, responded with a nod. "Seems fair enough."

"You'll think about it, then?"

"Sure. But right now, I need to take a leak."

"Not in the truck you don't."

"I'm not a damn savage," the Indian growled.

As the Ute was dismounting the cab, Pizinski glanced at the mirror mounted on the door. In the swirling gray mists, there was a peculiar amber light. Seemed to be rising up from the lake, like a whale surfacing. At first, the white man was startled. Then he laughed at himself and said: "It's just the moon coming up."

The Ute, now relieving the pressure on his bladder, squinted thoughtfully at the light. "It's too early for the moon to come up." He said this in a superior tone that offended his drinking buddy.

"How do you know what time the moon should come up?" Pizinski snapped.

"Us Indians know all about that kind of stuff."

Smart-ass redskin. "So if it ain't the moon comin' up, then what is it?"

"Could be a flying witch-egg."

"A what?"

The Ute explained the facts patiently, as if to a small child. "Witches fly around at night. Sometimes they fly in eggs."

Aeronautically speaking, the engineer decided, this was impossible. Eggs don't have wings. Besides, it was silly. "Why'n hell would they do that?"

The Ute shrugged; this caused him to pee on his over-sized boot. " 'Cause they can."

"It's the moon," Pizinski insisted.

"Is not," Tonompicket shot back.

This inane exchange might have continued, but the white man ended the argument with a "hmmmph" that galled the Indian into a sullen silence. The quiet was temporary.

The Ute zipped his fly. "Ouch!"

Pizinski cackled rudely. "What happened, Little Beaver—you catch it in the zipper?"

There was a smacking sound. "Some kinda bug bit me." Tommy Tonompicket stopped rubbing his neck long enough to inspect the flattened creature on his palm. "But it won't never bite nobody no more."

Though he continued to stare at the luminous form in the mirror, Pizinski was not concerned about this disputed appearance of the earth's largest satellite. The aeronautical engineer had more urgent matters on his mind. His troubles were very close at hand. And the moon, despite appearances, was a very long way off. He did not heed the enigmatic warning etched into the glass surface:

CAUTION!
OBJECTS IN MIRROR ARE CLOSER THAN THEY APPEAR

The amber light hung over the waters, then disappeared into the thickening mists. The low clouds swallowed the glowing object, then rumbled in dyspeptic dissatisfaction. As if attempting to disgorge an unsavory meal.

7:15 P.M.

Southern Ute tribal police officer Daniel Bignight squinted warily over the steering wheel at the wet road stretched out before him. As was his habit when alone, he mumbled to himself: "The rain's making that black-top slick as snail spit." Slip off into one of these deep arroyos, he imagined darkly, and they wouldn't find you till your bones had crumbled and turned to dust. The Taos Pueblo man eased off on the accelerator pedal, slowing the patrol car until the speedometer jittered around fifty.

An indistinct pulse of lightning flashed in the east; the policeman counted off sixteen seconds until he heard a barely audible rumble of thunder. *About three miles away . . .*

He flinched when the radio console burped static, then coughed up a mouthful of unintelligible words. The dispatcher snapped at him. "Car two-twenty-eight. Respond, please."

He ignored the rude summons.

The determined dispatcher disposed of the usual formalities. "Bignight—get on the horn."

She knows I can hear her. He held the plastic microphone under his chin and pressed the Transmit button. "Two-twenty-eight here. What's the problem?"

The radio sneezed like it had a snootful of juniper pollen, then found its voice. "Call from a citizen at Arboles. Reports peculiar activity along the lakeshore."

From Arboles you could see the lake seven ways from sundown. "What part of the shore?"

"Well . . . uh . . . to the east, I think."

Though most of Navajo Lake was in New Mexico, two pointy fingers tickled Colorado's underbelly. One digit poked north up the valley of the Piedra; another, east along the San Juan. Bignight keyed the microphone. "Dispatch, please describe the peculiar activity."

"Caller said she sees a funny light."

In spite of his dour mood, Daniel Bignight managed a half smile. "Funny light?"

"That's what she said—looked fairly big. Might be a boat on fire."

There was an optimistic side to Bignight's personality, and this was augmented by his fanciful imagination. *I'll stop and interview this Arboles lady who saw the funny light. She'll likely have a pot of java perking. Hello coffee. Maybe even offer me a piece of pie. Hola tarta.* He salivated. "Dispatch, who's the caller?"

"She didn't leave a name."

His mouth went dry. *Good-bye coffee . . . adios tarta.* "So how'll I find the ha-ha light?"

The dispatcher thought this was a dumb question. "Well, Danny, it shouldn't be all that hard to see a great big light in the dark."

"Smart-ass," Bignight grumbled to himself, then addressed the dispatcher. "What about the Park cops? Lakeshore's their jurisdiction."

"I called the Arboles campground. Mike's the only officer on duty and he's got a problem with a bear turning over garbage cans."

"How about the Archuleta County sheriff's office?"

"It'd take a good hour to get someone out there from Pagosa."

The Southern Ute Police Department had an unwritten policy. Regardless of whose turf the trouble was on, if one of their officers was close by, the Ute constabulary took the call. After the dust settled, jurisdictional matters would be worked out amicably.

Danny Bignight pressed the mike button. "I'll have to go way out on Carracas Road." It was gravel and rough as an alligator's back. "This'll take me some time to check out, so don't bother me with any more traffic for a while, okay?" *I'll park by the lake, watch the moon come up*.

"Roger that. I'll do what I can."

The road, which had recently been graded, was not so rough as the policeman had anticipated. Heading east, he drove slowly along the northern edge of the lake, watching to his right for any indication of an unusual light. Seeing nothing, he began to recall a dozen other false alarms. Then, flickering through the willows, was a brief glimmer of orange light. It was extinguished as he passed behind a low ridge.

"Campfire," Bignight muttered aloud. "I drove alla way out here for a damn *campfire*." The campers were on a thumblike peninsula that protruded half a mile into the lake. The light was suddenly extinguished. *Funny. Campfires don't tend to go on and off*. He turned off the pavement onto a sandy lane, slowing the patrol car to a groaning crawl. Again the police officer saw the glow of light. Dead ahead, just over a small ridge topped with a thick stand of cottonwood and willow. He watched the wipers swipe oily smears across the windshield. Above the crest of the ridge, the orange light flashed on again, reflecting off the soft, gray belly of the clouds. Much brighter now.

He muttered through dry lips, "What'n hell *is* this?"

There was but one way to find out. The policeman shifted into Low and pressed his boot toe lightly on the accelerator. The SUPD cruiser crept up the incline like a determined white beetle laboriously climbing a black dunghill. As he topped the ridge, the skin on the back of Bignight's neck prickled. Something didn't feel right. He cut the headlights.

A white-hot bolt of lightning sizzled at the top of a lone ponderosa snag. Briefly, his retinas recorded an image. Something was down there by the lakeshore. Something big. And it was coming up the ridge to meet him! The lawman, unaware that he had jammed the brake pedal almost to the floorboard, stared into the darkness.

A double flash of electric fire: two long fingers reaching down to trouble the lake's surface.

Briefly, through the rain-streaked windshield, he saw it again. More clearly this time. Still coming. Right at him. Instinctively—as if expecting a collision—Bignight flicked the toggle for the emergency lights.

Didn't help.

It kept right on coming.

Now a flash of sheet lightning made a neon blanket over the lake.

The police officer could not believe what he saw. Underneath the unspeakable *thing* was something smaller . . . trapped . . . wriggling like a worm on a hook. Bignight's jumbled thoughts were interrupted by a scream . . . a long, keening, hopeless wail. The *something* was a man. Whatever this monster was, it had a human being in its clutches. Bignight's blood turned icy in his veins. "Oh, God," he muttered. "Oh, God . . ."

Another wailing scream . . .

Daniel Bignight had always known it'd happen some-day. He could turn his tail and run . . . or stand and give an account of himself. The Pueblo man didn't think twice.

Tommy Tonompicket—twitching like a moth entangled in an ever-tightening web—saw the approaching head-lights of an automobile.

Now there was hope of rescue.

The headlights went out . . . hope was also extinguished.

Tonompicket felt himself being carried rapidly forward. Then there were blue-and-red flashing lights where he'd seen the car. It was the cops! And he was headed right toward the blinking lights.

He called out again.

And was rudely jerked, like a puppy on a leash who had misbehaved.

Officer Bignight was out of the squad car, his side arm at the ready. There was an angry roar, a flash of amber light. The brightness persisted for several seconds. He got a good look at the enemy. And trembled. *God in heaven . . . what is it?*

The unspeakable thing was almost upon him. Its long, spindly legs—dancing wickedly in the darkness—made a rustling, clicking sound.

The Pueblo man gamely stood his ground. *I will fear no evil . . . for you are with me.* He raised the 9-mm automatic. *Hail Mary, full of grace . . . remember us sinners at the hour of our death.* His finger tightened on the trigger.

And then it was gone.

Before he could squeeze off the first round, the shadowy apparition had simply vanished into the mists . . . as if slipping away into a parallel dimension.

Bignight stood like one frozen, staring dumbly into nothingness. There was another dismal scream, farther away now. He crossed himself, whispering an urgent prayer for the pitiful victim, now beyond the help of mere mortals.

The low clouds rumbled . . . and were illuminated internally by an unearthly amber glow. And then this too was gone.

Reluctantly, the policeman lowered his weapon. His heart thumped like an old well pump; the roof of his mouth felt like dry sandpaper on his tongue. The rain was beating hard against his face. He slipped inside the squad car and huddled there, wondering what to do. Every once in a while on your night patrols, you'd come upon something that seemed very queer. *Maybe I shouldn't report what I saw. Or . . . what I thought I saw.*

Unconsciously, he had squeezed his hands into fists. *Maybe I'm losing my mind.*

Bignight noticed that the Chevy engine wasn't running. Peculiar. *Maybe I turned off the ignition, then forgot what I did.* The policeman twisted the ignition key, heard the big Chevy V-8 shudder to life. He eased the vehicle down the ridge. As the policeman approached the shoreline, he toggled the spotlight switch and swept the beam along the rocky ground at the lake's edge. There was a GMC pickup truck. Parked right next to it was a big Ford flatbed. Looked like Tommy Tonompicket's truck. He eased himself out of the patrol car. "Hey," he said, "anybody here?" Afraid he might get an answer, he didn't call out too loudly.

The only response was a rolling peal of thunder overhead . . . like an avalanche of huge boulders tumbling down a mountainside.

The policeman approached the trucks warily. The

flatbed's engine was idling. And Tommy's big truck was missing its hood. From the appearance of the twisted hardware, it looked as if something had literally ripped it off. Fat raindrops sizzled into puffs of steam as they splattered onto the exhaust manifold. Bignight made a wide circle, poking the beam of his flashlight under the vehicles, behind bushes, along the rocky shoreline. Between the trucks, he spotted a pair of cowboy boots. One was sitting straight up, like somebody had been yanked right out of it. The tribal police officer backed all the way to the Chevy patrol car, his gun barrel and flashlight beam synchronously sweeping the darkened shore. He slid into the automobile quickly, locking the door, switching off the lights. He laid the pistol on the seat close beside him, picked up the microphone, pressed the Transmit button. "Dispatch—Bignight here." What'll I *report*?

The response was delayed for a few seconds that seemed an eternity to the lone policeman. "Dispatch here. What is your current position?"

"Shore of Navajo Lake, the peninsula—Buckskin Charlie's Thumb. I'm at the scene of . . . uh . . . a couple of abandoned vehicles."

AVs were pretty standard stuff. "I copy that."

"Dispatch—looks like we got a problem out here."

"What sort of problem?"

His hands trembled; the microphone rattled against his chin.

The radio squawked again. "Bignight, this is Dispatch. Is there something I can do for you?"

The policeman barely heard himself reply. "You'd better call the cops."

Tommy Tonompicket tried to assure himself that this was a terrifying alcoholic dream. He would wake up on the rocky beach, vomit up his socks—and then everything would be all right. But this all seemed so *real*. There were flashes of electric fire from the clouds. And much closer, flames of actual fire. From somewhere—very near, it seemed—he heard the white man's awful shrieks.

The cords around the Ute trucker's body were gradually tightening, shutting off the blood flowing to his limbs. He swung back and forth, a living, breathing pendulum.

He whispered hoarsely to himself. "Tommy, you sorry sonuvabitch . . . you're a dead man."

7:50 P.M.

A lone shepherd stood on the cleft of a rocky slope, tending his little flock. He was not under the misty clouds that shrouded the mountainside. He was in them.

His dog, whose honest face was decorated with one brown and one blue eye, lay contentedly at his master's feet. The sheep were also resting amongst the tender new spring grasses, though a few youngsters cavorted about quite gaily. Except for the occasional rumble of thunder to the south, all was serenely quiet. It was a time of such perfect peace as is rarely known upon the face of the earth.

Nothing so sweet can last.

The dog suddenly lurched to his feet. The short hairs bristled on his neck; a low growl rattled ominously in his throat.

The man leaned forward to rub his faithful friend's back. "What is it?"

As if in answer, from a few yards down the rocky slope—deep within the mists—there was a dull orange glow.

The sheep got jerkily to their feet and began to mill about, bleating pitifully.

The dog—who had once stood off a full-grown cougar—whined and pushed his side against his master's leg.

The light was extinguished. All was quiet for a moment. Then there was an odd rustling, bumping sound in the night. Like something was being dragged along the ground.

As one is naturally apt to do in such circumstances, Arturo Marquez leaned forward . . . squinted through the mists. It didn't help. He thought of shouting "Hallo—who's out there?" And thought better of it. A sensible fellow allowed Trouble to pass by unhailed.

He heard something different now . . . a pitiful moan.

"Who is it?" the shepherd whispered.

The crunching, bumping continued, then stopped. Then there was a metallic crashing sound.

The dog barked once, but stayed close to the shepherd.

Somewhat farther away, the light flashed again—and was gradually extinguished.

The herder of sheep sat very still. The dog, tail tucked between his legs, looked up imploringly at his master. Evidently with the expectation that the human being would do something.

"Be still," the old man said gruffly. "This ain't none of our business."

It seemed that the dog's face took on an expression of pity for this cowardice.

Embarrassed, Arturo Marquez got to his feet, brushed off his woolen trousers. His dignity thus restored, he touched a match to a rusted Coleman lantern. With the light swinging from one hand, a stout cudgel in the other, he headed warily down the rocky slope.

Something was there. It was a wicked-looking thing . . . like a devil from . . .

"Go away," he muttered.

There was no answer. And it didn't go away.

The shepherd paused, leaned forward, holding the lantern out as far as possible.

The dog, hackles bristling, approached more closely, one deliberate step at a time. Stretched his neck. And sniffed at the thing.

Whatever it was, Arturo thought, it wasn't moving. So it must be dead. And dead things—even dead devils—can't hurt you. But despite his curiosity, the sensible man kept his distance. And mimicking the dog, he turned his shaggy head this way and that . . . squinting at the mysterious object.

In spite of this effort, he did not understand.

The shepherd withdrew, sat down on a pine stump, and fed the embers of his campfire with aspen twigs. No matter how long or hard he thought, this night's peculiar events made no sense at all. But wait—what agency was it that continually performed perverse acts to annoy and endanger the citizens of this great country? The answer was clear enough.

The dog licked his master's hand, whining inquisitively.

Arturo understood that the simple-minded canine expected some sort of explanation. The fine-tuned product of a million years of simian evolution spoke these words to the shivering dog: "It's the damn government in Washington that's behind this. They're always up to no good." He nodded with the knowing air of one who understands such deep matters. "What they'll likely do next is drop a damn bomb on us. The United States of America is in a sorry state, old boy."

The dog—Australian by birth and suspicious by nature—seemed to agree with this gloomy observation. He barked twice to voice his approval, then began the difficult task of rounding up the terrified herd, which had scattered like . . . sheep.

The shepherd added more twigs to the flames. He watched a small pot of water bubble and boil, made a mug of green tea, lit a battered briar pipe. He inhaled a few thoughtful puffs of the fragrant tobacco smoke. *Some things are quite beyond human understanding.* He wisely decided to dismiss the whole matter from his mind. He was—like most men who live out-of-doors—a tough-minded fellow. But every minute or so, he could not help himself. He would stare into the deepening mists with a sense of profound unease. Wondering whether there was something wicked wandering around in the darkness. And whether it might come back.

7:58 P.M.

In the elderly Ute woman's home—a sturdy house trailer manufactured during the 1950s—the scene was one of domestic tranquillity.

Daisy Perika had washed the supper dishes and was in the process of drying them.

The child's black cat—hoping for a scrap of food—was pacing near her feet like a miniature panther in a cage.

Sarah Frank sat at the kitchen table. The child appeared to be devoting all of her considerable concentration to the crisp new pages of a history book. In fact, the Ute-Papago girl's attention was divided. Her dark eyes darted between the text and the flickering screen of a portable color television. The appliance was a Christmas present from Charlie Moon. It was an extravagant gift for a man who—aside from an occasional success in a poker game—survived on the modest salary of a Southern Ute police officer. Though the nine-year-old did not fully appreciate his generosity, she did appreciate the TV set—and Sarah was fascinated by the weekly show that dealt with all sorts of mysterious phenomena. A father's ghost that returned to warn his family about the impending danger of a mud slide that would destroy their hillside home. Great hairy animals (who walked upright like men!) that roamed the mountainous regions of the Pacific Northwest. And sundry odd things seen in the night sky.

This TV fare fascinated the child, who had almost managed to evict the shaman's lurid tale about Grandmother Spider from her mind. Almost.

If all was serene and peaceful inside the old woman's home, it was not so outside. For the past several minutes, a nervous pair of coyotes had been yipping almost constantly. Now they were coming very close to the trailer. The Ute elder normally let the coyotes strictly alone. These were sacred animals—earthly imitations of the Trickster. But they could be downright annoying. If Daisy Perika didn't do something about it, they would likely sit by her bedroom window and yip-yap all night. When the moon was large, coyotes just couldn't keep their mouths shut. Whether they were sacred or not, she was bound to put a stop to this. They could go and make their infernal noise somewhere else.

Mr. Zig-Zag leaped to a precarious perch on the windowsill. The black cat sat very still, blinking pale yellow eyes at the darkness.

Sarah watched with mild interest as the old woman opened the closet door. First, Daisy slipped on a woolen shawl. Then she removed the double-barreled twelve-gauge shotgun. Sarah's brown eyes grew large. "What're you gonna shoot?"

Daisy winked. "Gonna kill us a wild turkey for to-morrow's lunch."

Sarah did not appreciate being talked to like a five-year-old. "No, really."

The old woman inserted shells into both chambers. "I'm gonna scare off those loud-mouthed coyotes."

Pleased at any break in the monotony, Sarah slid off her chair. "Can I come outside and watch?"

"Sure." The old woman switched off the kitchen light, leaving her small home in darkness except for the flickering glow from the television screen. She opened the door that led onto the rickety wooden porch. It would be easy enough to scare the varmints off just by letting out a blood curdling yell. But it would be a lot more satisfying to sneak up on 'em and fire off a big blast from the twelve-gauge. They wouldn't drop their tails 'till they were in the Conejos County!

Mr. Zig-Zag, normally eager to slip outside and sniff around for small rodents, withdrew to his dark hide-away under the propane stove. Only the black cat's slanted yellow eyes were visible.

The child followed her guardian onto the porch. Though the sun had been down for some time, it was not very cold. With the warm southerly winds, the snow was gone except on the highest mountaintops. That was not entirely good news. The sudden melt had left behind gooey mud that was knee-deep in the low places.

The coyotes had fallen quiet.

Sarah, who had the typical patience of a nine-year-old, waited an entire three seconds before expressing her opinion. "I think they're gone, Aunt Daisy."

"Shhhhh." The Ute elder sniffed for coyote scent, then squinted into the darkness. "They're still close by. Stand here real quiet till they start yippin' again. Then I'll show 'em what a *real* noise sounds like!"

Sarah leaned close to the old woman and whispered, "Will it be really loud?"

"You bet," Daisy muttered. "When you see me wrap my finger around the trigger, put your hands over your ears."

And so they stood on the porch, the old woman with the heavy shotgun cradled in her arms, the little girl hugging herself in delightful anticipation of the great event.

They waited.

And waited.

The coyotes, it seemed, had lost their voices.

Though it was an almost balmy evening, Sarah began to feel a little chilly. She wished she'd slipped her sweater on before she came outside. Suddenly, the child drew a deep breath. "Aunt Daisy?"

"Shhhhh."

"But I *see* something."

The child was a regular chatterbox. But she did have good eyes. "Where?"

"Over there." The girl pointed to the south.

The old woman squinted. "I don't see nothin'."

"It's the stars."

"What's so interesting about the stars?"

"A patch of them close to the ground . . . they're gone."

The old woman was about to scold the child for such foolishness when she saw the shadowy form. It was large. Getting larger. The shaman felt her heart flutter. *This is something bad.* "Get inside, child."

Sarah—transfixed by the apparition that moved toward them—pretended not to hear the command. "I think it's like what they was telling about on the TV."

Daisy cocked both hammers. Snap. Snap.

Sarah tugged urgently at the old woman's skirt. "A

spaceship came down in Montana last January. This woman told how her car stalled when a beam of light came out of the spaceship. Then . . . then . . ."

"Then *what*?" Daisy barked.

Sarah swallowed hard. "Some little gray people with great big bulging eyes came out of it."

"That's a silly story—why would anybody go to Montana in the middle of winter?" But the shotgun was shaking in her hands. Daisy watched the shadow grow larger. It was coming almost directly toward them. "What happened then?"

"When?"

Such an annoying child. "After them bug-eyed creatures came out of—"

"Oh. The poor woman said she must've fainted. But later on, she woke up."

Daisy felt marginally better. "Good." So everything had turned out all right.

"No, it was bad. When she woke up, she was inside this big spaceship. And she was naked as the day she was born and stretched out on a table. They were doing all sorts of awful things to her . . . sticking long, shiny probes into her and—"

"Hush. I don't want to hear that kind of talk." The inkblot was flowing inexorably toward them. "Anyway, it's nothing but a little black cloud . . . blowing up toward the canyon."

Sarah shook her head earnestly. "I don't think so, Aunt Daisy. I think it's *aliens*."

"Well, if it is," the shaman said with a nervous laugh, "they can't see us here in the dark. They're goin' to pass right by."

"If it's space aliens," the child said in an authoritative tone, "then a beam of light will come out and . . ."

As she spoke, a bright beam of light flashed from the

inky blackness. It swept over the piñon grove in front of the trailer home.

Sarah shrieked.

The beam moved toward them.

Daisy Perika—who had no intention of being subjected to a humiliating examination by creatures from a far-off world—did not hesitate. She raised the shotgun to her shoulder. Pulled the trigger. The report was deafening.

Almost instantly, a most remarkable transfiguration occurred. Simultaneously, the shadowy apparition answered the boom of the shotgun with a horrendous roar of its own—and was transformed into a huge mass of blinding orange light.

Sarah continued to shriek.

The fiery thing lurched upward, as if about to pounce on them.

The old woman stood her ground. She raised the shotgun again. "Take *this*, you bug-eyed monsters!" She emptied the second barrel toward the orange blob.

The immediate response of the object to this second violent assault was a vanishing act. The thing was gone. Swallowed up in darkness.

Daisy's heart was racing with this victory—she had the little buggers on the run! The Ute elder raised the shotgun in both hands like a coup-counting stick, and shook it arrogantly at her unseen adversaries. "Hah," she snorted like an old war horse. "Hah. That'll teach you smart-ass foreigners!" She cupped her hand by her mouth and yelled: "This ain't Montana, you sneaky little bastards—this is Southern Ute airspace!" She leaned on the flimsy porch railing long enough to catch her breath, then turned to the child. "Go inside, get that box of slug-shells outta the closet. If the little varmints

are dumb enough to come back, I'll shoot their spaceship down."

The child, who was shivering uncontrollably, could
barely speak. "Do you think you could?"

"You watch me." Daisy's lips parted to make a
wicked grin. "Then I'll skin 'em alive and have 'em for
breakfast!"

Sarah Frank—who had never seen the old woman energized by the heat of battle—was greatly impressed by
such valor. She did not know that Daisy had wet her
pants. For the moment, neither did Daisy.

LATER THAT NIGHT . . .

The graveled road meandered up First Finger Ridge like
a two-mile bull snake suffering a multitude of dislocated
vertebrae. It slithered through fields of granite boulders,
past stately groves of bone-white aspen. Impassable in
the depths of winter, the lane had been plowed a month
earlier by the retired pharmacist who operated the
neighborhood association's aged Caterpillar grader.

Attorney Miles Armitage had arrived at his log cabin
just past noon. The snows were melting early for this altitude (nine thousand four hundred feet). The front yard
enjoyed a fine southern exposure; black mud was ankle-
deep here. There was still almost a foot of slushy snow
in the back, which was shaded by the two-story log
structure and a cluster of blue spruce. Because the cabin
had not been occupied during the previous winter, there
were chores to do. Empty a dozen mousetraps of their
miniature, shrunken mummies. Crank up the thermo-
stats on the downstairs under-floor propane furnace and
the space heater in the loft bedroom. Light a match to
the paper under the kindling wood in the fireplace that

had been laid down last October. Turn on a circuit breaker to power up the well pump.

Such minor domestic tasks were a distinct pleasure. Miles was exultant with this annual, wet taste of spring. He assured himself that he was free of the city, a man once more connected to the great mysteries of nature. The man from the city had felt very much like going out and shooting a mammal of some sort and roasting it over the crackling stack of pine logs in the fireplace. He might have attempted to fulfill this fantasy had he owned a firearm and known where to locate said mammal. Or had even a rudimentary idea about how to remove the skin from his furry victim.

Deprived of the sweet opportunity to wreak havoc on a fellow creature, he had turned to other manly outlets. Exhilarated with the freshness of the mountain air, Mr. Armitage, Juris Doctor, class of '83, had been inclined to sing very much off-key ("Springtime in the Rockies") and to mouth hackneyed phrases ("Miles, my boy: This is the first day of the rest of your life"). Indeed—he did a quick little soft-shoe step. Unfettered freedom, unrestrained joys . . . they are wondrous things indeed. Enough to make a sober man quite silly.

Lusty ballads about springtime amongst the peaks and bloom being on the sage are uplifting to a man's weary spirit. And it *was* the first day of the rest of his life. But though this statement was undeniably accurate, it was—for lack of certain critical data—somewhat limited in scope. This waning day was also something else. Alpha had become Omega.

Having started a fine blaze in the granite fireplace, having prepared a delicious pot of beef stew (contents disgorged from the round mouth of a steel can), having stood on the front porch admiring the stars and inhaling the balmy-sweet breeze on this first evening of April,

Miles had now reverted to form. He watched the big-screen television for some thirty minutes, soaking in all the raw pleasure a documentary on international currency issues could offer. For light entertainment, he read a piece in *U.S. News & World Report* on "The Coming Global Economic Meltdown."

Presently, he seated himself at a varnished pine desk facing a two-yard-wide window that looked south over a lovely valley wherein roared a stream filled with snowmelt. He did not gaze out the window at the soft curves of the San Juans, or at the sprinkling of stars above them. He was poring over a declaration from an expert witness on the subject of artificial corneas. Miles Armitage was a patent attorney of some fame; defending against infringement charges was his game. He used a Sony microcassette recorder to make his notes. Thus bent over his desk, occupied with arcane matters that totally fascinated him (Blessed is he who loves his work!), the attorney had lost all contact with the natural world . . . its awesome potential for surprise. And mortal danger.

Something at the edge of his visual field distracted Miles from his task. A yellowish glow. He laid pencil on pad and stared out the window. Nothing but darkness. For a moment, he thought he saw a shadowy something moving along the ridge. Then it was gone. He shrugged, returned to his labors.

Again, a flash of orange light outside the window.

Then darkness.

This was getting to be an annoyance.

The better to see outside, he switched off the gooseneck desk lamp—casting the cabin interior into darkness. The thing was no longer a shadow . . . it was now a solid *something*. And it was coming rapidly along the ridge. Toward the cabin. Moving like nothing he'd ever seen before. Something clicked in the logical brain of Miles Armitage. "My God," he said. The utterance was not a prayer. *This is an . . . could it just possibly be one of those . . . omiGod!*

He pushed the chair away from the desk, fumbled in his Italian leather suitcase for the new camera, rushed outside, oblivious to the chill breeze in his face or the soft mud squishing around his six-hundred-dollar shoes. The huge object was dark, a great blot over the stars. Dead silent. And approaching rapidly. He raised the camera.

The thing lit up again—not a hundred yards away. And roared at him!

Miles had mentally prepared himself for the unusual, the bizarre, the otherworldly.

But not for *this*.

It was as if something horrible had slipped loose from his worst nightmare. It could not be real. But there it was. Coming right at him. He did not realize that the expensive machine was set to manual focus. But a man under great stress does the best he can. And so he pressed the shutter button.

Click.

Click.

Click.

The roar from the apparition lowered to a soft sigh; the orange light was extinguished.

Miles' mouth was powder-dry.

The hideous thing was very close . . . about to pass by the cabin. He turned, sprinting up the porch steps, running helter-skelter through his summer home—knocking furniture aside—tripping over his feet. Determined to get another photograph, he burst out the kitchen door into the backyard, stumbling through wet, ankle-deep snow—and raised the camera.

But there was no orange light. Was it gone?

He heard a sharp report. Then . . . an ominous grinding sound. Like great molars crunching a mouthful of bloody bones. It struck him with full force.

Cleaving flesh from bone . . . spirit from body.

CHARLIE MOON GAZED over the glassy waters of Navajo Lake. A cool, damp breeze wafted off the waters, bringing a mildly fishy smell ashore. The morning sun was barely showing its pale face in the east.

Daniel Bignight—who had spent much of the previous night on the lakeshore—was grateful for this light from the nearest star. And for the company of the acting chief of Southern Ute police.

Charlie Moon followed Bignight toward the rocky shore where the abandoned vehicles were parked. The Taos Pueblo man was broad-shouldered and muscular. As he walked his stiff, bone-jarring gait, Bignight's heavy braid swung back and forth across his broad back. He stopped a few yards away from the trucks. "There they are. Just like I found 'em."

Charlie Moon gave them a once-over. Two things were interesting. The GMC pickup had New Mexico plates. And the hood was missing from the flatbed truck.

Bignight realized that Moon already knew most of the story, but he began his recitation at the beginning.

"Last night, Dispatch had a phone call from an uniden-tified citizen at Arboles. Said she saw a peculiar light on the lakeshore. Sounded like a campfire to me, but I thought I'd check it out. I found these abandoned vehi-cles." He stared thoughtfully at the GMC. "There's some empty beer cans on the pickup floorboard. The engine on Tommy Tonompicket's flatbed was still run-ning. And it looks like the hood's been . . . ahh . . . re-moved." *Forcibly*. He fell into a long silence.

Moon was wondering whether he should get some breakfast at a small restaurant in Arboles. "Anything else?"

As if he had momentarily forgotten to breathe, Big-night sucked in a lungful of air. "Footprints of two per-sons near the vehicles."

"What do you make of it?"

The question sounded less like a polite query than the first question on an examination. Bignight looked up warily at the Ute, who was almost seven feet tall in his bare feet. With his boots on, and the wide-brimmed felt hat on his head, Charlie Moon loomed over him like a giant. Bignight—who liked and respected the acting chief of police—knew he had no reason to be apprehen-sive. Charlie Moon was as fair and honest a man as he'd ever come across. But, as a few slipshod officers had learned the hard way, Moon was not a fellow to trifle with. Bignight was wishing he'd left the boss out of this. It would've been best to turn in a routine AV report and let the state cops take over. "It looks like a couple of guys was here last night. Now they're gone."

That was obvious. *Why is Bignight so worried?* Moon kicked at a tire. "Who owns the pickup?"

"Registration was in the glove compartment, along with some proof-of-insurance payment receipts. To make sure, I ran the plates through the computer. It all checks out—the truck belongs to a William Pizinski, who has a New Mexico address." Bignight pointed at the empty boots. "Those are Tommy's. His wife says he ain't come home yet. She said he picked up this load in Denver on March thirty-first. He was supposed to haul it down to Albuquerque this morning. Looks like he stopped out here late yesterday. Prob'ly to do a little fishing."

Moon recalled the beer cans in the GMC pickup. "And maybe a little drinking."

"I've searched the shore for a half mile both ways without findin' hide nor hair of Tommy. Or anybody else."

Moon walked slowly around the trucks, taking mental notes of what there was to see. Sometimes, it was what you didn't see.

The Ford flatbed had about half a load. He stepped up onto the sturdy bed and pushed back a heavy green tarpaulin. Immediately visible under the protective cover was a greasy commercial-size gas range, a large wall-mount oven, a two-door refrigerator, a walk-in freezer. All were secured with heavy straps.

"Tommy hauls equipment for an outfit that owns a chain of restaurants," Bignight explained.

"What kind of restaurants?"

Bignight strained to recall what Mrs. Tonompicket had said. "Seafood, I think."

Moon grinned. "Looks like he's got everything here but the kitchen sink."

"He's got that too—right behind the stove." Bignight said this with a poker face.

Moon peered under the tarp. There it was. A stainless-steel double sink. Like the other appliances, it was used equipment. He tied the canvas cover down, dismounted from the flatbed, and turned his attention to the GMC pickup.

A shiny aluminum shell covered the eight-foot bed. According to a nameplate riveted to the metal, it been installed by Camper World in Belen, New Mexico. The twist-latch was unlocked; Moon lifted the shell door and poked his head inside. Nothing much to see. A spare tire, heavy-duty screw jack, lug wrench. Some nylon tie-down straps. He opened the pickup's driver-side door, pressed a thumb lever on the bench seat, and moved it forward. Behind the seat was a nice-looking Zebco spinning outfit with a treble hook tied on the line. He pushed the bench seat back into position and slid onto it. Moon looked around the cab. Nothing unusual. There were, as Bignight had said, beer cans littering the floor. The cooler was empty, except for a couple of gallons of cold water. He examined the glove compartment. In addition to the registration and several insurance receipts, there were the usual things. Small flashlight. Several misfolded, coffee-stained road maps. New Mexico. Colorado. Utah. And oddly, he thought— Brazil. There was an assortment of small hand tools. A plastic cigarette lighter. A package of Beeman's chewing gum. Moon pulled the sun visor down. In an elastic strip there were a few odds and ends. Smoky-brown sunglasses. A wallet-size plastic calendar. And a couple of business cards. A Big-O tire store in Taos. A firm with addresses in Albuquerque and Colorado Springs . . . RMAFS. Moon was repelled by strings of meaningless letters. He longed for the days when businesses had sensible names. Acme Tool Works . . . Willie's Water Well Drilling . . . Mom's Delicious Donuts. He noted that the Colorado Springs address for RMAFS was near the airport. And Peterson Air Force

Base. He offered the cardboard rectangles to Daniel Bignight. "These might be useful."

Bignight pocketed the business cards. *Useful for what?* But he didn't ask.

Moon leaned easily on the aluminum shell and squinted at the great expanse of water. Shimmering pillars of mist moved about like the ghosts in *Cañon del Espíritu* who haunted his aunt Daisy. "These guys might've launched a small boat. Could be on the lake somewhere." *Somewhere* covered a lot of area. Navajo was a sizable lake.

The Taos Pueblo man shook his head slowly; the heavy braid writhed like a snake climbing his back. "They're not on the lake."

If another officer had made this statement, Moon would have asked how he knew. Putting such a question to the Pueblo man would be worse than a waste of time. It would annoy him. Bignight had his hunches—and something had him plenty spooked. "Maybe they wandered off somewhere and got lost. Or fell asleep."

The words fairly jumped out of Bignight's mouth. "I don't think so."

This time, Moon couldn't resist asking. "Why?"

"I'll tell you something, Charlie . . . on two conditions."

Moon fought back a grin. "Name 'em."

"First, you don't laugh at me. Second, it don't go in my written report."

Only a few months ago, Daniel had heard a wailing banshee. He was still sensitive about that encounter. The tall Ute shrugged.

Bignight took this as a "yes" to his conditions. "Last night, when I got here—I saw something . . . strange."

Moon, who was familiar with his fellow officer's sense of drama, waited patiently.

"When I was up there—near the top of the ridge"—Bignight pointed toward the willow-studded hogback—"I saw this . . . this great big *thing* comin' from the lakeshore." The Taos Pueblo man opened his mouth, but could not force the words past his lips.

"What'd you see, Daniel?"

The policeman looked sheepishly at the rocky ground. "I don't know for sure."

"Well, was it animal, mineral, or vegetable?"

This seemed to agitate his subordinate. "Dammit, Charlie, I don't even know *that*."

"Did it have a shape?"

"I couldn't see too good . . . it was raining catfish and bullfrogs. But I'd say it was sorta . . . well . . . roundish." The policeman looked like he might be ill.

"Roundish," Moon said. "That should narrow down the possibilities."

Bignight took a deep breath. "And it was *big*."

This was Bignight's game. Moon played along. "How big?"

He shrugged. "I dunno. Big as a house, I guess."

The Taos Pueblo man had been raised in the oldest continuously occupied apartment building in the United States. "Could you estimate that in more familiar units?"

Bignight's brow furrowed in painful concentration. "Hard to tell. Maybe fifty or sixty feet high. And about as wide."

"Danny, when did you make this—uh—sighting?"

The subordinate officer referred to his dog-eared notebook. "Lessee . . . I took the call from Dispatch at about seven-twenty P.M. and I was just the other side of Arboles. It's about twenty minutes to get here . . . must've been about seven-forty, I guess."

"With the storm clouds over the lake, it must've already been fairly dark," Moon said. *Dark enough for Bignight to see the moon rising and think it was some kind of monster.*

The troubled man rubbed his hand over his eyes. "Worst of all, when the thing came close to me, I heard somebody. A man. He was yelling like bloody murder."

"Any particular man?"

Last night was already beginning to seem unreal . . . a bad dream poorly remembered. "It could of been Tommy Tonompicket." Bignight nodded to agree with himself. "Yeah. I'm pretty sure it was Tommy."

The Ute wasn't surprised. When Tommy got serious-drunk, he tended to bellow like a bull elk.

Bignight rubbed a spotless white handkerchief across his forehead. "The—whatever it was—it'd grabbed him." He closed his eyes at the awful memory. "Tommy was screaming for help, Charlie. I was about to take a shot at the thing and then it just"—he sighed— "just wasn't there anymore."

"Did you see Tommy well enough to make a positive ID?"

Bignight shook his head.

"Okay. This thing was big. And orange. Any other distinguishing characteristics?"

"Well . . ." Bignight hesitated. *Maybe I shouldn't tell him.* He swallowed hard. "It had legs."

Oh boy. "How many legs . . . two . . . four?"

Bignight turned away. "More'n that. And they was . . . real long. And skinny." He looked toward the deep waters of Navajo Lake. *That's where it came from.*

"Well," Moon said, "lemme see. What's really big . . . has a bunch of long, skinny legs . . . Sure. There's only one thing it could've been."

Daniel Bignight's mouth gaped. "What?"

Moon seemed not to hear the urgent question. "We ought to be looking for some unusual tracks."

"Unusual?"

Moon squatted; he ran the tips of his fingers along the sand. "They'd be . . . round. Like suction cups."

This wasn't making any sense. "What makes that kinda footprints?"

The Ute looked like he didn't want to say it. But he did. "Octopus."

The word echoed off Bignight. "Octopus?"

Moon nodded soberly. "Must've been a sizable one."

Bignight cast a doubtful glance toward the waters. "How would an octopus get in Navajo Lake?"

Moon got to his feet. "Folks buy 'em at pet stores when they're little and cute. But sooner or later, those eight-legged fellas outgrow the aquariums. And you wouldn't want to flush one down the toilet."

"You wouldn't?"

The Ute shook his head grimly. "They stick their legs out and attach them suction cups to the inside of the pipe. Stop up a sewer line real bad. So people pitch 'em into the rivers . . . and lakes. And once they've got enough room, they can grow big. Really big."

Bignight was dazed by this revelation. "A giant octopus . . . you really think . . ."

"Sure. Tommy Tonompicket, he goes fishing last night. Hooks himself a big octopus. I imagine it must've put up one helluva fight. But ol' Tommy, he's no quitter. He hangs on. After a long tussle, he finally lands the thing. But what does a man do with a catch like that? Nobody around here eats octopus." Moon scratched thoughtfully at his chin. "Tommy must've figured he'll tie it down on his truck, haul it to Albuquerque, sell it to one of them seafood restaurants. But it must've got loose and grabbed him and . . ." He turned away, faking a cough.

Smart-ass Ute. Bignight glared at the tall man's back and muttered a few choice phrases in the Tiwa dialect. They were Greek to the Ute. It was just as well.

The acting chief of police was rescued by a warble from the radio mounted on his belt; this was followed by a jumble of static. He pulled the portable transceiver from its holster and pressed the red Transmit button. "Moon here. What's up?"

He heard the morning-shift dispatcher's gravelly voice. "Charlie . . . I've got the Ignacio Public Schools transportation manager on the line. With all the snowmelt, he says their bus won't be able to make it over that road to your aunt's home. Wants to know if you'll pick up the little girl today and bring her to school."

With the early-spring thaw and heavy runoff, this was getting to be a habit. Moon hesitated, then pressed the button again. "Sure. Tell 'em I'll bring Sarah in." *I'm not needed here. Tommy Tonompicket and the white man will turn up before the day's over. With skull-busting hangovers. Serve 'em right.* Moon stuffed the radio back into its holster. "Look, Daniel, I'm sorry I . . ."

Bignight waved off the apology. The Taos Pueblo man stared glumly at the abandoned vehicles. "What d'you want me to do about this?"

Moon thought about suggesting that he call the Air Force and submit a UFO report. But Danny Bignight might not appreciate the humor. "Have the trucks towed to the station."

Though Bignight often sought after guidance, he hated to receive instructions that created extra work. "Strictly speaking, they ain't in our jurisdiction," he grumbled.

This was true enough. Ute land was a few hundred yards away. Moon looked off to the northeast, toward Pagosa Springs. "If the Archuleta County sheriff's office or the state police want to mount a search for these guys—or take responsibility for their vehicles—it's all right by me. But we can't leave these trucks sitting out here on the lakeshore. Tommy's got a load of restaurant gear on his flatbed. And that GMC pickup's almost new."

Bignight nodded glumly at Moon's logic. The whole shebang might get stolen.

"Another thing, Daniel—see if you can lift some prints off the trucks. Forward 'em to the FBI for ID." *That'll give him something to do.* And so Moon departed. Happy to have an excuse to leave Daniel Bignight to sort out this silliness. It would be comforting to get back to the real world. *Maybe Aunt Daisy will whip me up some pancakes and eggs.*

———•

Sarah Frank sat across the kitchen table from Charlie Moon and continued her narrative of last night's encounter with the unknown. He heard a breathless account of a dark blotch against the southern horizon, a mysterious light beam searching for victims, the old woman firing the shotgun at the intruder, a glare of blinding orange light . . . "And then Aunt Daisy shot at it again!"

The Ute policeman glowered at his aged aunt. "You'd better stop unloading that old twelve-gauge at everything that passes by. Someday you'll hit something—and get into deep trouble."

Daisy Perika, who never took the least notice of her nephew's advice, sipped thoughtfully at a mug of black coffee. "If it wasn't space aliens, it could of been a

Navajo witch," the old shaman muttered to herself. "They say them skin-walkers can change their shape . . . and fly about like ravens."

"It wasn't anything *like* a raven," Sarah said decisively.

Moon looked at his plate and wondered. Daniel Bignight sees a whatsit, but he didn't get off a shot. Aunt Daisy was quicker on the trigger. His appetite having departed, he resalted his scrambled eggs. Then added a dash of black pepper. And picked at the food with his fork. Moon was almost full last night. Maybe it was one of those crazy times. When otherwise normal people see weird things in the sky and act downright silly. Not that Aunt Daisy was what you'd call normal. For that matter, neither was the Taos Pueblo man. Maybe nobody was *normal*. And then Moon was visited by an unsettling thought. What if the same whatever-it-was Bignight claimed he had seen was something *real*? And what if this same thing had passed by Daisy's home?

"It could've been a Navajo skin-walker," the old woman said stubbornly. "Or a ghost-light."

He smiled reassuringly at the child. "Tell me, sunshine—about what time last night did you see this . . . uh . . . thing?"

Sarah wrinkled her brow in concentration. "I'd been watching TV. It was right when *Amazing Mysteries* was going off . . ."

Aha!

". . . so I guess it was a little after eight o'clock."

Daisy muttered to herself. "It's just like on the TV. All these oh-so-smart policemen can ever ask is: 'When did this happen? Did you get its license-plate number?' They don't ever do anything, just waste your time asking useless questions."

Moon—who had tuned out the old woman's insults—was trying to remember when Bignight had had his encounter. A few minutes before eight o'clock, he thought. And a few minutes later, Daisy and the kid see something strange outside. A policeman who managed to stay alive learned to be suspicious of coincidences. If all three of these witnesses had seen the same thing, it had headed roughly north by northwest from the shore of Navajo Lake.

Daisy continued her mutterings. "Next thing he'll want to know is exactly what it looked like." As if such mysterious things could be explained.

He leaned his elbows on the small dining table; the spindly legs creaked. "Sarah, this thing you saw . . . what did it look like?"

Daisy cackled. "See—what'd I just say?"

Puzzled by this odd remark, Moon shot the old woman a dark look, then returned his attention to the little girl. "Could you draw me a picture of what you saw?"

"Sure." She slid off her chair and disappeared into the far bedroom. Moments later, the child returned with a lined notepad and a box of crayons. She sat at the table for some minutes, laboriously sketching an outline, then coloring the awful thing Aunt Daisy had chased away. Finally, she passed the drawing to Moon.

Daisy, who had been scouring an iron skillet at the sink, came to have a look. "Hmmmf," the old woman said. "It didn't look like that to me."

Sarah stared at her drawing. And stood her ground. "This is *just* what it looked like."

Moon studied the child's crude sketch. The thing had a bulbous, reddish-orange body. Several long, skinny legs. One of the legs was curled around a tiny object.

Something with a perfectly round head. Pair of arms. Two legs. The policeman didn't want to know. But he had to ask. "What's this?"

"That's the man," the child responded in a whisper.

Daisy snorted. "I didn't see no man."

"You didn't see Grandmother Spider's *legs* either," the child shot back.

Moon raised an eyebrow. "Grandmother *who*?"

The old woman scowled a warning that went unheeded by the little girl, who proceeded to explain the facts of life to the tall policeman. "When somebody kills one of her people, Grandmother Spider gets awfully upset. Sometimes—when she's really mad—she slips out of her cave under the lake—and gets even. I didn't really believe it," she said with an apologetic glance at the Ute elder, "but she came out last night."

Daisy Perika met her nephew's suspicious gaze with an innocent shrug. As if she didn't know what on earth the silly child was jabbering about.

Sarah leaned her head on Moon's shoulder and felt comforted. "Charlie . . . that awful spider is gonna bite that poor man's head off. And use her fangs to suck all the blood outta him. And then she'll put his body in a tree while she hunts for . . . a cow, maybe."

Moon's brow furrowed. "A cow?"

The old woman rolled her eyes as if to hint that the child was demented, then busied herself making a fresh pot of coffee.

Sarah continued breathlessly. "Grandmother Spider kills cows too. And horses. Some time later, she'll come back and get the dead man out of the tree." She closed her eyes. "And then she'll *eat* him."

Daisy, who was turning up the gas flame under the coffeepot, seemed not to hear the child's lurid prediction.

Moon had no doubt that the old woman had been filling the little girl's head with some of her foolish tales. The policeman was well aware of the power of suggestion. Sarah hears an awful story about a giant spider, so when something unusual happens, she naturally sees one in the dark. Whatever had spooked Daisy and Sarah—and Daniel Bignight—was probably an unusual display generated by last night's thunderstorm. Some kind of electrical phenomenon. He recalled a novelty lamp he's seen in Durango. Violet-tinted electrical discharges moved continuously over the inner wall of a hollow glass sphere. The same sort of thing might happen in electrical storms. Moon pictured a great mass of orange plasma, surrounded by long, writhing, electrical discharges. A child with an active imagination might interpret this as an incredibly large spider. Or, in Daniel Bignight's case . . . a monster of another sort, wading out of Navajo Lake to rip hoods off trucks and jerk luckless men right out of their boots.

Moon pushed his chair away from the table. "It's time we left for school." He patted the girl's head. "Sarah, I think you'd better keep this thing about— uh—Grandmother Spider . . . to yourself."

The little girl nodded obediently.

The old woman surprised her nephew by agreeing with him. "That's right. Some things is best kept in the family. Besides," she added opaquely, "loose lips sink ships."

Moon regarded his aunt with an openly suspicious look.

Daisy's mood was improving. "Long as you're hauling Sarah to school, you might as well take me into town. I got some shopping to do." *And some visiting.*

Two hours later, Sarah Frank—duly delivered to Ignacio Public School by Charlie Moon—was sitting primly at her desk. Watching the teacher do a math problem at the blackboard, which was actually green. Her best friend leaned over to whisper in her ear. "My momma said that Tommy Tonompicket went fishing over at Navajo Lake last night. And he didn't ever come home."

Sarah shrugged complacently. According to Aunt Daisy, Mr. Tonompicket was a notorious drunk who didn't come home most nights.

Best Friend—truly her mother's daughter—was not discouraged by this apparent lack of interest. "An Indian policeman came to talk to Miz Tonompicket way before daylight this morning and my momma went next door to see what was wrong. The reason Tommy didn't come home," the budding gossip whispered hoarsely, "was that somethin' came right up outta Navajo Lake. And grabbed him."

Sarah felt her blood turn cold. She turned and stared wide-eyed at her smug comrade. "Out of the lake . . . ?" Where Grandmother Spider's cavern was hidden under the cold waters.

Best Friend nodded importantly. "Something really *big*, they say. Yanked Mr. Tonompicket right out of his boots and took off, with him screaming something awful! Lordy," she added, imitating her mother's tone.

Sarah looked up to see the teacher towering over her. "You two want to share this fascinating conversation with the class?"

Sarah hung her head in abject shame.

Best Friend also seemed to be embarrassed. In fact, she was delighted at the opportunity offered by the teacher. *Oh no, ma'am, please don't throw me into that awful brier patch!*

The teacher—who believed she was in complete control of the situation—decided to make an example of the little motormouth. It would serve as a stern warning to others.

With just enough hesitation to lend credence to her story, Best Friend stood before the class and repeated the lurid account of Tommy Tonompicket's mysterious disappearance. The audience of nine-year-olds was entranced. The teacher, though officially disapproving of such tales, hung on every word.

At recess, the children talked of nothing else. The fact that everyone had seen Tommy Tonompicket in the flesh gave the tale an element of solid reality. He was missing, wasn't he? And hadn't the Ute cop found Tommy's empty boots right there by his flatbed truck? There were several theories, but the prevailing opinion was that some sort of hideous monster had grabbed Tommy. Something strong enough to jerk him right out of his boots and carry him away to some unspeakable fate. The tale was simply wonderful.

Sarah Frank was sorely tempted to tell what she knew, but the little girl did not repeat her bone-chilling account about how she'd seen Grandmother Spider carrying a man in her clutches. A man the eight-legged, two-fanged monster would undoubtedly dine on. She would have loved to tell the awful tale to her friends, but the child remembered her solemn promise to Charlie Moon. And Aunt Daisy's dark warnings about loose lips.

———•

Daisy Perika sat in Louise-Marie LaForte's cozy parlor. The elderly French-Canadian woman—who lived in a dilapidated house on the edge of Ignacio—came to see her Ute friend whenever the unpaved reservation roads permitted. And Daisy often returned the visits when Charlie Moon drove her to town. The Ute took a sip of weak coffee from her cup. *Like drinking warmed-over dishwater.* Daisy picked up the thread of her tale. "When she first spotted it, the little girl thought it was a gang of them bug-eyed little space-midgets—the kind that swoop down and carry folks off."

The antique woman rocked back and forth in the antique chair. "I don't much like them space-people. I think they mean to move into Ignacio someday. Take over the whole town." *Damn foreigners.*

The Ute elder—barely aware of the interruption—continued. "But later—when Charlie came by my place—Sarah told him it looked like Grandmother Spider."

Louise-Marie cupped a hand by her ear. "Who?"

Daisy explained about the giant spider who lived in a cavern under Navajo Lake. How, long ago, she had killed her husband and eaten him.

The elderly French-Canadian woman shuddered. "How *awful.*"

Daisy Perika, pleased at this response, continued with her report of the past evening's adventure. "All I saw was this big thing that could change back and forth from a black shadow to a bright light. I didn't see nothing that looked like no spider. I still say it was bug-eyed monsters in a spaceship." *Or a skin-walker. Or maybe a ghost-light.* Best not to mention that she'd taken a couple of shots at the thing. Louise-Marie had a tendency to talk too much.

The elderly French-Canadian woman—who was sipping delicately at green Japanese tea—nodded as *one who knows.* "There's lots of bad things that creep around in the night, looking for a chance to do some dirty work." This telling of monster tales was a delightful game. And Louise-Marie held a pretty good hand. Not to be outdone, she decided to see the giant spider, raise with a hairy monster. "Did I ever tell you about the *Loup-Garou*?"

Daisy rolled her eyes at the cracked plaster ceiling. *Only about six hundred times.*

"That *Loup-Garou*, he's all hairy. *Oui*, with a long tail, him."

"Sounds like a ring-tailed bush rat."

Ignoring the insult, Louise-Marie held an arthritic finger near each temple. "And he's got horns!"

The Ute woman snorted. "*Goats* got horns."

"And the *Loup-Garou*, he smells awful—like rotting flesh!"

"A goat with the mange," Daisy suggested innocently.

The French-Canadian woman stood her ground. "The *Loup-Garou*, why, he'll carry off little babies—right from their cribs." This dread pronouncement was punctuated with an appropriate expression of horror.

Daisy dismissed this doubtful claim with a disdainful wave of her wrinkled hand. "That old Loop prob'ly picks on little children because he's afraid to tackle something *sizable*. Grandmother Spider, she's been known to bite the head off a full-grown buffalo."

This preposterous claim brought a smirk to Louise-Marie's leathery face. "My, my, Daisy—that's quite a story." She sniffed. "Do you really believe such stuff?"

The Ute woman turned up her nose at the old smart aleck. "My father *saw* her, down by the San Juan. It was back in nineteen and twenty-one."

Louise-Marie's bright blue eyes twinkled. "And I'm sure he was cold sober."

Unperturbed by the malicious implications of this remark, Daisy went on. "It was on September the thirteenth, late in the day—just as the sun was goin' down." Small details provided authenticity. "Daddy—he was tendin' some sheep—said old Eight-Legs was wadin' right out into the deep water."

Pulled by the gravity of this tale, the French-Canadian woman leaned forward.

Now Daisy played her hole card. "Daddy said Grandmother Spider had a fine Hereford steer tucked under each arm." It still needed a final touch. "And both of them steers was still alive and kickin' and squallin' to beat the band."

Louise-Marie opened her mouth to respond, but could think of no praise for the *Loup-Garou*'s dark skills that would meet this last challenge. Indeed, compared to the Ute's amazing spider-woman, the Hairy One seemed almost pathetic. Thus defeated, she folded her hand.

The Ute elder—secure in her victory—smiled sweetly and reached into her grocery bag. "You want a chocolate chip cookie with your tea?"

Louise-Marie sighed despondently. "That would be nice."

———.·

By twilight, almost every household within ten miles of Ignacio had heard some version of the tale. Shortly after dark, a gathering of local barflies offered solemn opinions on the disappearance of poor old Tommy Tonompicket (bless his soul). As the dusky moon reached its zenith, small children had nightmares wherein they were chased by hideous monsters.

Shortly after dawn touched the sky, the lurid tale of how Tonompicket had been jerked right out of his boots by an unidentified something-or-other was discussed at great length on KSUT's morning show. A local drunk rang up the station to say he'd never liked Tommy Tonompicket overly much ever since the fellow had stole a whole case of beer out of the bed of his pickup and he hoped the monster had swallowed the little bastard whole. Because this citizen had not gotten into the spirit of the thing, his taped call was not played on the air. But most calls to the station were made by outraged tribal members demanding to know what had happened to Tommy Tonompicket. Exactly what were the tribal police doing about all this? Who would be snatched away next? Several children called, saying how awfully scared they were. It was fun to be On The Air.

When the weekly *Southern Ute Drum* hit the streets, there were several interviews and two dozen letters. Decisive action was demanded.

It was perfectly clear to the elected tribal leadership that this first wave of hysteria was but a hint of the tidal swell to come.

———•

The old woman should have slept well on this night. For one thing, it was a sweetly fragrant evening in early spring, when the pungent aroma of new grasses tickles the nostrils with a promise of life renewed. Second, on this particular evening Daisy Perika had not filled her belly with corrosive spices and caustic animal fats. Uncharacteristically, she had eaten a mild supper of twice-boiled potatoes, warmed-over pinto beans, and a heel of dark rye bread. It was not her habit to sup on such bland fare—but these were nutritious leftovers that must be consumed. Daisy did not practice such economies because she was a frugal woman, but on account of being habitually short of cash. There was a third reason that she should have slept soundly: The child, tucked in her bed in the far end of the trailer

home, was fast asleep, dreaming of fields of blue flowers. Sarah Frank was—so it seemed—as safe as a little
girl can be in this world.

But Daisy's world is full of restless spirits that linger
on from the misty past. And some will surely come calling. Tap-tapping on the door.

The old woman said her prayers, which were primarily a list of names for God to remember. The child led
the list, followed by Daisy's nephew, Charlie Moon. The
tribal policeman had a dangerous job to do for the People, who—she reminded the Creator—didn't pay him
nearly enough for what he did. She put in a good word
for Scott Parris. The Ute elder felt a strange kinship to
this *matukach* policeman who—from time to time—
also saw things beyond the edge of this world. Daisy
mentioned her cousin, Gorman Sweetwater, whose
drinking was likely to kill him. Unless she took it in her
mind to do it first. Gorman was a very annoying man,
and she didn't blame God much for not liking him. The
old woman did not neglect to mention her own needs.
She asked for relief from the arthritic pain that had settled in her left hip joint. And some extra money would
also be helpful; the child drank a quart of milk every
day. *Oh—and don't forget that I still need a telephone
out here. It would be nice if I could place a call to Ignacio now and then. Just for emergencies and such.*

Her prayer continued. *I'd never use a telephone for
foolishness, like gossip . . .*

God smiled.

Now she was slipping off to sleep. The aged woman
perceived a fleeting vision of Upper World. There were
familiar faces there, of those who had already passed
over that deep river. Her parents. All three of her hus-
bands. (She was surprised that one of them had made
it.) Some old friends waved to her. There were many,

many shining creatures—some whose faces were fearful to behold. In the midst of the angels . . . on a high place . . . was the Source of all that was Holy. She averted her eyes from this.

And then the heavenly vision faded.

As the aged pendulum clock above her bed ticked off the moments of this present age, the old woman slept without dreaming. The middle of night passed by without incident.

And on she slept.

Presently, just outside her trailer home, there was a sound. Like the scurrying of small feet. It might have been a wood rat.

Overhead, the sonorous flapping of great wings. An owl, perhaps. Hungry for a fat rodent.

And then she heard her name called. The shaman sat up on the side of her bed and rubbed her eyes. She might have been dreaming. Or perhaps not.

There was a flickering of light at the window.

Fire!

Daisy pushed back the curtains, expecting to behold a fearful vision of dry brush and piñon trees all ablaze—a wall of flames rushing toward her home.

What the shaman saw was something far more surprising. Perhaps even more dangerous.

It was the *pitukupf*.

She was stunned. It was virtually unheard of for the little man to leave his home between the towering sandstone walls. Yet here he was, dressed in a tattered green shirt, short buckskin trousers, beaded moccasins. On his head he wore a scruffy black hat, with a small blue feather in the leather band. The dwarf was tending a campfire, which he had kindled within yards of her bedroom window. *I shouldn't be so surprised. If I don't go to see him, sooner or later he's bound to come see me.*

The little man lived far up *Cañon del Espíritu*, in an abandoned badger hole. For more times than she cared to remember, the elderly Ute shaman had trudged up the canyon with a small bundle of gifts for the *pitukupf*. But for several months, she had stayed away.

The shaman wanted to apologize to the little man, to place the blame where it belonged. To make excuses. *It's all Father Raes' fault.*

The rector of St. Ignatius Catholic Church in Ignacio had warned Daisy of the terrible peril one courted when dealing with unwholesome spirits. Father Raes Delfino was a quiet, gentle man who would have much preferred an assignment on a university campus. Teaching anthropology . . . theology . . . church history. He was not, he thought, suitable for pastoral duties. But the scholar was transformed into a valiant, club-wielding shepherd whenever a member of his little flock was threatened by the wolves. The priest—who had spent years among the primitive people who lived in the dark rain forests of Brazil—had a store of hair-raising tales that illustrated the dangers of those peculiar spirits who inhabit places in the wilderness. The South American Indians talked to frog-spirits (Daisy found this quite amusing—what would you say to a frog?), and the consequences of this unholy communion had been frightful. An elder who communed with the pop-eyed spirit had gone stone-blind and thrown himself into a river. A mother—on orders from the frog-god—had killed her newborn son. A young man had gone mad and cut out his own tongue! And so Daisy Perika—a Christian nourished by the Catholic branch of the Vine—had tried to follow her priest's solemn instructions.

But it was very hard.

The dwarf—carrying on a tradition that had involved

her distant ancestors—was an important source of power for the shaman. Every Ute healer had a connection to a power spirit. Most such sources were archetypal animals, who conferred specialized powers to heal. If the redheaded woodpecker was the source of a shaman's dream-power, he could stop bleeding of any sort. The helpful vision of a badger-spirit would enable a medicine woman to heal diseases and injuries associated with the hands and feet. And so it went.

But such narrow specialization was impractical in a small band of hunter-gatherers that might have only one or two healers. What one wanted was a physician who could deal with a broad range of common ailments. And—at some forgotten time in the long history of the People—there came an answer to this need.

It arrived in a diminutive form.

Powers gained by an association with the dwarf were very broad. Daisy Perika was, in effect, a general practitioner of spirit-medicine. With assistance from the *pitukupf*, she could deal with every ailment (with the exception of fractured bones) from head to toe.

And so she valued her association with the little man.

The old woman stepped into worn night-slippers. She found her third husband's woolen overcoat in the closet, and pulled it on over her nightgown. Daisy hobbled into the small kitchen, the cold leather soles of her loose slippers popping across the cracked linoleum floor. The shaman reached up to open a cabinet over the propane stove; this was where she kept the jar of sweets for the little girl. And the little man. She selected an Almond Joy candy bar and a large oatmeal cookie, and slipped these into her coat pocket.

The Ute elder swallowed hard and prepared herself for the confrontation. She slowly turned the door handle, peeked through the crack of an opening, then stepped cautiously onto the creaky wooden porch.

The dwarf was squatted in what seemed an uncomfortable position, tending his small fire. He poked at the embers with a crooked stick. A pair of willow forks supported a resinous branch over the fire. This simple spit pierced the skinned carcass of a small rabbit. Yellow fat bubbled above the flames; savory juices plopped onto the juniper embers and sizzled.

Daisy Perika hesitated. Even though the uninvited guest was camped on her property, the *pitukupf* must be treated with due respect. One did not simply walk up to the dwarf-spirit and say: "Hello, little fellow. How are you tonight?" This particular *pitukupf*—like all his wee brethren—was a bit testy at best. At his worst . . . well, one did not wish to imagine him at his worst. The dwarf was capable of sudden flares of temper—he had once strangled a spotted horse that her cousin had taken into *Cañon del Espíritu*. Gorman Sweetwater had been very upset by the loss of such a fine mare. But, Daisy reasoned, it wasn't actually the *pitukupf*'s fault. Gorman should have known better than to tether his horse so near the little man's home. It was well known that the *pitukupf* detested these animals who had come with the invaders from Europe. Odd, she mused, that the dwarfs should have attached themselves to a tribe that so loved horses. But the little men had come to live with the People ages ago—long before the Spaniards had brought the strange, four-legged beasts to the shining mountains. The Ute elder pulled the overcoat collar tightly about her neck. And waited patiently for the *pitukupf* to acknowledge her presence.

He seemed in no hurry to take note of the shaman's arrival. His interest was apparently occupied by the preparation of his meal. The dwarf sniffed, evidently finding the aroma of the roasting rabbit quite fetching. Indeed, so engrossed was he in the preparation of his feast that the *pitukupf* might have been at home in the perfect privacy of his subterranean badger hole, sitting contentedly by the fireplace. The little man seemed quite at ease. He touched a glowing piñon splinter to his clay pipe, lighting a bowl stuffed with dried kinnikinnick leaf. He took a long draw. Coughed. Took the pipe from his mouth, frowned at the smoldering bowl. Then cast a nasty sideways glance at the old woman, who was descending the steps below her flimsy porch.

The shaman, who was quite familiar with his ways, understood this crafty little pantomime. *So you're tired of smoking kinnikinnick. Mad at me because I haven't brought you no tobacco for a long time now.* And there was none in the house. *But maybe you'll be satisfied with the sweets.* Her presence acknowledged by the grumpy little fellow, the shaman drew near to the fire. For some time she stood there, holding her hands out to the pleasant warmth, flickering orange light reflecting off her palms.

When it was apparent that the little man would not object, Daisy unbuttoned her woolen overcoat and sat down by the fire.

The *pitukupf*, after watching the progress of his cooking for some time, eventually removed the spit and sniffed tentatively at the hot carcass. Apparently satisfied with the aroma, he pierced a rear leg with a long thumbnail, presumably to test for tenderness. From the pleased expression on his narrow face, it seemed the rabbit was roasted to his liking.

Needless to say, he did not pause to give thanks for this food.

Daisy Perika sat in silence as he greedily stripped the roasted flesh from the skeleton of the rabbit, pitching the fragile bones unceremoniously into the fire. It was not a pleasant thing, watching the *pitukupf* devour his nightly meal. His teeth were yellowed, the canines unpleasantly long and sharp. Grease soiled his bony fingers and dripped from his chin. Moreover, he offered her not a morsel.

Good table manners were not the dwarf's long suit.

The old woman waited until he had quite finished his meal, then produced the sweets from her coat pocket. She offered him the candy bar and the large cookie. Without formality, he snatched these delicacies from her hand. The little man gobbled up the oatmeal cookie in a few bites, then sniffed suspiciously at the paper-wrapped Almond Joy. Cautiously, he pierced the wrapper with a pointed fingernail. And sniffed again. He popped a delicious chocolate-coated morsel into his mouth, and chewed with enormous concentration.

The Ute elder smiled. *So you like the coconut and the almonds.*

The *pitukupf* finished Daisy's treats without so much as a glance at the shaman.

Daisy was asking herself the obvious question: *Why are you here?* To visit her home, he had left his underground lair—even forsaken the protective walls of *Cañon del Espíritu.* So the little man surely must have something important to tell her. But thus far, he had said not one word. She decided to work her way up to it gradually. "Weather's been peculiar," she said. "Way too warm for this time of year . . . the snow is meltin' fast."

No reply.

"I expect we'll have some bad floods in the canyon—

you oughta be careful. That hole in the ground where you live might fill up with water."

She paused to shift gears.

"There've been some strange doings since the last time I saw you."

He sighed, and scratched indolently at his round belly.

But the shaman noticed a glint of interest in his eye. More than likely, he'd come here to tell her what he knew. He was a lonely little fellow. And he liked to show off how smart he was. But the *pitukupf* expected to be coaxed and cajoled. It was the way of men. Even little men.

"People on the reservation are all wondering what happened to Tommy Tonompicket down at Navajo Lake. Some people say one thing, some another." She hesitated. The little man knew everything that went on around here. But he wasn't very talkative. Not unless you made out like you thought he *didn't* know. She pretended to think hard about the issue. "I think maybe the bug-eyed monsters got 'im."

His thin lips twisted into a sneer.

When he was in a talkative mood, you might get maybe half a dozen words out of him. Tonight it looked like he might not say a thing.

But knowing that the *pitukupf* was a prideful little fellow, she pressed on. "Well, I don't suppose you have any notions. I guess you just sit out there in your badger hole and smoke your pipe." She sighed. "Old men get that way." She got up, as if to depart.

Her visitor also got to his feet, and stretched to his full height—which was not much above Daisy's knee.

Hoping something would come from her taunts, the shaman waited expectantly.

The *pitukupf* used the crooked stick to stir glowing embers in the dying fire.

Maybe he's going to leave without saying anything. Just to aggravate me.

As he stirred the embers, a sooty smudge arose from the ashes.

The shaman watched closely.

The fumes above the fire were flowing here and there. Much like any campfire smoke you might see. But the dwarf twirled the loopy stick. The smoke took on form.

The old woman shuddered; she would have preferred not to see this abomination.

It was a hideous shape. The thing had no true color; it was the mottled gray of dead, worm-eaten wood. The body of the monster was like a fat summer squash. Its legs—all eight of them—were long and spindly. And they wriggled anxiously below the bulbous body, as if the awful thing were attempting to escape the searing heat of the embers. Worst of all, a tiny, almost invisible thread hung from the belly of the repulsive creature. Entangled in this filament was something that struggled in a vain attempt to get free.

She leaned forward and squinted.

It was a tiny man.

Daisy, fascinated by what she saw, was rooted to the spot.

The *pitukupf*, who had been watching this singular development with professional interest, finally spoke. His words were clipped, his tone throaty and guttural. Though he used an archaic version of the Ute tongue, the shaman understood the meaning of his question. The teacher wanted to know whether his pupil understood what it was that had materialized over the ashes.

"Yes," the shaman whispered in utter horror, ". . . it's a spider." But she knew this was not something you'd find hiding under a rotten log, ready to plant poisonous fangs in your finger—or hanging on a trembling web, waiting for an unwary bluefly. Daisy took a deep breath and said what had to be said. "It's Grandmother Spider. She's making a web . . . to strangle the man. And the man is one of the People."

The *pitukupf* half smiled, exposing jagged rows of yellowed teeth. He vigorously stirred the crooked stick in the embers under the apparition, kindling new flames. The dwarf ceremoniously lifted the helical baton like a conductor calling dark chords from an unseen orchestra. The glowing sparks swirled up the column of heated air . . . and the hideous image of the eight-legged creature followed. As it ascended, the grayish form took on the bright orange hue of the yellow flames beneath it. The apparition grew larger, the entrapped man struggled vainly in hope of release. And screamed piteously for someone to help him.

But there was no help.

The shaman watched the horrific creature depart with the terrified man in its clutches. Daisy Perika was furious with the dwarf; the little man had done nothing to help the human being. She was ready to unleash a barrage of righteous protests.

But the *pitukupf* had vanished. And the small fire had no more light to give. The stars also flickered out, and no trace of opal moon could be seen. Indeed, the Ute elder could comprehend nothing around her—all had become utter darkness.

BETTY FLINTCORN, ELECTED tribal chairman just months earlier, had already earned a reputation for being a hardnose. She was proud of it. "No Nonsense" was the motto etched into a brass plaque on her wall. On this damp, cloudy morning, the plump, middle-aged woman sat quite alone in her office, sipping a cup of rose hip tea. The chairman reminded herself that she should not be alone. The acting chief of tribal police should be standing just beyond her desk, hat in hand, listening with great attention to what she had to say.

And acting on it.

Betty Flintcorn—a fanatical devotee of science-fiction flicks—saw herself in the role of admiral of the Federation's vast Starship fleet that patrolled the galaxy. Once again, those pesky Klingons were threatening—a sinister battle group was approaching Starbase Ignacio at Warp III, cloaking shields up, phaser torpedoes firing with deadly accuracy. The captain of the flagship vessel

(Officer Moon) would offer several options for action. Admiral Flintcorn, having listened with admirable patience to her subordinate, would reveal her own daring plan—and give the solemn order . . . *make it so.* Captain Moon would do her bidding without question; Klingons would fall in the thousands.

Like many citizens, the tribal chairman spent entirely too much time watching television.

She stared accusingly at the round, bland face of the quartz chronometer strapped to her wrist. Her own round face twisted into an ugly frown. Charlie Moon was already six minutes late.

The office door opened. The man—who was broad of shoulder and very tall—dipped his head to enter.

Betty Flintcorn held the wristwatch out for him to see. "Charlie Moon, you are six minutes late."

He bent to inspect the watch. "Looks closer to seven."

She snorted.

He offered an amiable smile in return. Betty used to be a fairly pleasant soul before she was elected by a two-thirds margin. He grinned. "Sorry, Mrs. Chairman. Had a flat. Didn't have a spare, so I had to do a hot-patch."

The new police station was a short walk from the brick building where her office was located. And she didn't like Moon's silly so-called sense of humor. "I do not intend to run this office on Indian Time. We have an appointment, I expect you to show up on the dot. Do you understand me?"

He nodded. And waited for her to get past the obligatory pleasantries and start talking. That's mostly what politicians did. Talk. And he was sure he knew just what she'd want to talk about—the Tonompicket disappearance. So her introductory remark caught him a bit off guard.

"Charlie, do you want to be permanent chief of police?"

He'd been acting chief since Severo retired. "Why should I?"

This was an unsettling response. She stirred the tea with a silver-plated spoon. "Don't you know it isn't polite to answer a question with a question?"

"Why not?" Though uninvited to sit, he turned a straight-backed chair around and straddled it.

Her dark eyes glinted. Charlie Moon was always joking. On the other hand, he was very competent. And more important, he was nonpolitical. Never took sides in divisive tribal issues, like what to do with earnings from the casino. Never openly supported a council candidate. Never bad-mouthed anybody. Never got a friend or relative hired on the police force. So Moon, though not uniformly liked, was trusted and respected by everyone. Especially the common criminals. He was known for hammering them hard when they needed hammering. And for finding some excuse to turn them loose when he didn't think jail was doing them or the tribe any good. "Do you know how much we were paying Roy Severo?"

He shrugged, like it didn't matter. It did.

She told him.

He took a deep breath. "That much?"

The chairman nodded.

"That's *twice* what I'm making."

"A little more than twice," she said. "You sure you don't want the job?"

He frowned at the plump woman. She was smarter than he'd given her credit for. "I'll have to think about it." He got up, towering over her like a great tree.

It was unnerving. "Sit down," she commanded.

"Thank you," he said politely. "I'd rather stand."

She pointed a yellow number-three pencil up at his forehead. "While you're thinking about whether you want to be permanent chief of police, think about this—Tommy Tonompicket is missing. There's talk he got carried away by a . . . something or other . . ." The dignified woman coughed, cleared her throat. She waited for Moon to say something. He did not. "Well, where is he?"

"If I knew, I'd be going to get him."

Her blood pressure climbed ten points. "When . . . do you expect to find him?"

Moon stared at the ceiling. "Hard to say. I've been experiencing some delays."

Betty Flintcorn clenched her jaw. "What delays?"

"For one, coming here to answer your questions."

She ground her teeth. "Do not mess with me, Charlie Moon."

Smiling happily, he put on his broad-brimmed black Stetson. "Betty, this has been fun. But I've got some work to do." Making a point of not asking her leave, he turned on his heel and departed.

Betty Flintcorn sat behind her massive walnut desk, looking twice as mean as the bull buffalo in the painting over her head. It was an innocent, pastoral scene done in oils. Rolling Thunder stood in knee-deep grass, glowering across a rolling prairie. The tribal chairman glared silently at the closed door. And thought her thoughts. *Charlie Moon is getting too big for his britches. Needs taking down a notch or two.*

SOUTHERN UTE POLICE DEPARTMENT, 8:30 A.M.

Nancy Beyal motioned Moon over to her desk, where lights on the telephone lines flashed like nervous fireflies. The normally unflappable dispatcher was fairly trembling with anxiety. She pointed a shaking finger at the blinking lights. "You've got to do something, Charlie!"

"About what?"

"About *what*? I'm getting a call a minute from people who say they've seen something strange near their homes. Giant bugs of all kinds. One old man swears he's had a half-dozen chickens stolen by hairy tarantulas the size of dinner plates. They all expect us to do something. I tell them we're shorthanded, that most of the officers on patrol are dealing with drunks and road accidents. They're frantic, Charlie—and they're making me frantic." Her lower lip trembled. "So you got to do something."

He managed an innocent expression. "Why me?"

" 'Cause you're the acting chief."

"Oh."

The telephone buzzed again. More lights flashed. "SUPD—please hold." She snapped the microphone headset over her ears.

Moon felt that he had to say something. "Where are the calls coming from?"

She didn't look up. "Mostly from Ignacio."

"That's out of our jurisdiction, except for complaints from tribal members. Refer non-Indian calls to the town police." *There. A command decision.*

She snorted. "The Ignacio PD dispatcher has already been instructed to refer all the *freaky* calls to SUPD." Nancy sighed. "They say we're responsible for this giant-spider nonsense, so we should take the calls."

"The department never said anything about spiders," he pointed out reasonably.

Reason infuriated the harried dispatcher. "Don't tell

me," Nancy Beyal fairly shrieked, pointing at the blinking console, "tell *them*."

Moon backed away. "Uh . . . excuse me. I got some business to take care of." On his way to his office, he paused at Bignight's desk. "Daniel, see Nancy gets a rest from the console."

Bignight squinted uncertainly at the duty roster. "We're kinda shorthanded."

"Then *you* take over Dispatch for a coupla hours." Bignight had started this mess.

The Taos Pueblo man's face went blank, which meant he wasn't too happy with this order. But he got up without a word and approached the dispatcher's console.

Moon hurried into the spacious corner office assigned to the chief of police and shut the door. He poured a cup of black coffee from the percolator, added six sugar cubes, and seated himself behind the desk that had belonged to Roy Severo before the man had had the good sense to retire. Being chief of police wasn't all it was cracked up to be. Being acting chief was worse. You got all the headaches and half the pay. But at least it was quiet in here so a man could think. The telephone hardly ever rang . . .

It rang.

"Shoot," Moon said. *Maybe if I don't answer it . . .*

The thing continued to jangle. Moon got up, headed for the door. When he opened it, Nancy Beyal was standing there, glaring at him. She had a wicked-looking letter opener in her right hand. Her knuckles were white.

"Answer the damn phone," she said evenly.

"Oh . . . the phone."

"Now," she barked. "Answer it!"

It was not, he told himself, like he was afraid of a

hundred-pound woman. But an effective manager knows when to humor the more neurotic members of his staff. So the acting chief of police backed into his office, closing the door softly.

He sat down. And reached hesitantly for the telephone.

Ten to one it'll be some kook, with a story about a goblin in his backyard.

His voice was weary, resigned. "Moon here." *Go ahead. Do your worst.*

"Charlie?"

The Ute policeman grinned with a mixture of relief and pleasure. "Scott?"

"Hey . . . sorry, but I can't make it for our one o'clock lunch at Angel's. I'll be a little late."

"How late?"

"Could be an hour. Maybe two."

Two hours? Moon's stomach growled in protest. "What's up?"

Parris grunted. "Routine call—way down by the county line. Another two miles south and it'd be out of our jurisdiction." *And into yours.*

"You could refer it to the state cops."

"They claim they're spread way too thin to be bothered with minor complaints. I could send out a patrol car, but I hate to waste the manpower when I'm heading in that direction anyway."

Moon, who hated the thought of a late lunch, was thinking fast. "That anywhere near Mining City?"

"Yeah. I gotta take a road up the mountain, just a half mile north of the junction."

"They got a restaurant?"

"Sure," Parris said. "And a gas station and a general store." It was a tourist stop.

"Tell you what . . . let's say I meet you for lunch. Save you a trip all the way to Ignacio."

Parris chuckled. "What is it, Charlie, that spider-monster flap you guys stirred up gettin' to be too much for you?"

"You heard about that?"

The chuckle grew into a laugh. "Heard about it? It's all over the TV and the newspapers. We're even getting some calls up here. Dispatch just took one from a little old grandpa who swears his pussycat was eaten alive by a hairy goblin that was big as a Volkswagen. One bite, good-bye, tabby. I sent Officer Slocum out to talk to him. He told the old guy to calm down, that it must've been a mountain lion that ate his cat. Grandpa swatted Slocum with a broom, and made disparaging remarks about his mother."

The Ute policeman groaned.

"Charlie—you there?"

Moon nodded absently.

Parris' voice was louder this time. "Charlie?"

"I'm here, pardner. What time you expect to show up at Mining City?"

"Oh . . . let's say noon."

"See you there."

Moon glanced at the clock on the wall. That'd just give him time to make a stop in Durango.

FBI FIELD OFFICE, DURANGO,
9:20 A.M.

Moon was silent as he read the FBI report on the latent prints Bignight had lifted from the GMC pickup. A thumbprint belonged to Tommy Tonompicket, who had been fingerprinted years ago when he joined the

Marines. Most of a whole set belonged to the man who owned the pickup—a Dr. William Pizinski, who had a New Mexico address in Bosque Farms, which was just south of Albuquerque. Pizinski, a bureau check revealed, had a Department of Defense clearance. The special agent had already put in a call to Pizinski's home and got an answering machine. The New Mexico State Police had been notified.

Stan Newman was pacing back and forth like a man who'd just heard that his wife had delivered twins . . . and was half expecting the count to increase. Triplets at least, maybe even quads. "We got your prints ID'd, Charlie—I hope you're satisfied."

Moon hid his amusement behind a serious expression. "Thing is, Stan, you're always reminding me that the FBI is responsible for investigating serious crimes on Indian reservations. So I figured it was my duty to keep you informed. I thought maybe you hadn't heard about our . . . uh . . . missing-persons thing. We've got a potful of misdemeanors to handle at SUPD and you know how we're understaffed."

Special Agent Stan Newman snapped at the Ute policeman. "Understaffed my aunt Minnie—there's just two of us working out of a cramped office in Durango and you got a fancy new police station with a fifty-five-bed detention center and two dozen staff and—"

"Twenty-three," Moon corrected. "And some of them are jailers and dispatchers."

Newman responded with something that was halfway between a snort and a laugh. "Anyway, how can the tribe afford the new building?"

"The wages of sin," the Ute said evenly.

"Casino profits, huh?" Newman didn't look at Moon, who was comfortably stretched out in a padded chair. He spoke in a hard-edged accent that hinted of

New Jersey. "Look, Charlie, I try to read the local rags. And when I get a chance, I even catch the news on the tube. These guys you've lost . . . this have anything to do with the—uh—thing from the lake?"

Moon managed to look puzzled. "Thing from the lake?"

The special agent grinned like a possum. "It was on the TV news last night. Said you guys are chasing after some great big . . . thing . . . that ran off with somebody."

The Ute policeman closed his eyes. "You watch too much television, Stan. I don't have time for such foolishness—I'm here on serious police business. What we have is a couple of missing persons. You FBI types are supposed to take an interest in major crimes on the reservation."

Newman waved his arms. "I didn't consider this thing down at Navajo Lake as something really . . . well, major." He stopped and stared blankly at an enlarged color photograph of the president of the United States. "So. We got two citizens presumably gone missing from the reservation—one of 'em a Native American, the other one some scientist from Albuquerque. And Danny Bignight's claiming he's seen some kinda . . . thing. And he hears somebody screaming. Bignight figures it's a tribal member . . ."

"Tommy Tonompicket," Moon said helpfully. "Only I don't think Daniel figured it was Tommy right away. He came to this conclusion sometime after he found Tommy's boots and flatbed truck. And learned that Tommy hadn't got home that night."

Stan Newman blinked at the president's smiling countenance. "And then your aunt Daisy, she—how is she, by the way?"

Moon shrugged. "Same as usual. Old as the hills.

Mean as a green-eyed snake. Seeing ghosts and goblins in every shadow."

Newman, who had not heard a word, nodded. "Good. Glad to hear it. And I hear your aunt Daisy and this little girl, Sally Whatshername . . ."

"Sarah Frank."

". . . claim they saw something skulking around Daisy's trailer."

"Where'd you hear that?"

The special agent grinned. "We're the FBI, Charlie. We hear everything."

"Including gossip," the Ute policeman said. Moon didn't think it advisable to mention that Aunt Daisy— scared by a TV show about flying-saucer abductions— had seen an alien spaceship. And Sarah Frank—prompted by Daisy's wild tales—had seen Grandmother Spider. Especially since his aunt had fired her shotgun at the . . . whatever it was.

Newman turned to frown at the big Ute. "Your old auntie reminds me of my grandmother back in Trenton. As she got past eighty-five, Grandma started getting kinda peculiar—always hearing sneak thieves in the backyard. She mistook me for a burglar one night, brained me with a bedpan. It was stainless steel—had sharp edges. I hadda have sixteen stitches," Newman added as he rubbed a thick ridge of scar tissue under his hairline. "You need to talk to your aunt about moving into Ignacio. Where somebody can keep an eye on her."

Moon tried hard not to smile. "I've talked to her. But she doesn't pay me any attention. I think it's because I'm her nephew." He raised his eyebrows as if an interesting thought had just occurred to him. "But she does respect people who represent the federal government. Especially the FBI."

Newman was pleased to hear this. "Really?"

"Sure. Maybe I should take you out to her place sometime. You could explain how she needs to move into town. Maybe into one of those 'assisted-living' facilities."

"You think she'd listen to me?" That old woman had a reputation for being mule-stubborn.

Moon nodded. "Aunt Daisy respects authority. But you'd have to get tough—lay the law down to her." He saw a shadow of doubt pass over the special agent's features. "That's the kind of thing that gets her attention." *This should make for some great entertainment.*

Newman, who wore both belt and suspenders, hooked his thumbs in the latter and tugged thoughtfully at the elastic. "Maybe I will. Maybe I'll just do that."

"Make sure I'm with you," the Ute policeman added quickly. "Aunt Daisy might be overly intimidated if there's no—uh—family there to lend some support." *I'll have to make sure she doesn't shoot you.*

"Okay, Charlie. First chance I get, I'll give her a good talking-to." He began to snap the suspenders with his thumbs. "Now what do we do about this Dr. Pizinski's disappearance? And Mr. Tonompicket? You want me to open an official investigation?"

Moon shrugged. "Your call, Stan. But it'd sure help my department."

Newman's gray eyes narrowed. "How?"

The Ute policeman hesitated. And avoided the special agent's suspicious stare. "Well, to tell you the truth, since this thing was reported publicly we've been getting a coupla dozen calls a day at SUPD. Mostly from people who claim they've seen all kinda giant bugs. And funny things flying around in the sky. All these complaints have to be checked out. It'd be nice if we could just refer these calls to your office and—"

"Whoa, now! Hold on. You have any hard evidence that a crime's been committed?"

Moon tried to look embarrassed. "Well, no *hard* evidence. But there's no sign of either Tonompicket or Pizinski yet and . . ."

Newman tapped his finger on Moon's chest. "Lissen. When you've got some solid evidence of a serious crime, like murder or kidnapping, general mayhem, you inform this office." He shrugged. "Maybe they had a boat in one of those trucks. I bet they went fishing. Those two jokers might be anywhere along the banks of Navajo Lake. The Bureau don't have enough manpower to go around searching the whole stinkin' lake for fishermen who would rather be left alone." He shook his head wearily. "I don't have time for this nonsense, Charlie. I got an unsolved bank robbery right here in Durango, a casino holdup on the Ute Mountain Reservation—I could go on . . ."

Moon nodded sympathetically. "Maybe I should refer this case to the BIA cops." Stan had not been getting along well with the Bureau of Indian Affairs. Some petty jurisdictional dispute. Like who investigated major cases of arson on the reservation.

Stan Newman's nostrils flared. "If and when it seems appropriate, I'll talk to the BIA police about your missing persons. I'd appreciate it if you just kept clear of 'em, Charlie."

Moon—his mission accomplished—got up. He patted the agitated man reassuringly on the shoulder. "Sorry I bothered you, Stan. But I didn't want you to think I wasn't keeping you informed."

The special agent, somewhat mollified, followed the Ute policeman to the door. "Don't mention it, Charlie. I know you meant well."

When he was on the street, breathing in the sweetly scented April air, Moon allowed himself a broad smile.

The FBI had been duly and officially informed about the Pizinski-Tonompicket disappearance. And had unequivocally stated their strong disinterest. Moreover, he had been instructed to leave the BIA cops out of the picture. So until he uncovered hard evidence of a serious crime on the reservation, the Bureau wouldn't be breathing down his neck. Pestering him about jurisdictional issues and proper protocol. And he had an excuse if the BIA cops started grumbling about jurisdiction.

Now for the hard part.

He had to find out what had happened to Tommy Tonompicket and the *matukach* scientist. It would be something ordinary. Daniel Bignight had probably seen a big tumbleweed blowing in the wind. Heard a coyote howl. Been temporarily befuddled by a close flash of lightning. Stranger things had happened. Stan Newman was probably right. Chances were, Pizinski (drunk) and Tonompicket (barefoot and drunk) were somewhere on the lake, baiting their hooks for rainbow trout. Or maybe they were somewhere *under* the lake . . . had become lunch for the bottom-feeders. At the back of his mind, this grim possibility nagged at the policeman— that they had slipped away to the other side of the rainbow.

But the early Utes had a saying: *Don't think bad thoughts*. So Charlie Moon attempted to exclude these unpleasant images from his mind. Time to get down to some serious work. The acting chief of Southern Ute police thrust his hands into his jacket pockets. He felt the smooth surface of the plastic instrument. He had—after relentless haranguing from Dispatch—grudgingly agreed to carry a cellular telephone. So the station could get in contact with the acting chief of police, wherever he might wander. Charlie Moon—who treasured the infrequent moments of quiet and solitude—fervently hoped that Mining City was not in the infernal instrument's range.

———•

Inside the Mining City Cafe, the lunch crowd had thinned. A scattering of long-haul truckers sat around munching extremely greasy cheeseburgers, which they washed down with scalding coffee. The lawmen retreated to a booth in a shadowed corner, where they spoke in low, unhurried tones. The main topic was Scott Parris' engagement. The date was not yet set. But Charlie Moon was to be best man. There were details to discuss. Jokes about whether there was a tux west of the Mississippi big enough to outfit the Ute. There were also serious questions. Why hadn't Anne set a date for the wedding? How would Scott deal with her being out of town chasing stories half the time? What would he do if the pretty journalist felt compelled to accept a job somewhere far away from Granite Creek?

When Scott's mood turned mildly blue, Moon sensed that it was time to plow some new ground. "So what's the police business that brings you down here?"

Parris rotated the heavy coffee mug in his hands. "Nothing important. A friend of the mayor's—some big-shot lawyer from Denver—he's got himself a cabin up on First Finger Ridge. Came down here a couple of days ago to open it up for the summer. His wife has called several times, but he don't answer."

It was common, especially after heavy snows, for trees to fall on the lines. The phone had probably been dead for months. Electric power was probably out too. "Must be a line down," the Ute said.

"Not according to U.S. West," Parris said. "Phone line checks out okay. Maybe he never got to the cabin."

"Or maybe he don't want to talk to his wife." Moon grinned. "I've heard that married life can get tedious."

"Tedious is a helluva lot better than lonesome, Charlie."

His tone was so earnest that the Ute did not respond. And then something bubbled up from the depths of Moon's subconscious. "When did this lawyer get to his cabin?"

Parris consulted a neatly kept notebook. "April first, assuming he got there at all. He was supposed to call his wife that night. He didn't. She started calling the next morning. No answer."

A cold something touched the back of Moon's neck. First day of April. That was when the men had disappeared from the shore of Navajo Lake. The same night, just minutes later, Daisy had taken a shot at something . . . and Sarah Frank had seen a "big spider." And now this lawyer wasn't answering his phone. There probably wasn't any connection. "Pardner . . . maybe I should go up to that cabin with you."

Parris laid his greenbacks on the table. "You think I'm gonna need some help?"

The rocky lane followed a wriggling line of utility poles up First Finger Ridge. There were no fallen trees to interrupt the flow of electricity or conversations.

There had been an uncommonly early thaw; several small streams were splashing their way down the slope. The sun was pleasantly warm, the temperature balmy. At higher altitudes there would still be thick white patches hiding under the blue spruce, but the winter's snow on this sunlit slope was completely melted. The insects knew this and were pleased; energetic deerflies buzzed through the rolled-down windows and hummed about the men's faces.

Parris pulled to a stop in a level clearing. The cabin was nestled among a picturesque grove of spruce and pine. In front of the structure, several naked aspen were showing tender buds.

The log structure looked quite normal in every respect save one.

The front door was open; a light breeze moved it back and forth on well-oiled hinges.

Moon remarked that on such a warm day, a man might well leave his door open to air out a place that had been shut up for the long winter.

Scott Parris added hopefully that telephones fail for all sorts of reasons.

But experienced lawmen develop a keen sense about such things. The policemen were filled with a sense of unease—even dread. This had the empty, abandoned look of a dead man's house.

They climbed three pine steps to a sturdy redwood deck.

"Hello," Parris shouted.

He was answered by a heavy, almost palpable silence.

Moon held the door steady and banged his knuckles on the varnished pine.

Still no answer.

Parris called out again. "Mr. Armitage?" A pause. "Anybody home?"

The place was quiet as a tomb.

The lawmen entered the cabin, still announcing themselves. There were cold ashes in the fireplace. But no sign of an occupant. Muddy footprints led through the front parlor, down a short hallway toward the kitchen.

Parris paused to study an array of papers on a desk by the front window. "Looks like he was doing some legal work."

Moon followed the footprints into the kitchen, which

was uncommonly neat and tidy. The back door was not latched. The breeze that had opened it was about to close it. The same breath of air brought with it a familiar, unpleasant odor. The Ute policeman pushed the door wide open, looked outside. The muscles in his jaw tensed. "Scott."

"What've you got?"

"Better come and see."

Parris appeared behind the Ute. "You find him?"

Moon, standing in the open doorway, nodded.

Charlie Moon was blessed and burdened with a formal education. He could trace the flow of electricity through a simple circuit, appreciate the lilting song of a Shakespearean sonnet, discuss the rise and fall of the Roman Empire. If hard pressed, he was able (should an urgent need arise in the course of his law enforcement duties) to find the solutions to a quadratic equation and plot the results in the complex-number plane. The concept that negative numbers had imaginary square roots did not lock the gears of his mind into neutral. But for all this, Moon was Ute to his very marrow. It would not have occurred to him to touch a dead man's body unless there was a very compelling reason to do so. There was no such necessity.

Scott Parris was also keeping a respectful distance between himself and the corpse. It was the medical examiner's job to poke the lawyer's mortal remains. Doc Simpson would probe and sample and sniff around like a bloodhound. Photographs would be made from a dozen angles. The Granite Creek chief of police was already planning his department's work. A thorough search would be made of house and grounds for any physical evidence that might remain. Neighbors—such as there might be—would be questioned.

"I've never seen anything quite like this," Moon said.

Parris tried to respond; the words hung in his throat.

The corpse's yellowed face was a reflection of horror. Shrunken eyes stared blindly from gray sockets. The mouth yawned open in an endless scream. And this was not the worst part.

The head was separated from the body.

The torso was unremarkable except for one feature. On each side of the breastbone, a pair of gaping wounds penetrated deep into the chest cavity.

Scott Parris broke the silence. "God Almighty."

Despite the stench, Moon was compelled to take a deep breath. "Looks like somebody took an axe to his neck." Within a foot of the man's pale, shriveled hand, there was a small camera. "Maybe he took pictures of whoever did it."

"We should be so lucky." Parris knelt by the corpse. He pressed a handkerchief over his nose and mouth, frowned at the chest. "These are way too big to be bullet wounds," he said in a muffled voice. "And there's hardly any blood on his shirt."

Moon's thoughts were running in dark channels. Evidently, the lawyer had seen something outside. Something so interesting that he wanted a picture. If he was working at the desk when he saw it, he would've grabbed his camera and headed out the front door. So whatever he'd seen had been somewhere to the south of the cabin. *Whence cometh the unknown thing that snatches men off the earth.* And then he headed back through the cabin, making muddy tracks all the way to the back door. So whatever he wanted to photograph had been heading more or less to the north . . . passing by the cabin. After he'd got outside the back door, he'd dropped the camera. And besides losing his head, the victim had suffered two mortal wounds in his chest. Overkill. The Ute stared up the steeply pitched roof of corrugated steel at a perfectly blue sky. Whoever . . . or *whatever* . . . it was didn't even bother to take the camera. Why? Didn't notice it? Didn't care about leaving evidence behind? Moon wondered whether there would be any images on the negatives. And, if there were, whether he'd want to see them. "What'll you do with the camera?"

Parris considered his options. The FBI Forensic Laboratory came immediately to mind. And the state police had a first-class photoanalysis team. But it would be nice to keep this investigation in the family. "I've got a friend at the university who's served as an expert witness in a half-dozen crimes where photographic evidence was submitted. Guess I'll ask him to have a look at the film."

Moon frowned at the flies buzzing around the corpse. "We better throw a sheet over the body."

Parris stared at the gruesome scene. "You know, I keep thinking something . . . really crazy."

Moon nodded. Whatever had happened here was crazy.

"These big holes in his chest." Parris pointed. "They're about the same size. It's just that . . . it looks like a damn snakebite." He was immediately embarrassed at having blurted out such an asinine remark. *Even in the tropics, reptiles just didn't grow big enough to . . . and monstrously large snakes don't bite big holes in your chest. They crush you to death.*

The Ute policeman was more circumspect. And economical with his words. Besides, a sensible man wouldn't care to mention the absurdly superstitious thought that had been tickling at the dark side of his mind. *Spider-bite.*

Three hours later, the remote cabin site was crawling with state police and officers from Granite Creek PD.

The elderly medical examiner had arrived with his two young assistants. Dr. Simpson was—as was his custom—grumbling. About having to work in this black mud, how those damn deerflies were "biting my ass off," and "why couldn't these slow-witted donut-eaters manage to find bodies before decay had set in?" He, of course, was having the time of his life. Within an hour, Simpson had completed a preliminary examination of the corpse and declared that sufficient photographs had been made. The ME barked instructions to his assistants, who eased the greater bulk of the attorney's remains into a black plastic body bag and pulled the zipper. The head—lifted indelicately by the ears—was packaged separately in a sealed container that resembled a hatbox.

The lawyer's camera was tagged and placed in an evidence bag. On the morrow, Scott Parris would deliver it to Rocky Mountain Polytechnic. And ask Professor Ezra Budd to examine the instrument . . . and develop the film.

Moon, disinclined to witness the gory proceedings, stood well away from the commotion. So detached he seemed, a casual observer might have assumed the policeman was daydreaming. But the Ute was staring intently at a profile on the far ridge—a single spruce standing among a great company of its fellows. Near the crest of this particular tree was a slight interruption of natural symmetry. This distortion alone was not sufficient to attract his attention. There were many ordinary causes for a disruption of branches. It was what Moon saw above the tree that most concerned him. A half-dozen large birds . . . circling patiently. They were neither hawks nor eagles.

He thought about it. Climbing a thick spruce would be quite a troublesome task. And this was Scott Parris' jurisdiction, his investigation. Moon eased his way over to his friend's side. "Scott?"

Parris turned. "Yeah, Charlie?"

"I think you'd best call in a medevac copter."

The *matukach* squinted, followed the Ute's gaze to the far congregation of spruce. "You spotted something?"

"Maybe." *Or somebody*. The buzzards circled high over Second Finger Ridge. So it might not be too late.

———•

Corporal Rodriguez spoke through the microphone built into his orange Kevlar helmet. "Sarge . . . it's a body. You copy me?"

The helicopter pilot had seen more than his share of corpses; his response was a professional monotone. "Roger that, Corporal. We'll descend to seven meters over the target. Prepare the sling."

The ungainly craft hovered low, flaying the spruce branches with a noisy whirlwind. Rodriguez buckled himself into an array of heavy canvas straps. On a signal from the pilot, he lowered himself toward the body, alternately cursing in English and praying in Spanish as he swung to and fro, a living weight on a perilous pendulum.

The pilot was pleased to hear the VHF radio report over the roar of the engine. "Sarge. It looks like . . . he's alive!"

GRANITE CREEK, COLORADO
INTENSIVE CARE UNIT,
SNYDER MEMORIAL HOSPITAL

MOON AND PARRIS loomed silently by the bedside, staring at the still form. Tommy Tonompicket—resting on an electrically heated pad—was fairly prickling with plastic tubes and color-coded wires. The monitor indicated a heart rate of forty-eight beats per minute. His core temperature was up to ninety-four. The patient's face was a sickly gray; his closed lids occasionally jerked with a spasmodic tic. This man slept the deepest of sleeps . . . but did he dream?

The patient's personal effects had been removed from his pockets and placed in a plastic bag. Moon made a mental note of the unremarkable items. A canvas wallet containing fifty-five dollars, two credit cards, and a Colorado driver's license. A few coins. Bone-handled pocketknife. Keys. Two packs of Juarez gold cigarettes. a little roll of string. A paper clip. A few pieces of cellophane-wrapped candy. Nothing to offer the least hint of what had happened to the man.

The attending physician—just three years out of medical school—shook her head. "If this poor fellow was really in that tree since the night of April first, it's astonishing he's alive at all."

"Tommy's a fairly tough little bird," Moon said. "And he was dressed pretty warm." *Except for his feet.*

"Still," she said, "I doubt he'd have made it for much longer. Lucky thing you spotted him." The physician was stimulated by this puzzle. "I guess you'll want to hear about the shotgun wounds."

The Ute looked at the ceiling. *Uh-oh.*

Scott Parris paled. "We didn't know he'd been shot."

She pulled a small plastic vial from the ample pocket on her white smock. "The ER surgeon removed these from his back. And buttocks."

Parris held the bottle close to his face, making an almost cross-eyed focus. "So somebody peppered him with bird shot."

Charlie Moon thought he knew who was responsible. *An excitable old woman who thought Tommy was a space-monster.* "Did the wounds from the shotgun pellets cause any serious injury?"

The physician shook her head. "No. They were all superficial."

The Ute policeman was considerably relieved. If Aunt Daisy was responsible for the gunshot wounds, both she and Tommy Tonompicket had been lucky. But another thought troubled Moon. *Maybe Danny Bignight did see something big and ugly on the lakeshore. And maybe that something really did pass by the old woman's trailer home on that same night. Something with Tommy Tonompicket in its clutches.* But the idea seemed far too fantastic.

Parris leaned on the headboard and glared at the unconscious man. "When'll he be able to talk?"

The physician shrugged. "Impossible to say whether he'll even survive. But if he can hold on for a few days, he may come out of it. There's measurable brain function. His core temperature will be up to normal in a few hours. We'll have to be patient." A buzzer whined on her pager; she checked the message and departed.

Scott Parris continued to frown at the still form on the hospital bed. "Charlie, this guy's boots are found on the shore of Navajo Lake . . . then he shows up miles to the north, in the top of a tree. With bird shot in his ass. What do you think happened out there?"

Sooner or later Mood would tell his friend about Aunt Daisy's shotgun. But not until he knew a lot more than he knew now. "It's hard to figure."

"That's an understatement." Parris jammed his battered felt hat down to his ears. "But it can't be just a coincidence that Mr. Tonompicket shows up within a few hundred yards of Armitage's corpse."

"I don't think Tommy Tonompicket killed that lawyer."

Parris scratched thoughtfully at a day's growth of stubble on his chin. "Maybe the missing guy from New Mexico killed Armitage. Then maybe Pizinski chased Mr. Tonompicket up that tree."

Despite the gravity of the situation, Moon grinned. "When's the last time you climbed a tree?"

The white man shrugged. "I dunno. When I was a kid, I guess."

"Well, if you get the urge to take it up again, don't start with a spruce. The branches are thick as bristles on a porcupine's back. And Tommy wasn't wearing his boots."

"He might've been highly motivated . . . maybe Pizinski was after him with a shotgun."

"Maybe. But the branches below where he was found didn't show any sign of being disturbed. Like they would've if he'd climbed the tree."

Parris gave his Ute friend a long, pensive look. "Okay. So how'd he get up there?"

"Hard to say." And it was hard to say something that sounded so downright silly. But say it out loud or not, it looked like Tommy was *put* in the tree. But how?

SNYDER MEMORIAL HOSPITAL CAFETERIA

Moon stared at his plate. Baked beans and franks. Macaroni and cheese. Green peas. His stomach knew it was time for lunch. There was nothing wrong with the food. He couldn't eat a bite.

Scott Parris—about to taste a tuna salad—frowned at his friend. "What's the matter, chum?"

Moon shook his head. "I never could enjoy a meal in a hospital. I don't know why."

Parris looked very thoughtful. Almost wise. "I know why."

The Ute gave his friend a warning look. "You just keep it to yourself."

The white man continued. "You been thinking . . . after the surgeons remove all them spleens and gallbladders and eyeballs . . . what do they do with 'em? Burn 'em up in a furnace? Throw 'em out with the trash? No. That's not what they do. This is the new Colorado, pardner. Everything gets recycled." Parris pointed a fork at the franks on Moon's plate and chuckled.

Moon groaned. "That ain't funny."

Now Parris laughed out loud. "I didn't know you was

so fussy. Did I ever tell you about the fella I knew back in Chicago who went deer hunting up in Minnesota? Fred Hill was his name. Old Fred was almost blind but wouldn't wear glasses. Thought it would ruin his good looks—you know the type. Well, Fred and some of his buddies split up and went out lookin' for their twelve-point buck. Old Fred, he wandered around most of the day, seein' nothing, which is about all he ever did see. Then he hears this rustlin' in the brush and takes a pop at it with his trusty thirty-thirty. Got it too, which, seein' as he couldn't find a fried egg on his plate, was almost a miracle. So he hauls the carcass back to camp and later on some of his hunting buddies show up. 'My God, Fred,' they say, 'you done shot Jimmy Harkness.' "

"I expect Fred was disappointed," Moon said. "A man who thinks he's killed a fine deer generally has his heart set on some fresh venison."

Parris nodded. "Well, you can bet your best saddle on that. Fred was awfully upset when he found out what he'd done. He insisted that they take Jimmy into town right away and find a doctor who could patch him up. The other guys didn't hold out much hope, but to humor Fred they took Jimmy Harkness into a little burg called Seven Lakes, and as luck would have it, there's a nice little clinic there. Old Fred, he's cryin' his eyes out by now. He pleads with the surgeon: 'Can you save him?' The doc, he says, 'Well, I'll do my best. But it woulda helped a whole lot if you hadn't already field-dressed him.' "

Moon put his fork down. "You know, for a man who's about to get married—give up his freedom forever—you're having way too much fun."

"Tell you what, Charlie—we'll go over to the Sugar Bowl Cafe. I'll treat you to a real he-man supper. Gobs and gobs of fat and grease and cholesterol."

"Now you're talkin'."

At this moment, someone tapped Moon on the shoulder. He looked up at an elderly man, his gangling body clothed in faded denim jeans, a new plaid shirt. A tattered straw hat was perched on his shaggy head. "Yeah?"

The stranger's words came through a bushy, unkempt beard that filtered his throaty syllables. "You Officer Moon?" His breath smelled of garlic and raw onion.

The policeman nodded.

"I went to the Indian police station over in Ignacio, they said you was up here in Granite Creek—at the hospital. I said how'll I know 'im when I see 'im and they said I couldn't mistake you for no one else 'cause you're big as a horse."

Moon stared blankly at the man.

"I'm Arturo Marquez." He said it proudly, as if the Ute policeman must surely have heard of him.

Moon got up from the cafeteria table; he looked down at the six-footer. "What can I do for you, Mr. Marquez?"

The bearded man was not about to be hurried. "I use some summer pasture just north of Navajo Lake for my sheep. Lease it from your tribe."

"If some of your sheep get rustled, you didn't need to see me about it. Any of my officers could have taken your report."

The shepherd continued without acknowledging the policeman's comment. "I wasn't going to tell a soul what'd happened, but I changed my mind because of Old Grinder."

Moon's puzzlement increased. "That's your dog?"

"Old Grinder's my hand-crank radio. Thirty turns on the spring and it runs for almost a half hour. Anyway, I was listening to some good music, and they started in to playin' that Eye-talian opera. I changed stations and heard the local news on KSUT. The man was tellin' about how those two men went missing down by the lakeshore."

Scott Parris hid his grin behind a Styrofoam cup.

Moon looked over the man's head at a display under glass of freshly baked pies. The pattern had become monotonously predictable. This would be another wild report about a spaceship. Five to one, it would be shaped like a cigar or a saucer. The old duffer might even claim he'd seen little gray midgets or huge hairy monsters or scaly lizard-people. One thing was for sure—he'd demand that the police do something about it right now.

The man's eyes had a dull, fanatical sheen. "Something's out there. Something *wicked*."

This one would have to be humored. Moon produced a small notebook from his jacket pocket. "If you could tell me a little more about . . ."

The shepherd took a deep breath, closing his eyes to remember the awful event. His voice was a raspy whisper: "It was after dark. Real misty, so's you couldn't see three yards in front of your nose. Then, just down the slope, there was this peculiar light."

"A light?" This was no surprise. They all saw lights of one kind or another.

He nodded his grizzled head. "And there was sounds."

"What sort of sounds?"

"It was all mixed up. Like something was being dragged along the ground. And there was this moaning and groaning. It was awful."

Parris offered the complainant a sober look. "Well, sir—you've come to the right man. My friend Charlie Moon knows all about such things. He'll take care of you—you can bank on it."

Moon sat down. He looked at his plate. The skin on the franks was wrinkling.

The shepherd leaned close to mutter in the Ute's ear, "I think you should come and have a look at it."

"At what, Mr. Marquez?"

"The . . . the thing."

Moon thought maybe he could eat some of the beans. "What kind of thing?"

The shaggy-haired man pulled at his beard. "I don't know how to describe it."

"Maybe you'd like to bring it to the station next time you're in town and then we'll—"

"No! I don't aim to touch it. You got to come and take it away." The old man shuddered. "It's from some infernal place."

Moon—at a loss for words—looked to his *matukach* friend for moral support.

Parris, who had lost the grin, wiped his mouth with a paper napkin. "Could you tell us what this . . . thing . . . looks like?"

The old man's glassy eyes looked through the lawmen. "It's awfully strange." He hesitated, then placed a finger by each temple: "Got *horns* on it. Like a devil."

———•

Moon and Parris followed the shepherd up a winding, rocky trail. After a lengthy hike in the warm sunlight, they reached the windswept crest of a long, sloping ridge. The old man's camp was under the shelter of an overhanging cliff. His dog—who had been keeping watch over the scruffy-looking little flock—awaited him. The stoic man barely nodded at the animal, which responded with a suspicious glance at the strangers who accompanied his master.

The shepherd led the lawmen along a deer path,

through a lonely gathering of scrub oak. He paused at the edge of a clearing, where tufts of tender spring grass sprouted among a scattering of mossy boulders. He pointed. "Down there."

Moon strode ahead of the sturdy sheepman, with Parris limping along behind, roundly cursing a prickly pear cactus that had pierced the soft bullhide of his bootheel. The Ute knew what to expect. The mysterious "thing" would be gone. And the shepherd would be greatly puzzled, even apologetic.

But there it was, in plain view.

Arturo Marquez kept his distance from the strange artifact. "See? Just like I told you—it's got a pair of horns. Upset my poor dog somethin' awful. Scared hell outta my sheep too."

The lawmen stared at the thing.

Moon asked the critical question. "When did this happen?"

"Night of April first."

Moon squatted by the object. "What time that night?"

The shepherd shrugged off the question as inconsequential cop talk. "I dunno. Don't own a mechanical timepiece; I watch the stars."

"So what'd the stars say?"

"I guess it was about an hour after dark." Emboldened by the presence of the lawmen, Marquez approached the hideous thing.

Scott Parris used a tuft of grass to wipe soil off the chrome plate.

The shepherd leaned, squinting at the logo. "It says . . . FORD."

The Ute policeman nodded. "It's the hood off Tommy Tonompicket's flatbed truck."

Arturo Marquez harbored dark suspicions that this

might be some devilish ploy hatched in Detroit. "How'd it come to have horns?"

Moon gazed toward the lakeshore. "Tommy mounted a steer horn on it."

The shepherd—who had once owned a fine Ford truck—was dismayed at such wanton vandalism.

The ornament was hanging loosely now, from a single twisted bolt. Wrapped around the rusting bolt were several thin blue fibers. Parris used the pointed blade on his pocketknife to unwind the delicate filaments. There were five in all. They ranged from about three to six inches long. He pulled on one of them. Gently at first. Then harder. Though it cut halfway through the callused skin on his fingers, the fiber would not break.

"Pretty tough stuff," the Ute observed.

Parris pulled harder. "What do you think it is?"

Moon shrugged. "Maybe . . . fiber from a rope."

The shepherd was beginning to be annoyed. "That still don't make any sense. How'd a blasted truck hood get way up here where there ain't no roads to drive a truck on?"

"High winds," Moon said. "There was a thunderstorm over the lake that night. Wind must've picked up the hood and dumped it here."

The shepherd cleared his throat and spat. "I figure the damn government is behind this." And these cops were, however indirectly, representatives of the government.

The Australian sheepdog came to sniff at Charlie Moon's hand.

He patted the noble animal's head. The dog was comforted.

Moon was not.

———•

The lawmen stood well away from the stainless-steel table where the medical examiner plied his morbid trade. Walter Simpson pulled a dark green sheet over the partial remains of attorney Miles Armitage. He turned to confront his reluctant guests.

The lawyer had met his demise in Scott Parris' jurisdiction, so the Ute waited for his friend to ask the questions. Parris' gaze was fixed on the form under the sheet. "So. What can you tell us?"

Simpson—normally a cocky little man—was oddly subdued. "I can tell you something about the trauma that resulted in Mr. Armitage's demise." He waved a liver-spotted hand to indicate the headless corpse. "The subject's neck was severed with a tremendous anterior blow that shattered the third, fourth, and fifth cervical vertebrae. As if that wasn't enough, there was major trauma to the chest cavity. A pair of approximately circular wounds penetrated the rib cage, rupturing the lungs. The penetration on the subject's left chest also ruptured the aorta."

Parris' forehead furrowed into a field of wrinkles. "What happened first, the chest wounds or the—uh—decapitation?"

The medical examiner ran his fingers through a thick mop of snow-white hair. "Well, that's the peculiar part. It looks like the head was removed and the chest cavity penetrated . . . virtually simultaneously."

"That would suggest two assailants," Parris said. "One swinging an axe, another striking the victim with . . . maybe a miner's pick."

Simpson shook his head. "Don't think so."

"Why?"

"First of all, whatever took his head off wasn't something sharp—like an axe blade. The spinal column wasn't severed in the normal sense—the cervical vertebrae were smashed. And as regards the chest trauma, pickaxes are generally rectangular in cross section, and curved along their length. The penetrators that caused these wounds had a more or less round cross section—and were straight as an arrow." The medical examiner shrugged off a blood-splattered smock, pitched it into a wicker laundry basket. "In addition to the major penetrations of the thoracic cavity, there are four minor wounds on the chest—barely penetrating the skin. And I'm fairly certain that all six penetrations were made at the same instant."

"How do you figure that?"

"If the victim had been struck several times," Simpson explained patiently, "the penetrations would appear in a fairly random pattern. But all six wounds lie on a perfectly straight line across the chest. And if you think that's peculiar, you haven't heard the strangest part." Simpson—who enjoyed playing his part in this drama—paused. Waiting for his cue.

Parris fed him the required line. "So what's the strangest part?"

The ME exhaled a deep breath. "Spacing between wound centers is precisely the same—seven centimeters. Hence, the victim was evidently struck on the chest just once—with something like"—the medical examiner paused to conjure up a picture of the implement of death—"like a great big garden rake. Two of the rake's teeth were large; the others, relatively small."

The lawmen exchanged puzzled glances. *Teeth . . . set seven centimeters apart?*

Simpson smiled coyly as he pulled off a pair of latex gloves. "I hope I've been of some help to you coppers."

Parris shook his head in weary disbelief. "So you're telling us Mr. Armitage got whacked in the chest with something like a giant garden rake. I imagine you must have some equally enlightening theory about how his head was taken off."

The ME dropped the soiled rubber gloves in a stainless-steel waste receptacle. "Maybe some heavy hitter took a swipe at the poor bastard with a telephone pole." The elderly physician removed his gold-rimmed spectacles and wiped at them with a linen handkerchief. "Boys, in my time I must've autopsied a couple thousand corpses. Several hundred of them were homicides—most of those done in by some mean bastard with a pistol or a butcher knife or a club. Your criminals are generally a sorry lot—cowards and pissants and perverts who prey on the weak. So I've never had an ounce of respect for any of 'em." He hooked the spectacles over his ears and glared at the lawmen. "But I'll tell you this—I would not like to meet up with the badass who did this. Nossir, that's one hombre I'd just as soon keep clear of." He climbed the stairs, leaving the lawmen alone in the basement mortuary.

Scott Parris turned to his friend. "What do you think, Charlie?"

"Well," the Ute policeman said thoughtfully, "I'm thinkin' . . . that I'm glad that poor fella didn't die in *my* jurisdiction."

———•

Daniel Bignight stuck his round head into Moon's office. "You got a minute, Chief?"

"I'm not chief of police yet, Daniel."

There was gossip around the station that the tribal council might—mostly as a formality—interview at least one external candidate. A Northern Cheyenne military cop who was about to finish a twenty-year stint in the Army had submitted an application for the job. Rumor had it the Cheyenne was married to a Ute woman.

But Bignight shared the generally held view that the job was Charlie Moon's if he wanted it. He grinned innocently. "Well, *Acting* Chief of Police, I got someone here who wants to see you."

"About what?" *Please, God, not another crazy.*

"About a relative." Bignight stood aside.

A tall, gaunt man, outfitted in an expensive but illfitting gray suit, stomped into the office, his ostrichskin cowboy boots clicking on the hardwood. He was middle-aged and looked older. Heavy bloodhound jowls hung loosely from his face; dark bags drooped under watery blue eyes. A garish silver-and-turquoise buckle covered most of his flat belly. A black cigar was clamped firmly between his teeth. He took a quick glance at Moon, then began a cursory inspection of the furnishings. "I understand you're the boss here."

Moon stood up behind the desk. "I'm Charlie Moon, acting chief of police. What can I do for you, Mr. . . . ?"

"Kenneth Bright, chairman of Bright Enterprises, Incorporated—headquarters in Albuquerque. You can call me Kenny." He stuck out a hairy hand.

Moon shook it. The grip was firm. "What can we do for you . . . Mr. Bright?"

"I'm here about my brother-in-law."

"He have a name?"

"Bill Pizinski. I got word through the New Mexico state cops that you guys found Bill's pickup down by Navajo Lake."

"We did. But Mr. Pizinski hasn't turned up yet."

Bright was looking around for an ashtray. "You got any idea what happened to him?"

"No."

The gaunt man shrugged. "My sister, Margie—that's Bill's wife—she's off somewheres in Europe, riding a bike." Bright's dismayed expression made it clear that he considered such frivolous activities a foolish waste of time. "My sister'll be pretty upset if she hears that Bill's . . . uh . . . *missing*." He obviously found the word distasteful. "I'd like to get it all sorted out before she gets back to the States. If he ain't turned up by the time she's home, she'll be all over me like ugly on ape." The cigar drooped glumly in the man's mouth. "Maybe you could let me know if you hear anything."

"We'll be glad to contact you soon as we learn something about your brother-in-law," Moon said. "You want to leave a phone number?"

Bright produced a business card from his coat pocket.

Moon rubbed his thumb across the raised lettering on the card that spelled out BRIGHT ENTERPRISES.

The businessman turned to look out the window. "Well, as long as I'm here, I guess I might as well take Bill's pickup home for him. I'm in a rental car—guess I could get somebody to drop it off in Durango."

Moon stared at the back of the man's head. "Your brother-in-law's truck is in the holding yard. It's evidence in a missing-persons case; we can't release it just yet."

The gangly man turned, intending to launch a protest. He weighed the man who stood before him and realized it would be for naught. He stared uncertainly at the Ute police officer.

Moon broke the uneasy silence. "So . . . what exactly does Bright Enterprises do?"

Kenny Bright chewed on the cigar as he spoke. "Oh, this and that. It's an umbrella corporation for several companies. Made mosta my money in the furniture business."

"Your brother-in-law—what kind of work does he do?"

There was a noticeable hesitation. "Bill—he works at one of my companies."

Moon pretended ignorance. "Making furniture?"

"He's . . . ahhh . . . chief scientist at my high-tech company."

This was like pulling teeth. "Which enterprise would that be?"

"RMAFS," Bright muttered.

Moon was making notes on a pad. "I bet those letters mean something."

"Rocky Mountain Advanced Flight Systems. I got almost a hundred people there—half of 'em with Ph.D.s." Bright waved the cigar, leaving a thin trail of smoke. "But don't ask me about the research—most of it I don't understand. Besides, it's all government work. Classified. See, I bought that RMAFS high-tech outfit so my brother-in-law could run it. But my real business is home and office furnishings." He looked around Moon's office with undisguised disapproval. "We're puttin' up a new furniture factory in Alajuela. That's in Costa Rica."

Moon shifted gears. "Any idea how Pizinski's truck come to be on the shore at Navajo Lake?"

This produced a bearish shrug. "Who knows?"

"Why do you suppose he was in Colorado—business or pleasure?"

Bright presented a poker face. "Business, most likely." The entrepreneur was staring intently at a photograph mounted on the wall: former SUPD chief Roy Severo, shaking hands with the governor of Colorado. "RMAFS has a manufacturing plant in Colorado Springs."

"Did your brother-in-law make regular visits to the plant?"

Kenny Bright frowned at the long ash building up on the cigar tip. "I expect Bill made a run between Colorado Springs and Albuquerque . . . oh . . . a coupla times a month. He didn't—doesn't tell me much about his work. I don't know what those eggheads do. Or much give a damn." He rubbed finger against thumb, and grinned. "Long as they make lotsa money for Uncle Kenny."

"You have any idea why Mr. Pizinski would abandon his truck down by Navajo Lake?"

Bright tapped the cigar ash into a wastebasket. "Guess it must've broke down."

"Seems to be in good shape. One of my officers drove it to Ignacio."

"Well, then . . ." Bright seemed to be wriggling under the ill-fitting suit.

"When's the last time you saw your brother-in-law?"

"Must've been a coupla weeks ago. Me and Bill had lunch in Albuquerque—at one of them nostalgia places. It's got jukes with forty-fives, ten cents a play. Big greasy cheeseburgers. Real milkshakes. Even peanut butter and jelly sandwiches. Brings 'em in by the droves, everything from teenyboppers to old duffers."

"I'll have to try it next time I'm down that way." Moon scribbled on a yellow pad. "When you and Mr. Pizinski had lunch together, did he seem okay?"

"Far as I could tell."

"Was he worried about anything?"

Bright shot the Ute a worried look. "Like what?"

"Debts. His health. Work. His marriage."

"I don't think so. Why? You don't think Bill's done something stupid . . ."

"We have to consider all the possibilities." The Ute policeman stared at the businessman. Waiting for him to say something. White men could not bear silence.

Except for this one. Bright patiently stared the Ute down.

Moon gave up the game. "Well, is there anything else I can do for you?"

Bright clamped his jaw down on the cigar. "You could let me have a look at Bill's truck."

Kenny Bright circled the vehicle warily.

The *matukach* reminded Moon of an old battle-scarred coyote he'd watched once. The animal had been half starved, hungry enough to stalk a wounded badger. Old coyote knew if he got too close too soon, his lunch would take a bite out of *him*. The businessman stayed at arm's length from the vehicle, staring. "You find anything in the truck?"

"Like what?"

Bright pulled his suit jacket off and draped it over a long arm. "Oh . . . anything to do with our business. Papers. Stuff like that."

"No. We didn't find anything like that."

Bright eyed the big Ford flatbed, which was parked beside the GMC pickup. "This the other truck that was found on the lakeshore?"

"Yeah. It belongs to one of my tribesmen—Tommy Tonompicket. He disappeared along with your brother-in-law. But he's been found." He expected the businessman to ask some questions about Tonompicket.

Bright was an unpredictable man. "Hood's missing."

"It's been found."

Bright turned to raise a bushy eyebrow at the policeman. "Where?"

"Couple miles north of the lake. On a hillside where some sheep were grazing."

"How'd it get there?"

"Don't know for sure."

The white man leaned closer to inspect the dangling hinges. "Looks like it got ripped off."

"Yeah. It does."

Bright approached the rear of the flatbed. The officer in charge of the holding yard had stored the bent-up hood on the bed; it was leaning against the side rail.

Bright reached out, as if to touch the steer-horn ornament on the crumpled hood.

"Don't," Moon said.

The businessman withdrew his hand quickly, as if a snake might bite him. He looked up at the tall policeman. "Why?"

"Evidence."

Bright eyed the tarp. "What's under that?"

"Restaurant equipment," Moon said. "Couple of stoves. Refrigerator. Freezer. Even the kitchen sink." Danny Bignight had contacted Ozzie Corporation and provided an inventory of the equipment found on the truck. The bean counter who handled Tommy Tonompicket's hauling contract had checked, then called back to report that nothing was missing. The franchise restaurant company had shown no great interest in Tommy Tonompicket's disappearance. Maybe because he wasn't their employee—just a contract trucker. They weren't even particularly concerned about the equipment—which was all used stuff. They'd send another truck for the appliances, they said.

When?

When they got around to it.

Kenny Bright seemed suddenly deflated. He looked through bleary eyes at a platinum Rolex strapped to his wrist. "Mr. Moon, I'm starved. Would you have lunch with me?"

"I'm pretty busy."

"I'm payin'."

The magic words. But there might be a catch. "Where do you intend to eat?"

Bright sighed wistfully. "I wanna go someplace where there's a juke with old-timey country and western songs. I want to hear Lefty Frizzell and Hank Williams and the Sons of the Pioneers." Tears wetted his pale blue eyes. "I want to go where they serve huge beefsteaks that melt in your mouth and mashed potatoes made from scratch and thick brown gravy. Hot apple pie. A place with pretty waitresses that smile and call me honey."

Moon grinned. "You want to die and go to heaven."

"Sooner or later," Bright said matter-of-factly.

"I'll take you to the closest thing we got in Ignacio; it's called Angel's Cafe."

The noon hour being yet over the horizon, Angel's Cafe was doing little business. While Kenny Bright pored over the grease-stained menu, Moon excused himself. Said he had some police business to attend to. This was true—if one was willing to stretch a phrase. When the common good was to be served, Charlie Moon generally found a few elastic words.

He located the owner of the establishment fussing about in the kitchen. And explained to Angel Martinez that he couldn't say exactly why, but the man in the three-piece suit was no ordinary patron. It would be wise to see that he got special attention. The best beefsteak in the house. Mashed potatoes made by actually mashing real potatoes. Brown gravy with fresh mushrooms. And the service should be special too. Esmerelda Sanchez, Moon suggested, should take care of their table. He'd want to talk to her as well, make sure she knew how important this was—how the man was to be handled.

Moon's tone was sufficiently mysterious that Angel

Martinez guessed that the fellow was some sort of modern-day Duncan Hines. Probably here to rate all the best restaurants in Colorado. Four stars (maybe even five?) were dancing before Angel's eyes. After an intense discussion with the cook, the manager-owner of the establishment was suitably discreet about calling Esmerelda into the kitchen.

The exceptionally pretty waitress listened to Moon with wide eyes and open mouth. If any other man had made such a suggestion, she would have dismissed such foolishness. But Charlie Moon was a special guy who was always very nice to her father when he was picked up on a drunk-and-disorderly charge in the Southern Ute casino. Before Daddy was transferred to the Ignacio town lockup, Charlie always saw that the old man got a good Mexican supper from Angel's.

On the way back to the table Moon stopped at the jukebox. He fed it with a half-dozen quarters. By the time he was seated across from Kenny Bright, Jimmie Rodgers—the Singing Brakeman—was wailing a woeful tale. Something about how he'd shot a cheatin' woman with a gun that had a long, shiny barrel.

Kenny Bright's eyes were closed, his expression serene. "Thank you for the music, Charlie."

"You're welcome."

Esmerelda appeared. She was, Moon estimated, the best-looking waitress in Ignacio. Maybe in all of southern Colorado. Today, she was a vision of loveliness. The frilly blouse had slipped off one smooth shoulder. Red lips were slightly parted to display her perfect teeth. She seemed not to see Charlie Moon; her enormous brown eyes were all for Kenny Bright. *The old man is kind of cute, in a sad, basset-hound sort of way.* She put pencil to pad. "What'll it be, sweetie?"

Bright looked up at this lovely apparition whose lips

dripped with honey. "My God in heaven," he whispered.

She leaned close to him. "You look like a man who likes his steak."

He nodded dumbly.

"How do you want it cooked, sugar?"

"Medium rare," he rasped.

"Right, honey." She gave him a sly wink.

She's overdoing it, Moon thought. *Sweetie. Sugar. Honey. Amateurs don't know when to stop.*

Her flowery perfume wafted hypnotically over Bright, who had never smelled honeysuckles half so sweet. "You want that with mashed potatoes and thick brown gravy?"

He nodded again.

"How about some coffee? I just ground a pound of Colombian beans."

"Black," he croaked.

She glanced at Moon. "What'll you have, sir?"

Sir? "The same."

"Well, you hungry men'll have to be patient for just a few minutes." She patted Bright on the arm. "Cook'll have to mash up a batch of Idahos."

Bright watched her walk away. Hips swinging just enough to make an old man wistful for his youth.

Moon was mildly hurt. Wouldn't have hurt Esmerelda to call *him* honey. Pat *his* arm.

Another 45 rpm disc was selected by the juke's marvelously dexterous mechanical arm. Lefty Frizzell began to croon. About how his sweetheart preferred candy kisses (wrapped in paper) to his own. It was unutterably sad.

Halfway through the meal, Bright looked over his plate at the Ute. "Charlie."

"Yeah?"

"I read a blurb in some rag about how you found that missing Indian guy . . ."

"Tommy Tonompicket." *So he is interested.*

". . . up a spruce. Said it wasn't too far from where that lawyer was . . . uh . . . decapitated. You figure this Indian fella offed the lawyer, then clumb a tree?"

Moon, maneuvering his knife close to the bone, sliced a savory chunk off the broiled beefsteak. "No."

The man is not a conversationalist. "Billy Pizinski is just a techno-dork. But my little sister seems to like him."

With a prime steak on his plate, the Ute had little interest in small talk.

"So when do you think you'll find my brother-in-law?"

Moon chewed thoughtfully. "Depends."

"On what?"

"On where he is." Moon took a long drink of sweet, black coffee.

The extremely pretty waitress approached.

"Lordy," Bright whispered.

Esmerelda leaned to fill the coffee cups. She smiled sweetly at the middle-aged businessman. "If you want anything else, honey . . . just call me."

Bright watched her leave, then pointed his greasy fork at the policeman. "There's one thing I want you to know."

Moon was thinking about hot apple pie. "What's that?"

"I can't remember the last time somebody did me a favor just to be nice—without wanting something in return."

The Ute policeman assumed an innocent, puzzled expression.

"I appreciate how you set up this great meal for me.

And played them old songs on the juke. And"—he hesitated, blushing like a schoolgirl—"sent that pretty waitress out here to sweet-talk me."

Moon shrugged. "Esmerelda just plain likes you."
Oddly enough, it seemed that she did.

"Nice of you to say so." Bright smiled sadly. "But I
know there's not much about me for a woman to like."
The bass voice rumbled up from a deep cavern in his
chest. "Anyway, you're A-number-one with me, Charlie
Moon. And you have made a friend for life."

"Glad to hear it," Moon said. And promptly forgot
about it.

Moon encountered Daniel Bignight's Chevrolet cruiser
nosing out of the SUPD parking lot. He waved the
Pueblo Indian down.

Bignight put on a sober face. "What's up . . . *Acting*
Chief?"

"Soon's you get a chance, run a check on that guy you
brought to my office."

"Mr. Bright?"

"Yeah. Kenneth Bright. The missing guy—William
Pizinski—is Bright's brother-in-law. And Pizinski works
for a company owned by Bright. Remember that business card we found in Pizinski's pickup—RMAFS?"

Bignight nodded.

"It's Rocky Mountain Advanced Flight Systems.
They're located in New Mexico and Colorado. Pizinski
was some kind of top-dog scientist. Couple of times a
month, he traveled back and forth between the Colorado Springs plant and the company headquarters in
Albuquerque. He might've been on a business trip when
he stopped off at Navajo Lake." Moon realized that he
was speaking in the past tense. As if the missing man
were no longer with the living.

FOR THE THIRD day in a row, the lawmen presented themselves at Snyder Memorial Hospital. As on the previous occasions, Moon and Parris visited Tommy Tonompicket's bedside.

They asked the same questions of the ICU staff. *How is he? Has he said anything at all?*

Got the same answers. *Vital signs are okay. But he hasn't said a word. Sorry.*

Charlie Moon left Tommy Tonompicket's cubicle to Scott Parris, who was asking the on-duty nurse for more details about the Ute patient's condition. Moon intended to inquire at the desk about when his fellow tribesman might be well enough to be moved to Mercy Hospital in Durango, where it would be more convenient for his relatives to visit.

Moon was distracted from this task by a pair of newcomers approaching the nurse's station. The man in the powder-blue suit was short and beefy. The woman, sheathed in a simple black dress, was everything the man was not. Her companion had oily black hair, combed sideways in a vain attempt to cover a shiny bald spot. She had long, golden tresses that fell over her shoulders in great waves. The ogre looked to be closing in on sixty and was flabby around the middle. The woman was half his age, half his weight, and anything but flabby. And she was, in particular, not ugly as original sin. She was extremely easy on the eyes.

The pear-shaped man, who had brushed by the Ute policeman, was waving his hands excitedly at the full-back of a nurse behind the counter. Moon caught only a few words of the exchange.

From the man: "We came all the way from L.A. . . . this Indian guy . . . demand to talk to him . . . what kind of hick-town hospital is this . . ."

From the nurse: "L.A. ain't my kind of town . . . Mr. Tonompicket is in no condition . . . don't mess with me, buster . . ."

And so it went, escalating toward some uncertain climax.

Until the young woman interrupted. "Calm down, Uncle Eddie. I'm sure the nurse knows best." She smiled apologetically at the older woman, who seemed somewhat mollified.

Moon digested this information. *So she's his niece. That's nice.*

Parris showed up at his friend's side. Took a long look at the mismatched pair. "What've we got here, Charlie?"

"Looks like out-of-towners."

"It's the princess and the frog," Parris muttered. "But if she's kissed him already, it didn't take."

Moon sensed an opportunity. "I think they're . . . nice enough people." *That'll set his teeth on edge.*

Parris snorted. "Looks more like a gangster and his moll."

"Moll? That shows how old-fashioned you are." The Ute leaned close to his friend. "I figure the guy's here to see some sick friend. And the young lady—she's probably his . . . *niece.*" He knew what the response would be.

"Niece my hind leg. I say she's his secretary. Assistant. Girl Friday. Something like that."

Moon shook his head. "Five'll get you ten the princess is Froggy's niece."

It was like taking candy. "You're on, Charlie."

The young woman watched with elegant disinterest while the heavyset man carried on a less heated conversation with the fullback nurse. "Thing is, Miss Balmy, we've made a long, tiresome trip. We *gotta* see him. This is really important to us."

The stern woman fixed the brazen little man with a withering stare. She pointed at the name tag pinned to her starched blouse. "The name is Palmy. *Palmy.* With a P."

"Fine, Miss Parmy. Now do we get to talk to—"

"For the tenth time, you'll have to wait till afternoon visiting hours." She glanced at the clock on the wall. "And that's not till two o'clock. For all the good it'll do you."

"We'll wait, then," the frog croaked. The out-of-towners turned abruptly, almost colliding with the policemen.

Retreating from the close encounter, the lawmen barely wasted a glance on the uninteresting man.

Parris muttered inane apologies to the blond vision of loveliness. Excuse me, ma'am. Hope I didn't step on your toe. If I don't start watching where I'm going, someday I'll get run over by a truck. Tread marks all over me. Ha-ha.

Moon found himself unable to utter a word.

Basking in their admiration, amused at their confusion, she smiled tolerantly at this pair of masculine oafs.

It was the frog who croaked: "Hey, it's no problem, gents. Nobody got damaged."

He was pointedly ignored.

To fill the vacuum of silence, Scott Parris addressed the woman. "So you're here to see a patient?"

She nodded, then gave both men the once-over. *The six-footer has nice eyes. And broad shoulders. But he looks married.* She gave Moon the twice-over. *Hmmm. Overly tall. But not bad-looking . . . and dangerous. I like him best.*

The man in the suit stuck his hand out. "I'm Eddie Zoog." He might as well have been invisible.

The Ute removed his hat. "Ma'am, if you're here to see Mr. Tonompicket, maybe I could be of some help."

Her reply was cool as an October breeze. "Why would you want to help me?"

"Well . . . Tommy Tonompicket is a Southern Ute. So'm I."

Zoog's face was swelling. "I take care of business. Camilla, she's my—ah—business associate."

Parris grinned at his partner. *Business associate. You owe me ten bucks.*

The Ute's attention was elsewhere. "Camilla," he said. "That's a pretty name."

Her enormous blue-green eyes caressed him. "Camilla Willow." She glanced at her homely companion. "This is my uncle."

Parris' jaw dropped. *How does Charlie know these things?*

She patted Zoog's round shoulder. "Uncle Eddie married my mother's sister."

The lawmen—who were close as brothers—shared the same thought. *The princess doesn't want anyone to get the mistaken notion that she shares a single gene with Froggy.*

"So you're his niece," Charlie Moon said.

Scott Parris ground his teeth. *She is also his business associate. That cancels out the niece.*

Moon turned his hat in his hands. "I sure hope you enjoy your visit to Colorado."

"So far, I'm liking what I see." She smiled at the tall Ute.

The beefy man in the expensive suit—accustomed to his companion's power to disable strong men with a glance—rolled his eyes in mock dismay. "Okay, gents. So you've met Camilla." He stepped protectively in front of his niece. "But *we* still ain't been properly in-nerdooced. Like I said once already, I'm Eddie Zoog. I'm—we're here to see this Indian guy. And find out what we can about William Pizinski."

Scott Parris took a moment to have a look at the odd fellow. Zoog had heavy-lidded black eyes, a broad, flat nose, thick lips. *No familial resemblance, but . . .* "You a relative of Pizinski's?"

"Nope. In fact, I never heard of this Pizinski joker or the Indian till they disappeared down by Apache Lake."

"Navajo Lake," Moon said helpfully.

Zoog waved away this fact like another man would swat at a pesky mosquito. "Whatever. Anyhow, me and Camilla, we come all the way from L.A. to find out what happened to these guys."

Charlie Moon was looking over the frog's head at the princess. "What's your professional interest in this case?"

"Who wants to know?" Zoog snapped.

"I'm Charlie Moon, Southern Ute tribal police. This is my friend Scott Parris. He's chief of police here-abouts."

"Aha—the two coppers," Zoog muttered. He fumbled with a small spiral notebook. "Yeah. I got the dope on the both of you." He stopped to read the entry on a dog-eared page, then squinted under bushy brows at Moon. "You're the Indian cop who's investigating this weird business, ain't you?"

"What weird business?"

"Hey, I know all about it, Tonto. The double snatch."

"Snatch?"

"Sure. The abduction down at Cherokee Pond—"

"Navajo Lake."

"—where these two guys got grabbed by who knows what. We'd already heard about the Indian guy turning up—"

Parris interrupted. "You're referring to Mr. Tonompicket?"

"Sure, who else? The Apache Joe who—"

"He's a Ute," Parris interjected.

"—was snatched along with this other fella. And then we hear that an Indian cop has seen strange lights on the lakeshore. So we're here to have a powwow with the Apache that got snatched. And we're hoping this Pizinski guy will turn up before long—so we can interview two birds with one stone, to kinda coin a phrase."

Parris frowned. "Interview?"

Zoog spread his hands in an expansive gesture. "Sure. I need to have a heart-to-heart jawbone session with Pizinski and the Indian about what happened to 'em. That's my business, or didn't I say?"

"You didn't say."

Zoog grinned, splitting thick lips to display a glistening gold tooth nestled in a row of pearly whites. "I put together packages."

The lawmen stared uncomprehendingly at the short, stout man.

"What I mean," Zoog continued with an air of exasperation, "is book and movie packages." He offered up a business card.

Parris read it, then passed the item to Moon. "What's the EZ Agency?"

"EZ stands for Eddie Zoog. We're authors' agents. Our specialty is representing some Joe or Jane who's had a really weird experience. If they've got a marketable story to tell, I set him or her up with a sweet book deal. Even make him or her a best-seller."

Parris said it with a straight face. "So all of these hims and hers are writers?"

Zoog snorted. "Writers? Get real, donut-eater. Most of these Joes and Janes that get snatched are average guys and dolls who couldn't write their way outta the third grade. So naturally I got me a stable of hotshot ghostwriters. After the book, then comes the made-for-TV movie. Or sometimes the movie comes first, then the book. Then again, we may do both at once. Depending on the state of the market and stuff my astrologer tells me and whatnot."

"Well," Parris said, "I guess that about covers the possibilities."

The stunning blonde, who seemed to have little interest in the conversation, was staring openly, appraisingly, at Charlie Moon. *Here I am, big man. Make your move.*

The Ute was frozen. It was like coming face-to-face with a she-cougar. One false move and you get your heart ripped out.

Zoog—unaware of the little drama—continued his spiel: "The EZ Agency specializes in *really* weird stuff. All kinds of monster reports. Like Bigfoot. Sasquatch. Abominable Snowguys. Ghosts that throw knickknacks around the parlor. Giant lizards that can swallow your mother-in-law, orthopedic shoes and all. And UFOs, naturally. Everybody's into flying saucers. 'Specially when there's an abduction."

"There's nothing like that associated with this case," Parris said gruffly.

Zoog shrugged dismissively. "That's what you badge-toters always say. But me, I got a nose for these things." To make his point, he placed a sausagelike finger on his flat nose. "I can *smell* UFOs. And alien abductions. And this thing with Pizinski and Tillywicket—"

"Tonompicket," Moon said.

"—smells like an alien snatch to me. Wait'll they talk. You'll see I'm right."

"Mr. Tonompicket isn't talking at all," Parris pointed out. "And Pizinski is still missing."

"I know all of this," Zoog continued, "but I intend to be around when the Apache guy finds his tongue. And when the Pizinski fella comes back from wherever he's been, I'll be there to throw out the welcome mat. In the meantime, I'd like to talk to you cops. Find out what you know about this weird snatch."

"Whatever we learn in the course of an official investigation is police business," Parris said firmly. "When we have some hard information, there'll be a public statement. Until then," he added, "me and Charlie have nothing to say. Right, Charlie?"

"Right, pardner." Unless *she* asks me.

The blonde sidled up to the tall Ute. "Hey, big man."

Moon swallowed hard.

She shot him the killer smile. "I'm famished. You want to take me to lunch?"

Moon considered Eddie Zoog's scowling visage. "Depends."

She reached out and touched his sleeve. "On what?"

"Well . . . on a coupla things."

She walked her fingers up his forearm. "Name 'em."

"First, on whether you're buying."

"Sure. I got an expense account. What else?"

He gave the beetle-browed man an uncertain look. "Uh . . . I wondered whether Uncle Zoog plans to come along." *I sure hope not.*

"What—do you think I need a chaperon?"

Moon pulled at his collar. "I was thinking more about me."

He's funny. I like that. "Sorry. Uncle Eddie isn't invited—you're on your own."

"Well," the Ute said bravely, "sometimes a man has to take a risk."

Feeling quite abandoned, Scott Parris watched his best friend depart with the lovely woman on his arm. "Mr. Zoog?"

Eddie, who kept a box of toothpicks in his coat pocket, was chewing nervously on one at the moment. "Yeah?"

"On the level now . . . this Camilla—she really your niece?"

"Sure she is." The balding man—donning his best facsimile of an injured expression—looked up at the chief of police. "Whaddaya think I am, anyway, for cryin' out loud—some kinda old leech?"

"Old lecher," Parris corrected. *Or maybe you are a bloodsucker.*

Zoog shrugged. "Whatever." He spat the shredded toothpick onto the spotless oak floor. "So, copper, you got a date for lunch?"

Parris did not look at the repellent man. "Is this some kind of disgusting proposition?"

Eddie Zoog chuckled. "Okay—Andy of Mayberry— let me lay it on the line: I'm payin' for the cheeseburger and cherry Coke. In exchange for my generosity, I expect you to tell me what you know about all this weird stuff that happened to the Apache Kid and Wild Bill Pizinski when they got snatched. The question is, will you spill your guts for the price of lunch or do I have to lay some serious money on the barrelhead?"

The chief of police closed his eyes. And posed that most thorny of theological questions. *Why me, Lord?*

Scott Parris had selected the Sugar Bowl Cafe for two reasons.

First, it was his friend's favorite restaurant in Granite Creek. So he expected to find Charlie Moon and Camilla there, secreted in a cozy booth in the back of the room. Where he could keep an eye on them. Charlie might need some looking-after.

Second, the chief of police had a running tab at the Sugar Bowl. He intended to use this line of credit to teach Eddie Zoog a beneficial lesson about police ethics in Granite Creek, Colorado. He would accomplish this by paying for both of their lunches.

As he had expected, Moon and his red-hot date were in the Sugar Bowl. Nestled in a quiet booth, far into the twilight end of the dining room. Smiling like lovesick teenagers. With eyes only for each other. *Sickening.*

But Eddie Zoog—who was quick from the starting gate—confounded Parris' object lesson about who would pay for lunch. He introduced himself to the skinny waitress with a crisp fifty-dollar bill and these memorable words: "I'm payin' up front, sweetums. Give the sheriff here whatever he wants. Grilled cheese, sirloin steak, lobster thermidor, whatever—it's on Eddie Zoog." He nudged her thigh with his elbow and winked. "This here copper's in my pocket, see. Me and the boys from St. Louie is movin' into Mayberry and takin' over the town. Roulette wheels. Cheap hootch. Floozies. The works." He winked at the wide-eyed woman. "You can run a bawdy house for me if you want to, madam."

The waitress slipped the fifty into her apron pocket and spoke to the chief of police. "This lunatic a friend of yours, Scotty?"

Scott Parris rested his face in his hands. "He's more like a nasty little growth that I need to get removed."

This exchange brought an appreciative guffaw from Eddie Zoog.

Parris peeked through his fingers with one eye. "Donna, please put both our meals on my tab."

The waitress fingered the crispy greenback in her pocket. "What'll I do with this?"

"That," Parris said behind his hands, "is your tip."

Zoog's eyes goggled. "What—a fifty-smacker bribe for Olive Oyl?"

The beanpole-thin waitress bent over and kissed his balding, greasy head. "Thank you so much, sweetums." The buss completed, she put pencil to pad. "So what'll you have, Scotty?"

"The special. And iced tea."

She turned to the flustered out-of-towner. "And you, sir?"

Zoog stared at her apron pocket and felt his stomach roll. "Glassa water. And some bicarb of soda."

The lady with the blue-green eyes used them to read the menu.

Charlie Moon used his brown eyes to stare. The young woman was so pretty it almost hurt to look at her. What's more, she smelled awfully good. Like spring flowers. Fresh clover, he thought. And here she was, within arm's reach. He was blissfully happy. Then things started to go sour. "Don't look now," he advised.

Camilla managed not to look, but she was blessed with a modicum of curiosity. "Why?"

Moon pulled down the brim of his black Stetson. The seven-foot-tall Ute often did this in the vain hope of avoiding recognition. "My pardner and your uncle are at a table by the salad bar."

"Salad," she said, making a face. "Ugh! Rabbit food."

Moon's heart did a double thumpety-thump. "Do I understand correctly . . . that you harbor a grievance against lettuce and carrots and stuff like that?"

She parted her full lips and pointed. "See this?"

He leaned closer, and squinted. "It's a tooth."

"It's a *canine* tooth."

"Uh . . . right."

"Camels do not have canines," she pointed out. "Neither do the cattle of the field."

"So what do you enjoy for a light lunch?"

"Beefsteak," she said without a microsecond's hesitation, "medium rare. If prime beef is unavailable, I will gladly settle for a grilled pork chop. Or deep-fried catfish. Either way, a baked potato is a must. With real butter, of course. And lots of it."

"I took you for a regular woman—not knowing that a lady could stay so slim eating real food."

Camilla shamelessly gave Moon the big-eye. "I have ways of burning up the calories."

"I figured you for a jogger."

"Don't have the time for running nowhere and back."

"So how do you . . ."

"I raise quarter horses on my ranch. I rope 'em. And ride 'em."

She has a ranch?

"And I shoot."

This sounded dangerous. "What at?"

"At whatever needs shooting. Last October, it was a couple of half-wit rustlers who tried to slip away with some of my prize stock. One's gone on to his reward; the other horse thief is still in traction." She smiled at the memory.

"Horse ranchin' and shootin' rustlers must keep you fairly busy."

"It does. But every once in a while, I help Uncle Eddie with one of his agency projects."

"So . . . you're interested in monsters and flying saucers and such?"

"Hardly." Her expression was suddenly quite sober. "But my uncle tends to be somewhat reckless. He needs looking-after."

"That why you come along on this particular trip—to keep him out of trouble?"

"That's part of the reason." Camilla fixed him with an enigmatic look. "And I had a strange feeling that I should visit Colorado. See if there's anything here . . . I might like."

"Hope you're not disappointed."

She responded with a faint blush.

Charlie Moon, who had never expected to meet *the perfect woman*, was suddenly suspicious of his good fortune. "You're not—uh—married or anything?"

"Not even going steady."

"Hard to believe."

She reached across the table to touch his hand. "I've been waiting for . . . the perfect man."

"How'll you know him when you find him?"

As she pondered this question, Camilla seemed to be lost in deep thought. Actually, she was gazing over Moon's shoulder at an advertisement for Thunder Cola. The blue-eyed poster boy—who was enjoying a sip of the caffeine-spiked beverage—was blessed with an immaculate mane of golden hair. Furthermore, the model had a leather-bound book tucked under his arm and leaned against a classic red Jaguar. This racy vehicle was parked on several acres of neatly manicured lawn that fronted a brownstone mansion. "Oh, I'll have no trouble spotting him. He'll be . . . let's see . . . about five-eleven. Blond. Sky-blue eyes. He'll be . . . a sensitive man. A literary type—who owns a big estate. And he'll drive . . . let me see . . . a red Jag, I think." She watched Charlie Moon's face gradually sag into a pitifully disappointed, hangdog expression. *He's so incredibly sweet and honest and innocent.* And then it dawned on her. *He's just . . . perfect!* Like the lonely cowboy drifter in one of those terribly romantic Zane Grey novels. A man who'd gladly face death to protect the one woman he truly loved. Or so he seemed . . .

"May I call you Charlie?"

He nodded.

"Charlie . . . I want to ask you something."

Moon was staring unhappily at his coffee cup. "Yeah?"

"If you really cared for a woman . . . would you kill for her?"

He raised his head. Looked her square in the eye. "Who'd you have in mind?"

In spite of all odds, Scott Parris was enjoying his lunch of baked salmon, which was, according to the note on today's special, "nestled in a luscious bed of fettuccine." Across the table, Eddie Zoog—who had finished his bicarbonate of soda—was attacking a tasteless tuna salad nestled between dry slices of rye toast. Miles away in the twilight—nestled cozily in the secluded booth—Moon and the young woman were having an earnest conversation. No foolish romance budding there, Parris decided. All was right with the world.

Or so it seemed.

Without the courtesy of knocking, Trouble came right through the door of the Sugar Bowl Cafe. Marched toward Scott Parris' table. Stood there with a ramrod-straight back, small chin jutting out.

Parris inspected the slim figure in the neatly pressed

gray suit. No uniform. No stripes or medals. But might as well have MILITARY tattooed across her forehead. He returned his attention to the baked salmon.

Trouble will not be ignored. She addressed him directly. "Sir!"

"At ease," he said without looking up.

She automatically relaxed, then blushed to have fallen for the civilian's tasteless ruse. "Sir, I assume that you are Chief of Police Parris. At the police station, I was informed that you regularly took your lunch here."

"I'm Parris." He rolled a wad of fettuccine onto his fork.

"Sir, when you have finished your meal, I would appreciate a few minutes of your time." She gave the Zoog a cold look. "In private."

"I'm as good as finished." Ignoring Zoog's suspicious glare, Parris pushed his chair away from the table. The young woman followed the chief of police to a quiet nook that housed public telephones.

He put on an official smile that strained his face. "So who'm I talking to?"

Glancing over her shoulder to confirm that there were no observers, she presented her ID. "Captain Teresa Taylor. United States Air Force."

She was amusingly proper. "You're out of uniform, Captain."

Supposing that he might be nearsighted, she held the ID closer to his face. "As you can see, I'm with the Office of Special Investigations. When pursuing an inquiry among the civilian population, we often work in mufti."

Eddie Zoog materialized behind her, flapping his arms like a small rooster. "Air Force copper," he crowed triumphantly. "Ha—I knew it! You're here about the abduction."

She turned on the heavyset man. "Who is this?"

"This," Parris said, "is Mr. Zoog."

The OSI special agent accepted this information calmly, as if one in her capacity encountered such specimens on a regular basis. She fixed the beefy man with a flat fish-eye stare. "Sir, this is a private conversation."

"Private my ass," Eddie Zoog bellowed. "I demand to hear what you've got to say." He pounded his fist against a telephone stall, frightening an elderly lady who was calling her sister. "The people have a right to know!"

Captain Taylor seemed genuinely puzzled. "What people?"

Zoog threw up his hands. "I *knew* it. It's a damn government cover-up!"

She decided to ignore the rude man; her next words were addressed to the chief of police. "Sir, my business is of a sensitive nature. I believe we should converse in a less public place."

"Captain, I will grant you a private audience in my office. And we'll include my friend Charlie Moon, who is acting chief of the Southern Ute police."

"That will be quite satisfactory. I need to talk to Officer Moon."

"I'll do this on one condition."

Her face—which was capable of remarkably subtle expressions—managed to frown with a single arc of plucked eyebrow. "And that would be?"

"You will 'sir' me *nevermore*."

"Yes, sir. I mean—of course, sir." She closed her eyes, as if considerable concentration would be required for this task. "I will do my best."

Scott Parris looked at her closely for the first time. She wore no makeup. The hazel eyes were large and expressive; chestnut-brown hair was tied in a prim bun at the back of her head. "That is all that is required of us, Captain Taylor. That we do our best."

"How shall I address you . . . Chief Parris?"

"My friends call me Scott."

She almost smiled. "Then you must call me . . . Teresa."

The literary agent was highly annoyed at being so coldly ignored. "Oh goody," Zoog cooed, "it's love at first sight. Maybe you'll name your first boy-child after me."

Teresa turned on the mouthy little man with tightly doubled fists. "Listen close, Rumpelstiltskin—one more smart crack outta you and I'll knee the family jewels right into your chest cavity."

It was clear to both men that this was not a bluff.

Parris decided to preserve the rude man's delicate parts—and some level of decorum. "You'd best run along, Mr. Zoog."

"Well," Eddie Zoog muttered at the OSI captain, "so much for her being an officer and a gentleman." But he backed off . . . out of knee range.

Moon felt someone looking at the back of his neck. He turned. It was his best friend. "Hello, pardner."

"Hi, Charlie." Scott Parris nodded at the extremely attractive young woman. "Hello again, Miss Willow."

Camilla flashed a novalike smile.

Charlie Moon was mildly displeased by the interruption, but this was his buddy. "Have a seat, pardner."

"I don't have the time, Charlie. And neither do you."

"How's that?"

Parris tipped his battered felt hat at Camilla. "Miss, would you excuse us for a moment?" Without waiting for a reply, he gave the Ute policeman a "this-is-important-business" look and walked away.

Moon shrugged at his date and followed his friend.

Parris jerked his head to indicate the young woman in

the gray suit who waited near the exit. "We have an official visitor. Air Force."

Moon had a look at the plainly dressed young woman. It was not that she was actually homely. Far from it. But after gazing over his plate at Camilla, a man's scale of measurement got recalibrated. She made this Air Force kid look like a muddy fence post. Moreover, the military woman had a mean, hard look about her. Like someone from one of those Middle Eastern countries who hates absolutely everybody and carries concealed pipe bombs. "*United States* Air Force?"

"Yeah. She's one of ours. OSI."

"Why does the Office of Special Investigations want to talk to us?"

"Captain Taylor did not say. She requires a private audience. In my office."

The Ute glanced back toward the booth. The pretty woman smiled. "Well, you go ahead, Scott, and get started. I'll show up . . . right after I finish lunch." *Next week, maybe.*

Parris shook his head. "I'd never think of starting without you, old buddy. I'll wait right here. Till you've swallowed your last bite."

"But . . . you really don't have to . . ."

"Don't embarrass me with a hatful of thank-yous, partner." Parris grinned cruelly. "You'd do the same for me."

"First chance I get," Moon muttered. He headed back to the booth to make his apologies.

Camilla patted Moon's hand. "It's okay, Charlie. You run along. I'll catch up with you later."

"You sure?"

"Lean over." She kissed the tips of her fingers, then touched his lips.

Moon walked unsteadily away from the booth.

Parris smirked. "She's not wasting any time."

The Ute looked over his shoulder.

Camilla waved at him.

He waved back. "You know what, pardner?"

Parris knew. "What?"

"I think . . . I admire that woman."

"How come?" *Silly question.*

"For one thing, she's awfully nice to look at."

"She's no wart hog. What's another thing?"

"Camilla's not a vegetarian." Moon shook his head in wonder at this. "Likes her steaks half cooked."

"Another point in her favor."

The Ute—whose face had a faraway look—was now talking to himself. "And she owns a big horse ranch."

"The truth finally comes out." Parris smirked. "You lust after her real estate."

Eddie Zoog joined Camilla in the booth. "So?" he said.

She gave him a blank, disinterested look. Just to make him squirm.

He squirmed. And waved toward himself with both hands, as if to forcibly withdraw words from her sensuous lips. "Okay, Blondie—give me the straight scoop!"

She smiled. "Very well. There are no slobbering monsters lurking in the darkness, Uncle Eddie. No hideous aliens in flying saucers abducting helpless earthlings for unspeakable medical experiments."

"So the agency deals in fiction—who cares? I turn a nice profit givin' the public what they want."

Camilla rolled the blue-green eyes. "The agency used to be a legitimate operation, representing a dozen first-rate authors. Now it's an embarrassment."

"So you're embarrassed—get over it." This was maddening. "What'd you find out from the Indian copper?"

"Nothing." *Except that Charlie Moon is a very nice man.*

He was practically bouncing on the upholstered seat. "Whaddaya mean, *nothing?*"

She was weary of the interrogation. "Zip. *Nada.* Zero."

He chomped on the cigar. "That's what happens, give a man's job to a girl and . . ."

Her eyes flashed green fire. "What did you learn from the chief of police?"

Eddie Zoog raised his palms as if weighing some invisible treasure. "Well . . . actually . . ."

"Nothing," she said. And smiled.

Uncle Eddie chuckled. "Well, anyway, kid, we're zero and zero. So it's even Stephen."

She looked over his head. "Who's that woman they left with?"

So I do know something Miss Smarty-pants don't. Triumphantly, Zoog consulted his dog-eared notepad. "Captain Teresa Taylor. U.S. Air Force—Office of Special Investigations. Wants a *private* talk with the cops. Same as always. It's a government cover-up." He scowled under beetle brows at the Sugar Bowl Cafe's grease-stained windows. Zoog suddenly recalled the fifty-dollar "tip" and felt a searing stab of heartburn. "First thing you know, the Feds'll claim those two guys wasn't snatched off Apache Lake at all—and the light that Cherokee cop saw was nothin' but the planet Venice."

The beautiful princess laughed.

The frog responded with an angry, guttural croak.

It is true, the Ute realized—rank does have its privileges. And because Charlie Moon was within a whisker of being appointed chief of Southern Ute Police, he was more than a little interested in the office of the Granite Creek chief of police. Scott Parris' new quarters occupied almost a third of the remodeled second floor of the GCPD building. This space was segmented into a large corner office, a private meeting room with a long oak table and a dozen cushioned chairs. Moreover—to the envy of all his officers—the chief had a private rest room. With a blue-tiled shower.

Moon was impressed by the meeting room. The floor was covered with a thick black-and-green carpet; the acoustic ceiling was equipped with cleverly concealed lighting. The walls were paneled with genuine knotty pine, the tall windows curtained with a heavy fabric that matched the carpet. At one end of the rectangular room was a mini-kitchen. Copper-tone refrigerator. Full-size microwave oven. Four-burner gas range. Stainless-steel sink with utilitarian fittings. On this warm April afternoon, refrigerated air moved soundlessly from unseen vents to regulate the temperature at precisely sixty-eight degrees.

Parris, attempting to be a good host, fumbled around in the hardwood cabinets until he found the makings for coffee.

The Air Force officer sat across the table from Charlie Moon. "I understand you found the abandoned trucks on the shore of Navajo Lake."

"One of my men found them," Moon said. "He was answering a call about . . . peculiar lights on the lakeshore."

She barely smiled. "Peculiar lights?"

"Officer Bignight thought it might be a big campfire. But when he got there, all he found was the trucks."

She used a ballpoint pen to draw concentric circles on a legal-size yellow pad someone had left from a previous meeting. "I'd like to examine the vehicles."

"We're holding 'em in Ignacio," the Ute policeman said. "You're welcome to have a look. But there's not much to see."

"I understand the hood was missing from one of the trucks."

The Ute policeman nodded. "Seemed to have been torn off."

She looked up from her doodling. "I beg your pardon?"

Moon couldn't think of any better way to say it. Silly as it sounded. "Hinge hardware was busted up . . . just hanging there. Like the hood'd been pulled off."

"That implies that *something* pulled it off."

He left that one alone. "It turned up later, in a high-country sheep pasture. Couple of miles north of the lake."

"The hood must've been ripped off by a sudden wind," she said.

"Could be. There was a thunderstorm over the lake that night."

Captain Teresa Taylor stared at the legal pad. "What do you think happened to those men?"

In a whimsical mood, the Ute policeman toyed with the notion of having some fun with this very serious young woman. He would start by suggesting that a giant spider had crawled out of the lake, bitten off the pickup hood just for the hell of it, grabbed the drunken men, and run off with 'em. Then Grandmother Spider had flung the truck hood amongst a flock of sheep, scared Aunt Daisy and Sarah Frank half to death, got sprayed with bird shot by the ding-ey old woman. Then—in a fit of rage—the huge spider had chomped off an attorney's head. No ordinary creature would dare mess with a lawyer. The oversized spider had then stashed Tommy Tonompicket in a tree. And William

Pizinski was, in all probability, dangling in a sticky web in some deep, dark cavern . . . waiting to be dined upon. But this stern-looking young lady didn't show much evidence of having a sense of humor. She was probably a vegetarian. "I haven't got any good ideas. Tommy Tonompicket's not been able to say a word since they took him outta the tree. But I expect he'll tell us what we need to know. Soon as he feels like talking."

Scott Parris—who had not missed a word of this conversation—brought a lacquered Japanese tray to the table. On the tray were three crockery mugs of steaming coffee and a small basket filled with assorted packets of sugar, sugar substitute, and powdered nondairy creamer.

Moon didn't conceal his disappointment. "No cookies?"

Parris muttered something under his breath. He searched the cabinets until he found an unopened package of Oreos. The chief of police slid this across the table to the Ute. "Anything else I can get for you?"

"Not right now."

"I could send out for some French pastries."

Moon pretended to miss the sarcasm. "Maybe later." He opened a wicked-looking blade on his pocketknife and slit the plastic wrap around the black-and-white cookies.

The young woman took a tentative sip of coffee. Too strong.

Parris took a seat at the end of the table. For a moment, he watched Moon stuff Oreos into his mouth, then assumed his official voice. "So, Captain Taylor . . . what, exactly, is the Air Force's interest in this business?"

"Teresa," she said.

Parris was momentarily confused by the response.

"It was your idea, if I recall correctly. No official titles. I'm Teresa," she said, "you're Scott. Otherwise, I'll have to address you as 'sir.' "

"Ahh . . . right." He blushed furiously. "Sorry. I forgot."

"Men." She looked at the acoustic ceiling and sighed. "How quickly they forget."

Moon addressed the young woman in a serious tone. "Teresa, you can call me Charlie."

She returned the smile. "Okay . . . Charlie."

Parris—aware that she had avoided his question—repeated it. "Teresa, why is the Air Force interested in the misadventures of Mr. Tonompicket and Mr. Pizinski?"

The OSI special agent tapped her pencil on the pad. "It's *Dr.* Pizinski, actually. He's a rather senior scientist . . . Ph.D. in aeronautical engineering."

"Okay. So what's OSI's interest in *Dr.* Pizinski?"

Captain Taylor chose her words with some care. "OSI takes an interest in any . . . reported event . . . that might affect the national security."

"Could you be a bit more specific?"

She drew several circles on the pad. "I'm afraid not."

Scott Parris propped his elbows on the polished surface of the table. He rested his square chin on doubled fists. And chose his own words carefully. "*Teresa*—let's cut right to the bone. Here's the way it is. If you want to cooperate with us on this investigation"—he glanced at the Ute policeman—"I assume that I may speak for Charlie Moon—we'll be happy to exchange information for the common good. The key word is *exchange*. But if you think you can march in here waving the national security flag and pick our brains without telling us zip about what you know—you're wasting your time. And ours."

Apparently unmoved by the speech, she continued to doodle on the yellow pad.

Moon was eager to see what would happen next.
This is great fun.

Captain Teresa Taylor laid the ballpoint on the pad,
then looked directly at Scott Parris. "I understand your
position."

"Good," Parris said easily.

She took a deep breath. "You must try to understand
mine."

"I'm listening."

"OSI investigations are—of necessity—of a highly
confidential nature. There's really very little that I am
authorized to tell you."

Parris got to his feet. "Good day, Captain Taylor."

Whatever happened to "Teresa"? She offered him a
bitter smile. "You're a tough customer."

"That's right. I'm not buying."

"Please sit down," she said. "Let's try to start afresh."

Somewhat reluctantly, he did. And, quite deliberately,
looked at his wristwatch.

"I'd appreciate it if what I say is not repeated outside
this room."

Parris adopted a conciliatory tone. "We'll do the best
we can. But no hard promises. You may tell us something we already know. Or something we'll learn from
another source tomorrow."

"Fair enough." She picked up the pen and began to
draw more circles on the pad. "As I said, Dr. William
Pizinski is an aeronautical engineer. Graduate degrees
from Illinois-Urbana and the University of Michigan. I
imagine you already know that he is a civilian employee
of a United States Air Force contractor."

"Rocky Mountain Advanced Flight Systems," Moon
said.

She nodded. "RMAFS works closely with Kirtland
Air Force Base in Albuquerque. Dr. Pizinski is a very
senior technical staff member. Chief scientist, in fact."

Parris was unimpressed. "So what kind of work does he do?" *Not that you'll tell me.*

"Other than the fact that it is highly technical—and highly classified—I am not privy to that information. I do know—and this is sensitive information—that he is involved in a number of RAPs."

The lawmen exchanged puzzled glances.

"Sorry," she said. "The government thrives on acronyms. Dr. Pizinski works on several Restricted Access Projects."

Parris frowned at the young officer. "If none of us—not even OSI's investigators—knows what the guy is working on, and whether it might be connected in some way with his disappearance, it's going to be pretty difficult to run a meaningful investigation."

She spoke in a monotone that reminded Moon of computer-generated speech. "There is no indication at present that whatever happened to Dr. Pizinski has anything to do with his work for the Air Force. I assure you, gentlemen, that if such evidence arises to the contrary, OSI has the means—through the Judge Advocate General's office—to kick the RAP doors down. If necessary, I can walk in and examine any research that might be relevant to this investigation. Because the work is classified, I could not, of course, divulge any details to those without proper clearances. And the need to know."

"Which means Charlie and me," Parris grunted.

"When circumstances warrant it," she said coolly, "Department of Defense clearances may be granted to civilian authorities—such as police officials and judges. In such cases, of course, those officials are forbidden by federal law from improperly divulging any classified information gained via the clearance."

The chief of police threw up his hands in despair.

"So what'll it be?" she said. "You want me to disappear?"

Again the lawmen exchanged glances.

"We'll play it by ear," the Ute said. "It'll help us all if we pool our resources. We could start by putting together what we know about Pizinski's movements just before he . . . uh . . . sort of vanished."

Captain Taylor withdrew a leather-bound notebook from her briefcase. "Dr. Pizinski left Albuquerque on the morning of twenty-eight March, at approximately zero seven hundred hours. His destination was the RMAFS plant in Colorado Springs. He was driving a GMC pickup truck. A check of gasoline credit-card receipts indicates that Dr. Pizinski took Interstate 25 north to Santa Fe, and on through Las Vegas, New Mexico, and Raton to—"

Parris interrupted. "Why'd he drive his truck? Why didn't Pizinski fly to Colorado Springs? That's a pretty short hop from Albuquerque, but a long drive."

She shrugged. "I don't know. I'll ask Dr. Pizinski if—when he shows up." She ran an immaculate fingernail along the neatly written script in the notebook. "According to OSI's preliminary investigation, Dr. Pizinski arrived at RMAFS in Colorado Springs that afternoon at about sixteen hundred hours. Subject completed his business during the following three days. On one April, Dr. Pizinski departed from the plant. This was at approximately eleven hundred thirty hours. Later that day—at thirteen hundred and ten hours—subject purchased eighteen-point-four gallons of regular gasoline on his Visa Gold card. Also a large coffee and a grilled ham sandwich."

The lawmen tried hard not to grin.

The earnest young woman continued. "Both purchases were made at a truck stop just north of Walsenburg." Captain Taylor closed the notebook. "That is the last solid information we have of Dr. Pizinski's where-abouts. Until he showed up later that day on the northern shore of Navajo Lake. And either abandoned his vehicle . . . or was forcibly removed from it." She looked expectantly at Charlie Moon. "But why didn't he head straight down I-25 to Albuquerque? Why did Dr. Pizinski turn west on Route 160 and end up on the shore of Navajo Lake?"

The conversation meandered around aimlessly for several minutes.

Finally, Captain Taylor pushed her chair away from the table. "With any luck, Mr. Tonompicket will recover enough to be able to tell us what happened." She got up and smoothed her skirt. "Or perhaps Dr. Pizinski will turn up. And clear this thing up once and for all."

Parris decided to end the meeting on a cooperative note. "If Pizinski shows up around here, I'll let you know."

"Thanks," she said with a smug expression. "But if he turns up anywhere on the planet—I'll know. Good day, gentlemen." With this, the OSI special agent departed.

Parris frowned at the door, still swinging behind her. "There goes a smart young woman who's quite sure of herself. And she's interesting—wouldn't you say?"

Charlie Moon was inspecting the legal pad the OSI investigator had doodled on. "Yeah. Interesting." Scattered over the yellow page were several simple sketches. There was a grouping of concentric circles—an ancient shaman's symbol for a passage between worlds. Over this, a single slender oval, bisected along its long axis with a straight line. From the bottom of the figure, wavy lines flowed. Looked oddly like a cartoon drawing of . . . a hovering spacecraft?

But what interested the Ute far more was an array of single circles scattered randomly over the page. Each of these disks had precisely eight rays emanating from its periphery. They were, he assumed, happy drawings of the sun and its warm rays. Not unlike sketches a bored schoolgirl might make on her drawing pad. But to the Ute's wary eye, each circle represented a body. Each line, a leg. The things *crawled* across the page. Like spiders.

———·

Orville Stamm—who had just celebrated his eightieth birthday by baking a small blackberry-jam cake—eked out a meager living by gathering firewood from the national forest and selling it to whoever would pay eighty dollars for a short cord. His mother, Vera, who was ninety-nine, worried about her son. Orville had never been overly bright. Now that he was getting on in years, Vera shared this worry with her friends in the nursing home. "Orville's got the hardening of the arteries—can't remember where he is half the time. I'm afraid he'll get lost out in the pine woods sometime and starve to death before anyone finds him."

Mrs. Stamm's morbid fear was unnecessary. It was true enough that her octogenarian "boy" was often confused about exactly where he was in the forest. This was partly because one dirt road winding among the pines and aspen and spruce looked pretty much like another. But Orville never had any trouble finding the paved highway, or remembering which way to turn to get to Granite Creek, where all those "rich folk" lived who bought his loads of hand-sawed wood to burn in their fancy brick fireplaces and trendy cast-iron stoves.

On this particular day, he was nosing the creaking Dodge pickup along a lane that was gooey with black mud from the recent thaw. He pulled to a stop under the partial shade of a leaning spruce and cut the ignition. He squinted up at the sun, then removed the seven-jewel Elgin watch from his pocket. Yes, just as Old Sol's position had suggested, it was lunchtime. Ten minutes past noon, in fact. Orville opened the brown paper bag he'd prepared before daylight. There was a banana, which he set aside for dessert. The skinny old man unwrapped the aluminum foil around a thick sandwich. Black rye around slices of Velveeta cheese and pickle-pimento loaf. A generous gob of mayonnaise and dill pickles for seasoning. He also had a thermos of sweetened coffee.

Orville Stamm sat there under the spruce, the sandwich clamped in his grimy hands, and thought about how fortunate he was. A man should express his gratitude for God's many blessings. He bowed his head and silently thanked the Creator of worlds and universes for his food. And for his good health. And, oh yes . . . for the privilege of being in this lovely place. And asked God for this one additional blessing: that he, lowly among men as he was, might still be useful in this world. "Amen," he said aloud.

Orville took his first bite of the sandwich, then a swallow of steaming coffee directly from the thermos. Ahhh . . . Life was so good.

As if in affirmation, a black-crested Steller's jay lighted in a branch near the truck window and immediately began its clicky monologue. It was a refreshing delight to the old man, a happy song of the sweetness of spring. He did not understand that the aggressive bird was protesting his very presence in this place, to which Mr. Jay held a clear title. In such circumstances, there is much to be said for the blissful ignorance of innocents.

But even the innocent do not remain oblivious forever. Life has a rude way of intruding.

Orville didn't see the thing at first.

He heard it.

The sinister sound of a shuffling walk, the huff-huff of raspy breathing.

It assaulted his nostrils—smelled like some awful filth that'd been burned at the city landfill.

The old woodsman—who had heard tales of the loathsome monsters that roamed these deep forests—was almost petrified with fear. His mind worked slowly, but came to this very sensible conclusion. *Need to start the engine. Get outta here.*

Too late. The thing appeared a few yards away. It had a shape resembling a man, but this thing could not be human. It was half covered with sooty-black rags, like something that had climbed right out of hell's chimney. The matted hair was straggly and covered with pine needles; it hung over the bestial face like a mop. The eyes were white and wild; the mouth hung open. Slobber drooled disgustingly from bluish lip to hairy chin.

"Oh, God," Orville muttered, "protect me from this . . . this . . . *whatever it is.*"

The unspeakable creature approached the open truck window.

The stench was sickening; the old woodsman attempted a friendly smile. "Hello there," he said lamely. *As if you'd understand English.*

"Aaaarrrrgh," the thing croaked. And reached out with a filthy paw.

Orville leaned away and swallowed hard. "Uhhh . . . something you want?"

There was.

The grubby apparition snatched away the woodsman's sandwich, gobbled it up in an instant.

Then belched loudly.

THE LAWMEN—WHO knew better than to barge into Intensive Care without permission—dutifully appeared at the nurse's desk. It was actually an L-shaped counter that served as a bulwark between ordinary citizens and those starchy-white members of the healing profession.

Moon, who harbored a childlike dread of hospitals, stood a yard behind the *matukach* lawman. The least scent of rubbing alcohol—or the mere sight of a hypodermic—made him uneasy . . . even queasy.

Parris leaned with both hands on the spotless Formica counter and blinked sleepily at the petite duty nurse perched on the stool; her small feet dangled two inches above the floor. Her skin was white as parchment, her hair flaming red and—despite her continued attempts to "do something with it"—wild and stringy. Nurse Mulligan looked up from her work on a patient's chart, recognized the popular chief of police. She flashed him a toothy smile and spoke with a hint of Irish brogue: "Well, toppa the mornin' to ya!"

"Unngh," Parris said miserably. It was way too early in the day for an encounter with Miss Happy Face.

Moon nodded and smiled at the little woman. "Good mornin' right back at you."

Parris made a valiant effort at civility, but her good humor was annoying. He had been awake half the night with an upset stomach. "Me'n my buddy are here to see William Pizinski. And after we see him," Parris growled, "we'll want a have a look at Mr. Tonompicket."

"We're kinda hoping one of 'em will be able to talk to us on this fine morning," Moon added.

Parris' voice took on a sarcastically sweet tone: "So, my dear young lady—can we go into the ICU?"

"I would not hazard a guess as to whether you *can.* But you certainly *may.*"

The lawmen turned and headed for the double doors that were labeled AUTHORIZED PERSONNEL ONLY.

"Of course," the nurse called out merrily, "goin' into ICU won't do you all that much good."

Parris turned slowly. "And why may that be?"

She placed a pair of rimless spectacles neatly on her narrow nose and squinted at a sheaf of papers on a clipboard. "The patients in question—Pizinski and Tonompicket—have been moved, you see. Pizinski is in room AN-201. Tonompicket is right next door—in AN-202."

"They've been moved to the Annex?"

She nodded. "Aye, that they have, sir."

Moon enjoyed hearing the Irishwoman's voice. "And who's in 203?"

"Mrs. Snyder," she whispered. "Poor old thing, she's mad as a . . . a . . ."

"Hatter?" the Ute said helpfully.

"Yes. A hatter."

Parris stared suspiciously at the nurse. "Why were these patients moved to the Annex?"

She met the stern look without flinching. "Well, I'm sure I don't know, sir."

The lawmen were several feet below the greening sod and budding elms. The damp air smelled like rotting wood. Every thirty feet, there were flickering fluorescent lights overhead. The cinder-block walls were painted a sickly shade of green. The floor was concrete; the soles of their boots echoed along the underground corridor.

"I think it's kinda strange," the Ute said.

"What?"

"Way the hospital moved Tommy and the *matukach* out of the ICU. And put them in rooms side by side."

"Stranger than you think, Charlie. There are only rooms for five patients on the second floor of the Annex, which is what's left of the old Snyder mansion. And those spiffy lodgings cost a bundle."

"So who's paying for 'em?" Tribal medical insurance barely covered bare-bones hospital accommodations.

"That I don't know," Parris muttered. "But I intend to find out."

Moon shortened his long stride so his friend could keep up. "Who're the Snyders?"

"That I do know. Great-Grandpa Snyder made most of his money in silver mining. When the price of silver fell through the bottom, the family turned to dry goods and hardware. Sometime back in the 1950s, they built the Snyder Memorial Hospital on the family estate and gave it to the county. Then the last of 'em started to die off or move away. When there was no one left around here but Matilda, she deeded the family mansion to the county. That's what they call the Annex."

"She the patient in room 203?"

Parris nodded. "The very same. Matilda Snyder—

folks around here call her Mattie—she must be at least ninety. And strong as a plow horse. But her mind wanders. Sometimes she thinks she's a young gal waitin' for her husband to come back from the war. He never did come home, though. But no matter how confused she gets, Mattie always knows she's still living in her own house. So she gets pretty high-handed, gives the nurses lots of orders. And she bugs the patients something awful." For the first time this morning, Parris felt his good humor returning. "I think the main advantage of putting patients in the Annex is that being there with Mattie is a strong incentive to get well and go home."

At the end of the long tunnel that connected the main hospital with the Annex, the lawmen climbed a concrete stairwell to the first floor. Emerging from the near darkness of the tunnel into the warm light of an April morning was a startling but pleasant experience. They found themselves in an enormous circular parlor. On the west side was a massive sandstone fireplace, still outfitted with cast-iron cooking utensils. Shelves radiated out from the fireplace; they were empty except for a few clumps of leather-bound books and marble statuary. The room was furnished with an array of antique chairs that faced the center of the circle, where a massive round table had been placed. Its centerpiece was a bronze casting of six yelling cowboys, six-shooters pointed skyward, reared exultantly on muscular horses that snorted and pawed at the air. Moon wondered whether the sculpture was a Remington. This didn't look like a place that would display a knockoff, and an original would be worth a fortune. There was no visible security.

There were mullioned windows on the east side, nine feet high and a yard wide. Yellow sunlight filtered through ivory-tinted curtains. There were long, dark hallways leading off into north and south wings, which seemed to be unoccupied. Except, perhaps, by ghosts of the long-dead former inhabitants.

The chief of police, who often came here to visit the sick and the maimed, knew something of the history of the Snyder house. In the late-nineteenth century—so he had been told—this fabled "round room" had been the scene of many dazzling parties, humming until dawn with the sweet melodies of lush Austrian waltzes or fat Italian sopranos. Now it was a plush sitting room for the few convalescents and their occasional guests.

Today, the lawmen were quite alone in its vast spaces.

Moon peered out the east windows, which overlooked the banks of Granite Creek. He pulled back the almost translucent curtains. They were edged with age-yellowed lace; the linen fabric felt oddly stiff and shroud-like in his fingers. As if it were disintegrating along with the Snyder clan. Outside on the red-brick patio, everything looked new and vibrant—alive with the eternal promise of spring. Above the pavement of zigzag bricks, a broad second-floor balcony extended to the stream's edge. At each end of the patio, identical wrought-iron latticeworks reached up to the balcony. These black metallic structures supported entanglements of Virginia creeper that were just beginning to show soft green shoots. The view to the east was interrupted by a half-dozen massive pine posts that supported the balcony. The swollen stream, high on its banks, roared along only a few feet away from the French windows. Moon looked to the heavens. The mottled gray clouds were already clearing, exposing great expanses of turquoise sky over the San Juans.

Scott Parris whispered, as if they were touring a great cathedral, "Some place."

The Ute nodded. The family might be down to its last Snyder, but you could still smell the money.

Parris looked up the long, sweeping stairway ascending to the second floor. "The nurse's station is at the top of the stairs. There are six good-sized rooms up there, three in each wing. The far end of the north wing is where they've put our guys. Mrs. Snyder has the room closest to the nurse's desk. The three rooms in the south wing include two for patients and a TV room."

The Ute followed his friend to the magnificent curving stairway. They didn't hurry. In contrast to the dank, twilight climb from the basement, this was a very pleasant ascent. A deep blue carpet was centered along the varnished steps, which were hewn from thick slabs of solid oak and fastened in place with wooden pegs the size of a man's thumb. A seamless, sculpted mahogany banister meandered along beside them like a skinny cat who wanted her back rubbed. The wall was lined with flaking paintings of dour-looking men and haughty women, presumably members of the Snyder tribe. A crystal chandelier that had once supported forty-eight tallow cylinders hung on a heavy brass chain from the high conical ceiling. The candles had been replaced with decorative twenty-watt bulbs, which were not energized on this brightening morning. This magnificent pendulum was suspended precisely over the geometric center of the parlor; the daggerlike projection on the bottom seemed to be moving slowly, tracing a tight ellipse.

At the top of the stairs, a stern notice was mounted on a wooden tripod.

ALL VISITORS MUST REPORT
TO THE NURSES' STATION

The station would have been difficult to evade; it was directly in front of them.

The lawmen paused and removed their hats. This was

quite a contrast to the bustling ICU nerve center. Here the atmosphere was serenely quiet. A slender woman in her late forties sat behind a massive walnut desk, pretending not to notice their arrival. She wore a gray skirt and a yellow silk blouse. Her round face might have been attractive if visited by a smile. Raven hair was pulled tightly over her ears; a long braid hung down her back, precisely aligned with her spine. A lovely cameo on a black velvet band adorned her throat. Single pearls were fastened to each earlobe. She might have been the curator of a small museum.

On the desk were three items, arranged with geometric precision. A black, old-fashioned dial telephone was on her left. A small panel—also black—occupied the corresponding space on her right. On this instrument were a pair of lights for each of the five patients' rooms. A white light for the call-button attached to each bed. A red light—in case monitors were attached to the patient—to indicate that some vital parameter was out of limits. Centered on the desk was an elegant crystal vase. It was occupied by an astonishingly perfect yellow rose, precisely the color of her blouse. The stem of the blossom was carefully trimmed so that the lowest leaf sprouted just one centimeter above the rim. The water in the vase was dyed a light hue of blue—which matched the nurse's nail polish.

Like the cold blood flowing in her veins, Scott Parris thought.

Moon—who felt transported back in time—stared at this vision with childlike fascination.

"Hello," Parris said. He rotated an elbow to indicate his friend. "This is Charlie Moon. He's chief of the Southern Ute police."

"Acting chief," Moon muttered modestly.

The nurse put on her professional smile for the tall,

dark stranger. "I am Miss Helene Shrewsberry, R.N. In the Annex, we do not wear uniforms. Not even name tags. The intent is to provide the ward with a more homelike atmosphere. The patients seem to approve of this policy." There was a hint in the sudden tilt of her chin that she did not.

Parris nodded toward the north wing. "We heard that Pizinski and Tonompicket have been moved over here."

"Yes. They were transferred to the Annex late yesterday. You may visit either of them if you wish. Mrs. Tonompicket has been with her husband most of the morning. A very devoted wife," she said approvingly. "And Mr. Pizinski also has a visitor."

Moon leaned easily on the desk. "And who's that?"

She glanced at the massive hands that were making prints on the polished oak. Then at Moon. He retreated.

She found a tissue in her purse and wiped at the oily marks.

Parris grinned at his Ute friend. *Met your match, haven't you?*

This little matter dispensed with, she closed her eyes and consulted the infallible record inside her skull. "Mr. Pizinski's visitor is a Mr. Kenneth Bright, of Albuquerque, New Mexico. He claims to be the patient's brother-in-law." It was apparent that she did not care for this visitor from the south. Or necessarily trust him to be who he said he was.

Parris glanced at Moon. "Pizinski's brother-in-law didn't waste much time getting here."

"Evidently a very devoted relative," the nurse said with a cynical expression.

Moon offered her his best smile. "Who's paying for these ritzy rooms in the Annex? Mr. Bright?"

She almost smiled in return, momentarily baring a dozen perfectly aligned teeth. As if to prevent such a breach of protocol, she bit her lower lip. "Well . . . I ordinarily would not discuss such matters. But because you are the police, I suppose it is the correct thing to do. Yes. He is." Her lips pursed to express her distaste for Bright. "Boasted about it, in fact. Said he could afford it."

"Pizinski is Bright's relative and employee," Moon said almost to himself. "But I wonder why Bright's taking such good care of Tommy Tonompicket."

"Mr. Bright," Parris observed, "is apparently a generous man."

Shrewsberry sniffed. "If Mr. Pizinski has himself a brother-in-law, perhaps he also has a wife. If so, it seems odd that she has not come to see her husband."

"His wife is on a trip," Moon said. "She'll probably be hard to find."

Her barely raised eyebrow asked why this should be so.

"She's riding a bike," the Ute explained. "All over Europe."

Nurse Shrewsberry—who would not have thought of straddling such an unseemly contrivance—raised the immaculate eyebrow another two millimeters. Which was sufficient comment.

Parris popped an antacid tablet into his mouth. "How long has the brother-in-law been here?"

She consulted a platinum-plated wristwatch. "Thirty-two minutes."

"We'll look in on Mr. Tonompicket first. How's he doing?"

"Physically, he is improving rapidly. His vitals are satisfactory. But he hasn't said a word. I don't think he knows who he is. Or where he is, for that matter. I feel so sorry for his poor wife."

"Miss Shrewsberry, if Mr. Bright should get done with his visit while we're in 202 . . ."

She understood. "I will detain him for you, Chief Parris."

Moon followed Parris into 202. Tonompicket's room was sandwiched between Mad Mattie's and William Pizinski's, on the far end of the north wing. He'd never seen a hospital setup like this. For one thing, the room was quite large. For another, there was thick blue carpet on the floor. Blue-and-white paper on the walls. Immaculately plastered ceiling, with a chandelier that was a miniature replica of the massive fixture suspended over the downstairs parlor. The furniture was heavy and dark and old. An IV stand by the headboard of the four-poster bed was a glaring reminder that Tommy Tonompicket wasn't in a fancy hotel in downtown Denver. There was an ivory-tinted control pad pinned to the bed sheet by his pillow. The buttons could be used to adjust the configuration of the mattress—and to summon the nurse. Neither of the policemen could imagine Miss Shrewsberry removing a bedpan.

Tommy's chubby wife was sitting by the bed, staring at her spouse's still form. She turned to have a look at the unexpected visitors. "Hello, Charlie."

"Hi, Bertha. This is my pardner, Scott Parris."

Parris took his hat off. "Good morning."

She ignored the white man's greeting. Charlie Moon's close friendship with the *matukach* policeman was puzzling to the Utes. But Charlie had always been different from regular people.

The lawmen looked down at the man on the hospital bed.

Despite Nurse Shrewsberry's optimistic appraisal of Tonompicket's condition, her patient looked more dead than alive. His eyes were half open, staring, unfocused. He probably didn't even see the plastered ceiling. He was breathing, it was true. But Moon estimated the man had lost a good ten pounds. The skinny fellow didn't have that many pounds to lose.

"He can't talk," Bertha said to Moon. "I don't think they can do anything for him." She gave no outward sign of being dismayed.

The policeman put his hand on her shoulder. "He'll be up and around in a few days."

"I think it's soul-loss," the wife said hollowly. "Whatever happened to Tommy has scared his spirit away." Bertha Tonompicket rubbed her husband's forehead with the tips of her fingers. "Maybe your aunt Daisy could help Tommy get his soul back." She paused to consider this possibility. "I should ask her to come up here. See what she can do for him."

The Ute policeman shook his head wearily. *Aunt Daisy doing her mumbo jumbo over Tommy. That's all I need.*

Parris approached the bed and cleared his throat. "Mr. Tonompicket?"

No response.

He raised his voice by several decibels: "Mr. Tonompicket—can you hear me?"

Not a flicker from the patient.

"Yelling won't help," Bertha pointed out reasonably. "Tommy's soul is gone." *Don't these* matukach *understand nothing?*

Moon lifted the patient's forearm. Let it go. The limb fell limply to the starched cotton sheet. He knelt by his tribesman. "Tommy—I don't know if you can hear me. But you're safe now. In a real nice hospital room. Bertha's right here with you. You're gonna be okay."

Tonompicket's eyelids fluttered. His mouth opened; he made an odd rasping sound.

The Ute policeman fought off a dreadful premonition

that Tonompicket would never leave the hospital alive. "He'll be okay," he said. As if the power of the spoken word would make it so.

Parris retreated to a far corner of the room; Moon followed. The white policeman shook his head sadly and whispered: "Might as well be talking to a baked potato."

Moon could not disagree with this assessment.

Bertha, now oblivious to the visitors, was stroking her husband's arm. And whispering. "Come back, Tommy . . . come back."

The Ute policeman wandered aimlessly around the room until he found himself facing the French windows. He turned a brass latch handle and stepped outside onto the redwood planks. A fresh breeze blew over the river; it felt good in his nostrils. Alive with hope.

The balcony spanned the entire length of the east face of the Annex. The identical glassed doors to William Pizinski's room were to his right. Just past Pizinski's room was the north end of the structure, which terminated in the upper portion of a wrought-iron lattice. Long brown fingers of Virginia creeper were tentatively feeling their way over the railing. A few steps to his left—near the nurses' station—was the entrance to the old woman's room. Matilda Snyder. Mad Mattie. Behind the nurse's desk, a massive bay window jutted onto the center of the balcony. The French windows at the three rooms which comprised the south wing were hidden from his view by the central bay window. Long ago, all would have been family bedrooms where a half-dozen Snyders dreamed their dreams. With ample glazing to catch the first light of morning.

The balcony was bare except for a scattering of uncomfortable-looking metal chairs and tall, spindly terracotta flowerpots that had been made somewhere south of the border. There were no plants in the heavy pots. Someone—perhaps to prevent the winds from toppling them—had filled each vessel with large, smooth stones. Most were dark-speckled granite. Mixed in with this common stuff were shiny chunks of gray flint, gold-bearing rose quartz, dark basalt.

Moon, who had been in a fine mood all day, felt a sudden surge of melancholy.

He would have leaned on the blackened iron railing that surrounded the redwood deck, but the banister was just over knee-high. So he stood there, hands in his jacket pockets, staring down at the river rushing underneath the balcony. These troubled waters hurried down the Granite Creek to join the Piedra. And then on to Navajo Lake. And, finally, to the sea. He felt himself also rushing downstream—as the great cosmic clock ticked away the minutes and years of his life. The policeman mused about how wildly unpredictable life could be. Tommy Tonompicket had probably been fishing off the lakeshore on that first afternoon of April. Expecting things to go on pretty much as usual. But something unexpected had cropped up in Tommy's life.

For one thing, he'd met up with the *matukach* scientist in the pickup truck.

And something very peculiar had happened to both of them. The hood had been ripped from Tommy's flatbed, then discarded among the shepherd's frightened flock. Officer Bignight had experienced something that spooked him pretty bad. Minutes later, Aunt Daisy and little Sarah Frank had encountered something outside the old woman's home. Something that terrified them. The unfortunate lawyer—who had evidently gone outside his cabin to get a better look at something or other—had literally lost his head. And suffered something like enormous bite marks in his chest. Now

Tommy Tonompicket, who had been found in the top of a tall spruce, was stretched out on a hospital bed. Staring at nothing. Saying nothing. *Like a baked potato*, Parris had said. A potato was, of course . . . a vegetable.

Moon turned on his heel, suddenly coming face-to-face with his best friend.

"I'm sorry about Mr. Tonompicket. He looks bad." Parris didn't look much better. Like death warmed over. "But I expect he'll get better."

"Sure he will," Moon said brightly. "Let's go see the other guy."

"Let's," Parris agreed wearily. "Maybe we'll find out what'n hell's been going on."

They said polite good-byes to Mrs. Tonompicket, who was hunched over in the chair, staring intently at her husband's masklike face. She did not bother to acknowledge the lawmen's farewells. There was nothing they could do.

Nurse Shrewsberry approached the policemen with a mildly conspiratorial air. "Mr. Bright is still in 201, visiting with his brother-in-law. Mr. Pizinski also has some newly arrived visitors—in there." Shrewsberry made a slight nod to indicate the waiting room. "I thought you might want to check them out," she whispered. "They are certainly not family. And I'm sure they're not from around here." Out-of-towners were always suspect.

The lawmen had a quick look. Eddie Zoog and his gorgeous niece were seated in the waiting room. Zoog, who had not noticed the appearance of the policemen in the outer hall, was perched on the edge of a massive padded chair, staring blankly at a television screen. A black cigar butt was clamped on the left side of his mouth. The other side was hungrily chewing a fingernail to a pulp while he watched an old soap. Camilla, who was filing her nails to a point, noticed the lawmen. And smiled at them. Especially one of them. Moon returned the smile and tipped his Stetson.

She did not alert her uncle to their presence.

As Parris urgently tugged at his sleeve, Moon retreated from the encounter. They passed room 203, where the elderly Mrs. Snyder was housed. As they entered 201, it became apparent that Pizinski's plush quarters were an exact duplicate of Tonompicket's. When the intruders were noticed, there was a sudden hush in the intense monologue Kenny Bright was directing at the pale figure on the bed. The businessman got to his feet scowling, as if ready to protest this invasion of familial privacy. Then he recognized the tall Ute policeman. "Charlie." He ambled across the thick carpet, his hairy paw stuck out.

Moon shook Bright's hand. He nodded to indicate his companion. "This is my pardner, Scott Parris—Granite Creek chief of police."

Bright stuck his hand out to the broad-shouldered policeman. "Glad to meet you, sir. Any friend of Charlie's is a friend of Kenny Bright."

Parris shook the hand, then shifted his gaze to the man on the bed. "How's your brother-in-law doing?"

Bright lowered his voice to a mutter. "Well, there's glad news and there's sad. The glad news is that he's alive at all after whatever he's been through." He waited for the question.

"And what's the sad news?" Parris asked amiably.

Now Bright was whispering. "It's his so-called mind." He glanced at William Pizinski, who was straining to hear the conversation. "He's a scientist, so you know right off he's not normal. But now it looks like ol' Bill's gone completely wacko."

"Why d'you think that?" Moon asked.

Bright rubbed at his large, melancholy eyes. "I ask Bill questions, but he don't have nothing to say that makes any sense. Not that he ever did, but now it's a lot worse." He made a jerking nod toward his brother-in-law. "See for yourself."

The lawmen approached the sickbed. They went through the necessary formality of introductions. Pizinski was an ordinary-looking fellow. Except for his ears, which were large and protruded comically at right angles from his head. The patient was silent, responding with barely perceptible nods. His eyes glistened with a wild, frightened expression. Pizinski's gaze darted about the room, as if searching dark corners. A troublesome tic jerked rhythmically at his jaw.

Parris pulled a comfortable chair near the bed and sat down heavily. He smiled at the wary patient. "You were kinda beat up when old man Stamm found you wandering around in the national forest. I guess you must've had a rough time." He waited.

Pizinski's fingers fidgeted with a corner of the blanket.

"We've figured out some of what happened," Moon said. "You must've met up with one of my people—a Southern Ute—down by Navajo Lake. Tommy Tonompicket."

The voice was hoarse. "Yeah. I remember him." He didn't look up. "We had a coupla drinks. I . . . uh . . . understand he's in the room next door. Is he okay?"

"No," Parris said. "He hasn't said a word."

Pizinski sighed. "Me'n the Indian, we were just having some beers. Looking at the lake. Talking about . . . well . . . things, you know."

Parris managed a friendly smile. "What kind of things?"

Pizinski stared at the chandelier. "Fishing. The weather. Women. That kind of stuff."

"Sure," Moon said. "Nice way to spend an evening. Then what happened?"

"Then . . . then we saw this light coming up from the lake. I thought it was the moon rising. But the Indian, he said no it wasn't." He took a deep breath. "Said it was the wrong time for the moon to come up. Starting talking about witches flying in eggs and stuff like that."

Kenny Bright tapped his dead cigar on a crystal ashtray. "Well, hallelujah! That's more'n I've been able to get out of him. But ask him where he's been since that night." He pointed the cigar at this relative by marriage. "Go ahead, ask the silly sonuvabitch."

Parris gave the entrepreneur a flinty look. "Mr. Bright, I'd appreciate it if you waited outside while we talk to Dr. Pizinski."

"Oh, *Doctor* Pizinski, is it? Well, let me tell you something—" Bright's speech was halted by a warning look from Charlie Moon. The entrepreneur shrugged as if it didn't matter. "Silly bastard. I told my sister not to marry an egghead—but she was *in love*. What a crock." With this parting shot, he stalked to the door, slamming it behind him.

The patient had fallen silent.

They waited.

Scott Parris finally broke the silence. "So what happened—where've you been since the evening of April first?"

Pizinski looked up with a pleading expression. "That's what's got Kenny so pissed at me—*I don't remember!*"

Parris scowled at this response. "You must remember *something*."

The man in the bed shuddered. "Now and then, a few things come back to me—but it's like a bad dream. Unreal."

"Tell us anyway," Moon urged.

Pizinski closed his eyes. "I seem to hear that Indian guy—Mr. Tonompicket—screaming. And I remember being scared silly. Unable to move a muscle. I felt like I was kinda . . . slipping away. That's about all. Until that old guy found me in the woods and gave me his sandwich. And then the paramedics brought me here."

Parris glared at the unfortunate man. "That's it?"

"Sorry. I can't remember another thing. Maybe if I could get some decent sleep, it'd all start coming back to me."

Moon pressed on. "Let's go back to April first. Before you got to the lake. Where were you coming from?"

"Colorado Springs. I was on my way back to Albuquerque."

"You'd kinda wandered off course," Moon said gently. "Why not head straight down Interstate 25—through Raton . . . Las Vegas . . . Santa Fe?"

Pizinski avoided the lawman's steady gaze. "My wife's on a biking vacation in Europe, so I wasn't in any big hurry to get home. I took a little side trip."

"What had you been doing in Colorado Springs?" Parris asked.

Pizinski's face went blank. "Business."

"What kind of business?"

The bewhiskered man hesitated. His large ears seemed to blush. "I work for a . . . uh . . . contractor in Albuquerque."

"What kind of contractor?"

"We mostly do . . . ah . . . government business."

"For the Air Force?"

Pizinski frowned suspiciously. "How do you know about my work for the Air Force?"

"An agent from the Office of Special Investigations paid us a visit," Parris said. "She was worried about you. Wondering where you were."

The man paled. "OSI?" He pressed his palms over his eyes. "Oh, crap."

Parris pulled on this string. "Captain Taylor is very persistent. I imagine she'll want to have a word with you."

"But I haven't done anything wrong. And I don't know what happened to me."

"On this trip to Colorado Springs, what was the nature of your business?"

Pizinski set his jaw. "The work I do is classified."

The chief of police clasped his hands and shifted to a congenial mode. "I understand that there are aspects of your work you can't discuss. All I want to know is whether some research you're doing for the Air Force might have something to do with—well, with your unexplained disappearance."

The patient took a sip of tepid water from a plastic cup. "How could it?"

Parris looked thoughtfully at the ceiling. "Oh, I don't know. Unless maybe you were transporting something important. Something somebody had a hankering for. Maybe that somebody knocked you on the head and took what they wanted. Then dropped you and Mr. Tonompicket off in the national forest."

"That's absurd."

"This whole business is pretty absurd," Parris said. "And I'm wondering why this Air Force investigator is so interested in you."

Pizinski was suddenly pugnacious. "If you want to know about Air Force business—ask the Air Force."

Moon, sensing that this was a good time to break off the questioning, glanced at the door. "After you've had time to get some rest, we'll want to talk to you again, Dr. Pizinski. But right now, you have some other visitors waiting."

The patient's look was apprehensive. "Is my wife back from Europe?"

"Afraid not."

"Then who?"

The Ute policeman smiled. "I think I'll let them introduce themselves."

It must be OSI. "I don't want to talk to anybody."

Moon put his hat on. "Okay. We'll tell 'em." The lawmen turned to leave.

"Hey—these visitors—you got any idea why they want to talk to me?"

Moon nodded. "I think they want to make you rich."

"And famous," Parris added dryly.

Pizinski's face was pinched into a puzzled frown.

"We'll run 'em off," Moon said.

The man on the bed—who should have been satisfied—pulled nervously at an oversized ear. He was normally a cautious man who did not invite trouble into his life. But curiosity got the better of him. "Wait. I'll talk to them. But I want you guys here. If they bug me, *then* you can throw them out."

Scott Parris—who could not see himself playing the role of William Pizinski's personal bouncer—glanced uncertainly at the Ute policeman.

Moon leaned close to his friend and muttered, "I say we bring 'em in. See how he reacts."

Eddie Zoog—who had been staring blankly at an antique rerun of *Days of Our Lives*—was delighted to hear that Dr. Pizinski was ready to receive him.

"Great," he said, jumping to his feet and pulling on an expensive pinstriped jacket. "Now we'll get offa our butts and do some serious business."

The astonishingly pretty woman, who had been thumbing through a tattered copy of *Reader's Digest*, kept her seat.

Moon looked down at her with deep appreciation. "A visit from you might help Pizinski's recovery."

She rewarded him with a dazzling smile. "Interviewing prospective clients is Uncle Eddie's department."

Zoog darted a quick look at his niece, then pointed his bulbous nose toward the north wing and hurried away with Parris at his heels.

Charlie Moon remained behind, looming over the attractive woman like a dark pine peering down on a dazzling sunflower. "So. How've you been?"

"Well enough." *He's so awfully cute.*

He waited for her to inquire how *he'd* been. She didn't. "Well, if you have to know, I've been okay. Except for an old gunshot wound that acts up now and again."

"How sad." Her pretty eyes twinkled. "The injury from the bullet—is it in your head?"

"No." He avoided her gaze. "It's in . . . well, an unmentionable place."

"Then I trust you won't mention it." She leafed through the *Reader's Digest.*

"Not unless you twist my arm."

"I would never do that." Camilla was smiling at a story entitled "Will Resistant Bacteria Kill Millions?"

He was about to try another approach when he noticed Scott Parris holding off Eddie Zoog at Pizinski's door. Moon's friend was giving him the look that said, *You arranged this little circus, so come and join the fun.*

The Ute tipped his hat. "Well, see you later."

Camilla looked up from the magazine. *I hope so.*

The promoter—unlighted cigar clamped between his teeth—approached William Pizinski's bed with all the finesse of a runaway locomotive rolling downhill. He stuck out his stubby hand. "I'm Eddie Zoog."

The wan-looking patient yielded a pale hand to Zoog's meaty grasp. The enthusiastic little man did the shaking for both of them, jerking Pizinski's limp arm up and down like a broken pump handle. "I know you've been through a helluva experience, pal—so I won't stay long. This is just a get-acquainted visit."

Judging from his expression, the patient seemed relieved by this promise.

Zoog seemed oblivious to the fact that he was under the watchful eye of the police—and the duty nurse, who had appeared in the doorway. He pulled the cigar from his mouth and pointed it at Pizinski. "I'm general manager of EZ Agency, in L.A."

The patient smiled wanly. "Your initials?"

"Yeah. EZ—Eddie Zoog." He stuffed the cigar between thick lips. "Hey, your brains ain't so scrambled after all."

Pizinski closed his eyes. "What do you want?"

"Hey, I like that. A sharp blade cuts right to the bone." He spread his hands expansively before the patient. "EZ's main business is package deals. Books and movies. Our agency handles all kinds of material. Movie-star romances. Celebrity biogs. Insider exposés. The works. But mostly we specialize in"—he paused to search for the right words—"really *weird* stuff. Bizarre adventures. Big hairy bug-eyed monsters. Flying turnips from the planet Bazorg. Earth-mothers impregnated by philandering space cadets. Stuff like that."

Pizinski opened his mouth to protest. He managed just two words. "I don't—"

The locomotive, now hissing with a full head of steam, rolled mercilessly over him. "We've set up combo deals on all kinds of famous stuff. Like that giant sea serpent those Tallahassee schoolteachers spotted last year at Atlantic City, just off the Steel Pier. And you remember that sweet little all-American family in Michigan that was snatched by aliens? And the UFO scare down in the Yucatán? Well"—he jabbed a thumb at his chest—"EZ set up the books. The TV-movies of the week. We handled alla those, see?"

The patient raised a hand to ward off this assault, and got in three words this time. "I don't think—"

"You don't think you could write about your experience—am I right?" The Zoog waved his short arms. "Well, that don't matter, don't you see? Lissen, most of the people who have these weird experiences couldn't write a grocery list. Some of 'em can't spell their own names. But it don't matter none, pal. EZ Agency has a potful of down-and-out ghostwriters. You tell 'em your story. We provide 'em with a bowl of red beans and rice, a bottle of cheap wine—they sit up all night pecking at the keyboard and before you know it—shazam! You're a best-selling author."

"The thing is, I—" Four whole words before he was interrupted.

"Hah—I know what you're thinkin'. You're thinkin—what's in this for me? Am I right? Tell me, am I right?"

Pizinski, astonished at the unexpected silence, took a deep breath. "I'm sorry. I can't tell you anything."

"Damn." Eddie Zoog scowled, and chewed thoughtfully on the corpse of the cigar. "Somebody's already got to you. Who was it? The Morris bunch? No." He held his palms up and shook his head. "Don't tell me—it wouldn't be ethical." His face brightened. "But hey, have you signed a contract? If you haven't scribbled your John Henry on the dotted line, baby, it don't mean a thing. I mean, if you just got a verbal agreement with one of them fly-by-night agencies, it ain't worth a pint of donkey spit. Whatever they promised you, EZ will go one better. You know what I mean?"

With some effort, Pizinski raised himself on his elbows. And fixed his gaze on the Zoog. "Listen to me."

The promoter wiggled his fingers to pull the words his way. "Hey, baby—I got ears itchin' to hear what you got to say. Talk to me. Tell Uncle Eddie all about it."

"About what happened—I don't remember a thing."

Zoog was unmoved. "That's a good sign."

"It is?"

"Sure. Mosta the people who get snatched by Gosh Knows What—at first they don't remember what happened."

Pizinski seemed genuinely surprised to hear this. "Really?"

"You heard it from Eddie Zoog's mouth. Read my lips, fella—you not remembering what happened, it don't matter."

Pizinski stared blankly at this supercharged madman. "It don't . . . doesn't?"

The promoter shook his head to emphasize the point. "Not an atomic particle. Not a flea's eyeball. Not a mouse-nut. In fact, amnesia is a strong point in your favor. Gives your story traction, my lad."

"I don't understand. If I can't remember, then how can you . . ."

Zoog reached out suddenly toward the patient—who recoiled until his head was pressed hard against the pillow. The promoter gingerly touched the tip of a horny fingernail to Pizinski's forehead. "It's all in *here*."

The patient frowned cross-eyed at the finger. "What's in . . . here?"

"Your memories." The cigar stub bobbled as Zoog

spoke. "And we have ways of making you remember. And making you talk."

"You mean . . . ?"

"Trust me, Pizzy. You don't wanna know." Zoog's lip curled into an ugly snarl.

"What . . . exactly . . . do you do?"

The short, beefy man leaned very close, his dark eyes inches from Pizinski's pale gray orbs. "We pull out your toenails one at a time. Until you spill your guts."

Pizinski blanched and made a peculiar choking sound.

The duty nurse found her voice. "Really, now—I think I've heard about enough of this nonsense . . ."

The Zoog turned and grinned broadly. "Take it easy, Florence N. I would not extract a single toenail from this man's foot. In fact, I do not even have a podiatrist on my staff."

Shrewsberry stared at the Zoog. *He's an idiot.*

She's a touchy wench. But comely, for all that. "It was merely a joke, madam. A witticism. A quip."

The lawmen were trying hard not to grin. And failing.

She blushed and departed in a huff from this knuckle-dragging gathering of male oafdom.

Zoog patted Pizinski's pale hand. "Tell you what, pal—I got a standard contract right here in my coat pocket." He produced the document and unfolded it. "You ink your J-H in right here at the bottom of the page and we'll get started tonight, helping you remember what happened. If you've got a story the people of this great nation need to hear, I guarantee you fifty percent of the net. Think about it, baby—fifty percent."

Pizinski closed his eyes. "No."

Eddie Zoog cringed; he detested the n-word. "Okay, pal. You got me by the nuggets. Tell you what—we can talk about an advance. I'd say maybe—"

Pizinski amazed them all—even himself—by interrupting. "No."

The promoter repeated the hateful word. "No?"

"No. I mean yes . . . no."

This was confusing. Zoog leaned forward. "I don't get it."

The man on the bed shuddered. "Sometimes I seem to see little flashes of what happened out there. I don't know whether it's real or not—but it scares hell outta me." He glared defiantly at Zoog. "I don't want to remember."

The promoter assumed a patently false air of sympathy. He tapped the cigar butt on his knuckles. "I understand, fella. You need a coupla days to get your noodle rested." He licked his thick lips. "But when you start feeling better, Eddie Zoog will be here for you."

Pizinski stared at the squat figure. "Thanks. If I ever remember anything . . ."

If? In desperation, Eddie Zoog played his last card. "Hey, Willy P.—something really important happened to you and this Apache guy, Tompucket . . ."

"Ute," Moon said. "Tonompicket."

". . . and this Indian bird is not able to sing a note. So it's *your* duty to inform the honest, tax-paying citizens of this great nation." Now Zoog drew himself up to his full height. And puffed out his chest in preparation for the mantra of his ilk: "The public has a right to know."

Charlie Moon winked at Scott Parris. "Mr. Zoog is right. This could be big news. Important to public safety. Dr. Pizinski, as soon as you can remember what happened, we'll arrange a press conference. I'm sure there'll be lots of interest from the media."

This brought a shriek of righteous anger from Eddie Zoog, who looked ready to pounce on the enormous Ute policeman. "Press conference my ass!" He bit the cigar butt in half; a portion plummeted to the plush carpet. He swallowed the remainder and succumbed to a wild coughing fit.

Parris slapped him hard on the back, ejecting the plug.

Zoog, recovering from his strangling coughs, was shaking a finger at Moon. "Don't let me hear no talk about no . . . aghh . . . no press conference," he gasped. "I was here first."

"But the people have a right to know," Moon reminded him.

The promoter, still weak from ingesting bits of tobacco into his lungs, leaned on the bed. He pleaded with the patient. "Don't lissen to this Indian cop, Pizzy—he don't know the score. When you've got something the rubes are willing to pay for, you'd be a prize dimwit to *give it away!*"

The lawmen followed the furious promoter to the Annex waiting room.

Camilla looked up from the *Reader's Digest*. "How did it go?"

Eddie Zoog waved his short arms at the lovely young woman. "It was a bad scene, kid. The worst. I should be depressed, but I'm not. It's bad enough that the Apache fella—Tombucket—ain't able to say a word about what happened. Now the Pizinski guy says he can't remember what happened to him. And he don't want to—'cause it was all too horrible. So he must've had some fantastic experience." He rubbed his palms together. "This is a book and movie for sure. Maybe even T-shirts and toys. We're talking seven figures for certain, kid—maybe eight. I tried to get Pizinski to sign an options contract and then this oversized Navajo cop tried to queer my deal."

Camilla raised a questioning eyebrow at the Ute.

Moon assumed an innocent expression.

Zoog turned to glower up at the offender. "Press conference. That was a dirty rotten thing to say. Right when I had him ready to sign."

"I apologize." Moon looked at the ceiling. "I didn't really mean it."

The promoter frowned suspiciously. "You didn't?"

"No. It was merely a joke. A witticism. A quip."

Zoog jammed a fresh cigar into his mouth. *Smart-ass copper.* "By the way, my offer is still open."

Moon looked down at the indefatigable deal-maker. "What offer?"

"Didn't I tell you? I got contracts ready for the botha you cops. Not as much dough as for Pizinski and the Apache—if Timwicket's ever able to talk. But there's some serious money for exclusive rights to what you guys already know about this weird business. And what you can find out."

The Ute found himself interested. "How much money?"

"We couldn't do that," Parris said quickly.

"And why not?" Zoog asked.

"A couple of reasons," Parris snapped.

The promoter was losing his patience. "So don't keep me guessing, Name 'em."

"For one," Parris said, "ethics."

Zoog shrugged. "I don't get it."

Camilla smiled sadly at her uncle. "He really doesn't."

Scott Parris was the soul of patience. "Mr. Zoog, what we may learn in the course of performing our official duties is police business. If and when we find out what happened to these fellows, we'll make a public statement. What we know is not for sale."

Zoog waved away this inconsequential objection. "So

you're worried about getting into trouble. Okay, we'll keep your names out of it. No written contract—a handshake deal works for me. And no checks; I'll pay cash on the palm. So what's the other reason?"

The chief of police chose his words carefully. "It has to do with . . . physiology."

The promoter shrugged. "Hey, I'm just an ordinary guy. I don't know much about Pluto and his Greek pals and their deep thoughts—so speak regular American."

Parris sighed. "I'm referring to the gag reflex."

The Ute policeman left with his friend. "So what've you got against making a little cash on the side?"

Scott Parris pretended not to hear.

The promoter watched the lawmen depart, then turned on Camilla. She was wearing that amused smile that annoyed him. *Gag reflex?* "This ain't no gag—what'n hell was he talking about?"

She got up and smoothed the wrinkles from her skirt. "Let's go back to the hotel, Uncle Eddie. It's been a long day."

He chewed on the unlighted cigar. "I know it looks grim, kid, but don't you worry your pretty little noggin. There's a big story here. It's a whiz-bang movie-book deal for sure. And EZ Agency is going to represent it."

The blond woman pulled on her coat. "Sure. You've got two great witnesses. A comatose Indian and a scientist who has amnesia."

"The Indian's not really in a coma, babe—he's just sorta feeling punky. He'll get well, and he'll talk to me. And Pizinski's memory'll come back sooner or later. Either way, EZ Agency will get the story." He tapped his temple. "I'll think of something."

"I've no doubt you will." *Something stupid.*

"Lissen, kid—Eddie Zoog holds on to a deal like a starving bulldog with a bloody pork chop." He shook his jowls and growled to demonstrate. "And he does not know the meaning of the word *defeat*!"

Camilla sighed. "Does he know the meaning of the word . . . *demented*?"

"Never heard of it." He clasped his hands at the small of his back, and performed a heel-thumping jig on the hardwood floor. For a heavyset man, Zoog was astonishingly light on his feet.

As the lawmen approached the head of the circular staircase, they were confronted by a most formidable apparition. The white-robed figure was tall and thin as a beanpole. Silvery-white hair hung well past the narrow shoulders. Dark, beady eyes peered at them from a leathery face. A heavy wooden staff was raised in the right hand. Its end bulged with a massive knob. "Halt," an aged voice croaked. "Stand fast, or I'll smite you!"

Charlie Moon stopped in mid-stride and looked to his friend for guidance. "Who's this . . . Moses' older sister?"

Parris, in spite of his weariness, laughed. "Mrs. Snyder, meet my friend Charlie Moon."

The old crone lowered the staff. But her dark eyes were filled with suspicion. "You're an Indian."

Moon made a slight bow. "At your service, ma'am."

She looked hard at his dark face. "You're a Ute. Like that new patient who don't talk."

"I appreciate your not taking me for a 'Pache."

She shook her head vigorously, tossing the white hair. "I don't like Utes."

Parris patted the old crone on the shoulder. "It's all right. Charlie's quite civilized. More like a Navajo."

"Damned Ute savages," the old woman hissed. "My poor grandmother was slaughtered by a band of renegades from the White River Agency. I'll never forget it. Summer of 1879."

The Ute policeman removed his hat. "I'm sorry about that, ma'am. But I wasn't old enough at the time to participate." He paused, his dark eyes twinkling. "Were you?"

"Please don't get her started," Parris muttered.

But she was already started. Matilda sidled up to the tall Ute, waving the wicked-looking knobby cane like the club it was. "You got any smokes on you?"

"No," he said, backing away. "But you can have my lunch money. Even my watch."

The hint of a smile passed over the wrinkled face. "I need a cigarette," she snapped.

"I don't believe the hospital allows smoking on the premises," Moon pointed out.

"Don't talk to me about rules, Tonto. If you're holding out on me, I'll give you a good whack across your big watermelon head. We understand each other?"

"Yes, ma'am. But I don't smoke. Honest."

Snorting at this unlikely claim, she turned on the white policeman. "And another thing."

Parris looked at the ornate ceiling. "What's that, Mattie?"

She pointed the heavy stick to indicate the dimly lighted north wing of the Annex. "It's about them two fellas."

"Tonompicket and Pizinski."

"Whatever—I haven't been able to remember names too good since the last election." She squinted at Moon. "You know, that Truman fella is a damn suspicious character. He didn't get my vote. Never trust anybody in dry goods, that's my motto."

"I like Ike," Moon assured her.

"She's kidding," Parris said wearily. "Mattie pretends to be crazy so she can get away with being rude."

"You'll have to meet my aunt Daisy," the Ute said. "She could give you some pointers."

"I kind of like you," the old woman said. "Even if you are one of them damned murderous Utes. I could be wrong, but you don't look like you'd slaughter women and children."

"All compliments are gratefully received," Moon said graciously.

She chuckled, and tapped his elbow playfully with the knobbed cane.

Moon winced at the sharp pain.

Parris was beginning to feel better. "So, Mattie—what is this about Tonompicket? And Pizinski?"

"Who?"

"The new patients in 201 and 202. Just on the other side of your room. You were going to tell us something about them."

"Oh, them." She was stealing little glances at Moon. "Yeah. I been reading the newspapers and watching the TV, so I know all about 'em. Strange pair."

"Are they troubling you?"

"Nobody troubles Matilda Snyder," she snapped. "I'm the one who causes trouble around here. It helps keep me young and perky," she added by way of explanation. "When a soul can't get into some mischief no more, they might as well just go curl up in their grave and pull the sod over 'em."

Moon decided that the old troublemaker had a point.

Parris glanced at his wristwatch. "Look, Mattie, it's always nice to pass the time with you. But I've got some work to do . . ."

She tapped his broad chest with the knob on her walking stick. "You better put a guard on 'em."

"On who?"

"Who've we been jawin' about? Them fellas in 201 and 202."

"Why should I post a guard?"

She leaned so close he could smell a faint hint of bourbon on her breath. "Because whatever it was that kidnapped 'em in the first place—late some night, it'll come back. And grab 'em again." She touched a long, bony finger to the transparent skin on her nose. "I know what I'm talkin' about—that's how these things work."

Parris patted her thin shoulder. "You don't need to be frightened, Mattie. Nothing's going to bother those men—or you."

"I'm not scared of anything that walks or crawls or slithers through the mud." She waved the walking stick. "Anybody messes around with Matilda Snyder, he'll get a good whack that'll splatter his brains and eyeballs all over the wallpaper."

Charlie Moon moved out of range.

She looked warily down the darkened hallway. "It's those men in 201 and 202 that should be worried. When it shows up some dark night, it'll be comin' for *them.*"

SNYDER MEMORIAL HOSPITAL . . .
THE ANNEX

THE NURSE LOOKED the old woman up and down. *She must be over ninety.*

Daisy Perika returned the brazen stare without flinching.

The *matukach* cleared her throat. "Are you a close relative . . . his grandmother, perhaps?"

Tommy Tonompicket's grandmother? It was insulting. Daisy Perika shook her head.

"I'm sorry, then. Only immediate relatives may visit the patients. It's a hospital rule."

The Ute elder drew herself up to her full height, which was a head shorter than her pale adversary's. "I got a right to see him. He's my patient."

The nurse smiled slyly, like a teacher who has caught a naughty student in a preposterous lie. "You are . . . a physician?"

"Sure. Dr. Perika. I cure cramps, nosebleeds,

snakebites—you name it." Daisy leaned forward, pointing a crooked finger at a small "beauty mark" artfully applied to the nurse's cheek. "Give me five minutes and ten dollars, I'll conjure that ugly wart right off your face."

GRANITE CREEK POLICE DEPARTMENT

Charlie Moon paced around Scott Parris' spacious second-floor office. He paused by the coffeemaker long enough to pour himself a steaming cup.

The chief of police regarded his Ute friend with some amusement. "You seem a little edgy this morning."

Moon sipped at the dark brew. He stared at the morning traffic in the broad street below. "I need to get back to the Rez."

"What's the matter—the folks at SUPD can't get along without their acting chief?"

"They do fine without me around to pester 'em."

"What, then?"

"It's my aunt Daisy. And the little girl . . ."

"Sarah Frank?"

"Yeah. There's no telephone out at Aunt Daisy's place. I need to go check on 'em—make sure they're all right."

"Uh-huh." Parris grinned. "And make sure your aunt isn't up to some mischief."

Moon drained the cup. "That too." All night long, he'd had a worrisome feeling.

"Charlie, you worry too much."

"But before I head south," Moon muttered, "I'd like to know what's happening with Dr. Pizinski. And Tommy Tonompicket." He refilled his cup, adding several sugar cubes. "Maybe I'll stop by the hospital and check on 'em."

"No need for that. I'll give the Annex a call."

"It's hard to learn anything over the phone."

Parris assumed a smug expression. "Obviously, Charlie, you do not realize what a great gulf there is between being a mere *acting* chief of police and the real McCoy."

"Hmmmpf," Moon said.

"Humph if you will. But I am well known in my jurisdiction. When the chief of police calls and requires information, he damn well gets it."

"And it's not like you'd ever brag or anything."

Scott Parris picked up the telephone, dialed the memorized number, and waited patiently until the switchboard operator answered. "Hi, Zelda. Yeah, this is me. No, we still don't know what happened to those guys." He paused impatiently. "Zelda, I'd like to chat with you, but it's a busy morning. Please connect me to the Annex. Okay, sweetheart." As he waited for the Annex nurse's station to respond, Parris smirked at Moon. "See what I mean? Around here, citizens know who the chief of police is. And fall all over themselves to help him."

"You are practically a celebrity."

He heard a feminine voice he didn't recognize. "Good morning. This is Scott Parris, GCPD. I need some information on a couple of your patients." He listened to a monotone statement about how patient information was not released over the telephone, except to members of the immediate family. Was he a member of the immediate family?

"No," he said evenly, "I am not. But this is official business, and I'm—"

He was interrupted by a pointed query.

Parris' face reddened. "No, ma'am, GCPD does not stand for Granite Creek Parks Department; we're the police. Those nice people in blue uniforms, here to protect and serve. And," he added with a hint of menace, "we carry guns."

She asked whether they were also allowed to carry bullets.

"Enough to do the job," he muttered, mystifying Moon.

There was a brief pause as he listened to a hopeful request.

"No, ma'am, I do not fix traffic tickets. If you weren't actually speeding, then you should—"

He was interrupted by a curt request for clarification. Would he repeat his identity?

He enunciated the words with exaggerated care: "Chief—of—Police—Scott—Parris. Granite—Creek—Police—Department." Dark blue veins on his temple were beginning to throb. "You want my badge number?"

Astonishingly, she did.

Dumbfounded, Parris recited the number.

Moon managed to keep a straight face. The day was looking up.

Parris shot his Ute friend a dark look and snapped into the telephone, "How about my mother's maiden name?"

No, she thought not.

Parris had escalated to white-knuckle mode. "Do you want me to come down there and show you my driver's license?"

The nurse supposed that this would not be necessary. And she reminded him—somewhat frostily—that she also had a job to do. And firm rules to follow.

Defeated, he nodded—as if her vision could transit the telephone circuits. "Yes, ma'am. I do understand. Now about your patients—Tonompicket and Pizinski— please tell me: Are they alive?"

She responded in the positive to this query.

"How's Mr. Pizinski doing?"

His condition was, she said, stable.

"Any improvement in his memory?"

Not that she was aware of.

Now he was getting somewhere. "Good," he said wearily. "Is Mr. Tonompicket talking yet?"

He was not. But she volunteered some additional information about Mr. Tonompicket's visitors, which she found quite troubling. Parris—who was quite pleased at this development—nodded again. "Yeah. I understand. But you shouldn't worry. I'm sure it'll turn out all right. Thank you. Sure, Miss—uh—Peters? You've been a world of help. Good-bye." He placed the telephone receiver in the cradle ever so gently, and smiled upon his Ute comrade.

Moon didn't like the silly grin on his friend's face. "So . . . what's up?"

Parris leaned back in the comfortable chair and placed the heels of his new boots on the immaculate desk. "Oh, nothing much. Pizinski is about the same."

"Memory still on the fritz?"

Parris shrugged, as if it did not matter. "Sounds like it."

"Tommy Tonompicket . . . he doin' any better?"

"Nope." Parris appeared to be quite satisfied with life. "But I think we can count on a significant change in his condition fairly soon now." He took a sip of luke-warm coffee. "Yeah, with the new therapy, he'll either get a lot better real quick or . . ." He assumed a glum expression, as if the other possibility were too melancholy to voice.

Moon sat his cup down. "What new therapy?"

Parris' brow wrinkled into a thoughtful frown. "Well, how would I describe it? Aggressive? Risky?" He nodded to himself. "Yeah. It'll probably be sorta like . . . shock therapy. From what I'm told, sometimes it works pretty well. Other times"—he made a thumbs-down gesture—"the patient never quite recovers from it."

The *matukach* was having way too much fun. "Spill it."

Parris' tone was apologetic. "Oh—didn't I say? The nurse at the Annex, she told me that Mrs. Tonompicket showed up this morning—with an old Indian medicine woman who insists on treating Mr. Tonompicket. Claims she has the power to bring his soul back to his body." He shook his head in wonder. "Now isn't that something?"

Moon closed his eyes and prayed. *Please, God. Don't let this be who I know it is.*

The white man continued. "If the hospital doesn't let this . . . uh . . . medicine woman have access to her patient, there's a pretty broad hint that there'll be some serious hell to pay. Nasty publicity about discrimination against Native American religion and healing arts. Curses on the hospital administration. Cows will go dry. Crops fail. The usual sort of thing."

The Ute stared blankly into space. "Aunt Daisy."

Scott Parris nodded thoughtfully. "That'd be my guess too."

Moon was pulling on his jacket, jamming his black, broad-brimmed hat down to his ears, heading for the door.

Parris bounced up joyfully from his chair. "Hey, Charlie—wait for me." The day was looking up.

The Annex duty nurse led the lawmen down the hall, then paused near the entrance to room 202. "I couldn't stop her—she's in there now. With Mr. Tonompicket and his wife."

Moon muttered hopefully to himself: "Maybe it's not Aunt Daisy." *Maybe Bertha Tonompicket brought that old Navajo woman from Many Farms. The hand-trembler.*

Parris grinned happily at the nurse. "Please describe the—ah—suspect."

The young woman—who had large, protruding eyes—frowned sourly as she called forth the unpleasant recollection. "Short. Awful posture; sort of hunched over. Looks like she could be a hundred years old. And," she added firmly, "she's a really hateful old woman. When I told her she couldn't see Mr. Tonompicket, she said she'd put a curse on me—all of my children would be born with big, bulging eyes." She glanced at her pale fingers. "And webbed hands and feet."

The policemen seemed not to get the point.

"Like frogs," she explained.

"My goodness," Parris muttered, "now who do we know who'd say such things?"

Charlie Moon dreaded the unavoidable confrontation. He hesitated, took a deep breath. Then manfully turned the doorknob—and entered Tommy Tonompicket's hospital room. The Ute policeman was followed closely by Scott Parris—who was in turn trailed by the pop-eyed Annex nurse.

Daisy Perika was indeed present at Tommy's bedside, leaning to counterbalance the considerable weight of her oversized purse. Bertha Tonompicket was at the Ute shaman's side, evidently ready to catch her elderly companion should Daisy lean too far and begin to topple.

Moon approached his aunt carefully, like a wary soldier tiptoeing across a minefield to confront the enemy. He removed his hat. "Hello."

A heavy silence hung in the stale air of the sickroom.

"Didn't expect to find you here," Moon said.

The Ute elder didn't bother to look up at her nephew. Nor did she respond to his somewhat critical greeting. Daisy did speak to the *matukach* lawman, who was far more understanding of her arcane craft than her nephew. "Hello, Scott."

The chief of police happily tipped his hat. "Good day, Mrs. Perika."

The Ute policeman leaned close to his aunt. "That remark about the nurse's babies turning out looking like frogs—that wasn't nice. You should apologize."

"It was just a joke," Daisy snorted. "But if you think the frog-people would be insulted, I'll tell 'em I'm sorry."

Parris suppressed a snicker.

The nurse—who had paused near the door—looked down her long nose at the old woman. And directed her words to any who might receive them. "Mr. Tonompicket has been in a state of shock since he was admitted. He's getting the best care available. Within a few days, he may come around. We must all be patient." The steely tone of her voice conveyed the unspoken message: *I don't hold with any of this Native American hocus-pocus.*

Daisy Perika pointedly ignored the *matukach* nurse. After pushing aside a plastic pitcher of ice water and a stack of old magazines, the tribal elder began to assemble her queer paraphernalia on a narrow table. There were several odds and ends. An assortment of polished river stones. A handful of bleached raven bones. Several small cotton sacks with red drawstrings. And a striped drinking straw from a hamburger restaurant.

Despite her annoyance at such reprehensible practices, the nurse was curious. She leaned forward to see what foul things the old woman had produced. And felt it necessary to hurl an insult at the so-called medicine woman: "What, no eye of newt—no deer's gallbladder?"

"I fresh out of newt parts," the shaman said amiably. "And deers don't have gallbladders." Daisy—who detested having skeptical folk rubbernecking as she plied her trade—spoke to her nephew. "For the healing ceremony to work, we've got to have some privacy."

For other reasons, Charlie Moon wished himself rid of the nurse. It would be best if there were few witnesses to this embarrassment. He cleared his throat. "Uh . . . thing is, my aunt just wants to make sure that—"

"I know what she wants," the nurse snapped. "But Mr. Tonompicket is a patient in this hospital and I have a responsibility for his welfare. I've absolutely no intention of leaving." She folded thin arms across a flat chest.

Moon looked to the heavens for help. The plastered ceiling obscured his view.

The old shaman turned, fixing the nurse with a soul-piercing stare. "Stay if you want, young woman." She shook her head and sighed. "But I can't guarantee your protection."

The nurse jutted out her chin. "Protection? From what?" *Fussy old barbarian.*

Daisy arranged the chalky raven bones in a roughly circular pattern. "Tommy's soul left him because . . . because something *bad* came into his body."

"Something . . . bad?" The nurse tried to sneer, but her upper lip was oddly numb. "Like a . . . an evil spirit, I suppose." *These Indians are so superstitious.*

"Sure." These *matukach* were so superstitious. "See, that's what's keeping him from waking up. But I'm gonna bring it right outta him. And when I do, it'll want to get into somebody else. Now I can keep the bad spirit from slipping inside myself, and Tommy's wife—even my big jug-headed nephew. But I can't do anything for you. You . . ." There was simply no nice way to say it. "You're not one of the People."

Scott Parris—who was also not one of the People—wondered just where he stood. And decided to stand closer to the exit.

The nurse took a deep breath. "I don't believe in such things."

The shaman shook her head sadly. "That's the very reason I can't protect you. Just last summer—it was late in August, down at Dulce—there was a nosy white woman who watched me take a bad spirit out of an Apache woman. I warned her to go outside the old woman's house while I brought it out. Told her to wait under an elm tree, but she wouldn't listen. So when the spirit did come outta the sick person—it went right into that white woman's left ear."

I'll humor her. "What happened?"

"That bad spirit, he made her go loco as a hydrophobic fox." Daisy grinned maliciously. "Poor white woman, she threw herself into the horse pond."

The nurse's skin switched from blush to blanch. "Was she drowned?"

"No. Some Apache fellas pulled her outta the water."

"Then she's all right."

"Depends on what you mean by 'all right.' " Daisy loosened the drawstring on a yellowed cotton sack. "She's still in that lunatic asylum down at Albuquerque. Making little baskets outta straw."

The nurse consulted her wristwatch. "I have rounds to make. But I'll be back directly." The door clicked behind her and she was gone.

Moon frowned at his aunt. "You shouldn't make up stories like that."

"Who says I made it up? That white woman who got

the bad spirit is still in the crazy house. They say she laughs all the time, day and night. And spoons oatmeal into her ears." A little embellishment always helped a tale along.

"What was her name?"

Just like a policeman. A sly smirk spread over Daisy's wrinkled face. "I don't exactly remember."

Moon tired of the game. "So what're you gonna do to Tommy?"

"It's what I'm gonna do *for* him." She pulled a small clay pipe from her medicine bag.

Moon groaned. "Not the smoke treatment."

"Sure." She laid the striped drinking straw on the table by the pipe. "The *Ajilee Natoh*—the Navajos call it 'the powerful smoke'—it always works."

"Didn't work on Sarah Frank."

Daisy, who had been tamping a pinch of the expensive Navajo herbs into the sooty pipe bowl, paused to squint suspiciously at her nephew. About three years ago, she'd used the *Ajilee Natoh* on Sarah when the child had been struck mute by a dreadful experience. But "the powerful smoke" had not worked. Amazingly, the child had been restored to health by ice cream Louise-Marie LaForte had brought from Ignacio. But how did Charlie come to know about it? "Who told you about that?"

It was Moon's turn to smirk. "I don't exactly remember."

"Hmmpf." It had to be Louise-Marie. *That meddling old French-Canadian woman can't open her mouth without telling somebody's secret.*

"He won't mind the smoke," Bertha Tonompicket said. "Tommy smokes at least a pack a day." She lifted her arms in despair. "I've told him it'll kill him, but you know how men are. If he gets well, I think I'll tell him

he can either have his cigarettes or share his wife's bed."
Her round face took on a flint-hard look. "One or the
other. But not both."

Daisy touched a kitchen match to the pipe's bowl,
then took a long draw on the short stem. Her lungs
filled with the smoke, she placed one end of the drinking
straw between her lips, the other into Tommy Tonompicket's left nostril. She used her thumb to press the
right nostril shut.

"He won't be able to breathe," Moon pointed out.

"Shut up," she hissed. "Don't disturb the doctor
when she's working."

Sure enough, Tommy opened his mouth and gasped
for breath.

Daisy clamped her hand over his mouth and blew
hard through the straw in his nostril. The effect of "the
powerful smoke" was powerfully dramatic. The unfortunate patient rose off the mattress, flailing arms wildly
about, groaning. Indeed, he uttered his first word in
days: *Turusi . . . turusi!*

Daisy withdrew the straw from his nostril and shot a
triumphant look at her skeptical nephew. "See, I told
you . . . it never fails."

"He's begging you to stop," Moon pointed out.

Tommy had collapsed on the bed, his complexion a
dirty gray.

Mrs. Tonompicket was quite composed.

Moon leaned over the corpselike figure. "You've
damn near killed him."

The stubborn old woman would not admit defeat.
"I've *cured* him."

"Then," Moon asked, "why don't he jump up and
dance around the bed?"

The shaman glared at her uncooperative patient. "Because he don't *want* to, that's why."

Mrs. Tonompicket nodded. "Tommy was always lazy. Never did want to get out of bed in the morning."

"I know just what he needs." Daisy rolled up a tattered copy of *Field & Stream.*

Moon, optimist that he was, assumed his aunt was going to direct the smoke through this stiff cylinder—right into Tommy's mouth.

Just as the nurse peeked through the doorway, Daisy smacked her patient sharply across the forehead with the magazine. Mrs. Tonompicket nodded to indicate her approval of this tactic.

Tommy's eyes rolled upward, showing thickly veined whites.

Daisy shouted at him. "Tommy, your soul is back. Now get up before I really give you a swat!"

The nurse—outraged to witness such barbarous behavior—gasped.

Moon smiled stiffly at the hospital employee. "It's all right—just part of the ritual." He forcibly removed the magazine from his aunt's grip. "But you're finished now—aren't you, Aunt Daisy." This was clearly not a question.

The mystical physician, determined to have her say on the matter, leaned over Tommy and spat the words in his face. "Wake up, you dumb yahoo—you're *cured*!"

The nurse marched to the patient's bedside, speaking through clenched teeth. "I've seen quite enough. Take her away. *Now.*"

"Yes ma'am." Moon tipped his black Stetson. "That's just what I'm gonna do."

They were in the SUPD Blazer when Charlie Moon finally trusted himself to speak. "That was embarrassing."

The Ute elder was lost in thought about proper diagnosis and therapy. And muttering to herself. "Maybe the *Ajilee Natoh* was way too powerful to hit Tommy with all at once. I should've worked my way up to the strong stuff. Could've started with the *Hozhooji Natoh*, the Beauty Way smoke."

Moon, fairly grinding his teeth, turned the ignition key to crank the engine. "I can't take you *anywhere.*"

"You *don't* take me anywhere," she shot back. "And you didn't bring me here. Bertha Tonompicket brought me in her pickup—so I could cure her husband."

He glared at the sand-blasted windshield. "That's beside the point."

Though oblivious to her nephew's petty complaints, the shaman was aware that her treatment of Tommy Tonompicket could not be called an unqualified success. She muttered to herself: "I could've tried *Atsa Azee*, the Eagle Smoke. Or maybe the smoke that comes from the mountains, *Dzil Natoh*. Them Navajos swear by it. Yes"—she nodded to agree with herself—"that's what I should've done."

William Pizinski was, for the first time in days, feeling quite comfortable. The stabbing pain in his side had subsided after an injection in his butt. His head no longer throbbed with each heartbeat. Pizinski thought that his wife would be located soon. Margie would grab the next flight to the States and rush directly to the hospital. And, just on general principles, give him hell. But for now, he would enjoy the blessed quiet. He closed his eyes. The velvety soft voice materialized at the foot of his bed. "Dr. Pizinski?"

He cracked his eyelids to see who had invaded his territory. A nurse, most likely. *Maybe she's got some sleeping pills for me.* But this was definitely not a nurse.

"Just for the record, you are Dr. William Pizinski?"

He managed a nod against the firm pillow. And was not surprised when the straight-backed young woman presented her credentials.

"I am Captain Taylor. U.S. Air Force Office of Special Investigations."

Pizinski felt a wormy coldness start at his feet, crawl up his legs to make an icy nest in his groin. He managed a weak grin. "I'm honored. But why's OSI interested in my welfare?"

Captain Taylor sat down on the edge of his bed, crossing her slender legs. "You are entirely too modest." She removed a leather-bound notebook from her brief-case. "According to our records, you hold a top-secret clearance. And you're chief scientist at Rocky Mountain Advanced Flight Systems. Furthermore, you are chief investigator on a contract to the United States Air Force—the very subject of which is classified information."

He shrugged. "Still, I don't see why—"

"On the way back from Colorado Springs, you disappeared for several days." Her face was without expression. A blank page. "Please tell me precisely where you were. And exactly what transpired during . . . your absence."

"I'd like to do that. Thing is, I can't remember anything about it. Doctor says I'm in some kind of shock."

She smiled, baring the chiseled edges of a perfect set of teeth. "You're claiming amnesia?"

Claiming? "Well—I can't remember anything. But," he added in a hopeful tone, "it's probably only temporary."

Captain Taylor entered the date and time of day on a fresh page. Under this heading, she took her time recording the identity of the subject to be interviewed. "Dr. Pizinski, do you wish to have counsel present during questioning?"

"You mean like . . . a lawyer?"

She nodded. *That ought to make him sweat.*

Beads of perspiration were forming on his forehead. "Why should I?" The chill worm squirmed in his gut. "I haven't done anything . . . wrong."

The OSI special agent continued in a roundish hand: *Dr. William Pizinski states that he does not wish to have counsel present.* She didn't look up from the notepad. "Upon your return from Colorado Springs—on the first day of April—did you have in your possession any classified documents?"

"Of course not! Why would I . . ."

"I understand you have suffered injuries." She jabbed the ballpoint at his bandaged side, almost touching it.

The patient flinched. "Ouch—don't do that!" His skin was white as the linen sheet.

"It's painful? I'm so sorry." She tilted her head quizzically. "On April first, upon your return from Colorado Springs, what sort of transportation were you using?"

"What?"

"It is a simple question." The OSI agent tapped the pen against his knee. "The type of conveyance you were using. A vehicle restricted to rails? Greyhound bus? Motorcycle?" She paused. "Flying machine?"

He thought of asking whether she rode a broom. And thought better of it. "I was driving a pickup truck."

She made another entry in the notebook. "Was this a government vehicle?"

You know damn well it wasn't. "No. It was mine."

"Were you transporting any U.S. government property in this private vehicle?"

He raised up on his elbows, almost to a sitting position, and tried hard to look insulted. "What sort of a question is that?"

"It is," the OSI special agent said slowly, "the sort of question that requires an answer."

The young woman unbuttoned her white cotton blouse, stretched her legs out on the padded footstool to intercept the chilly gust from the air conditioner. After a few minutes of blissful silence, she picked up the telephone, dialed 1-202. Then the familiar number. At this late hour, there would be no one at the trouble desk—but a cryptic voice-mail message would suffice to let the colonel know she was on the job. She waited through the terse message, then began to speak:

"This is Captain Taylor. I'm in Granite Creek, Colorado. Silver Mountain Hotel." She recited the hotel's telephone number. "I've made initial contact with the subject, who is hospitalized with a few minor injuries. He is evasive, providing no useful information about the so-called abduction. Claims amnesia. Subject is involved in restricted-access projects, so we would be justified in requesting a polygraph. Please advise." She hung up without any formality and smiled to herself. It wasn't that she needed the colonel's advice. But the vain man would be pleased that she had asked. Ninety percent of this job was politics.

———.

Eddie Zoog, muttering under his breath, stomped around a floor lamp, flapping his short, muscular arms in exasperation.

Like an enraged moth, Camilla thought. She tried not to smile at her irascible uncle.

The ever-present cigar dangled between his thick lips. "I'll tell you what you are. You are"— he paused in his pacing long enough to spit the ugly word at her—"a defeatist!"

She suppressed a yawn. "I'm tired of living in a hotel room. And I've got a horse ranch to look after."

"So why'd you come along in the first place?"

"Because you asked me," she reminded him gently. "Besides, some of these so-called abductees you've represented in the past have been borderline lunatics. Worse still, your conduct in dealing with them has been—let us just say—unprofessional. Gives the agency a bad name."

He jerked the cigar from his mouth, pointed it at his niece. "Bull-hockey."

She threw up her hands. "There's nothing useful for me to do here. I'm going home."

A more conciliatory tone was called for. He approached her with hairy hands folded prayerfully. "Please don't go, kiddo. I need you."

"For what?"

"To help me get to the bottom of this thing with Pizinski and Tonypucket. It ain't right to leave me all alone in this cow-pie of a town." He sulked. "You and me, we're family."

Such a helpless baby. "Look, it's late and I'm sleepy . . ." The yawn slipped out.

The Zoog pulled a shiny new quarter from his pocket. "Tell you what, Buckwheat. I'll flip the two bits—you call it in the air. You win, we both head back to L.A. and forget the whole thing. I win, we stay another week. Just on the off chance there's a story here."

Her blue-green eyes narrowed suspiciously. "Let me see the coin."

He offered the quarter with an injured expression. "You don't trust your uncle Eddie?"

That didn't deserve a response. She inspected the silver-clad copper disk, it looked legit. She dropped it into his hand. "I call it correctly, we both go home?"

"You got it, babe. But if you're wrong, you stay around and help old Eddie sort out this mess." Zoog had already palmed his "special" quarter. Camilla was a bright kid, but predictable. She always called tails. He flipped the two-headed disk. It ascended into a parabolic curve, tumbling . . . tumbling . . .

She clenched her fists. "Tails!"

COLORADO
WEST OF LEADVILLE

THE ALL-DAY meeting had taken place in a rented cabin. The sturdy structure was perched on a mossy granite bluff, two miles from Turquoise Lake.

The squad leader was a short, muscular man, approaching his fifth decade with little sign of wear. He wore lightly tinted horn-rimmed spectacles and had a nervous habit of running a callused hand over his steel-gray burr-cut hair. The other eleven men in the spacious room—all at least a decade younger than the leader—had sat quietly and listened to Cassidy. It was his first name. In their profession, last names were not used.

Cassidy spoke in a soft West Texas drawl. "We've gone over the operational plan till I imagine you're sick of it. But it's pretty simple. We go in at night. Locate the target. Do the job. Then move out without being seen. Any questions?"

A black man raised his hand and grinned sheepishly. "What if we're spotted?"

Cassidy's jaw took a grim set. "If you encounter any-one—order them to stand aside. If necessary, state that what you are about is . . . government business."

This produced a few appreciative chuckles.

"And if they don't stand aside?" The black man, un-like many of his less experienced comrades, was deter-mined to know up front what the ground rules were. In that Balkan fiasco during the previous summer, his team had abducted a middle-aged man and performed a sum-mary execution. It had been a tragic error. The poor fel-low was not the Serbian paramilitary leader known to be responsible for torturing and murdering hundreds of Al-banian civilians—he was a Belgian official of the Inter-national Red Cross who bore a remarkable resemblance to the notorious Slav. Sadly, the innocent was in the very hotel room just vacated by the Serb war criminal. There had been very stern complaints from very high places.

Cassidy stared at his audience for a long moment. "If someone gets pushy, deal with them. But use the mini-mum force necessary. I need not remind you—this oper-ation must not attract attention."

———•

The thunder rumbled like churning boulders, rattling the shutters behind her. A gusting wind moaned around the bay window. It was fortunate that the young woman was not bothered by storms.

Nurse Mulligan sat behind the immaculate walnut desk, grimacing as she attempted to run a plastic comb through her matted red hair. Though she had just fin-ished eight frantic hours on ICU duty, she was pleased to spend the night shift in the Annex. Being selected to watch over the second-floor ward in the former Snyder mansion was a feather in one's cap. And it was relatively easy duty. Only three of the five patient rooms were occupied, so the long hall was wonderfully quiet. Far better than duty at the Intensive Care Unit desk, where bloody accident victims might be brought in at any hour of the night.

Nothing exciting ever happened in the Annex.

She slipped the comb into her purse and smoothed a small wrinkle in her blue skirt. Miss Mulligan always kept a fresh change of civvies in her locker, just in case Annex duty was offered. It was fun to pretend that she was not really a nurse. More like a hotelkeeper to Matilda Snyder, her rich, eccentric guest. At the moment there were two other rather notorious "guests" in the Annex. The Indian patient would be no trouble tonight; the silent Mr. Tonompicket never pressed the call-button pinned to his pillowcase. Dr. William Pizinski—the scientist from New Mexico—could be a bit cranky. Mostly wanting pain pills to ease the ache in his fractured ribs. And sleeping pills to see him through the long night. But the doctor had him on a strict regimen of narcotics. Miss Mulligan opened a plastic compact and powdered her freckled nose. What had actually happened to these unfortunate men? Last month, she'd watched a frightening TV movie about a young lumberman in Arizona who had vanished after he and his buddies saw a very strange object hovering over a clearing in a pine forest. The disoriented man had shown up several hours later, quite far from the scene of his abduction. And unable to recall much of what had happened during his "missing time." But what he had remembered had been horrifying. Could such things actually be true—monsters from other worlds who treated human beings like cattle?

Miss Mulligan dropped the compact into a purse and

glanced at her wristwatch. Almost one o'clock in the morning. Time for rounds. Then, if there were no complaints from her "guests," two hours of blessed peace.

She stopped first in room 203. The gaunt old woman was sitting in a plush armchair, staring out the French windows at infrequent reflections of lightning on the mountains. "And how are we tonight, Mrs. Snyder—ready for bed?"

"Hullo. It's the little redheaded woodpecker." The elder of the Snyder clan turned in the chair to shoot Miss Mulligan a vicious glare. "I don't much like shanty Irish."

"My, aren't we sweet tonight?"

It was highly annoying when people didn't know they'd been insulted. "I need a smoke."

"You know that hospital rules forbid smoking." Nurse Mulligan's good nature was irrepressible. "It's very late. We need our sleep."

"If you need some rest, then go crawl into a hole in some dead tree." The old woman cackled. "That's where woodpeckers nest."

The nurse patted the old crone's shoulder. "My, my—we're a little cranky, aren't we? Maybe we have a temperature. I could get a rectal thermometer."

Matilda curled her thin fingers into a fist. "You could get a knuckle sandwich, Woody."

Miss Mulligan laughed. "We *do* need our rest."

"I won't do any sleeping tonight," Matilda grumped.

"Don't you feel well, dear?"

"I feel it . . . coming back."

"Feel *what* coming back?"

"Trouble," she said, staring through the rain-splattered panes into the outer darkness.

"I've got to check on my other patients. But I'll be just outside at the desk if you need me. Just press the little button if—"

"You're beginning to annoy me," the old hag snapped. "Piss off."

Tonompicket's eyes were closed, his chest moving rhythmically with the breath of life. Nurse Mulligan put her small hand on his forehead; it was cool and dry. No need to disturb this poor fellow with a thermometer. She closed the door gently behind her.

William Pizinski was propped up on three pillows. Wide awake. "Hello," he said glumly.

"Hello yourself, laddie." The nurse stuck a cold thermometer under his tongue. "And how are you feeling?"

His tongue flapped over the glass cylinder. "Abouda glame I geg."

"That's nice." She waited for the red column to stabilize.

There was a bright flash of lightning, followed almost immediately by a deafening electric crack that left a pungent ozone odor in its wake. Hard pellets of rain began to hammer the windows.

She removed the instrument from his mouth and squinted at the graticule. "Ninety-eight-point-eight. Very good. How're your ribs?"

"Medium rare," he said, gently massaging his side with the tips of his fingers. "I could use something to help me sleep."

It was the expected request. She smiled tolerantly. "You had your last medications at eleven P.M. Can't give you any more until three A.M."

He grunted to show his displeasure.

She pulled one of the two pillows from under his neck, then pressed a button to lower the head of the bed. "Close your eyes. Think about something nice and peaceful, that'll help you slip off to dreamland."

Another bright flash of lightning, followed almost immediately by a sharp electric crack.

"Close one," he muttered.

Minutes after the nurse had departed, the telephone by Pizinski's bedside rang. Who would call this late? He pressed the receiver to his ear. "Yeah?"

It was Kenny Bright. Pizinski listened intently.

"Sure. I understand. She'll be here in the morning." There was a pause as he listened to his brother-in-law's voice. "Look, don't worry so much. Okay." He sighed. "Good night, Kenny." Pizinski plopped the instrument into its cradle.

Now she would have some time to herself. The nurse slipped stealthily into the waiting room. Miss Mulligan did not bother to switch on the lights, but she did use the remote control to energize the large television set. She pulled a comfortable chair quite near the doorway, where she would be able to hear the buzzer at the desk if one of her patients pressed a call button. From this vantage point she could also command a view of the long, curved staircase. And be at her desk in the flicker of a sheep's whisker in the unlikely event that a supervisor dropped by on this fine, stormy night.

She rested her aching feet on a cushioned stool, and began to scan the microwaves. She paused at the Arts & Entertainment channel. It was showing a rerun of the Horatio Hornblower series. *Fine-looking young man he was. And so good. Not at all like the beastly men in my life.*

For some time, Nurse Mulligan suffered from the conviction that someone was watching her. Because of her practical nature, she put this down to a guilty conscience about being away from her station.

*   *   *

William Pizinski—in spite of the odds—was drifting off into a half sleep. He might have completed the pleasant transition had he not sensed the presence in the semi-darkness. It was as if the indistinct figure had—by some dark magic—materialized in the shadows at the foot of his bed. *Must be that graveyard nurse. Maybe she's brought me some sleeping pills.* He squinted hopefully at the shadowy form. "You got something that'll help me get some serious sleep?"

It seemed to Pizinski that his visitor nodded.

2:59 A.M.

Nurse Mulligan switched off the television. She got up, stretching her small frame until the muscles relaxed, then padded down the darkened hallway. She paused to open the first door. *The old woman should be in dreamland by now.* Matilda was still sitting in the chair, her back to the hall door. She was either asleep or staring through the rain-soaked French windows as if she could see what was happening out there in the blackness. *Poor old thing.* If she was asleep, it would be very unwise to disturb her. *Let sleeping bitches lie.* But, propelled by some perverse nursely instinct, Mulligan tiptoed across the room. And whispered: "Mrs. Snyder—are you asleep?"

"Yes," the old woman growled, "sound asleep."

The nurse tittered a little laugh.

"It came," the old crone muttered in a hoarse rattle. "Just like I told you it would."

"Yes, of course. Now, shall I help you into bed?"

Matilda waved the knob-headed cane menacingly. "Get out of my bedroom, you redheaded floozy!"

"Well, really now, I must say—"

"Move your arse, you little Irish hen—or I'll knock your chicken-brains all over the furniture!"

* * *

The kindly nurse closed the old woman's door with a sense of relief, whispering nervously to herself. "It must have been the storm that upset her." She moved briskly to room 202 and opened the door. The Indian patient was breathing evenly. She closed the door ever so gently.

Nurse Mulligan made her way to the end of the hall. *Perhaps the poor man is finally getting some sleep.* Most insomniacs slept more at night than they believed. She allowed her eyes a moment to become accustomed to the near darkness of the room. *Odd. He's not in his bed.*

She tapped on the bathroom door. "Dr. Pizinski—are you all right?" There was no answer. Nor any light coming from beneath the door. She stepped inside, switching on the light. Pulled back the shower curtain. "Well, that's peculiar," she muttered, and backed out of the bathroom. She flicked the switch by the door to illuminate the room. Sometimes patients did the strangest things. Nurse Mulligan knelt to look under the bed. No sign of him. She checked the wardrobe. Then she noticed that the French window was swinging gently. *He must've gone out onto the balcony to watch the storm. Silly man. He'll get soaking wet and catch pneumonia. And it'll be all my fault.*

She removed a small flashlight from her pocket and marched resolutely onto the balcony, prepared to remind this naughty patient a thing or two about rules. The Annex might seem like a hotel, but it was still a part of Snyder Memorial Hospital. The rain had stopped; a full moon, now well past the zenith, was peeking through misty clouds. *He doesn't seem to be out here.* To make certain, she directed the beam of light to the north end of the structure, then to the south. The nurse walked the entire length of the balcony. No. There was no doubt about it. Mr. Pizinski was nowhere to be seen. *My word . . . isn't that just the strangest thing?*

She hurried down the hall, put in a call to the night-shift supervisor. The supervisor summoned Security. The supervisor then called the hospital administrator, who was at home, snug in his bed. Fast asleep. Dreaming a very pleasant dream.

The administrator, who was not pleased to be awakened at this ungodly hour, snapped unkindly at the nurse supervisor—who was responsible for whatever happened on her watch. This done, the administrator made a call to the Granite Creek Police Department.

The night-shift dispatcher took the call, hurriedly scribbled Pizinski's description on the duty log, and promised to alert the GCPD night patrol to watch for the patient who had walked away from the Snyder Memorial Hospital Annex. Once this was done, the dispatcher remembered that Chief Parris had a special interest in this particular patient, who had already disappeared mysteriously on a previous occasion. And was apparently suffering from amnesia. *If I wake the chief up, he'll be very testy. If I don't call him, he'll yell at me later.* This was definitely a lose-lose situation.

The dispatcher dialed Scott Parris' number. And gritted his teeth in anticipation.

There were nine rings before Parris answered. "Ahhh . . . hullo."

"Chief—that you?"

Parris recognized the dispatcher's voice, and groaned. "Who did you expect—Marshal Matt Dillon?"

"No, sir." The twenty-two-year-old wondered who in hell Marshal Matt Dillon was.

"What is it, Beardsly?"

"It's that William Pizinski guy, sir. We got a report he's walked away from the hospital. I got the night patrol looking for him." He waited for a response. "Thought you'd want to know, sir. Seeing as you've been personally involved in this giant-spider investigation—" Realizing his error, the dispatcher caught his breath.

"Beardsly?"

"Yes, Chief?"

"Read my lips."

"I'll try, sir." The dispatcher closed his eyes in an attempt to picture the chief's face. Including his lips, which in Beardsly's vision were snarling.

"There—are—no—giant—spiders."

"Yes, sir. Is there anything you want me to . . ." He was talking to a dial tone.

Scott Parris sat on the side of his bed, face resting in his hands. He absolutely hated to be yanked from his peaceful slumbers. Loathed it. Detested it. Felt like strangling the man who'd done it. In fact, Parris was certain that in the whole world, absolutely nobody abhorred getting rousted out of his warm bed in the middle of the night as much as he did. Except for one person.

Charlie Moon.

Parris' mouth relaxed into a satisfied smile. He reached for the telephone.

IT WAS, BY the conservative standards of the Snyder Memorial Hospital, a veritable flurry of activity. The private company that provided security was present in force. The uniformed guards were primarily managing to get in the way of the GCPD, which had six officers detailed to searching the spacious grounds and questioning hospital employees.

Charlie Moon—who had skipped his breakfast and made the drive from Ignacio to Granite Creek in fifty minutes flat—met Scott Parris in the hospital parking lot. They headed directly to William Pizinski's empty room in the Annex, where they listened to a terse report from one of Parris' most competent young officers. She still carried scars from a violent encounter with a terrified man in a local bar. It had been two years ago, but if the offender had not been dead, Scott Parris would have still been searching for him. But he was dead. And the young lady was healing.

Alicia Martin, who had been working the missing-patient incident since well before first light, read crisply from her notes. "I got a list from the nurse of what had been in Pizinski's closet. All of his clothing, which wasn't that much—just what he had on when he was picked up in the forest—is gone. Underwear. Dark blue socks. Roper boots. Khaki pants, torn. White shirt, also torn. A few things Mr. Kenneth Bright brought to the hospital for his brother-in-law are still here. Electric razor. Comb. Toothpaste. Stuff like that. The nurse couldn't remember every item, but she's pretty sure it's all in the room. Just his clothes are gone."

Moon rubbed his sleepy eyes. "What about his wallet?"

Officer Martin checked her notes. "The most valuable stuff Pizinski had in his pockets when he was admitted—wallet, credit cards, a wristwatch—that was locked up for him. The safe's over in the main hospital building. His keys and a few other things are still here." She nodded to indicate an antique chest of drawers.

Parris frowned at the empty bed. It looked like Pizinski had got tired of being cooped up in the hospital. So he'd got out of bed in the middle of the night, put on his duds, and walked away. He had left a few things behind. But maybe he was in a hurry. "Any indication of violence?"

She shook her head. "No traces of blood. Nothing in the room was disturbed."

"What about the balcony door?" Moon asked.

"Unlocked. But there are no stairs on the balcony." She smiled at the tall Ute. "I don't think Pizinski would have shinnied down the vines; he had fractured ribs. Anyway, it'd make more sense to leave by the hallway. It wouldn't have been too hard to get past the nurse." Alicia lowered her voice to a conspiratorial whisper. "I've got a cousin who works here—in Pediatrics. She tells me that Annex duty is considered a plum assignment by the nursing staff. Late at night—once the patients are quiet—it's common practice to slip into the visitors' waiting room, have a seat in one of those reclining chairs. And watch the TV. Maybe even catch a little nap."

The lawmen made a quick check of Tommy Tonompicket's room. The skinny Ute was lying on his back. Lips parted to expose nicotine-stained teeth, empty eyes staring vacantly at the ceiling.

Moon sat on the bed. "Hey, Tommy. How you doin'?"

There was no response. Not the flicker of an eyelash.

"Sad case," Parris said.

The Ute policeman got up; the bed creaked gratefully. Moon wandered around the room. He began to open the drawers of an immaculate cherry chest. Unlike Pizinski, who had not yet been favored by a visit from his wife, Tommy had an ample assortment of clothing. Moon wondered how long it might be before Tommy would need something besides a hospital gown.

Parris looked over his friend's shoulder. "Well, if this one decides to take a walk some night, he's well supplied with stuff to wear."

Moon opened the small drawers at the top of the chest. There were several items that had been in Tommy's pockets when he was found. Keys. A small Case pocketknife. A few peppermints wrapped in cellophane. Paper clip. Hank of string. If Tommy's wallet wasn't in the hospital safe, his wife, Bertha, would have it. But something else was missing.

Parris had also noticed. "So Mrs. Tonompicket's taken her husband's cigarettes away. Just like she threatened."

The Ute grunted. "Looks that way."

Matilda Snyder was seated in a comfortable old chair. A mobile tray was positioned over her lap, a white cotton napkin tucked under her lace collar. The elderly woman was picking at her breakfast. She took a dainty sip of orange juice, then looked up at the pair of policemen. "It's your fault that man's gone. I told you to put a guard on the both of 'em."

Parris removed his hat. "Yes, ma'am. We need to know whether you saw anything at all last night."

She sawed on a greasy sausage with a dull knife. "I saw lots of things."

"Did you see Mr. Pizinski any time after dark?"

"Maybe I did. Maybe I didn't." She snapped the corner off a piece of rye toast, and spoke as she chewed. "What's it to you, Flatfoot?"

Parris took a deep breath and fixed his gaze on the small chandelier that hung over her head like a hornet's nest. *Maybe it'll fall on her.*

Moon squatted by Matilda's chair. "I haven't had any breakfast. That sausage sure looks good."

"They're too greasy for me. Too much fat messes up my colon—gives me the squirts."

"You've sure got a way of honing a man's appetite."

She cut her eyes at him, almost smiling. "Slaughtered any helpless settlers since I saw you last?"

"No, ma'am," the Ute said apologetically. "I've been feeling way too poorly for any slaughtering. But I did push a little old lady off a curb into noon-hour traffic."

Now the smile played at the corners of her mouth. "Why'd you do such a horrible thing?"

"She wouldn't give me her sandwich."

Matilda forced the smile away. "You're a heathen savage. But go ahead—have a sausage. Just one."

"Thanks." He took two; this earned him a poisonous look. Moon chewed them thoughtfully before speaking. "You gonna eat that other piece of toast?"

"Go ahead, take the last bite out of my mouth." She

waved her hand to dismiss the slice of rye. "My good-ness, don't they feed you at home?"

"Not since Daddy lost his job at the mine."

"You're a dreadful man."

"Yes, ma'am. There is one other thing—"

"Don't tell me—let me guess. You want my coffee?"

"No. Looks too weak."

"Then what is it?"

"I had a question."

"Well, I can't wait all morning. Spit it out."

"Did you notice anything unusual last night?"

Mattie's eyes glazed; she began to pat her hand ner-vously on the breakfast tray. "There was a bad storm. Lightning flashing. Thunder shaking the house. Wind screaming like ten devils. That's when they come out, you know."

The Ute wasn't sure he wanted to know. "Who's . . . they?"

"The monsters," she said. "Some nights they go traipsin' up and down the hall after the lights are out. One of 'em has six eyes . . . long black legs go clickety-clack when she walks." Matilda reached for a small carafe. "Would you like some orange juice?"

The lawmen were leaving Mattie's room when they en-countered Kenny Bright in the wide hallway. He saw the policemen and waved. "Hey, Charlie."

Moon returned the wave.

Bright was trailed by a tall, slender woman who might have been attractive a decade earlier. It was not so much that age was taking its toll. Her face was pinched in a perpetual, petulant scowl. As the policemen ap-proached, she was venting her white-hot wrath at Nurse Shrewsberry.

"This is outrageous! My husband was here last

night—and he's gone this morning. And you have no idea where he is?"

"That is my understanding of the situation," Shrewsberry replied evenly.

The tall woman noticed the scruffy-looking men, who were taking an unwarranted interest in her personal business. "Who are you?"

Parris pulled his jacket back to expose the gold shield pinned to his shirt pocket. "Police, ma'am. You are, I presume, Mrs. Pizinski."

"I certainly am. Margaret Pizinski."

"We're also interested in your husband's whereabouts. If there's anything you could tell us, we'd appreciate it."

She patted her perfectly coifed hairdo. "I've just returned from Europe. Flew all night after I got my brother's telephone call."

Bright, who imagined his sister crossing the Atlantic on a broom, grinned.

She paused to glance suspiciously at Kenny, who swallowed the grin. "I'm exhausted, naturally. And probably look a mess." A pale hand smoothed the skirt over her hips. "And now I learn that this so-called hospital can't keep track of its patients."

There was a warning glint in Nurse Shrewsberry's eyes. "It looks as if Dr. Pizinski simply got out of bed some time late last night, put his clothes on, and left."

Margaret's face was contorted with rage. "That is completely absurd. Kenny had called Bill last night about my arrival—my husband knew I'd be here this morning. So why on earth would he leave?"

The three men exchanged wry glances. And shared the same uncharitable thought.

The lawmen strode into the hospital administrator's office. The redheaded Irish nurse was standing near the windows overlooking the brick patio. Her back was very straight, her already pale complexion chalky white. Parris attempted a smile. "Hope we're not interrupting anything."

The administrator cleared his throat. "I was just getting a report from Nurse Mulligan." He shot her a steely glance. "About how a patient under her care last night . . . has vanished."

The chief of police nodded to indicate the Ute. "This is a friend of mine from SUPD, Charlie Moon."

The administrator frowned at the tall, dark man. "And what is his interest in this matter?"

"Pizinski and Tonompicket disappeared in Charlie's jurisdiction."

Moon let the minor error pass. *Within a few hundred yards of Ute jurisdiction.*

"Oh. Then perhaps Officer Moon will have some sympathy with my situation." The administrator was spitting the words out between clenched teeth. "I cannot fathom it—how can a patient simply walk away without being noticed?"

Parris glanced at the nurse, whose color was rising. "I'd say it was easy enough. He just got out of bed, put on his clothes. Then he walked out."

The administrator glared at the nurse. "Then why did you not see him go?"

She licked her thin lips and frowned with concentration. "Well, that's certainly the question, isn't it? I was right there for the whole shift"—*in the waiting room*—"watching"—*the television*—"like a hawk. And I never saw anybody leave. No, not a solitary soul."

Parris rubbed his bloodshot eyes. "Maybe Pizinski waited till you went to the ladies' room." It was at the south end of the long hallway. "And then he slipped out." Wouldn't hurt to toss a bone her way.

She grabbed it in midair. "Aye, that must be just what he did—wait till I was pressed by"—she blushed prettily—"an urgent call of nature. Why, the sneaky rascal!"

The administrator sniffed. "So you went to the rest room, did you?"

"I'm altogether repentant, sir." Her face was a picture of childlike innocence. "Would you prefer that I kept a coffee can under the desk?"

It was the administrator's turn to blush. *Redheaded witch.* As was his normal practice with difficult problems, he forthwith pretended that she did not exist. He directed his frustration at the lawmen. "But this patient—Pizinski—he didn't have any transportation. Surely he could not have gotten far away."

"Maybe it was planned," Moon said. "All of these rooms have a private telephone line. He could've called someone with a car. Asked 'em to meet him in the parking lot."

The administrator thought this unlikely. "But why would he leave—so abruptly?"

Parris grinned. "Have you met his wife?"

The administrator scowled at the lawman. "Well, however he got away, you've got to find him."

"Look," Parris said amiably, "*I'd* like to know why your patient wandered off in the middle of the night. And where he is now. But it's not exactly a felony to walk away from a hospital."

"Or even a misdemeanor," Moon added helpfully.

The administrator was appalled. If it was not against the law to depart from the hospital without being properly dismissed, it certainly ought to be. "But he's a sick man. Dr. Pizinski has cracked ribs—he's suffering from memory loss. He needs medical treatment."

Parris was tiring of this exchange. "We'll do what we

can. But even if we find the guy, we can't force him to come back."

The dumbfounded administrator sat down, shaking his head in disbelief at this undeserved calamity. "It makes no sense. I just don't understand why a man in his condition would simply walk away."

"Maybe he intends to admit himself to another hospital," Moon said with feigned innocence.

"That's absurd—why would he want to do that?"

The Ute could still taste the sausage grease. "Maybe he didn't like the food."

The lawmen stepped out of the administrator's office onto the brick patio that spanned the long, shady space under the Annex balcony. They stood, hands in pockets, staring at Granite Creek.

"Running high and fast," Parris said. "And muddy."

"We had an early snowmelt," the Ute observed.

"Yeah. Late in March, it turned unusually warm. TV weather guy said it was a forty-year record."

Moon nodded. "Then we got the rains. Warm rains."

Parris sighed. "We sound like a couple of old farmers. With nothing to talk about except the weather. And we got important police business to sort out."

"Weather's important," the Ute said. "Helps to know which way the wind's blowing."

"Right."

A thin young man in oversized coveralls appeared. He had a grimy canvas sack slung over his shoulder, a long wooden rod in his hand. A sharpened spike protruded from the end of the implement. He went about his task methodically, ignoring the lawmen. There was not that much work to be done. At the far end of the patio, he expertly speared a Styrofoam cup. Then a pink tissue. Both of these went into the canvas sack. As he passed between the police officers and the river, he aimed the sharp spike at a small white object.

"Wait," Moon said. "Leave it there."

The assistant groundskeeper turned to stare at the taller of these intruders. Their clothes were rumpled and they looked like they hadn't slept all night. The white man had a day's growth of beard and the bloodshot eyes of a wino. The lean, dark one had a hungry look. Like he hadn't eaten a bite in days. Obviously a couple of bums— out of work and wandering around the hospital grounds looking for a handout and a place to sleep. He'd report them, of course. But he didn't bother to speak to them.

Moon knelt to pick up the cigarette butt.

The assistant groundskeeper experienced a sudden mix of pity and anger. "Hey, mac, this is the United States of America. You need a smoke, you don't need to scrounge around in the dirt for throwaways."

"Actually," Moon said, "I don't intend to smoke it. I—"

The young man smiled knowingly. "Sure you don't— it's for your rich uncle's butt collection. Look, you don't need to make no excuses." He jerked a thumb to his thin chest. "To look at me, you'd never guess it, but I been down on my luck a coupla times." He pulled a pack of Luckies from his coverall pocket and thumbed out a pair of cigarettes. "Here, pal."

The Ute policeman graciously accepted the offer.

Before Moon knew what had happened, the assistant groundskeeper had pressed a few coins into his hand and hurried away. Moon stared at the coins. "He gave me sixty-five cents."

"He's a Good Samaritan who took you for a vagrant." The chief of police smiled at the young man's receding form. "I need not remind you that he did not offer *me* a handout."

"You're right," the Ute said. "It's not fair." He stuffed the Luckies into Parris' shirt pocket.

———•

Parris braked the aging Volvo to a halt in front of the Silver Mountain Hotel. It was a three-story brick building. Almost a century old, but loath to show its years. A dark green canopy extended from the entrance to the curb, providing cover from a pelting rain. *Beautiful day.* Indeed, a film of oil floating on a puddle made a lovely rainbow reflection.

Moon ducked to look through the water-streaked window. "So this is where Camilla and Mr. Zoog are staying?"

The chief of police nodded. "Where else? This is the best hostelry in town. That OSI investigator—Captain Taylor—she's got a room here too."

"So why're we here—you figure William Pizinski's checked in?"

Parris chuckled. "It'd be a helluva lot cheaper than Snyder Memorial Hospital. Especially the Annex. And the food's infinitely better."

Moon felt his spirits soar. "Then we're here for breakfast?"

"And it's on me—so you can make a glutton of yourself."

"I'm just medium-hungry." *Pork chops and eggs, maybe. Home fries and gravy. About a half gallon of coffee.* "But thanks. You're an all-right guy."

Parris pushed a button to lower the window. "I'm an all-right guy with an expense account."

"Even better."

A uniformed hotel employee sheathed in a transparent raincoat appeared at the driver's side and accepted Parris' key with a perfunctory smile. He gave the aging

automobile a sadly disparaging look, then drove it into
the hotel parking lot as the lawmen slipped under the
canopy.

Once inside the hotel lobby, Moon was dismayed to
note that his friend was not leading him to the restaurant,
whence delicious aromas beckoned to his nostrils. Parris
was headed toward an office. The small sign on the door
said MANAGER. "You go on ahead," the Ute said. "I'll
check out the restaurant—see what's for breakfast."

The short, balding man looked up from his work at the
computer terminal. Well, now. Here was the chief of police with an unshaven face and road-map eyes, dripping
rain. Looked like a derelict who'd slept outside all
night. But Scott Parris was an honest public servant and
a decent fellow. Such folk were always welcome at the
Silver Mountain Hotel. The manager's smile was genuine. "Good morning, Scott."

Parris removed his rain-spotted felt hat. "Hiya, Andrew."

They spent a short time discussing the weather and
local politics and baseball. Andrew liked the Dodgers
this year. Parris, though years away from Chicago,
gamely followed the hapless Cubs. This happy conversation was interrupted when a very tall, dark man—
who also had the look of a policeman—appeared
behind the chief of police. *Looks like a Ute,* Andrew
thought. *Must be Parris' Indian chum from Ignacio.*
Not much went on in Granite Creek that was missed by
the manager of the Silver Mountain Hotel.

Parris introduced his friend. "Me'n Charlie stopped
by for breakfast, but first we've got a little police business to conduct."

"Oh, dear," the manager was deadpan, "you've heard
about the crap game in the cellar."

"Yeah, but as long as the payoffs keep coming, we won't roust you." Parris was too tired to grin at his own joke. "Actually, I'd like to get the room numbers for a couple of your guests. Middle-aged man. Pretty young woman."

"You could have asked for that at the desk." Andrew's lips curled into a sly smile. "But I suppose you prefer to be more discreet."

"Yeah. Discreet."

The manager turned to the computer terminal. "Love nest and all that sort of thing?"

Moon cringed inwardly. And outwardly.

Parris smiled at his friend's discomfort. "They *claim* to be uncle and niece."

Andrew selected a menu entitled GUESTS. "Names?"

"Eddie Zoog. Camilla Willow."

He tapped the keys, then pressed ENTER. The hard disk whined like a bloodthirsty mosquito. "Willow, Camilla. Zoog, Edward." He looked up. "Sorry. They've already checked out."

"When?"

"Let's see." He raised an eyebrow. "Quite early this morning. Four forty-eight A.M. for Mr. Zoog. Four forty-five for Miss Willow."

"Seems pretty early."

The manager shrugged. "Not necessarily. They had a rental car in the hotel garage. If they're driving to the airport at Colorado Springs, they'll need a good two hours."

Moon had a question. It was of a somewhat personal nature. "Could you tell us what rooms they were in?" He clasped his hands behind his back. *Please, God— don't let them be in the same room.*

The manager hoped these policemen did not have a search in mind. That would suggest drugs. Or something equally distasteful. He squinted at the flickering monitor. "Mr. Zoog was in room 245. Let's see, Miss Willow was in . . ."

Charlie Moon, encouraged by this prompt answer to prayer, pressed his luck: *Thank you, God. Now don't let it be 243. Or 247.*

". . . room 312."

The Ute was greatly relieved. But being somewhat pessimistic on this rainy morning, he was suspicious of any good news. "Were you . . . uh . . . short of rooms when they checked in?"

"Certainly not. This is our slow time—well after the ski season when the young and beautiful have departed, but before hordes of smelly fisher-folk show up with rod and reel."

The pair of fishermen did not take offense.

Parris whispered in Moon's ear, "Relax, Charlie. Camilla really is the Zoog's niece."

"It's kinda hard to believe they could be related— even by marriage," the Ute muttered. *Or have the same number of chromosomes.*

Parris stood before the manager's desk, turning the shapeless felt hat in his hands. "How about a room number for a Miss Taylor. Teresa Taylor." The OSI special agent wouldn't be registered as Captain Taylor.

"Well, two down, one to go," Moon said glumly. "Ten bucks will get you twenty—Taylor's checked out too."

"You're on," Parris said quickly. He had made a call from the hospital. Captain Taylor was having a leisurely breakfast in the hotel restaurant.

The Ute laid a twenty-dollar bill on the desk. *Ten bucks the easy way.*

The chief of police covered the twenty with two fives. Again the disk hummed. The manager shook his head. "Sorry, Scott—you've struck out. Miss Taylor checked out about twenty minutes ago."

Parris' mouth dropped open.

"Imagine that," Moon said. And scooped up the greenbacks. While Parris was having a chat with the manager, he had checked at the front desk.

Scott Parris—who had finished a bowl of cornflakes—sipped at a glass of extra-pulpy orange juice. And watched his Ute friend put away three fried eggs, two pork chops, a heap of home fries smothered in brown gravy. The Ute had washed this down with several mugs of steaming coffee, each laced with a handful of sugar cubes.

"Well, Charlie, we haven't made much progress. The two missing guys show up, but can't tell us what happened after they disappeared from the shore of Navajo Lake. And now one of 'em's gone again. And we don't know where to start looking for him." This was not the worst of it. "I've heard through the grapevine that the FBI's starting to show an interest in the matter."

"Life is tough for us small-town cops," the Ute observed.

"Uh-huh. Sometimes you're the windshield, sometimes you're the bug. But we should've expected it. Once a case makes the TV news five or six nights in a row, the Bureau gets interested."

"I hope," Moon said sternly, "you are not suggesting that employees of our federal government—who take an oath to serve the great white father in Washington—would be motivated by the least desire for publicity."

"Ha—don't tell me you've never wanted to see your picture in the paper. And a big headline, like LOCAL INDIAN SAVES ENTIRE TOWN FROM TERRORISTS."

"Well, of course I have," Moon said. "But you got the wrong headline."

"Which is?"

The Ute held his hands up, thumbs extended to frame the words. "CHARLIE MOON INHERITS HUGE FORTUNE FROM DEAD RICH PERSON. RETIRES FROM POLICE FORCE. BUYS CATTLE RANCH ON THE GUNNISON."

"That's way too long for a headline."

"The editor of the tribal newspaper owes me a favor or two." There was a long silence while Moon entertained fantasies about how to spend his inheritance.

Parris' mind was occupied with the real world. "The whole thing don't make any sense. Couple of guys get into some kind of peculiar trouble at Navajo Lake and end up miles to the north—in the middle of the national forest. Tonompicket is up a tree and almost dead, the scientist is wandering around in the woods with busted ribs. One's not able to say a word, the other one can't remember what happened."

"Or don't *want* to remember," Moon said.

"The whole story smells like boiled Brussels sprouts."

The Ute nodded. "Like a beached carp. With green flies on it."

"Like a maggoty, rotten—"

The Ute raised his hand. "Enough. I'm still eating."

"However you slice it, it's still stale bread."

"What we need," Moon said, "is some hard evidence."

"Ahh . . . excuse me."

Moon looked over his friend's head. Standing behind Parris was a slender man of average height. His rumpled gray suit was too small for his lanky frame. Unkempt hair the color of carrots crowned a narrow face; his pale blue eyes were wide with anxiety. "Excuse me," he said again.

Parris turned. "Hey, glad to see you, Ezra. Grab a seat."

The flustered man slid onto one of the padded chairs. He directed his continuing apology at the Ute policeman. "I am sorry to interrupt your breakfast. I was on my way to the police station to see Chief Parris when I noticed his car in the hotel parking lot."

"That rusty old Volvo *is* distinctive," Moon said. "Also an eyesore. A pox . . . a blight . . ."

The slender man, confused by Moon's jest, turned hopefully to Parris. "I hoped I might find you in the hotel."

The chief of police pointed his fork at the Ute policeman. "This big smart aleck is Charlie Moon. He claims to work for the Southern Ute police—but some say he's working *against* 'em. Charlie, this is Professor Ezra Budd, a tenured professor over at Rocky Mountain Polytechnic. Ezra's agreed to do me a big favor, for which I'll probably be fixing parking tickets for years and years."

Somewhat shyly, the newcomer stuck a hand out to Moon. "I'm pleased to meet you."

Moon shook the hand, which was cold. "Same here."

"The professor is a busy man, Charlie. But someday when he eventually gets around to it, he'll develop the film in that dead lawyer's camera. See if Miles Armitage took a photograph of . . ." *Of what?*

Budd managed to look even more apologetic. "I'm so sorry I haven't gotten back to you sooner, but dealing with the film turned out to be—well, rather an involved process."

Parris gave him a worried look. "The film was okay, wasn't it—not ruined or anything?"

The professor scratched at thinning hair; a light snow of dandruff drifted down to his jacket collar. "The film wasn't damaged. Only three of the frames had been exposed."

Moon gently prodded the academic along. "You find anything on the exposed film?"

"Indeed I have." Budd nodded. "Found something, I mean."

Parris leaned closer to the professor. "So tell us."

Budd glanced around the restaurant, as if someone might overhear. There was a scattering of customers left over from the breakfast crowd, nursing cups of tepid coffee, reading the local newspaper. He lowered his voice to a hoarse whisper. "It's rather hard to describe. The results are . . . one might say . . . inconclusive." He saw disappointment slip over Parris' face like a dark shadow. "You'd best have a look for yourself." Budd removed a sealed manila envelope from his inside jacket pocket, slid it across the table toward the Granite Creek chief of police. "The camera and developed negatives are locked in my safe at the university." He knew something about the rules for handling evidence. "But I made you some prints."

Parris ran his thumbnail along the seal and opened the stiff envelope. There were three glossy photos. To indicate chronological order, the professor had numbered each print. The top of each photo was also indicated. The chief of police sorted quickly through the trio of black-and-white photographs. His brow twisted into a puzzled frown. "What'n hell is this?"

Moon got up to stand behind his friend, who had spread the prints on the restaurant table like a face-up poker hand. Three of a kind. In each of the photographs, there was a fuzzy-looking whitish splotch on a dark background. The splotch was more or less egg-shaped. From the bottom of the egg, slender tentacles reached out toward the earth.

The Ute felt the hair stand up on the back of his neck.

The professor's glance darted nervously between one

policeman and the other. "Well, as you can imagine, I was surprised to see what was on the film. It was necessary, of course, to understand the environment where the exposures were made. To this end, I went to the cabin on First Finger Ridge where the lawyer's body was found. I performed a careful survey of the grounds. I'm certain that all three of the photographs were made from within a yard or so of the cabin's front porch." Budd pointed to a feature on the left side of the prints; it reached out in front of the central object like a skeletonous hand. "Despite the new leaves, I was able to positively identify this specific branch on an aspen. It is located on the south side of the Armitage cabin. You will note that the limb is well in the foreground—between the camera lens and the . . . uh . . . object. The limb is about three meters above the ground. Note that the limb is in perfect focus . . . the central object is not. The central object—whatever it is—is of substantial size."

Moon posed the same question he'd asked Officer Bignight. "How big?" *Big as a house?*

The professor pondered this issue carefully before he replied. "It is difficult to say with any precision, because one cannot determine the exact distance of the object from the camera, which was set for focus at about four to five meters. But the object was obviously farther away than the tree limb in the foreground—at least twenty to thirty meters. An arm-waving estimate"—he waved his arms—"would be at least ten meters in horizontal diameter." He muttered to himself: "At least ten meters. And almost twice that in height. Could be much larger, of course."

Moon drummed his fingers on the table. *So. Big as a house.*

The professor pointed out another relevant feature of

the evidence. "In successive photos, though it remains behind the aspen limb, the object is larger—about twelve percent. And in slightly better focus. Therefore, as successive photographs were made, it was moving closer to the camera."

Right at him. Parris imagined Armitage's panic. "How fast?"

"If one assumes that the time between shots was two seconds . . . an estimate on the approach velocity would be on the order of, say, ten miles per hour. But this is no better than an educated guess."

Parris pointed to the bottom of the white blob. "What're these?"

Professor Budd hesitated. "I'd say . . . ahh . . . appendages of some sort."

Parris stared. *They look like legs.* But appendages was a nice, neutral term that didn't conjure up the inhabitants of nightmares. "Off the record, Ezra—what do you make of this?"

The academic shrugged under the ill-fitting jacket, and blushed pink. "I don't really know what to say." He fiddled nervously with his string tie. "Never seen anything remotely like this. Wouldn't know what to say in a court of law. Quite peculiar . . . yes . . ." He glanced at an inexpensive wristwatch without noting the time of day. "Sorry. Really must be going. Departmental meeting. Summer-school schedules, course plans for the fall semester. That sort of thing."

The policemen watched the professor's hurried departure.

Parris pushed the three prints back into the manila envelope. "Weird," he muttered.

Moon nodded. That was the word, all right.

The *matukach* stared thoughtfully at his Ute friend.

And repeated the question he'd asked the professor. "What do you make of this?"

Moon managed a weak grin. "Don't have a clue." But he did. He gave his friend a searching look. "What do you think, pardner?"

The chief of police pushed the envelope around the table with his thumb, as if this might coax some intelligence from the eerie images. "Maybe it was some kind of atmospheric discharge. You know . . . electrical. A plasma."

"Yeah. Like ball lightning." Moon liked this explanation. Even though ball lightning or any other kind didn't make a habit of biting off lawyers' heads and making puncture wounds in their chests. Or, in the instance of Tonompicket, stashing its stunned victims in the tops of tall trees.

"So what do we do next?"

Moon thought about it. "Some hard thinking."

Parris ran his thumb along the envelope seal. "What'll we do besides some hard thinking?"

"Don't know about you, pardner—but I'm headin' home. Got my chiefly duties at SUPD to attend to."

Parris tapped a spoon against the cereal bowl and began to think out loud. "What if Pizinski never shows up again? What then?"

"Just as long as he never shows up on the Southern Ute Reservation." Moon wiped his mouth with a linen napkin. "That fella—along with Tommy Tonompicket—has caused me a pile of trouble."

Parris shared the feeling. *But where is he?*

———•———

He sleeps, it seems . . . and dreams his dream.

The naked biped floats effortlessly on his back, arms

outstretched in an expansive gesture. Beyond the reach
of his pale hands are sweet pastures of yellow and blue
blossoms. Beneath him—breathing the crystalline
fluid—are darting blue-gray creatures. Shining stones
pave the underside of this slippery highway. Above
him . . . they seem so near . . . the snow-white clouds
drift lazily across an azure sky. Moreover, a breeze
sighs . . . caressing his face. It is such peace as men cannot know in that world he leaves behind.

He rises and falls with the undulating waves.

———•

Charlie Moon was secluded in his office, seated comfortably behind the massive desk. Until quite recently,
this had been the domain of retiring Chief of Police Roy
Severo. It was finally beginning to feel like his own comfortable sanctuary.

But it is written that a man must sweat for his daily
bread. To this end, Moon tackled a thick stack of paperwork. He made a quick survey, then began to sort tasks
into categories. Mail and faxes to be read. FBI statistical
reports on regional criminal activity. BIA reports to be
glanced at and filed away. And SUPD paperwork. Duty
rosters. Proposed vacation plans. All to be cross-checked
and signed off on. A couple of recommendations for
commendations. Another for a reprimand—officer
sleeping on duty. And there was some useless stuff that
would be dropped into the round file. Moon was sorting
the diminishing stack when Daniel Bignight lumbered
into the office. "H'lo, Charlie. I got some stuff for you."

"That's what I need, Daniel—more paperwork."

"You asked for it."

Moon aimed his response at Bignight's cheerful face.
"I never asked to be deputy chief of police."

The Taos Pueblo man was unfazed by the missile.

"That's not what I meant. You asked for *this*." He pitched a folder on the desk.

"What's that?"

Bignight enjoyed a smirk. "You already forgot? You told me to find out what I could about that Kenny Bright guy. And his business interests. That's my report."

"Oh, yeah. Thanks, Daniel." He opened the folder. Bignight's "report" was a series of computer print-outs—mostly stuff from the Internet. *Wonderful. Thirty minutes of dull reading.* And it looked like Bignight intended to stand there and watch him suffer through every minute. Time to counter-punch. "Daniel, why don't you give me a one-minute summary?"

One minute! I spend hours putting this junk together and you don't have time to read it? A bland mask spread over Bignight's features, barely concealing his annoyance. "Well, I guess there's not much there you didn't already know. Bright Enterprises is a half-dozen businesses. The high-tech firm is RMAFS. It's an acronym for Rocky Mountain Advanced Flight Systems."

Moon nodded. "Kenny Bright told me about it. They live off government contracts—mainly with the Air Force. Dr. Pizinski worked out of the Albuquerque division, but he made occasional trips to the manufacturing plant in Colorado Springs. Which was where he was returning from when he decided to take a detour to Navajo Lake." He glanced over Bignight's head at the clock on the wall. "Anything on the computer about the company?"

"Yeah. On the last page." *Read it.*

Moon found the printout.

Bignight peered over his shoulder at a copy of the firm's home page.

RMAFS, Inc.
A Bright Enterprises Corporation
Locations in Albuquerque
and Colorado Springs
*Specializing in State-of-the-Art Research and
Development*
Advanced Propulsion Concepts
Adaptive Control Systems
Air Frame Development
Artificial Intelligence
Innovative Robotics
—Custom Designs Are Our Specialty—
Watch This Site for Announcements of
New Product Development!

There was a "Contact Us" e-mail address, phone and fax numbers, a street address in Albuquerque. "What does Bright Enterprises do besides the high-tech stuff?"

The Taos Pueblo man rocked back and forth on worn bootheels. "Real estate. Insurance. Law firm in Los Angeles. And there's the Bright furniture stores. They got factories all over. Trinidad, Dominican Republic, Venezuela."

He's altogether too pleased with himself. "And Costa Rica," Moon added casually. There were other ways to get information without pecking away at a computer keyboard. Like talking to human beings.

Bignight was doubtful. "Costa Rica? That one wasn't mentioned on the Web."

"It's new." Moon got a small satisfaction from one-upping the smug policeman. "Anything else?"

Bignight dropped a thin sheaf of papers on the desk.

"This was faxed in a few minutes ago. It's from your buddy at Granite Creek PD."

Moon thanked the officer, who departed.

The fax consisted of three pages. The first two were a summary of information Scott Parris' staff had put together on some recent visitors to Granite Creek.

With no thought for alphabetical order, Zoog and his niece headed the list. Edward P. Zoog had served an undistinguished hitch in the Navy, was a graduate of the Mexico City College of Dentistry. He had practiced his craft in Los Angeles for nine years. Moon tried to imagine Zoog with a dental drill in his mitt. Not a pretty picture. Perhaps his patients had shared this view. For whatever reason, he had sold out the dental practice, investing the proceeds in the booming California real estate market. With amazing timing, he made his move just as prices were at a historic peak. History is a puckish playmate. Within months, California dirt took a long, downhill slide. Eddie Zoog went along for the ride.

Camilla's résumé was brief. The young woman had an MBA from UCLA and a sizable inheritance from her paternal grandfather. Granddad had also left her the family horse ranch. Shortly after Eddie Zoog took a hit in his real estate ventures, she had bought a moderately successful literary agency in Los Angeles and appointed her uncle to run the show. Zoog had named the business after himself. Judging by EZ's credit rating, the literary agency was teetering on the edge of bankruptcy. Camilla, Moon guessed, had come along on this Colorado snipe hunt to bird-dog her uncle. Probably hoped she could keep him from driving the business into the ground. *Good luck.*

The Ute policeman thumbed his way to the third page and read a paragraph on Captain Teresa Taylor. She was as she had represented herself—a special agent with the United States Air Force Office of Special Investigations. Also a magna cum laude law graduate from the University of Kentucky. Captain Taylor was currently assigned to OSI headquarters at Bolling Air Force Base. Which was in the District of Columbia. He pondered this. Dr. Pizinski worked for an Air Force contractor in Albuquerque that had a plant in Colorado. So if the OSI was running a routine investigation on the disappearance of one of its contractors' key scientists, why not send someone out from the Denver OSI office—or Albuquerque? Possibly because the OSI didn't consider the Pizinski-Tonompicket misadventure to be a routine matter?

IN THE MISTY *depths of Hip Pocket Canyon, there are shadowy places on the south slope where direct rays from the sun have never warmed the soil—not since the earth was formed from stellar dust. The thick forest on this steep incline absorbs energy from reflected light . . . and photons scattered from minute dust particles. In this eternal twilight, bright green pines spring forth from moldy cones. When old age comes, they sprout pointy gray-green tufts of the parasite called Old Man's Beard. As they weaken, the aged trees lean wearily on the knotty shoulders of a neighbor. Where they touch, thick bark is worn away. When winds whistle down the canyon, the pines rub pulpy bone against bone . . . and whine a painful lament. Many die without falling to the ground.*

And so it continues.

From year to year . . . millennium to millennium—as in a thousand other dark wounds in the mountains—there is a perpetual sameness about the moist depths of Hip Pocket Canyon. Lichen-encrusted granite boulders. Mosses of emerald green and silver gray. The stream—

frozen almost solid in winter's cold sleep—spills happily over shining stones as the crusty snowbanks melt. Though it cycles through endless seasons, this place has never changed in any remarkable way.

Except this once. Not far from the snag-choked, boulder-strewn stream, there is something quite new in the forest. This deep, narrow, dead-end canyon has never known the like of it. A mule deer, come to drink silently from the stream, has seen it—and fled, bounding panic-stricken over impediments of moss-sheened boulder and moldy log.

The hideous presence that frightened the deer remained almost motionless. True, the bulbous body did occasionally pulsate, like a great bladder inhaling and exhaling. The long, slender appendages twitched now and then . . . but not in preparation for anxious flight. The hideous form merely tarried as the storm clouds gathered. It was quite incapable of fear. Or pity.

——·

The assembly point was a high mountain pasture, contained well within the fenced boundary of a six-thousand-acre ranch. The property was owned by a family who had connections with the powers that be. Land transport—an assortment of four-wheel-drive pickups and SUVs—was secured under the cover of a thick stand of aspen. Where it was thought prudent, camouflage netting had been used. Team C—comprised of three men and a woman—would remain behind at the temporary tent headquarters. Two of the men would provide emergency communications. And—if necessary—would secure the camp from the prying eyes of the unlikely hiker who would climb an electrified barbed-wire fence to trespass on the ranch property. The woman and one of the men comprised the medical team; a small but well-equipped surgical tent had been set up.

The operational troops were comprised of Teams A and B.

A pair of helicopters was stationed fifty yards away from the gathering. The machines were spray-painted a sooty gray. And unmarked. The aircraft were loaded with the necessary gear. Infrared night-vision equipment. Chain saws. Shaped charges and detonators. Flamethrowers. And a few other odds and ends. Their black rotors—drooping like bruised, wilting blossoms—were beginning to turn slowly in a preflight test.

The commander stood by a sturdy wooden tripod that supported a plasticized map board. Cassidy—who wore no indication of rank—paced back and forth before his subordinates. All of these tough young men were seasoned by previous clandestine operations. Six were veteran SEALS; four were former Special Forces. The team members wore charcoal jumpsuits. Each man carried a firearm of choice; most preferred 9-mm automatic side arms with NATO-issue ammunition. The black man—who was considered somewhat of an eccentric—carried a .22-caliber Ruger revolver. It was loaded with magnum hollow points. Cassidy noted that several men had M-16 assault weapons. *Lot of good it'll do 'em. Unless they come eyeball-to-eyeball with a black bear or mountain lion.* But going into an operation without a serious firearm made them feel naked. He tapped a pointer on the map stand. The murmurs among the men were hushed.

"Okay, fellas—here's the deal. With information provided by an eyewitness, a scouting party was deployed yesterday. They've located the target here." He pointed to a small red circle on the map, almost halfway up the narrow canyon. The commander glanced at his wristwatch. "At eighteen hundred hours, the copters take off. Flight time will be approximately forty minutes. At nineteen hundred hours, A-Team goes in up-canyon from the target, rappels down the north wall, then moves down-canyon." He touched the tip of the pointer to the red circle on the chart. Each team member had a smaller version of the map. "B-Team will be deposited at the mouth of the canyon, then proceed up-gradient toward the target location." He would go in with B-Team. "We will converge at the target no later than twenty hundred hours. If either team is unduly delayed, the group that arrives first shall commence the operation. Radio communications will be used only in the case of emergencies that require immediate helicopter assistance or evac. Any injury that cannot be managed by the team medic shall constitute such an emergency."

He inhaled a deep breath of the bracing mountain air. You had to tell them a dozen times, then remind them six more. "The mission objective is simple—total destruction of the target. Whatever cannot be obliterated must be removed. Once the basic objectives have been accomplished, both teams will move west to the mouth of the canyon for pickup by the choppers." He frowned. "This operation has risks that you have all agreed to assume. Absolute secrecy is paramount; our sponsor is adamant about this. Any leak will compromise our sponsor . . . and our future employment."

This was greeted by expressionless stares from the blackened faces. The teams had been assembled with more than ordinary care—there was not a man present who had a tendency to talk about his work.

"Any questions?"

The black man raised his hand, a bright grin flashed across his face. "One thing you still ain't told us, boss. And you said you'd tell us when the time had come."
The time has come.

Cassidy managed an innocent expression. "Which is?" *As if I didn't know*.

The black trooper directed the disarming grin at his comrades. "Just what *is* this target?"

All were aware of those wild-assed stories on the TV. Giant insects and space goons and whatnot. The men exchanged sheepish looks. What a load of crap.

Cassidy looked over their heads. "For security reasons, you will find out when the teams converge at the target location." There was another reason, of course. If these young gladiators knew what they were going into the canyon to destroy . . . some of them might well have second thoughts. "Anything else?"

A short, barrel-chested man—one of the older team members—waggled his hand. There was general, good-natured laughter.

Cassidy—pretending to be exasperated by this expected ritual—rolled his eyes. "What's on your mind, Aristotle?" The curly-haired man had majored in medieval philosophy at Princeton.

He posed the questions. "Boss—why are we here? What is our ultimate destiny? I mean, what the hell is it all about?"

"Beats me." Cassidy smiled. "Unless it's for the money." There was a light but appreciative applause from the men. "Any other questions?"

There were none.

"All right." Cassidy nodded toward the dark helicopters, engines now throbbing throatily, coughing thick puffs of gray fumes into the sweet afternoon air. "Let's go do it."

Winds were light and westerly. B-Team was deposited at the mouth of the narrow canyon precisely on time, without incident. It was a textbook operation. Each member of the team was thinking more or less the same thing. *Piece of cake. Easy money. Home in twenty-four hours.*

A-Team's arrival was somewhat more interesting. It was not yet dark, but thick cloud cover at the higher elevation swirled like blue smoke through the pines. The weather was effective for concealing the operation, but the limited visibility made navigation in the rugged terrain a white-knuckle affair. Even with GPS-correlated instruments and high-resolution topo maps, this was what the helicopter pilots referred to as a tight-rectum approach. Members of A-Team were finally put down in a light crosswind. It was a short hike from their initial destination—a sheer cliff over the north wall of the canyon called Hip Pocket. Within minutes, the half-dozen men were rappelling down to the narrow canyon floor.

A-Team's dark-skinned aircraft droned away to meet the B-Team chopper at an abandoned sawmill on Third Finger Ridge, where both pilots would wait for the pickup signal after the mission was completed. And pray that there would be no emergencies that would require a descent into the narrow canyon. The rules of operation had been agreed upon by vote. If a man suffered a minor injury, like a sprained ankle—or an untreatable condition, like death—the teams were prepared to carry the victim out of the canyon to the helicopter rendezvous. In between these extremes, there might be a serious injury where rapid hospitalization would be essential to preserve life or limb. Then all bets were off. Come hell or high water, a chopper would go roaring into the narrow canyon to evacuate the wounded comrade for emergency medical assistance. Straightforward surgery would be performed back at base camp. For complicated cases, two county hospitals had already been selected. Snyder Memorial at Granite Creek was preferred, especially for head injuries or serious burns. Mercy Hospital at Durango was the second option. Plastic stencils had been cut; identity numbers associated with a Cortez air-ambulance service would be spray-painted on one of the aircraft. Cover stories for the ER had been rehearsed. The patient—depending on his wounds—had taken a bad fall, been involved in a drunken brawl . . . or attacked by a wild animal. If the nature of his injury was particularly difficult to explain—he had been found on the highway by passing motorists.

Members of B-Team, equipment strapped firmly on their backs, were prepared to enter the mouth of Hip Pocket Canyon. Aside from the raucous complaint of a tuft-eared squirrel perched on an aged ponderosa—flipping its black tail and protesting the outrageous presence of the invaders—the evening was supremely quiet. The men checked firearms that didn't need checking, whispered wary comments—and waited impatiently for Cassidy's order to begin the trek. There was a well-worn deer trail beside the rocky streambed, so it would be—almost literally—a walk in the park. But the boss wasn't ready to move. So what was he waiting for?

Cassidy was squatting on a rough basalt outcropping, meticulously scanning the terrain with a Belgian-manufactured infrared viewer. *Everything looks okay. So what am I waiting for?* And then he heard the slight noise . . . turned the IR sensor toward its source. There were two green spots. One considerably larger than the other. He mouthed a curse, then waved to summon the philosopher. "Aristotle," he whispered, "c'mere."

The short, curly-haired man materialized from the darkness. "Sir?"

Cassidy pointed. "Company's coming."

The footsteps were now clearly audible. Aristotle listened intently to the rhythm. "Sounds like three guys."
And two of 'em are big.

The commander, who had the advantage of the IR display, smiled thinly. "Or maybe it's one man and a horse."

The remainder of the team had drawn near, to learn what the trouble was.

Aristotle peered through his own infrared optics. "It's a guy . . . and a damn *mule*."

Cassidy's reply was curt. "A mule . . . I stand corrected."

Aristotle, though a stickler for detail, did not think it judicious to point out that the commander was squatting. "What'll we do?"

"We cannot tolerate any interference. You will confront this . . ." The word was repugnant. "This *civilian*. And see that he withdraws immediately."

The philosopher did not ask for advice as to how this might be done. Aristotle, like the other knuckle-draggers, was being paid twenty thousand dollars for a single night's work. Cassidy would expect him to show some initiative. And so off he marched, to do his duty.

Aristotle sized up the intruder with a practiced eye. From his slow, halting gait and bent frame—this was an old man. The wrinkled face was almost covered by a wild sprouting of gray whiskers. The pilgrim's spare frame was hung with a faded denim jacket and stiff new overalls that were three sizes too large. He was shod in four-buckle rubber overshoes which flopped comically as he walked. He led the scruffy-looking mule by a hank of clothesline rope. The animal was burdened by a jumbled pack. There were miscellaneous bundles of food, tattered blankets, a large canteen, an iron skillet, a rusty pickaxe, a square-blade shovel. *So. A prospector.* The mercenary stood in the path, one arm raised like a traffic policeman waving down a motorist. He cleared his throat. "Who goes there?" *That sounded cool.*

The elderly man—who had thought he was quite alone—was startled by this unexpected challenge. He stopped in his tracks. "I'm Pinky Packer." He leaned forward, the better to peer through thick spectacles at this peculiar-looking young man who had smudges of burned cork smeared on his face. "Who wants to know?"

"Me," Aristotle said with an authoritative air.

The man leading the mule began to chew on a jawful of tobacco. "Who's *me?*"

The philosopher was surprised when the acronym came forth from his mouth. "FBI." *Not bad.*

Pinky chortled, and spat tobacco juice dangerously near Aristotle's shiny black boots. "Me, I'm with the CIA. I may look old as hell, but it's a disguise—I'm only twenty-six. And this ain't really no pack mule behind me. This here's a African zebra that can speak sixteen languages." He paused to laugh and wheeze. "I painted over the white stripes with road tar."

Old smart ass. "I'm sorry, sir, but you'll have to turn around immediately. And withdraw from the area. We're sealing off the whole canyon."

"Now why would you do somethin' like that?"

Aristotle searched his brain. "Uh . . . mad cow disease." *That sounded good. Damn good.*

This here's a sure enough dumb-ass city boy. "Well, I don't care whether the cows hereabouts is downright mad or just mildly pissed off. Me'n this Ginny mule has to get up the canyon to my diggin's."

The trooper glanced at the heavily laden animal. "What do you mine, old fella—silver? Or maybe you're taking big pokes o' gold nuggets outta *them thar hills*." To this he added a "heh-heh."

The old man chewed thoughtfully on the tobacco; he stared toward the mountains with a sad, wistful expression. "Mosta the gold and silver was worked outta here years back." He concealed a sly grin behind the whiskers. "But I got me a claim staked to somethin' that's rare as frogs' teeth."

The younger man grinned. "Like what—zinc?"

The prospector lowered his voice and uttered one terrifying word. "Plutonium."

Aristotle lost the grin; his dark eyes goggled. "Plutonium . . . like for making atom bombs?"

Pinky nodded. "It's what puts in the boom in the kaboom."

"But isn't mining something like that . . . illegal?"

Would be if there was any to mine. "Not if you got a federal license it ain't." Pinky's wrinkled features assumed a modest expression. "Now, I'm not sayin' it's the real high-grade stuff like the government makes in them nuc-yuh-ler thingamajigs, but the ploot vein I'm workin' assays out at six hundred dollars a ton. Not enough make a man filthy rich, but it keeps beans and taters on the table."

Amazing. "Well, I'm sorry to keep you from your plutonium mine, Pops—but this whole area is off limits." Aristotle pointed to where the prospector had come from. "You'll have to backtrack."

Backtrack my ass. The aged man dropped the rope; the mule took this opportunity to taste a sweet bit of spring herbage at the path's edge. Pinky moved close to the stocky man who blocked his way. So close that Aristotle could smell the sickeningly sweet scent of the chewing tobacco. Pinky gummed his wad thoughtfully. "Nope."

"What?"

"It's a free country, soot-face. Don't think I'll go back."

Aristotle was unprepared for such obstinate behavior. "Listen, old-timer—you don't have any choice in the matter. I . . ." He paused. And for an excellent reason.

The old geezer was grinning, displaying a mouthful of toothless gums. "You feel something under your crotch?"

Aristotle's voice was a harsh, froglike croak. "Yes, sir . . . I do."

"Know what it is?"

Aristotle nodded his curly head.

"This ain't some pissant foldin' knife, sonny—this here's a genuine Arkansas toothpick, fired in a Pine Bluff forge. Blade's a good fourteen inches long . . . and sharp as a Birmin'ham barber's best straight razor." He lifted the heavy blade a half inch.

To compensate, Aristotle was compelled to raise his bootheels off the sandy ground. By precisely one-half inch. "Look, mister—you don't know who you're messing with . . ."

"You're not FBI, are you, sonny? You're not near smart enough."

Aristotle swallowed hard. "Well . . . no, I'm not. Not exactly." He remembered Cassidy's instructions. "But I'm with the *government*."

This produced a barkish laugh. "Which one—the North Vietnamese?"

Under the circumstances, Aristotle thought it might be imprudent to mention the fact that the north and south portions of that unfortunate nation had been ruled by a single dictatorship for more than two decades. No point in irritating a senior citizen. Especially this old lunatic.

The elderly man shook his head sorrowfully. "Seems like nobody minds lyin' nowadays." He squinted at his victim through bleary eyes. "So what'll I do with you . . . slit you from asshole to Adam's apple?"

Aristotle jerked his head backward. "I got buddies backin' me up. They're heavily armed. You harm one hair on my head, they'll make hamburger outta you."

"It ain't your *head* you got to worry about," Pinky reminded his victim. And wiggled the tip of the blade.

Aristotle got the point.

Pinky winked. "So what kinda no-good *are* you up to—somethin' to do with drugs?"

The commando muttered through clenched teeth, "If you back off right now, I'll ask my buddies to hold their fire."

"Now there's the problem with lyin', sonny—you lose your credibility. I don't believe nothin' you say. Even my mule don't believe you—do you, Blacky?" The animal twitched its long ears and snorted.

Cassidy was watching the encounter through his night-vision optics. Aristotle seemed to be having a friendly chat with the intruder. But he was certainly taking his time.

The old prospector thought about it. *This here doodle-brain sure don't work for the government. Even those melon-headed sons of bitches has their standards.* Most likely, this one was involved in drug smuggling or claim-jumping or cattle rustling. All hanging offenses, and rightly so. But the long knife was getting heavy, and Pinky had bad arthritis in his wrist. And though this fella was a liar, Doodle-Brain might be telling the truth about having some buddies. So it'd be best to do some backtracking. *But not without something for my trouble.* "You got a wallet on ye?"

Surprised by this question, Aristotle nodded. *So he wants to see some ID.* But everything with Aristotle's name on it was back in base camp, sealed in a plastic sandwich bag.

"Where?"

"Hip pocket." The wallet, though stripped of credit cards and driver's license, did contain a bundle of bank notes.

"Get it. Slow and easy."

"No way. You can go straight to—"

Pinky lifted the Bowie knife a quarter inch.

Aristotle obligingly made himself a quarter inch taller.

The commander squinted at the green images on the infrared viewer. Aristotle was standing on his tiptoes—and he was showing the civilian his wallet. *What the hell is going on out there?*

Aristotle's ankles and insteps were beginning to throb.

Pinky—whose right hand was occupied with the Arkansas toothpick—used his left to inspect the wallet. There was a bunch of folding money, but there was not enough light to make out the denominations. "Here's the deal, Special Agent Dodo. I'll let you go for . . . a wad of these greenbacks."

"Take 'em, you damned old thief." *Please, God—don't let him see my side arm, or he'll take that too.*

Cassidy adjusted the focus on his IR viewer. *Well, I'll be . . .*

* * *

Aristotle marched briskly back to meet the commander. The remainder of the team had withdrawn discreetly into the shadows.

Cassidy spoke softly. "You got rid of him. Good work."

"Sure." Aristotle was perspiring. "No sweat."

"You weren't too rough on that civilian, were you?"

He managed a sneer. "Had to push the old fossil around a bit. But I didn't leave no marks on him."

"Why did you have your wallet out?"

Aristotle swallowed hard and thought quickly. "Well . . . he was a poor old soul. Didn't own a thing but what he wore on his back and what that swayback old mule could carry. So I . . . ah . . . let him have a few bucks." It wasn't a really coal-black lie. Sort of gray. Dark gray.

Cassidy patted him on the back. "I'm proud of you." The barest hint of a smile crossed the commander's face. "I'd say you . . . *stood tall* out there."

Despite the delay caused by the unexpected arrival of the elderly prospector, A and B teams met at the predetermined location within seven minutes of the prescribed time.

The clouds had parted, allowing a sliver of moon to spray a diffuse light over a stark landscape of gaunt trees and sandstone boulders. The stream that had sculpted the canyon slithered over shining rocks like a gleaming serpent. Under the bows of a leaning willow was an oval shallow where the waters were not troubled; it reflected moonlight like a pool of mercury. The men huddled at the rim of this silver puddle.

"Where's the target?" a black-faced man asked.

Cassidy pointed uphill, to a stand of aged ponderosas. "It was spotted up there by the cliff. In one of the trees."

The youngest trooper jammed a magazine into his M-16. *Click-clack*.

"Keep that strapped to your back." Cassidy looked up-slope. "It'll be of no use up there." He explained the nature of the target.

The men—who always had something to say about anything—were stunned speechless.

Cassidy fixed a filter to his flashlight, then directed a dull red beam onto a pile of gear assembled near a mossy granite boulder. "Okay, let's do it."

The student was squinting at her text, painfully pondering the mystery of linear differential equations. There were several ways to approach a solution, but Yolly Cassias preferred the series-expansion method. It seemed so sensible, compared to— The dispatcher's thoughts were interrupted by a burst of static, instantly followed by the familiar call. "Aspen Blue to Firewatch Base."

Yolly turned away from her homework assignment. She pulled the old-fashioned pedestal microphone close to her mouth and pressed the Transmit button on the base. "Aspen Blue . . . this is Firewatch Base." Blue's hourly check-in call was almost fifteen minutes early. "What's up?" Only Blue and Yellow were flying tonight. There was always the possibility of lightning-induced fires, but the forest was good and wet. Once things got powder-dry, she would be handling at least four fixed-wing craft and a couple of helicopters.

"This is Blue." There was a throaty background rumble from the twin Cessna's engines. "I got an initial sighting. Not large—must've been caused by a lightning strike. Looks to be near . . . uh . . . the Finger Ridges. I'm going to peel off to the east and get me a bearing."

Yolly assumed the professional monotone. "Ten-four, Aspen Blue. I'll alert the crew. When do you estimate you'll have a location?"

"Ahhh . . . maybe five or six minutes."

"Roger that. Firewatch Base signing off."

Suddenly, the pilot's voice had an edge. "Hey. My sighting is—is—"

"Say again?"

Silence.

The dispatcher tried again. "Come in, Aspen Blue. Repeat last transmission."

The pilot dispensed with formalities. "Yolly—this ain't no damn forest fire. I never saw . . ." Static smothered the pilot's voice.

She pressed the black Transmit button so hard that the delicate pink tissue under her thumbnail turned blood-red. "Aspen Blue, you are breaking up. Please repeat."

". . . somethin' down there is . . . spittin' fire."

"Spitting *what*?"

Silence.

She closed her eyes, as if this would pull the pilot's voice to her. "Aspen Blue, please repeat transmission."

"Base . . . this is Aspen Blue. I no longer have a sighting."

"The fire's gone out?"

"Base, I repeat—I no longer have a sighting. Ahhh . . . please ignore previous transmissions."

"Roger that, Aspen Blue." The dispatcher pushed the microphone away. And should have been content to return to her study of mathematics. Instead, she turned to the south window of the dimly lit forest-service cabin, pushed her hands deep into the coarse coverall pockets. She stared toward where the Finger Ridges lay like fat, sleeping snakes. Nothing out there but inky darkness . . . forever and forever. *Or maybe something moved about in the darkness.* The young woman felt a clammy coldness slip over her shoulders . . . prickle her skin.

11

IGNACIO, COLORADO

CHARLIE MOON WAS heading south along Goddard Avenue when the radio crackled static. This burst of noise was immediately followed by Nancy Beyal's staccato voice. In machine-gun fashion, she fired a short burst of four words: "Chief. This is Dispatch."

Who else? He held the microphone by his chin and used his left hand to steer the blunt nose of the Blazer along the wet street. "I'm not chief yet."

"Hey—it's as good as done. Gonna be a tribal council meeting on Friday. First item on the agenda is naming the new chief of police. Betting in the station has you sixteen to one over the Northern Cheyenne military cop."

"Odds are tempting. I might want a piece of that."

"You'd bet against yourself?"

"Sure, if the stakes were high enough—and then pull my application."

"Don't even joke about it—I got twenty bucks riding on this."

249

"For me or against me?"

She fired a single shot. "Guess."

"I guess . . . that placing wagers while on duty is strictly prohibited. Pass the word around. If the staff wants to gamble, tell 'em to go to the casino—on their own time—and donate their money to the tribe."

"They won't like that, Charlie." She laughed. "You'll drop to . . . maybe ten to one."

He didn't have time for all this gab. "So what'd you want?"

"You've got a summons."

"A what?"

"Tribal chairman wants to see you in her office."

"When?"

"Five minutes ago."

Betty Flintcorn was getting to be a nuisance, demanding his presence at every whim. Then Moon recalled that he did have an appointment with her. He had agreed to show up at ten sharp this morning. To discuss, as the chairman had put it: *your progress in the matter of what is generally known around Ignacio as the Grandmother Spider Rampage.* He glanced at his wristwatch. Seven minutes after ten. "Nancy?"

"I'm still here."

"Tell the chairman that I'll be running a little late and—" He was interrupted by a nerve-jangling alarm from the cellular phone in his jacket pocket. "Hold on, Nancy. I got a call on another line." It would probably be Betty Flintcorn dialing him directly. He could imagine the chairman, hunched over the great desk, gnashing her little teeth over being kept waiting by a mere policeman. He did a quick juggling act that ended up with the radio microphone cord draped over his shoulder, the small black telephone pushed against his ear. Moon prepared himself for the tribal chairman's complaints.

Maybe he'd tell her he was responding to an invitation to a bank robbery. Would she like to come? Then again, maybe not. Betty had about as much a sense of humor as a brass doorknob. "Hello. Moon here."

"Charlie. It's Scott."

Moon took a deep breath. "Thank God."

"What—you been trying to contact me?"

"No. I'll explain it later, pardner. What's up?"

"I'm still getting three or four giant-spider sightings every day."

Moon smiled at his grainy reflection in the sand-blasted windshield. "Glad to hear they're dropping off."

"I got one you'll want to hear about. This old prospector, Pinky Packer, just got back to town. Three days ago, he had some kind of peculiar run-in at the mouth of Hip Pocket Canyon."

"Where's that?"

"It's bordered on the south by Third Finger Ridge. Which is about two or three miles north of First Finger Ridge."

"That's not too far from where that lawyer was decapitated," Moon said.

"And where we found your Mr. Tonompicket up a tree."

"Tell me about it."

"Pinky says he ran into a guy in camouflage fatigues—talked like a Marine drill sergeant and had charcoal smudged on his face. And from how Pinky describes it, the guy may have been wearing night-vision IR equipment on his helmet. This soldier told Pinky to take a walk. And to forget where he'd been."

"Could be an out-of-season elk hunter."

"That's what I figured. But Pinky claims he took Blacky—"

The Ute frowned. "Who's Blacky?"

"Pinky's mule. Anyway, Pinky tied up Blacky about a quarter mile away in a scrub oak grove, and snuck back. He swears there was at least a half-dozen guys. Some were armed with automatic weapons. And they had a couple of chain saws."

"Did you say chain saws?"

"You heard me right. And some equipment Pinky couldn't identify for sure. High-pressure cylinders with hoses and hand-operated nozzles."

"Chain saws. Fire extinguishers. Sound like firefighters. But with automatic weapons." Moon laughed. "Firefighters with an attitude."

"Whatever. Anyway, they marched off into Hip Pocket Canyon, single file. Very military, according to Pinky."

"Sounds like we'd better go have a look."

"I've already got a couple of horses in a trailer. Meet me at Mining City."

"Be there in forty-five minutes." Moon pocketed the cell phone. He grabbed the microphone and pressed the Transmit button. "SUPD. Moon here."

Nancy Beyal answered immediately. "Go ahead, Charlie."

"Tell Betty Flintcorn I can't make the meeting. Something has come up."

"So what excuse do I give the chairman for you not showing?" Nancy Beyal had been through this more times than she could remember. Moon always had some trumped-up reason for avoiding meetings with tribal officials.

"Tell her I had to leave town on an emergency."

The dispatcher's tone made it clear she didn't buy a word of this. "What kind of emergency—an early lunch at the Strater?"

He thought about it. "Tell her I'm hot on the trail of Grandmother Spider."

Charlie Moon rode the larger of the chestnuts. It was a deep-chested horse, with a pounding gait that rattled the Ute policeman's spine. Moon was happy to rein the animal in as they approached the mouth of the canyon. He got off stiffly and led his mount along a deer trail. The sandy ground was still moist from a recent rain.

Parris—who was behind his friend—stayed on his mount and waited for the Ute to make some comment on the tracks. For a hundred yards they had followed prints of Pinky Packer's rubber overshoes and the mule's large, iron-shod hooves. Now there was a junction of prints. Where Pinky had backtracked along the trail with his pack mule, then veered off to the southwest. Moon paused and shaded his eyes from the afternoon sun. There was a patch of scrub oak up against a mottled-gray sandstone outcropping. That must have been where the old prospector had tied his mule.

Farther along, they found a spot where Pinky's trail, meeting toe-to-toe with deep-heeled boot prints, had stopped. It looked like both men had rocked back and forth. Like they were deciding what to do. Fight or retreat. In the end, they had both retreated.

The lawmen continued along the trail until it entered Hip Pocket Canyon. Moon squatted, peering at additional prints. And several odd indentations in the wet sand. Some were hard to figure. One was not. It had been made by the butt of an uncushioned rifle stock. An M-16, Moon thought. He squatted, drawing zigzags in the sandy soil with a dry stick. "Well, pardner—a first-year Cub Scout could read these prints. And they're consistent with the old man's story. Looks like about half a dozen men." He raised his head to frown at the canyon's open mouth. "They milled around some while they were unpacking their gear. Then headed into the canyon." He followed the deer trail for a dozen paces. And whistled. "Now this is peculiar. Six guys go into the canyon. Twice as many come out again. Then they all leave together."

The *matukach* got off his mount and stretched his back. "Maybe they had horses tied up somewhere."

Moon stared at the wide prints. These men weren't booted for riding horses. "When they left, they were headed toward another box canyon. If they were walking out or had horses tied somewhere, they would've taken the same trail we came in on." The Ute looked to the south, where the tracks were headed. "But there's no way out down there. Not unless you're a bird."

Parris shook his head. "You think these guys had helicopters? That's a very expensive way to travel, Charlie. It'd make this . . . pretty serious business." Maybe . . . *government business.*

Moon looked warily up the canyon. Even in the early afternoon, it was a place of deep shadows.

It was a long walk along the narrow deer trail, which paralleled a deep, rocky streambed where silt-yellowed water cascaded over a series of waterfalls. The north slope, exposed to eons of frost-sun-frost cycles, had slowly eroded into a crumbling assembly of boulders. The south wall was almost vertical in places, but there were recurrent humps of talus where spruce and pine grew thickly.

It was late in the afternoon when they arrived at a wide place in the trail. The stream was making its way through a shallow meadow where there was a shimmering pool. Moon tied his horse to a willow and knelt to have a closer look at prints that were now in the cool shadow of the towering wall.

Parris secured his own horse to a piñon branch and looked over his friend's shoulder. "What've we got?"

"This is where the two bunches of guys met up. The up-canyon group must've started somewhere up there"—he pointed to the east—"on the mesa."

"So they meet here. Then walk out again." Parris took a long swallow from his canteen, then wiped his mouth with his sleeve. "Charlie, I think I owe you an apology. This is beginning to smell like a snipe hunt."

The Ute didn't respond. The ground was stony here, so prints of man or beast were not so obvious. Charlie Moon was bothered by something that didn't fit. The needles under a leaning pine were strewn in an oddly uniform pattern. And along narrow tracks, they were aligned. As if someone had used a branch to sweep them about. To cover up something . . . tracks, maybe? He headed along an almost invisible trail toward the south wall. The Ute paused. And sniffed the sweet mountain air. Something hung on the freshness. An odor that was out of place.

Scott Parris stood bemused, watching his friend. Charlie Moon was determined to find something. Well, let him get it out of his system. But there would be nothing here.

Moon's tall form disappeared among a thick stand of scrub oak. Within a minute, Parris heard the Ute's deep voice. "Up here."

The white man made his way through the trees until he found the Ute. "What is it?"

Moon pointed toward the cliff. "There."

The lawmen approached what had been a tall ponderosa. The tree had been burned to a cinder. Only stubs of limbs remained along the charred trunk. At its base was a scattering of black ashes.

Parris stared at the sooty corpse. "What do you figure . . . lightning strike?"

Moon kicked at the ashes. "This wasn't done by lightning."

"What, then?"

Moon chuckled. "You know what my aunt Daisy would say?" This being a rhetorical sort of question, he did not wait for an answer. "She'd say these dozen guys came into the canyon to find Grandmother Spider. They found her—chased her up this tree. Then maybe they burned it."

"Sort of like a Tennessee 'coon hunt," Parris said vacantly.

"Yeah." Moon's eyes had a faraway look. "Sort of."

"So what happened to the elderly spider-woman?"

"I don't see no burned spider parts lying around. So it looks like she got away."

"Away where?"

"According to my aunt, Grandma Spider would have headed back south. To her cave under Navajo Lake."

Parris entertained geographical thoughts. "That'd take the—whatever it was—back across the reservation."

Moon nodded. "A long walk, even for a critter with eight long legs." He allowed himself a thin smile and glanced toward the small creek, where their mounts were secured. The big chestnut was pawing and snorting nervously. "All that exercise, Grandma Spider'd work up a big appetite. She'd need a good-sized meal to fill her belly. Like a horse." He glanced at his friend. "Or maybe . . . a man."

Scott Parris knew his friend well, and was accustomed to the teasing. Charlie Moon was determined to believe that all mysteries—no matter how inexplicable the evidence—must have ordinary explanations. And surely they were in no danger. But Parris was comforted by weight of the short-nosed .38 holstered under his left arm.

Moon knew his friend as well. This *matukach*—despite the paleness of his skin—was much like Aunt Daisy. Scott had a gift. He could see things that weren't really there. A gift like this should be returned. "What's up, pardner—you feelin' the spookies?"

Parris was staring intently into the gloomy forest of pines . . . where the sun never shines. In the shadows, there was a snapping sound. Then another. Like an elk stepping on dry twigs. Or something else . . .

"Maybe Grandma Spider is still close by," Moon muttered.

Parris had paled pasty-white. "I don't think so."

"Me neither." But the Ute glanced longingly toward his horse, where a .30–.30 carbine was sheathed.

There was another snapping sound. Not quite as loud . . . maybe farther away.

"Charlie . . . what if there *is* something out there we don't understand?" *Something really big. And really bad.*

Moon patted his friend on the back. "Don't worry about it, pardner. This Grandmother Spider stuff—it's just an old woman's story."

Sarah Frank was in her bed. The little girl was also in *Cañon del Espíritu* . . . quite alone, walking along in a nightmare. In her dark dream, the vast canyon was even larger than in her waking life, where it was very large indeed. In this night vision, the sandstone walls towered out of sight into swirling clouds. The small stream that watered the canyon floor was a rushing river. In it floated all sorts of horrid things. Hideous insects, legs jerking, wings flopping. Rotting carcasses of large animals, throbbing entrails visible through ivory-white rib cages.

She ran downhill . . . toward the sunny mouth of the

canyon. Aunt Daisy would be waiting there . . . and Aunt Daisy would protect her no matter what. Maybe Charlie Moon would be there too.

At the end of the canyon, there was something waiting for the child.

Not the old woman.

Nor the tall, dark policeman.

It was not a human.

It was—of course—the gigantic spider. Mouth gaping wide, curved fangs raised with hungry anticipation. Legs quivering like dry reeds . . . clickety . . . clackety . . . ready to spring.

Daisy was on her feet a moment before she was even half awake. She heard the child's screams; the old woman moved as fast as she could toward the trailer's end bedroom.

Sarah, comforted by the strength of Daisy's arm, buried herself in the old woman's bosom and sobbed.

The Ute elder rocked back and forth, as if the nine-year-old girl were a small baby. "Hush . . . hush . . . you're all right."

"Sh-sh . . . she's coming back."

"Who?"

"Grandmother Spider."

Poor little thing. "It was just a bad dream. You ate too much of that green chili right before you went to bed. And sweet pickles. And leftover pizza. I warned you."

"It was her. Sh-she was about to grab me . . . eat me up!"

Daisy realized that it was to be a long night. So the Ute elder sat with the child and talked and talked. About all the scary dreams she'd had when she was a little girl. About how it was bad to eat the wrong kind of food right before you went to bed. Pickles were especially bad. And pizza was invented by Christopher Columbus for one diabolical purpose—to kill Indians. No matter how much Sarah might beg, Daisy promised, she would buy no more of that Italian junk food. She talked incessantly—until Sarah's eyes finally closed. She pulled the covers up to the child's chin and wondered: *Who'll take care of you when I'm gone?*

Daisy went back to her bedroom. But the weary old woman did not immediately get into bed. Not until she got the double-barreled twelve-gauge out of the closet. She broke it down and loaded two shells into the chambers. But not with bird shot. Or even buckshot. This time the artillery piece was loaded with grape-sized slugs. This accomplished, she got into bed. And took the shotgun with her.

Grandmother Spider will not come to my home. But if she does . . .

At the first gray hint of dawn, the shaman's eyes were still open. Staring at the ceiling. Where a tiny red spider was weaving a most delicate web . . .

THE UTE ELDER and the slender, dark-haired girl strolled along. The black cat followed the child, but not without making several interesting detours to sniff at rodent holes or chase fat gray crickets. The trio followed the crest of a long, narrow ridge that stretched out from the fat rump of Three Sisters Mesa, then curved sharply at the tip. The early Spanish settlers had called this feature the cougar's tail, and the name had stuck.

From this height they could see well into the entrance to *Cañon del Espíritu* on the north . . . and into Snake Canyon on the south. The slit of *Cañon del Serpiente* was narrower and darker than the broad, bright thoroughfare preferred by the departed spirits. In the mouth of the serpentine canyon, there was a narrow stone monolith that stood upright . . . like a great incisor. On the pinnacle of this projection was a small basin—a cavity in the tooth. For eons, it had been an occasional watering place for owl and raven. In more recent times—which is to say during the past ten millennia—the shallow concavity in the stone had also served as an altar for fresh blood.

Even at noonday—should they find themselves within the confines of its shadowy walls—Snake Canyon is not a place where sensible folk would tarry long. Here the deer hunter takes his prey near the mouth of the canyon and is away well before dusk. Like most of the older Utes, Daisy Perika flatly avoids setting foot in the place. Even the *pitukupf*—and the dwarf is certainly not a timid soul—prefers to make his home in the Canyon of the Spirits.

And so the Ute elder and the Ute-Papago child kept themselves high on the ridge, bathed alike in diffuse morning sunlight. They were well away from the serpent's hungry mouth, the stone tooth that beckoned only to impale.

Sarah Frank was pleased to be invited on this wonderful trek with her guardian, who had come to gather the tender herbs of spring. Daisy used the tip of her oak walking stick to pry up the roots; the child carried a small cotton pillowcase wherein the prized medicinals were stored. They exchanged few words on these walks. Partly because there was little to say. And also because walking used most of the old woman's wind; little was left to be spent on speech.

And so along the ridge they went, the bent woman leaning forward on her stick, pointing here or there at a small plant to be gathered by the child. Mr. Zig-Zag, happy to be out-of-doors, purred like a well-tuned motor. It was a happy, wholesome outing. Thus far.

And then Mr. Zig-Zag paused, one paw raised as if quick-frozen. The purring ceased. Black fur stood up on the feline's neck . . . and the cat hissed at something unseen.

The shaman, who was straining her old eyes to see velvety green shoots along the flinty ridge, also paused. Something had stirred in the gray mists down there . . .

near the great stone tooth. She cocked her head inquisitively, and squinted. Yes. Something was there. Not a coyote or a fox. Too small to be deer or elk . . . and certainly not a mountain lion (thank God!) or a black bear. This was something that stood upright, like a man. But it was not quite a man. It was, she thought, something that had once been a man.

Unaware of the specter, Sarah Frank noticed something just behind a cluster of prickly pear cactus. A short cluster of green leaves protruding from the sandy soil; there was even a hint of purple blossom, though this was still wrapped in a transparent film. In spite of the old woman's detailed instructions, all these new plants still looked much the same to the child's unpracticed eye. She pointed the toe of her shoe at the herb. "Aunt Daisy—is this anything?"

There was no answer.

The child turned her gaze first to the aged woman's wrinkled face, then to the statue-cat. Next she looked downhill, toward where the cat and the shaman were staring so intensely. Sarah saw nothing all that interesting in the misty breath flowing from the mouth of Snake Canyon. So she looked all that much harder. And strained her very considerable imagination.

Well . . . there was a *little* something.

It seemed that a hollow pillar of nothingness parted the fog. This nothingness was about the size of a grown-up person. And it looked a little bit like a man. *Oh my.*

Now it was moving up the slope toward them. Slowly at first, like driftwood floating on a stagnant stream. Then more rapidly. Now much faster than any human could close the distance.

The black cat bolted with a shrill yowl, retreating in the general direction of the old woman's trailer home.

Sarah instinctively moved behind her protector. She

dropped the cotton pillowcase and held tightly on to Daisy Perika's skirt. For additional protection, she closed her eyes.

"Aaaaaiii!" Daisy shouted. The shaman raised her right hand, palm held outward to repel this brazen thing that dared come so near in the light of day.

The approach slowed. Daisy stamped her foot, raising a small puff of yellow dust.

Sarah heard the shaman bark a Ute word: *Turusi-kway*. Stop moving.

Sarah opened one eye to have a peek. The Whatever-It-Was stopped. Close enough to spit on.

Daisy rattled off a few more Ute phrases, but so rapidly that Sarah could not understand. It seemed that the thing also did not understand, because the shaman tried a few words in Spanish. Then switched to English. "Who are you?" There was a brief pause while Daisy Perika listened. Then she took a deep breath and raised her walking stick in a menacing fashion. "What do you want with me?" Again she listened.

Sarah opened both eyes, and looked around the old woman. She saw Nothing. Nothing was an empty void in space. The breeze did not blow dust through it. You couldn't actually *see* it—but neither could you see *through* it. The awful Nothing was real, like a fence post or a tree . . . or a person.

After a long silence, Sarah was startled when the old woman spoke again.

"You don't belong here." Daisy pointed the oak rod toward the broad, sunny entrance of the greater canyon. "Go rest in *Cañon del Espíritu*—that's where you belong. And wait there . . . someone will come for you."

Sarah tugged urgently at the skirt. "Aunt Daisy—what *is* it?"

The Ute elder seemed unaware of the child's presence.

She listened, shaking her head, then grunted. "Okay . . .
I promise—I'll tell him. But he won't believe me. Never
does." She shook the stick again. "Now vamoose! And
don't come back to see me again . . . not in this condition. You're an awful sight—ugliest thing I ever saw."

———•

Sarah was sitting on the porch, watching the fluffy mid-
day clouds gather. They were spread like umbrellas over
the squat forms of the three Pueblo sisters who sat forever on the mesa top. It must be awfully lonely to sit up
there, the child thought. Day after long day . . . nobody
to talk to.

A red-tailed hawk, floating on a rising plume of warm
air, circled serenely above the smallest of the sisters.

The little girl heard the familiar hum of the V-8 engine in the distance, the creaking and groaning of
protesting springs and rusty joints. After months of
sharing the Ute elder's isolated home, the child could
now easily distinguish the sound of Charlie Moon's big
black police car from Gorman's red truck and Father
Raes' black sedan and Louise-Marie LaForte's old rat-
tletrap. Sarah decided that she wouldn't tell Daisy
Perika that her nephew was coming. That way, she'd
have Charlie to herself for a little while, at least before
he went inside to find out what was cooking for lunch.
That'd give her time to ask him some really important
questions. And tell him some of the secret stuff she'd
been thinking about.

Moon rolled to a stop, shifted to Park, and cut the ignition. It was a pleasantly warm day; the little girl was
standing in the shade of a juniper. As he slammed the
Blazer door, Sarah came to meet him. Mr. Zig-Zag

trailed indolently behind the child, taking no notice of the visitor.

The policeman tipped his black hat. "Hello, sunshine."

She looked shyly at his boots. "Hi."

Moon glanced toward the trailer. His aunt evidently hadn't heard him arrive. "How's the old grouch doin'?"

Sarah rocked back and forth on skinny legs. "She's okay, I guess."

"And how're you?"

The child shrugged.

He squatted, to level his face with hers. "No scary things coming by at night?"

Sarah seemed embarrassed by the query.

He reached out and gave her braid a yank.

It was what those dumb-head boys at school liked to do—but Sarah managed to smile so Charlie wouldn't know how much she hated it.

"So should we go inside and see what's cookin' for lunch?"

"Aunt Daisy's in a really bad mood."

"What's set her off this time?"

"Oh, just stuff." Sarah scooped up Mr. Zig-Zag, hugging him to her chest. "She says the only reason you come out here is for her to slave away at the stove and cook you a free meal. And I think she worries about me eating so much. Food costs an awful lot."

"Don't worry about that old fussbudget—you eat as much as you want." The tribe was providing Daisy with more than enough financial aid to support the child. But she was bound to worry about something.

Sarah didn't think it right to mention what had happened on the ridge this morning. Anyway, she wasn't too sure what *had* happened. She took his hand. "Charlie?"

"Yeah?"

"I heard on the television—about those men."

"What men?"

"You know. Those two men that the giant spider ran off with—"

"Listen, runt, there's no such thing as a—"

"—and put one up in a tree and the other one got away. The TV woman said they were both put in a hospital, but that one—the white man—had disappeared in the middle of the night. When it was real stormy. You know what I think?"

"I never know what you think."

"I think Grandmother Spider came and got that man. And she'll come back to that hospital again . . . and get Mr. Tonompicket."

He tried to smile. Didn't quite pull it off. "Now why would she do that?"

"Same reason she grabbed him in the first place."

"Which is?"

Sarah avoided his gaze. "Aunt Daisy says Grandmother Spider comes out every so often and grabs a cow or a deer . . . or a person. Sometimes she'll leave what she catches in a tree till she finishes hunting. But she always comes back. And takes whatever she's caught away . . . to eat it. She's already got the *matukach*—and she'll come back for Mr. Tonompicket."

"Well, I don't know about the white man, but nobody—not even Grandmother Spider—would take more than one bite outta Tommy. He's all skinny and dried up—tough as old saddle leather."

She looked up at the policeman with enormous dark eyes. "Charlie?"

"Yeah?"

"I'm not a child anymore. So don't humor me."

"Okay."

"Promise? Cross your heart and hope to . . ." Her words trailed off.

He solemnly drew a large X across his chest. "I promise. From now on, I'll treat you like you were really old. Say . . . twelve."

That produced a smile from the nine-year-old. "Sixteen."

"You got it."

She squeezed his hand. "Okay."

"And I guarantee you—no spider nabbed that white man. I figure he got up in the middle of the night, put on his clothes, and walked away. He'll show up in a couple of days."

Sarah seemed a little bit relieved. "I hope so."

Moon's thoughts turned to matters of more immediate concern. Food. And who would prepare it. "So if the old biddy won't cook for us, what'll we do—eat bugs and worms?"

"I been thinking about that. You could drive us to Ignacio for lunch."

"Well, *there's* a notion."

"To a nice restaurant."

"Any place in particular?"

"Aunt Daisy likes Angel's Cafe."

"You got it, sunshine."

"Charlie—"

"Uh-huh?"

"Please don't call me sunshine. Or runt. It is so *lame*."

He tried not to grin. "So what'll I call you?"

"Sarah."

"Well. I'd never have thought of that."

When Moon entered the kitchen, the Ute elder was busy at the propane stove. Stirring the pot.

The Ute policeman removed his dusty black Stetson, tossed it on the table. "Hello, my favorite aunt."

"Hmmmpf," she said. And stirred all the harder.

"It's a fine day. Bluebirds singing. Wildflowers blooming. Bumblebees bumbling. Little old ladies stirring about." He winked at Sarah. She giggled.

"I know what you want," Daisy said gruffly. "Me to cook you a meal."

"Actually, what I had in mind was . . ."

She turned on him, waving a heavy cedar spoon. "A free meal—that's all you ever think about. Only reason you ever come out here is so I can sweat myself to death over a hot stove cookin' up posole and beans and eggs and gravy and biscuits—just so you can stuff your big face!"

"Well . . ."

"Don't you think I got nothing better to do than cook for you? You're getting more like Gorman Sweetwater every day. Must be in the blood."

"I thought Gorman was your favorite cousin."

"Sleep and eat, that's all you men want to do." She shook the spoon under his nose. "Except for chasing young women."

"I didn't know you objected to me chasin' . . ."

"Chasing don't get the job done." She turned her back on her nephew, jamming the spoon into a steaming pot. "You have to *catch* one. And settle down. Have some children."

"Thing is, I thought maybe you and Sarah might like to go into town."

Daisy looked over her shoulder. "For what?"

"For lunch. At Angel's."

She turned around slowly, fixing him with a beady-eyed stare. "You got a real mean streak, Charlie Moon."

"What . . ."

"Don't *what* me, you big jughead. You wait till I've got a big pot of pinto beans cooked, another pot of potatoes boiling. And after I've already thawed out a big slab of ham—"

"But I just got here and didn't know . . ."

Daisy looked upward for a heavenly witness. "He waits till I've got the meal practically finished, and *then* he says he'll take me into town for a meal."

"But I didn't have no way of knowing . . ."

She raised the spoon over her shoulder; great drops of thick brown pinto soup splatted on the cracked linoleum. "I ought to whack you right across the head."

"Okay." He sat down at the small table. "Forget about going to Ignacio. We'll eat here."

She was already turning the burners off. "Oh, you'd like that, wouldn't you? Get a poor old woman's hopes up for a fine meal in town—and then let her down. And how do you think the little child feels—she's been wanting to go to town as much as I have. Sarah, get some of them little plastic bowls with the tops. We'll put all these eats into the refrigerator, have 'em for supper." She waddled across the kitchen toward her bedroom. "Now where did I put my summer coat?"

On the drive to Ignacio, Daisy Perika stared without expression at the passing landscape. The Ute elder was silently recalling her many years in this lonesome land between the Pinos and the Piedra . . . wondering how many she had left.

Sarah Frank, who sat between the policeman and his aunt, was not so silent. Happy to be with Charlie Moon, she chatted on and on about many things that were of considerable interest to a nine-year-old girl.

Moon listened to the child's seemingly endless accounts of exciting conversations she'd had with her friends at school. Mostly about the mysterious disappearance of those two men from the shore of Navajo Lake. To divert her from this subject, Moon inquired about what she was learning at school.

"Oh, lots of stuff. Arithmetic. History. Biology. And geology . . . I think that's my favorite subject."

"And what're you learning about geology?"

"Caves. And how they're formed."

They passed over Devil Creek. "So tell me about caves," Moon said.

She did. About how rainwater percolated down from the surface to dissolve minerals like limestone. And once a cavern was formed, how water dripped off the ceiling to form stalactites. And dropped onto the floor to make stalagmites. These formations were usually made of either calcite or aragonite. This process took a very long time, she explained. Millions and millions of years. There were also underground rivers that were completely dark. The child told of strange creatures that moved in their murky depths.

What sort of creatures?

Well, blind salamanders, for one thing. And there were eyeless albino catfish.

Blind white catfish, Moon thought. *Interesting.* And there was something else the child had said about that dark underground world that rattled around in his mind. Something that might be important . . . though he didn't know why.

Angel Martinez hovered nervously over his customers. "We're kinda short of help today, so I'll wait on you myself."

Charlie Moon looked around the crowded restaurant. "Where's Esmerelda Sanchez?"

A dark scowl passed over Angel's round face. "She ran off with a guy. Down to New Mexico, I hear."

"No kidding. Anybody I know?"

"I expect so." He shot an accusing look at Moon. "You brought him here. Told me Esmerelda ought to wait on him."

The Ute policeman was stunned by this news. *Surely not Pizinski's brother-in-law.* "You mean Kenny Bright—that rich businessman from Albuquerque?"

"That's the one." His lips pursed in an expression of distaste. "He's old enough to be her daddy."

"If he's got tubs of money," Daisy said, "she won't mind all that much. What's the specials?"

"Chicken-fried steak with brown gravy and two vegetables. Blue-corn enchilada plate. Deep-fried catfish." Angel leaned forward to smile upon the little girl. "What'll you have, sweetie?"

Sarah pointed to a grease spot on the menu. "Cheeseburger. And a Pepsi."

Angel made a notation on his order pad. "And you, Mrs. Perika?"

"Don't rush me. I'm still looking."

"Sure, you take your time. How about you, Charlie?"

Moon still couldn't believe it. "Esmerelda Sanchez . . . ?"

"Sorry," Angel said dryly, "we're already out of that dish."

"And Kenny Bright. Ain't that something?"

"How about a double chicken-fried steak?"

Moon sighed. "I'll have the catfish. Fries. Coffee."

Angel made another notation on the pad. "I'll be back in a jiffy."

"Hey," Daisy said, "what about me?"

The proprietor forced a weary smile. "You ready now?"

"Sure." Daisy stared at the menu over her bifocals. For another full minute.

Angel's ballpoint was poised, the perfunctory smile painfully frozen on his face. "What'll it be?"

"I can't decide."

"How about the enchilada plate? It's delicious."

"Mexican food gives me gas." She flipped the menu aside. "Just bring me a grilled cheese. Glass of milk."

"Yes, ma'am." Angel hurried away before she could change her mind.

Moon was exchanging a smile with the little girl. "Well, there's nothing like a great meal at a fine restaurant."

"Oh, I don't know," Daisy said glumly. "I'd rather have home cooking, where I *know* what I'm eating. In these places"—she aimed a suspicious look at Angel's back—"you never know what they'll drop in the pot."

"That's right," Moon said. "Like maybe . . . a prickly porcupine."

"Or prairie dog puppies," the child chimed in.

"Alley cat ears," Moon said.

Sarah grinned. "Gopher snake eyes."

"Polecat tail," he countered.

"Spotted skunk tongue!"

"That don't count," the policeman protested mildly. "A polecat and a skunk are the same animal."

"Road kill guts," she yelled.

At a nearby table, a sedate family of tourists paused in their meal. The mother of the clan raised a thinly plucked brow and shot a full dose of the Evil Eye at the Ute and his party. It was highly effective.

"I guess we'd better keep our voices down," Moon whispered. He cupped his hand by his mouth and whispered, "Armadillo liver."

"Coyote kidneys," Sarah whispered back. She put her hand over her mouth and snickered.

"You two are such children," Daisy snapped. "Embarrasses me to be seen in public with you." The old woman rubbed her stomach. "I hope that sandwich don't give me the constipation. I still remember the last time I ate some of Angel's cheese. Next day, it was like trying to pass a brick."

Following the meal—which was greatly enjoyed by man and child—Sarah Frank asked to be excused. This request was granted. After the little girl had left for the ladies' room, Daisy Perika inhaled a deep breath and gave her nephew a warning look. "I've got something important to tell you. And I don't want to hear none of your smart remarks. I already know you think I'm a crazy old crackpot."

He sawed off a sizable bite from a thick triangle of cherry pie. "I never think of you as old."

She took a nibble at the cold cheese sandwich. And waited for her nephew to do the respectful thing.

Moon knew he was supposed to coax her to tell her tale. So he didn't. "This is good pie."

Hateful man. "Me and Sarah was out walking this morning. Up on the ridge above Snake Canyon."

"Nice morning for a stroll." He waved to Angel for a refill on the coffee.

The old woman held her tongue until the proprietor of the establishment had finished this duty and hurried away to take an order from a cranky truck driver. "While we was up there, I saw something."

Naturally. "What'd you see?" Not that he needed to ask. It was always the same thing.

"A ghost."

Bingo. "What kind of ghost?" They came in various shapes and forms.

She thought about this. "At first, I couldn't tell. Then

it kinda took on shape . . . and color. It was a man. A *matukach*."

Moon dropped six sugar cubes into the coffee. She often had conversations with the old man who had owned the Ignacio hardware store forty years ago. That was about how long he'd been on the other side of the River. "This *matukach* . . . anybody we know?"

"Nobody I know. But he knows you."

He took a long, satisfying swallow of sweet, black coffee. And wished he'd ordered ice cream with the cherry pie. Well, it wasn't too late. "This white man give you a name?"

She shook her head.

"What'd he look like?"

"He was naked as the day he was born, and all wet. And awfully bloated. Like he'd been drowned. One of his arms was almost torn off. Hanging by a little shred of meat."

At this—and with much scraping of chairs—the family of tourists withdrew from the adjacent table.

Moon pretended to consider the description. "Don't think I know anybody who looks like that. Bloated. Goes around naked. Arm hanging by a thread. No, that'd be kinda hard to forget." He sawed off another man-sized bite of cherry pie.

"And he had a funny little beard. Sort of reddish. And great big ears, like wide-open doors on a pickup truck."

The forkload of pie slowed in its trajectory toward Moon's mouth. When she was visiting Tommy Tonompicket at the hospital, Aunt Daisy must've gotten a look at William Pizinski. Sure. The *matukach* was in the room right next door to Tommy. Now she'd had a bad dream about him.

"And he had a big crack in his head." She put her finger on the center of her forehead. "Right about here."

Moon returned the pie to the plate. And stared at the remaining dessert without seeing it. "This . . . uh . . . ghost. He say anything?"

She nodded. "He wanted me to tell you that he didn't run away from the hospital."

Moon's mouth went sandpaper-dry. But she must've heard about Pizinski disappearing from Snyder Memorial. *Even if she's not making this tale up, her mind is playing tricks on her.* "Well, if this naked, bloated haunt drops by your place again, you tell him to get in touch with me. He could drop by the station." *That'd sure create a sensation. Empty the place in about ten seconds.*

The shaman's black eyes sparked fire. "Some dark night, Charlie Moon, a troubled spirit is gonna come calling on *you*. Then we'll see if you make jokes."

Moon considered this. "I don't want any unexpected visitors showing up at night. If this ghost wants to chat with me after dark—it'd be better if he phoned." He paused and looked thoughtful. "If he can come up with the spare change for long-distance charges."

"Don't mock me, you big jughead. Or you might get what you're asking for."

Moon looked over her graying head at the glass case on the counter. "You want some dessert? Angel's cook bakes the best pies this side of kingdom come."

Without as much as a glance at the tempting pastries, she turned up her nose. "They look stale to me."

"They put some fresh ones in there just a minute ago. Bet they're still warm from the oven."

Daisy shook her head and sighed. "There's lime Jell-O in the refrigerator. I'll have some of that when I get home."

———•———

Two miles north of Ignacio, on the rocky banks of the
Pinos, there is a dwelling that is considered quite peculiar by most of Charlie Moon's tribesmen.

It is round.

The modern Utes—whose great-grandparents lived in
teepees—now take it as self-evident that homes should
be rectangular in shape. The creeping influence of the
Bureau of Indian Affairs is an insidious thing.

The center of Moon's ceiling is supported by a massive
pine post. From the top of this hub, hand-peeled logs ra-
diate to support the conical roof. The effect is like a
great wheel on the end of a sturdy axle emerging from
the earth. On the western arc of this circular cabin, under a broad window that looks over the river, there is a
nine-foot bed, custom-made by its tallish owner.

On this berth the policeman sleeps tonight, eyes darting rapidly under the lids, his mind seeing that which is to
be perceived in dreams. Before him is an ever-changing
vista of sandstone mesas . . . cloud-shrouded peaks
where waist-deep snows are not yet melted . . . a roaring chocolate-brown river that rolls and crashes its way
under drooping red willow boughs. Now he sees his
aunt; she shakes a spoon at him. In the bowl of the
spoon there is a small, dark dot . . . a black bean? It
grows . . . sprouts eight spindly legs . . . dances happily
on the spoon . . . grows still larger. And larger. The old
woman throws back her wrinkled head and laughs.
"See, Charlie Moon—I told you so!"

The spider is now huge.

Sarah Frank appears; she shrieks at the sight of the
horrible creature. The spider advances on the child,
deftly weaving a web around her until she is enclosed in
a fuzzy cocoon. As the creature now scuttles away with
Sarah, Daisy chases behind with the cedar spoon,
screaming lewd Ute curses. Moon also tries to run—to

rescue the child. But his legs are impossibly heavy. The policeman reaches for the revolver . . . withdraws the pistol from its holster . . . hears a rude, jangling noise. The firearm is transmuted into a useless object; Moon holds a rectangular plastic object in his hand.

Someone speaks to him. "Mr. Moon?"

"Ahh . . . hello . . . who's there?"

The woman's voice comes from very far away. "Long distance. Please hold for your party."

The dream dissipates like a fog on a sunny morning.

Charlie Moon untangled himself from the sheets and swung his legs over the side of the bed. *Peculiar nightmare.* But there is, indeed, a telephone in his hand. He pressed the instrument to his ear. Listened. Except for a low hiss of static, there was nothing to hear. "Hello," he muttered sleepily. "Anybody there?"

He heard a clicking sound, followed shortly by a flash of lightning through the window over his bed. So that was it. The storm must have knocked out the telephone line. He was about to hang up when he heard the familiar voice.

"There are waves on the lake . . . it's stormy. Raining some. We're just sitting here in the pickup, me and this Indian. Having us a few beers—"

Moon thought he recognized the voice. "Dr. Pizinski? Is that you?"

"—and then the moon comes up—like it was comin' right out of the water. You can't actually see it real clear because of all the clouds and mist. The Indian, he says it's not the moon at all. Says it's not the right time for it to come up . . ." There was another clicking sound. From the window, a flash of lightning.

"Dr. Pizinski . . . where are you calling from?"

". . . and he says that Indians know about that kinda stuff. So we just have another beer and . . ."

As the disembodied voice droned on, the Ute policeman didn't bother to interrupt. He switched on a lamp by his bed, pulled a thick blanket over his shoulders, and listened to the extraordinary tale unfold. It took less than three minutes for William Pizinski, Ph.D., to give an account of his misadventures.

"That's about it—all I can remember." There was a long, sleepy sigh.

Moon tried again. "Dr. Pizinski, listen carefully. This is Officer Moon, Southern Ute Police Department. Where are you . . . are you okay?"

The only response was another click in his ear.

"Where are you calling from?" There was a crackling sound, several clicks, then a dial tone. He punched out a string of familiar numbers. There were four rings before the night dispatcher answered in a lazy West Texas drawl. "SUPD—how can I help you?"

So Officer Patch has graveyard dispatch tonight. "This is Moon."

Patch was instantly alert. "Yes, sir. What's up?"

"Just had a call at my home. Long distance, I think. Put a trace on it."

"Right. Hold on."

Moon pressed the Speaker button on the telephone, then slipped into his shirt and jeans. He was pulling on his boots when the dispatcher's voice crackled out of the instrument. "Charlie?"

"I'm here. You make the trace?"

"Tried to. But the thunderstorm's got the phone company's computers all bollixed up. Right now, they can't find a record of your incoming call. Said I should get back to them later, maybe they'll be able to tell us something after they've had time to clean up some of their software data problems."

He stifled a yawn. "Okay."

"Long as you're already awake, there's another thing you'll want to know. State police down in New Mexico pulled a body out of Navajo Lake today. It was in pretty bad shape, but they were able to lift some prints off one hand."

Moon felt a sudden chill. "Why just one hand?"

The dispatcher hesitated. "Poor bastard—they said one arm was . . . well . . . ripped off. Body must've gotten battered somewhere upstream from the lake. Those rivers are runnin' awful fast."

The coldness was settling slowly on Moon's shoulders like a heavy yoke of glacial ice. But it *couldn't* be . . . His voice came out in a hoarse whisper: "They have an ID yet?"

"Roger that. Just got it over the wire about thirty minutes ago. Knew you'd be interested, but I didn't want to wake you up." There was a pause. "You know how you hate to be woke up in the middle of the night."

Patch is a chatty fellow—never uses two words when two dozen will do the job just as well. There was an edge to Moon's voice. "So don't keep me in suspense— who'd they pull outta the lake?"

"That guy who disappeared from the hospital up at Granite Creek." The dispatcher sounded mildly hurt. "You know—William Pizinski."

Moon sat down on the bed. Staring at the shadows moving just outside the yellow cone of lamplight. It was flat-out impossible. *Dead men do not make phone calls.*

"Sir . . . you there?"

Moon nodded dumbly.

"Charlie—can you hear me?"

"I hear you."

"So . . . anything else I can do for you?"

"No." Moon rubbed his eyes. "You've done enough."

SOME TIME LATE in June, when most of the snow had melted, the roaring stream would revert to its normally sedate self—a shallow mountain creek, meandering over a hard path of shining stones. There would be a few deep holes where the larger trout lurked, but there would also be shallows in Granite Creek where a man could wade across without getting water over the top of his boots.

But now—a few yards below where the silent man waited—the swollen river rumbled along under the Annex balcony, scattering hundred-pound boulders along its slippery bottom. It was almost forty feet across, ten feet deep. So much water, moving so fast . . . a force of nature to be taken seriously. Drop a good-sized horse in these roiling waves, it would be swallowed up within seconds—its broken carcass spat up somewhere downstream in Granite Creek. A smaller creature—if it didn't get caught on a snag—might make it all the way to the Piedra . . . or even farther.

Matilda Snyder lay in her hospital bed and listened intently. For her, the voices of the waters were like a gathering of restless souls groaning . . . dead ancestors whispering dark secrets of deeds darker still.

Charlie Moon was on the Annex balcony. For him, the waters laughed and called. *Get on board . . . get on board. There's always room for one more.* Ten thousand cars coupled to a smoke-puffing locomotive, rolling relentlessly through the night. Heading toward some distant depot . . . some uncertain destiny.

The policeman ignored the tempting invitation.

Moon—his heavy boots propped on the steel banister—sat on a metallic chair that was evidently designed to remind its occupant that this earthly existence is one of unremitting pain. Occasionally shifting his weight in a futile attempt to relieve the aches, he waited patiently in the darkness. It occurred to him—not for the first time—that much of police work is a matter of waiting. Waiting for crucial information to surface . . . for an inconclusive report from a befuddled medical examiner. Or for a dozen pages of incomprehensible technobabble from some distant forensics laboratory. Most of all, waiting for an undeserved piece of luck.

Tonight he waited for a murderer. He estimated the odds of success as less than fifty-fifty. How much less was a depressing thought, so he didn't think about it.

He looked toward where the sky must surely be. There wasn't much up there a man could see. Like being under a deep puddle of ink. Now and again a patch of stars sparkled briefly through the blackness. Heavy, thunder-grumbling clouds were slipping eastward off the San Juans. There was a scattered sprinkle of lights on the mountain slopes where a few recluses occupied cabins in the pine forests. And beneath him was the eternal stream. A fan-shaped portion of the noisy river reflected a feathery glow of yellow light from a first-floor window under the balcony. *Somebody else must be working late. But they're inside. All snug and warm.* A cold drizzle began to descend from the upper darkness. Moon buttoned the black raincoat around his chin, pulled the equally black Stetson down over his forehead.

And waited.

He heard the nurse fussing about Tommy Tonompicket's bed; then the light went out in the Ute patient's room. Within seconds, a lamp was switched on next door in Matilda Snyder's room. The nurse raised her voice so the old woman could hear. "You should be in bed by now, Mattie. Why don't we turn the TV off . . ."

There was an unintelligible but belligerent reply from the old woman.

"Well, have it your way, then."

The lamp in Matilda's room was extinguished with an audible click.

The nurse naturally didn't bother to enter the room William Pizinski had recently occupied.

Minutes crawled by like snails on a long, pointless journey. The rain continued steadily. Moon's feet grew cold. The policeman noticed a bluish flicker of late-night television from Mattie Snyder's room. The old woman probably didn't get half the sleep she needed. And so the drowsy policeman felt a strange kinship with the poor, demented soul. *A man who'd sit out here all night—and for not a dollar of extra pay—must be a little bit demented too.* Presently, he noticed something odd—the river had fallen quiet. Like maybe it was tired from running so hard all day and needed rest. *Stay frosty, fella. You're getting sleepy.* He went through the multiplication tables up to twelve times twelve equals one hundred and forty-four . . . a grossly correct calculation.

There was a distant flash of lightning, a quick electric kiss between white-hot clouds passing in the night. Nevermore to meet again.

Maybe this stakeout is a dumb idea.

The policeman stretched his limbs. *A cup of coffee would be just the thing.* He hadn't brought a thermos, because of that immutable law. You took fluid in, it eventually had to get out. But in spite of this admirable bit of self-denial, his bladder was protesting.

Maybe if I took a break for just three minutes . . .

Though the rain had slacked off, it had not quite stopped. Water dripped slowly, one clinging drop at a time. Off the left side of his hat brim. Onto his shoulder. Plop . . . plop . . . plop. He recalled Sarah Frank's geology lesson. And could almost hear the little girl explaining how rainwater seeped down from the earth's surface to drip off the ceilings of dark caverns for millions of years to make stalactites. And stalagmites. But he didn't intend to sit here quite long enough for pointy formations to appear on his hat brim and shoulder.

A shaft of moonlight penetrated the rolling clouds, illuminating the stark landscape of night. And other formerly hidden things.

Of course . . . that's how it must have happened.

The policeman was interrupted from his thoughts by a hint of movement . . . no more than a wrinkle in the fabric of darkness. *I'm probably just seeing spooks in the shadows.*

But this was not a product of his imagination.

There was a distinct clicking sound at the French windows on Tonompicket's room. A dark form—wrapped in a blanket from the hospital bed—stepped onto the balcony . . . into the moonlight.

Moon watched the man fumble with a package of cigarettes. There was a snapping sound, then a small flame. He touched fire to the tip of a white cylinder, then inhaled deeply. Tonompicket leaned over the steel banister and happily sighed a fog of smoke over the roiling river.

The Ute policeman kept his place in the uncomfortable metal chair. "Hello, Tommy."

Tonompicket's bent frame straightened as if pricked by a cattle prod. He turned, squinted into the darkness. "Charlie Moon . . . that you?"

The words came back from the darkness. "You've made an amazing recovery."

It dawned on Tonompicket that he was in an awkward situation. "Yeah—I feel lots better." He barked a mirthless laugh. "Musta been your aunt's smoke treatment that fixed me up."

Moon's Cheshire grin flashed in the darkness. "She's always said that Navajo tobacco was powerful medicine. But it must be habit-forming. You just had to have another smoke. And another."

Tonompicket stared at the blackness that cloaked his fellow tribesman. "What're you doin' out here?" *Spying on me?*

Moon leaned forward in the chair. "Now that's the wrong question, Tommy. The right question is . . . what are *you* doing out here? You're supposed to be a pretty sick fellow. Don't even know where you are . . . not able to talk to anybody. Can't even get out of bed. But here you are . . . out on the balcony puffin' on a cigarette. And you seem to be pretty spry. I figured you'd wait another week or so before you decided to get well."

"What d'you mean—*decided*?"

"If I was a suspicious man, I'd figure you was up to no good. And I am. So I do."

Tonompicket turned away. "What's on your mind?"

Moon had been sitting in the cold rain far too long to mince words. "Pizinski's dead. You killed him."

Tonompicket's hand trembled as he pressed the cigarette to his lips. "I didn't even know the man. Why would I want to—to do that?" He inhaled the fragrant smoke.

"We both know why, Tommy."

The blanketed man glanced down the balcony at the dim light in Matilda Snyder's room. "Who you been talking to . . . that crazy old white woman? You can't believe nothin' she says."

"Mrs. Snyder didn't accuse you."

"Then why're you thinkin' bad things about me?"

"Lots of reasons. First of all, you've been pretending to be a basket case."

"You can't prove that."

"After Pizinski was reported missing, me and my pardner checked your room. Your cigarettes weren't in the drawer with the other stuff you'd had in your pockets when you were admitted to the hospital. I figured you'd stashed 'em somewhere—under your mattress, most likely—so your wife wouldn't take 'em away."

"My cigarettes was gone—that's all?"

"There was more."

Tonompicket pulled the blanket tightly around his shoulders. "Like what?"

"Like you'd been dropping your butts off the balcony. Most of 'em probably went into the river. But at least one of 'em ended up on the bank."

"I'm not the only person around here with a nicotine habit."

"Not many folks smoke Juarez Golds. And the butt was found just below where you're standing now."

The thin man snickered. "So I'm a litterbug. String me up and hang me."

"All in good time."

"Cigarette butts don't prove I did nothing to the *matukach*. Anyway, why would I want to hurt him?"

"You want to tell me?"

"Why should I help you?" Tonompicket snapped his fingers at the lawman. "You don't know diddly-squat."

"I know all about your adventure that night on the lakeshore. How things went from fairly bad to downright awful. I even know why you played possum in the hospital for days—pretending to be barely alive. You were making plans, Tommy."

It seemed an eternity before Tonompicket spoke. "You don't know nothin' about nothin'."

"I know how you ended up miles to the north of the lakeshore . . . where that lawyer was killed."

"There's no way you could know nothin'. You wasn't there."

"Pizinski was."

The smaller man turned his head to stare at the dark spot where Moon's voice came from. "You sayin' *he* talked to you?"

"Sure he did. Pizinski told me what happened that night when you showed up at his truck. You asked for a beer. And ended up drinking half a dozen. He told me everything that happened after that. You've been up to no good, Tommy. And two men are dead." Moon, who knew his man, waited for the inevitable response.

"Lissen, Charlie, it wasn't my fault—it was that damn *matukach*." Tonompicket shook his head; the burning cigarette tip traced thin red ovals in front of his face. "I should of known better than to trust that big-eared, hairy-faced bastard. He got me all boozed up and . . ." His voice trailed off uncertainly.

For no particular reason, Moon was feeling reckless. And lucky. "I already know what happened. I'm not much interested in hearing you tell me a pack of lies."

Tonompicket turned his back on the stream, leaned his slender thighs against the metal railing. "You know what that mean-assed white man did?"

"Sure I do." Moon pressed his luck. "And I know what you did that night Pizinski vanished. After the nurse had made her rounds, you went out on the balcony for a smoke. But like all those other times, you were careful. You didn't want to take any chance Miss Mulligan might come back and find your bed empty. So you went along the balcony to those big windows behind the nurse's desk."

Tonompicket turned his head to gaze toward the bay window, where filtered light spilled out onto the redwood planks.

"She wasn't there. So, knowing her habits, you went to the next set of windows and had another peek. Sure enough, there she was in the visitors' lounge, watching television. And the thunder was loud enough to cover any noise you might make. It was just what you'd been waiting for—the perfect chance to get even with the *matukach*. So you slipped into Pizinski's room through the glass doors. Did what you'd been planning to do."

"You're blowin' smoke . . ."

"You were pretty clever, Tommy. Clever enough to realize that it'd be better if everybody thought Pizinski had got up in the middle of the night, put on his duds, and walked away. So after you got rid of the corpse, you also got rid of his clothes. And his boots. But you forgot to do something before you disposed of the body. Something important."

The thin man's face was a question mark in the moonlight.

"It was his hospital gown, Tommy—just like the one you're wearing under that blanket. When we searched his room the next morning, it was missing. Now, Pizinski wouldn't have had any need for a hospital gown if he'd gotten dressed. So he must have still been wearing it when you got rid of the body."

Tonompicket shrugged. "So—his hospital gown wasn't in his room. That don't prove it was *me* that dumped his sorry carcass into the river."

Moon, who hadn't been absolutely sure of Tonompicket's guilt up to this point, sighed. "Tommy, I never said anything about Pizinski's body being pushed into the river."

Damn. "Nothing I've said can be used in court." He added confidently: "You're some sorry kind of cop—ain't even read me my rights."

"You want me to Mirandize you?"

"No. Then you could use whatever I said to put me in jail. What do you think I am—dumb as a rock?"

Moon diplomatically evaded this question. "Pizinski was a heavier man than you, Tommy. He must've put up a fight. It's a wonder you didn't end up in the river with him."

Tonompicket nudged his big toe against one of the terra-cotta flowerpots. "I'm not saying I did anything to him, see? But if I'd wanted to, I coulda took one of these big rocks outta this pot, gone into his room. Bopped him on the head two or three times. Not enough to make him bleed, just enough to take all the fight outta him." He smiled crookedly. "Not that I'm saying I did."

"Sounds like an effective plan," the policeman murmured. *Also like premeditated murder.*

"Then I coulda threw the rock into the river after him—if I *had* killed him. Then—like you said—I coulda thrown his clothes in after him. I could've gone back into my room and got in bed—for the best night's sleep I've had in weeks." The unrepentant assassin took the cigarette from his mouth. Looked at the pale cylinder, then stuffed it back between his lips and took a long drag. "If I *had* killed him, that mean-assed bastard would've got what he deserved. Eye for an eye, that's what I say."

Moon looked across the stream toward the hunched shoulders of the San Juans, shrouded in a billow of rolling clouds. "Old Testament justice always sounds pretty good when we want to get even. But that blade's got two edges, Tommy—and it cuts deep."

Tonompicket spent some time thinking it over. One particular thing didn't make sense. He tapped the cigarette on the steel banister. A spray of fine sparks fell toward the frothy stream. "You claim the *matukach* spilled his guts to you . . . when did this happen?"

Moon, who had been waiting for this question, smiled in the darkness. "Last night."

"Bullshit," Tonompicket muttered victoriously, and laughed. "You didn't see that white man last night."

Moon's tone was casual, as if they were discussing the weather. "Never said I'd *seen* him." He allowed time for this unnerving implication to worm its way into Tonompicket's brain. "But I did listen to what he had to say."

"Hah," Tonompicket snorted. "Never trust a cop." He took a long suck on the cigarette; the tip glowed ruby-red. "That *matukach* bastard didn't say nothing to you last night. Couldn't have."

"Couldn't have? Why's that?"

Suddenly sensing the smell of a trap, Tonompicket hesitated.

Moon pushed himself up from the wrought-iron chair. "You know Pizinski wouldn't have been able to talk to me last night . . . because he's been dead for days now—ever since the night you dumped his body in the river. He floated down Granite Creek, into the Piedra, into Navajo Lake. Those are rough waters, Tommy . . . ripped one of his arms off."

The thin man pulled silence around him like a protective garment.

"But what I told you was the truth. I woke up last night and heard his voice. Several days after he'd died." He paused. "Pizinski's voice came from . . . someplace a long way from my cabin." *It had been a long-distance connection.*

Tonompicket shivered under the blanket. "It's bad luck to talk about . . ." He swallowed hard, bobbling his Adam's apple. "About . . . ghosts. I don't like to hear that kind of talk."

"Well, I sure wouldn't want to upset you—you're not looking all that well."

Tonompicket missed the sarcasm. "Last night or two, I've not been feeling very good," he whined. "Been having trouble getting any sleep."

"Imagine that. What's been keeping you awake, Tommy?"

The thin man flicked the spent cigarette over his shoulder, into the stream. "It's that damned white man . . . his *uru-ci.*"

Moon was not surprised. Any Ute familiar with the old ways knew what was bound to happen when you killed a human being. After the unhappy soul had made the obligatory trip to Lower World, his furious *uru-ci* would come back. Tommy would expect Pizinski's spirit to hover over his murderer's resting place at night—moaning, making horrible faces, muttering dark threats—all so his intended victim couldn't get any rest. This ordeal, the elders claimed, went on for several days. The final order of business for Pizinski's vengeful shade would be to kill Tommy. Usually, the *uru-ci* would cause a fatal illness and the guilty person would slowly waste away. But on occasion, the end was more dramatic—the disembodied spirit might even slay its victim with an act of dark magic. There was no point in telling Tommy Tonompicket that he shouldn't be afraid of ghosts. Any traditional Ute worth the salt in his blood knew that a man who did not fear *uru-ci* was a fool. Moon decided to direct his tribesman's attention to a more pressing issue. "What you need to do is get yourself a smart lawyer. Somebody who can get you off with manslaughter."

This produced a derisive snort. "A lawyer won't do me no good. Once the *uru-ci* comes to visit, nothing on earth can save you. Just last night I had this bad dream. The *matukach* stood by my bed. Said he'd come back some night and . . ." Tonompicket paused, turned. Stared at the French windows.

It happened very quickly, before Charlie Moon could get close enough to make any difference in the outcome.

A pale, indistinct form emerged from Tonompicket's darkened room . . . moving purposefully toward the stunned man. There was an unintelligible muttering . . . a long, pale limb reached out. As if grasping for its victim.

Tonompicket threw his arm in front of his face, stumbled backwards. "No . . . no . . . Aaaiiieee!" He tumbled over the iron banister, thin arms flailing at nothingness.

Moon rushed forward, pulling off his raincoat, pitching his hat aside.

The apparition was pounding her walking staff on the balcony floor. "Wahoo—wahoo! Little Beaver has jumped into the river!"

The Ute policeman had pulled off his boots, preparing to leap into the rolling waters. But it was apparent that any attempt at rescue would be a futile gesture. And almost certainly fatal. Though Tonompicket's blanket floated away several yards downstream, there was no sign of the fallen man.

Matilda Snyder tugged anxiously at the policeman's sleeve. "Why'd he do that—was it my fault?"

"No," Moon heard himself say. "He lost his balance." *And for just a second or two . . . so did I. Both of us thought you were Pizinski's ghost.*

"Dammit—all I wanted was to ask him for a smoke." Matilda leaned over the railing. Moon grabbed the old woman's arm to make sure the river didn't claim another victim. She shrieked at the dark waters. "Hey, Little Beaver, don't blame me—being careless is what killed you!" Very gently, Moon eased her away from the railing.

The odd pair stood on the wet balcony, staring at the river. Moon heard something in the sounds of the waters . . . many anxious voices calling to him. Wanting something . . .

More to the point was the old woman's voice. "All I wanted was a smoke."

The Ute policeman estimated that Tommy Tonompicket was already a thousand yards downstream. Dashed against countless boulders. Most of the bones in his lifeless body were already broken like dry sticks. Moon pushed his wet feet into the cold boots, then draped his raincoat over Matilda's thin shoulders. Lastly, he pushed the Stetson down to his ears. He began to shiver; wondered if he'd ever be warm and dry again.

The old woman took a deep breath and repeated her

monotonous plea. "All I wanted was a smoke." Matilda Snyder shook her knob-headed cane at some phantom in her memory. "Here I am—in my own home. It was my family who gave the county the land for this hospital. I even let 'em use my house for the sick people. And now these goody-goody nurses won't let me smoke a cigarette—not even in my own bedroom."

After witnessing a pointless death, Moon found it oddly comforting to engage in small talk. "They don't have any choice, Mrs. Snyder. It's an ordinance."

She shook her head at the injustice of it; a comical mat of wet gray hair clung to her forehead. "It's them nitwits in Denver and Washington, making all these idiotic rules for other people to live by. I say we ought to get rid of all these regulations. And hang all the politicians."

The Ute policeman could think of no satisfactory response.

Her voice crackled with age. "My husband always smoked Kentucky black leaf tobacco in his pipe—and he'd have a big Havana stogie on Sunday afternoons. And he was healthy as an ox till he was killed in the war."

"So he lived to a ripe old age?"

"He was just twenty-four when a mortar hit the trench where he was sleeping. And I smoked whenever I felt like it, and I'm still sound as a dollar in body and mind. I just celebrated my eighty-fourth birthday." She looked puzzled. "Or maybe it was my ninety-fourth. I don't remember for sure. But I've lived to see my only grandchild. He's very smart, so they say. Graduated from Harvard Law School. Far as I'm concerned, he's an overeducated pipsqueak." Matilda looked over the banister, wiping salty tears from bleary eyes. "Poor little

Indian. He was dumb plumb to the marrow, falling in the river when it's running fast. Stupid, stupid man." She turned to blink at Moon. "You don't have any smokes, do you?"

"No, ma'am. Don't use 'em."

"Naturally," she huffed, "it was you redskins that invented tobacco. Got all us whites addicted, but you—oh no—you don't touch the noxious weed yourself."

"I apologize."

"Apologies don't help none."

"Then I'll start smoking first thing tomorrow."

She smiled. "How about whiskey?"

"I think your people invented that."

"No." She rapped her walking stick on the redwood planks. "I mean—do you drink it?"

"Had to give it up." There was an entire year he could not remember. Except for barroom brawls, tripping over his feet, vomiting on his shirt . . . and waking up in some exceedingly strange places.

Matilda Snyder shook her head. How pitiful today's young folk were. Here was a so-called policeman—size of a plow horse—and he didn't smoke tobacco or drink hard liquor. And he was all worked up because some crazy person had drowned himself. What this big fellow needed was a fat stogie between his teeth, a half-pint of Jim Beam in his hip pocket, some river gravel in his craw. She remembered back when Sheriff Bob Wallace had strung up three Nebraska horse thieves with his own hands—and then sat down not six feet from their kicking boots and had his lunch of lamb stew and corn dodgers and rye whiskey whilst them rustlers gasped and turned blue as bullfrogs in a tub of ice. After his meal, he'd lit up a big cigar. Sheriff Wallace enjoyed at least three cigars every day of his life and always had a hot toddy right before bedtime—even if he was in the saddle. After the hanging, there had been no more horse stealing in Granite Creek County for almost five years. Not until well after Sheriff Wallace got poorly from a bout of consumption and liver trouble and double pneumonia. That was when one of the Nebraskan rustlers' kinfolk had slipped into town and shot old Bob six times, right through the back of his wheelchair. Over two hundred folks had come to the sheriff's funeral the next morning, and more than that to the back-shooter's hanging that afternoon. What a glorious time to be alive!

But this big Indian cop would probably feel bad if he ran over a squirrel runnin' across the road. *Well, I've lived too long in this world.* Matilda felt the need of some comfort. She spoke to no one in particular. "What I need is a good smoke. And a double shot of Kentucky bourbon."

"Well," Moon said, "I don't have any bourbon with me." He retrieved Tonompicket's package of Juarez Golds from the balcony deck. "But I guess Tommy wouldn't mind you having these smokes." Poor old woman wasn't long for this world. She might as well have a little pleasure before she crossed that wide, deep river.

Matilda Snyder accepted the unexpected gift with a trembling hand, then ruthlessly ripped the package open. "Dammit," she hissed, "there's only three smokes left."

"Sorry. Guess you'll have to ration yourself."

She looked up at the tall Ute through moist eyes. "Even though you are a wild, uncivilized savage—you are a *nice* man. I take back most of the bad things I've been thinking about you."

"Thank you kindly."

"I can't forgive you *completely*—your tribe did murder my grandmother."

"Yes." He sighed. "I remember. Summer of 1879. Renegades from the White River Agency."

"Aha! Then you *were* there."

"Sure," the Ute policeman said helplessly. "It was probably my arrow that killed your poor grandma."

Matilda pulled a cigarette from the package, sniffed it. "Well, I forgive you—even for that. After all, you were just an ignorant heathen."

DURANGO

CHARLIE MOON STOOD, hat in hand, waiting for the woman behind the counter to turn around. And notice him.

She did. And did. Somewhat startled by the sight of this towering figure, she gasped.

"Excuse me for sneaking up on you." She was old enough to be retired. The watery blue eyes were magnified by thick spectacles, the wispy gray hair thin enough to expose brown spots on her scalp. Incongruously, the elderly lady had a pink blossom stuck over her ear. A plastic badge on her blouse said HELLO I'M DOTTY. And she was.

The dark-skinned man had a gold shield pinned on his shirt pocket. *So. An Indian cop.* "May I help you, sir?"

"Could you send somebody some flowers?"

"That's how I make my living, young man." Dotty smiled lopsidedly, then popped her loose dentures back into place. "What did you have in mind?"

He turned the black Stetson a slow half-rotation. "I don't know much about flowers, so maybe you could give me some pointers."

"They're for a lady?" *These days, you never knew . . .*

"Yeah. A lady."

"A relative . . . or a friend?"

"Friend."

Dotty pried a little harder. "A *special* friend?"

Moon pulled at his collar. "Sorta. Maybe."

Well well well. The clerk decided that she'd just about dipped this bucket dry. "Roses are always nice." *Nice and expensive. And I get a fifteen percent commission.*

"Roses'll do fine."

"How many—a dozen?"

"Sure."

He hadn't asked about price, so he was either well heeled or just plain dumb. She voted for dumb. "What color do you want . . . red? Or a mixture?"

So many decisions. "Mix 'em up."

"And who shall I send them to?"

He gave her a page torn from his notebook.

She looked over her spectacle frames at the policeman. "What do you want on the card?"

"Make it . . . ahh . . . 'Thank You, Charlie Moon.' "

" 'Thank You'?" She grimaced. "How terribly romantic."

He grinned. "It'll get the job done."

After the tall man had departed, she retired to a small office and seated herself at the computer terminal. The clerk had three troublesome characteristics. First, she was a romantic. Second—being certain she knew what was best for her customers—Dotty felt not the least guilt about meddling in their private affairs. Third, Dotty was somewhat . . . dotty.

She stared thoughtfully at the bluish halo around the

computer screen. *What an oaf. But how lucky he was to have come to this shop.* She began to compose the brief message that would be transmitted via satellite, then carefully handwritten on a card by an anonymous scribe. Her ambition was to compose country-western songs that Willie Nelson would use for a big comeback. For some peculiar reason, the fuzzy-faced Texan had never responded to her sterling submissions. Old Willie must still be distracted by those tax problems, she figured. Dotty made her first attempt:

```
       Since you said good-bye,
         I can't sleep a wink.
  All I do is moan and cry-and drink.
```

No. That didn't quite do it. The florist tapped out another bit of doggerel:

```
    I'm all alone and blue
    But roses remind me of you
```

That wasn't too bad. But Dotty knew she could do better. "I must consider the customer's persona," she muttered. "This is a taciturn man. Looks awfully melancholy, like he misses his sweetie something fierce. And he carries a big pistol on his belt." She tapped at the keys:

```
    Can't live without you.
      I'm loadin' my gun.
            Good-bye
```

"Yes. Nice touch of drama." She smiled, typed "Charlie Moon" at the bottom, and pressed the Send key. *That ought to do it.*

Indeed it would. By such careless words, the fates of men and nations oft go askew. And the die was well cast. Electronic bits and bytes zip along at the speed of light—and, once launched, cannot be recalled. In a distant city, the colorful wheels of flowery commerce had already begun to turn.

———•

She decided that it was quiet. Too quiet. The illiterati must be restless tonight . . . up to something sinister. Dancing obscenely around their television sets . . .

"Hi."

The librarian looked up from her desk. And smiled. "Charlie Moon. I didn't know you had time for books."

"Reading is my life," the Ute policeman said earnestly. "And I am urgently in need of the services of a librarian."

"Well, you stumbled into the right place. What can I find for you—a history of some sweet little oasis in the Baltics, a biography of some obscure person, a sizzling Jane Austen novel?"

"What I had in mind was something more . . . practical."

She pointed a leather bookmark at the policeman. "I know—a how-to volume."

He seemed doubtful.

"We have everything from African Art to Zenography. Name your poison."

He leaned on her desk. "What's Zenography?"

"I've no idea—I made it up."

"Shame on you."

She blinked innocently through round spectacles. "We librarians are a whimsical lot."

"So I've heard."

"So what, exactly, do you want?"

"A newspaper."

"Poor thing—you can't afford to buy your very own newspaper?"

He sighed pitifully. "Try living on a policeman's salary."

The librarian smiled slyly. "Is that some sort of . . . proposal?"

———•

FIRST FINGER RIDGE

It was a sweet, mild morning in late spring. The birds knew it. The bees knew it.

Charlie Moon eased the big SUPD Blazer to a creaking stop in front of the dead attorney's cabin. There were yards of broad yellow tape fixed across doors and windows. A stern-looking sign had been nailed on the front door.

CRIME SCENE—DO NOT TRESPASS
Granite Creek Police Department

The Ute policeman sat in the squad car for a long moment, staring at the empty cabin. Once the sign and the tape had been removed, this would be a nice little place again. And most likely it would be on the market. Considering what had happened here, it might go at a bargain price. *It hasn't been that long since . . .* He wondered whether there would be any odor left from the dismembered corpse. Probably not. There was lots of fresh air up here. *Well, might as well get this job done.* He removed a tape measure from the glove compartment and dropped it into his pocket.

This wouldn't take long. And then he'd know for sure.

———•

IGNACIO

Charlie Moon lifted his foot off the accelerator. There it was. Long cobalt-blue Cadillac. Going about fifty in a zone posted at thirty-five. The Ute policeman did a hard U-turn behind the luxury car. New Mexico plates. He flicked the emergency-lights switch.

The chrome-plated vehicle glided slowly, serenely to the curb. Like the *Queen Mary* docking.

Moon ambled up to the Cadillac. Kenny Bright was behind the wheel. The entrepreneur looked up, ready to protest that he was driving a good ten miles an hour under the limit. At the sight of the tall Ute, the bloodhound-jowled face brightened. "Charlie Moon—well, am I glad to see you."

The Ute pushed the black Stetson back a notch. "I'm kinda surprised to see you in Ignacio."

"You shouldn't be. You're part of the reason I'm here."

Moon rested his hands on the luxury car's glistening roof. "Is that a fact?"

Kenny Bright's eyes darted back and forth, as if passing motorists might be bending an ear to overhear their conversation. "Look . . . can we go somewhere and talk?"

"Just what I had in mind."

Moon closed his office door. And turned the latch. He took his hat off and sat down on the edge of his desk.

Bright searched his jacket pocket and found a fresh cigar. "Mind if I enjoy a stogie?"

"Smoke till it comes out your ears."

The heavy-jowled man rolled the wheel on a gold-plated cigarette lighter.

"So what brings you to the tricultural community of Ignacio?"

"Romance."

Moon raised both eyebrows. "Say again?"

Bright inhaled. "I know I'm almost twice her age. And I'm not much to look at. But I'm really fond of that little gal."

The Ute swallowed a grin. "I heard about it . . . Esmerelda Sanchez."

Bright nodded happily. "The very same."

It would be a great loss to the community. "She's Angel's best waitress."

"*Was* his best waitress. You know"—he pointed the cigar at Moon—"Esmerelda's not only good-looking, she's sharp as a tack. And she's almost a college graduate."

"I didn't know that."

Bright nodded. "Sweet little thing majored in accounting at Rocky Mountain Polytechnic. Two more semesters and she's got her sheepskin. I'll find something for her to do in one of my companies. But first things first. We get married next month."

"So soon?"

Kenny Bright waggled the cigar between his fingers. "Women like June marriages. We're gonna tie the knot in Las Vegas—at the Chapel of Everlasting Love. Sixteen dancing girls, cake the size of a fifty-gallon oil drum, parson in a pink tux."

This image boggled the mind. "Sounds like a ceremony she won't forget."

"I always go first-class, Charlie. Hell, I'm spending a tub of money. Thing is, I drove up here to ask you to be my best man. Whatta you say?"

"Well, I'm flattered, but . . ." *Parson in a pink tux . . . ?*

" 'Course, I'll put you up in a suite at the MGM. There'll be a bucket of quarters for the slots. And you'll have a full expense account. Shoot, you ought to clear some serious cash on the deal."

On the other hand, there was no fundamental reason why a parson should be held to a strict dress code. Moon slid off the desk; he sat down heavily in the padded chair. "I'll have to check with my pardner, Scott Parris. I'm supposed to be best man for him—and they haven't quite settled on a date . . ."

"Well, work out whatever you can. If you're not available, I'll have to settle for the junior senator from New Mexico—but he's sort of a sad sack. Thinks weddings should be in churches. So you try real hard, Charlie."

Moon stared at the wall. Esmerelda's departure would be a great loss for Angel. Lots of important stuff happened when you weren't looking.

Bright chomped on the cigar. "You said you had something to talk to me about."

The Ute policeman had almost forgotten. "Oh, yeah."

The businessman leaned forward. "So what is it, my friend?"

Moon got up. And gave Bright a look that would have disturbed a lesser man. "I know what happened to your brother-in-law."

"You mean . . . how he ended up in the lake?"

"Yeah. And more than that—I know how Dr. Pizinski and Tommy Tonompicket left the lakeshore that night.

And ended up miles to the north—by that patent attorney's cabin."

Bright removed the cigar from his mouth and stared at it. "You do . . . really?"

Moon nodded. "And I know how that lawyer died."

The businessman's eyes narrowed; he tapped glowing ash from the cigar into a wastebasket half filled with paper. "Tell me about it."

Moon told him.

It was some time after the Ute finished the tale before Bright found his voice. "That's some wild story, Charlie."

"Sure is. But that's what happened."

"How'd you—"

"Dr. Pizinski told me."

Bright's eyes were hard, like gunmetal-blue ball bearings. "When did he tell you?"

"A few days after he died."

"*After* he died?"

The Ute policeman nodded.

Bright banged the heel of his hand against his temple, as if to rattle his brain back into place. Didn't help. "Excuse me for sayin' so, Charlie—but that don't make no sense."

"It's a strange world we live in."

These Indians are a peculiar bunch. "So what do you intend to do?"

"Haven't quite decided. The FBI is showing some interest in the case."

"Listen, you and me, we can still—"

Moon aimed his finger at Bright's nose. "*You* listen. I kinda like you. But if you offer me a bribe . . ."

Bright raised his hands in a defensive gesture. "Charlie, I know you better than to offer you money."

"Good."

Bright grinned. "Not that I wouldn't if I thought it'd help."

Moon stared at the ceiling. Wondered how much cash he was passing up.

"But listen, I got a fine ranch up by Salida I hardly ever use. You ever need a place to get away—relax for a while—you just say the word. It's a regular Shangri-whatsit. Wildflowers thick as ticks on a dog's back. Bluebirds singing their dumb little heads off. The place is practically crawling with deer and elk. And the fishing is downright incredible."

Fishing?

Bright grinned ear-to-ear. "And it's all on the up-and-up. Letting one of my buddies use the ranch don't break no laws whatsoever."

Moon was surprised to hear himself asking the question: "Fishing's really that good?"

"Best in Colorado. I can almost guarantee you a trophy trout. And it's way out in the boonies—real quiet."

Sounds like Paradise. "I'll keep it in mind."

Bright exhaled a cloud of cigar smoke. "If you should ever find yourself in trouble . . ."

This sounded almost like a threat. "What kind of trouble?"

"Well, it could be almost anything." The entrepreneur winked. "You might wake up some fine morning . . . and staring you right in the eye is this great big hydrophobic wolf. He's licking his slobbering lips—about to put the bite on you. What would you do?"

"Hammer him good," the Ute said. "Nail his fuzzy hide on my door."

Bright rolled the cigar on his tongue. "There is wolves, Charlie . . . and then there is *wolves*. You meet up with the wrong kind, I expect you'd wish you was someplace else."

"Where?"

"My Salida ranch is the perfect place to go and rest for a spell."

"Thanks for the advice. And the offer."

"No matter how things turn out, I want you to be my best man next month. I told you once before when you set me up with that fine meal and introduced me to my future bride—when Kenny Bright is your friend, he's your friend for life. No matter what. Even if you was to put me in jail, why, we'd have the wedding there. You could bring the rings to my cell."

"Rings we could manage. But we couldn't provide you with a fifty-gallon cake. Or dancing girls."

Kenny Bright didn't crack a smile. "This is no joke, Charlie. I'm your friend through thick and thin."

This man was crooked as a ball of snakes. But the Ute found himself oddly moved by Bright's earnest speech.

GRANITE CREEK
FIESTA CAFE

CHARLIE MOON REQUESTED extra napkins for Scott Parris, who—he explained to the waitress—was a messy eater. The pretty Hispanic girl flashed the Ute a shy smile, then hurried away to order blue-corn enchiladas. Moon dropped a quarter in the jukebox terminal in their booth. Punched B4. The ghost of Hank Williams began to wail. The man from Tennessee was exceedingly lonesome. Lonely enough to cry.

Parris waited until the mournful song had played out. "Okay. Talk to me."

Moon was searching his pocket for another two bits. "It happened three nights ago. I was sound asleep—heard the phone ring. Thought it was just one of those peculiar dreams where you wake up thinking you heard something, but it's all in your head. But it wasn't. He just started talkin' into my ear."

Parris watched the waitress deliver a wicker basket of

308

hot sopaipillas. "You want me to ask *who* it was who was talking in your ear."

"It would help move my story along."

"Who?"

"Dr. William Pizinski."

Parris frowned at his friend. "What night was this?"

"Last Tuesday." Moon pushed his spoon handle through a hot sopaipilla, and used this orifice to squirt honey from a plastic bottle into the hollow cavity.

Parris did a quick mental count, then repeated the math on his fingers. "Pizinski couldn't have called you on Tuesday night. He'd already been dead a couple of days."

"Three days. But it was like he didn't know he was dead. He talked and talked. I wasn't able to slip a word in sideways. But there were some funny clicking noises, mostly in between Pizinski's statements. When the call came that night, there was a big thunderstorm. At the time, I thought all the clicks on the phone were from lightning. But most of 'em were where somebody's questions to Pizinski had been removed."

Parris was beginning to get a glimmer. "Tape recording?"

"You betchum."

"But who got Pizinski to talk?"

"Had to be Zoog."

"Why?"

"It was in those investigative reports you faxed me."

The Granite Creek chief of police frowned. "What?"

"Mr. Zoog used to be Dr. Zoog. He was a dentist."

Parris stared thoughtfully at his Ute friend. "You're still sore about that bad root canal you got down in Juarez."

Moon grinned to display a fine set of teeth. "On the contrary, I admire dentists. Especially when my teeth start hurting and I need help right away."

"Then what's so important about Zoog being a dentist?"

"I had Danny Bignight do some more checking. Dr. Zoog was a specialist. Catered to patients who couldn't take the needle."

Scott Parris began to see the dawn breaking. Needles were used to inject anesthetic. "Zoog used hypnosis?"

"That he did."

"So you figure Eddie Zoog, desperate for a monster story, slipped into Pizinski's room that night—and put the bulging-eye, wiggly-finger whammy on him." Parris shook his head doubtfully. "Just to help Pizinski remember what happened that night at the lakeshore."

"He'd never had any trouble remembering. Pizinski didn't want to *tell* anybody what'd happened."

"Then why would he submit to hypnosis?"

"Ever since he got to the hospital, Pizinski was having a hard time catching some z's. Maybe he thought Eddie Zoog was just helping him drift off into dreamland."

"I see you've been reading books again. But go on."

"Well, Eddie Zoog slips into Pizinski's room—"

"How does he accomplish this?"

"Maybe he dressed up in a nurse's uniform. Might've even wore a curly blond wig. Smeared on a little lipstick."

Parris made a face. "Please—not while I'm eating."

"I expect Zoog just waited till after the nurse had made her rounds. The hall lights were out. Wouldn't have been that hard to get into Pizinski's room without being spotted."

"Okay. But once he'd heard Pizinski's tale, why did Zoog and his pretty niece hotfoot it out of town?"

"Eddie Zoog hoped Pizinski had a red-hot monster story to tell. If it'd turned out that way, Zoog would have pursued the matter. But when he learned what'd really happened to Tonompicket and Pizinski, he knew it was likely to involve criminal charges. Too hot to touch. So he got out of town."

"There's a big hole in your theory."

"You're thinking Eddie Zoog wouldn't be public-spirited enough to call me up and play the tape in my ear."

"Astonishing—you have read my mind."

"And you're right as rain, pardner. Zoog wouldn't spit on me if I was on fire. It had to be Camilla. She found out about Uncle Eddie's hypnosis session. And, being a public-spirited citizen, she wanted me to hear what was on the tape."

"So Zoog puts Pizinski in a trance, is appalled at what he hears, leaves town. His niece places a long-distance call to her friend Charlie Moon and plays the tape for him."

"You have a way of boiling things down, pardner."

"But you left out the part about how Eddie Zoog, who is highly dissatisfied with his mesmerized subject's anecdote, murders him."

"Zoog never laid a hand on Pizinski."

"So who did?"

"I was getting to that. See, sometime after Zoog left his room that night, Pizinski is probably having his first good sleep in days. Tommy Tonompicket, who is bedded down next door, pays his former drinking buddy a visit. Bops him on the head, drags him onto the balcony, pitches him into the river."

"Why does he do a thing like that?"

"Tommy is highly annoyed with Pizinski."

"Wouldn't a good punch in the nose have sufficed?"

"Not for Tommy. He had a yen for that old-fashioned kind of justice. Eyeball for eyeball, bicuspid for bicuspid—"

"But what had Pizinski done to deserve—"

"I'm getting to that."

"Before you get to that, convince me it was Eddie Zoog that made the recording. Why not Captain Taylor? It was that OSI cop's job to find out what'd happened to William Pizinski. Maybe she twisted his tail hard enough to make him squeal. And when she found out what'd happened wasn't Air Force business, she called you up and played the tape."

"You really think Special Agent Taylor would go to all that trouble to help us local law-enforcement types?"

"You've got a point."

"I did have my doubts—wanted to be absolutely sure it was Camilla who'd placed the call. So I did something to find out. But I was going to skip that part."

"Why?"

Moon assumed a noble aspect. "Modesty." *And because it went sour.*

"Go ahead, brag about it till you make me nauseous."

"Well, if you have to know—I hatched me a nifty little plan."

Parris rolled his eyes.

"Don't get your eyeballs all out of joint—this was a first-rate plan."

"We both know I can't stop you from telling me, so go on—get it out of your system."

"I sent some flowers to Camilla Willow."

"What a swell guy you are. But no blossoms for Eddie Zoog?"

"Somehow, pardner, it just didn't feel right."

"I'm glad to hear it. But you oughta be careful, Charlie. Giving a woman flowers is a serious business."

"Sure is. Set my SUPD credit card back sixty-five bucks." *Wait'll the auditors see that.*

Parris arched an eyebrow. "So you figure when the pretty blond gal gets the bouquet, she'll be so overwhelmed at your thoughtfulness that she'll just break down and admit that she played Uncle Zoog's Pizinski tape over the phone for you?"

"That wouldn't be much of a plan."

"I won't argue the point."

"I included a thank-you note." Moon looked inordinately proud of himself. "Figured Camilla would understand right away *what* I was thanking her for. Women are curious by nature, pardner. I figured she'd stew for a while, but finally she'd *have* to call me up and find out how I got onto her."

"You're altogether too clever."

"Not clever enough."

"Why this sudden attack of humility?"

"Well, Camilla never called me."

Parris grinned. "Imagine that."

The Ute sighed. "Women are hard to understand."

"So I understand."

"So I figured I'd call her. Tell her straight out how much help she'd been—playing the Pizinski tape over the phone for me."

"So did Miss Willow own up to impersonating a long-distance operator?"

"Never got to talk to her. Camilla's home phone isn't listed, so I rang up the EZ Agency—which was where I'd sent the flowers." Moon looked utterly dejected. "Some days you can't make a dime. The receptionist at EZ Agency wouldn't give me Camilla's phone number— and she said it wouldn't do no good if I had it because Camilla wasn't at home. Gone somewheres and nobody knew when she'd be back. So I asked for Eddie Zoog. Turns out he's gone too. On a business trip to Brazil. Something about a fifteen-foot-tall jungle monster who eats goats whole, including feet, horns, and whiskers. Locals say it's half alligator and seventy-six percent snapping turtle."

"Likely story." Parris nibbled at the corner of a sopaipilla. "Zoog knows you're onto him. And Camilla's laying low because she don't want to implicate her uncle." He suddenly looked hurt. "Once Miss Willow had that tape, why didn't she call me instead of you?"

" 'Cause she likes me better."

"Or figured you'd be more likely than me to believe a dead man could place a long-distance call."

"Camilla might've known Pizinski was missing—it'd been in the papers for a coupla days. But she couldn't have known he was dead. His body had just been fished outta the lake a few hours before I got the phone call. Anyway, everybody knows I'm the sensible one—*you're* the fellow who sees ghosts and goblins. You and Aunt Daisy are peanuts from the same shell."

"Thanks," Parris said. "I needed that."

Moon looked longingly at an hourglass-shaped sopaipilla, and sighed. "Camilla's a fine figure of a woman. Sure like to see her again sometime."

"Don't get your hopes up, Charlie. That one's a big-city gal. Won't come back to these parts ever."

Moon responded to this dose of reality with a distant, melancholy look.

"So what was on the Pizinski tape?"

The Ute stirred his coffee. "Oh, nothing much."

"How much is nothing much?"

"Well . . . just about everything we needed to know."

Parris shook his head in awe. "And it was handed to you on a plate. You are the luckiest policeman I ever heard of."

"I'd rather be lucky than smart, pardner."

"So you got your wish. But tell me about the tape."

"First of all, William Pizinski mentioned some stuff he'd already told us. About how him and Tommy Tonompicket met up at the lakeshore. Sat around in the pickup, had a few beers, talked about lots of stuff. Women. The weather. Money. How peculiar the moon looked that night, coming up over the water. That's what gave Tommy Tonompicket his notion. That and about six cans of beer." The Ute assumed an innocent expression. "But you may not want to find out what actually happened."

Parris played along. "And why wouldn't I?"

"Well—there's no goblins or ghosts or monsters. You might lose all your faith in fairy tales."

"Let me guess." Parris had a sip of iced tea. "Pizinski and Tonompicket get drunk as skunks, tear the hood off the flatbed and throw it amongst the shepherd's flock, hitch a ride to Mining City, hike up First Finger Ridge, knock the lawyer's head off with a two-by-four and sink a pickaxe in his chest several times just to make sure he gets the point. They steal a shotgun—Pizinski shoots Tonompicket in the ass with bird shot and chases him up a tree. Then Pizinski—having completely lost his mind—runs off into the national forest, where he lives on grubs and locusts until he is found by the kindly wood gatherer."

"Pardner, you have a certain flair for telling tales."

"You are too kind. But if you've got a better version, tell me."

"Don' mind if I do. See—it was what Tommy Tonompicket had stashed on the back of his flatbed truck."

"If memory serves me, his rig was loaded with used restaurant equipment."

"When Danny Bignight found Tommy's truck, there was some stoves and refrigerators and stuff under the tarp. But we should've wondered what *wasn't* there. That flatbed was carrying some special cargo when Tommy got to the lakeshore."

"I'm too tired for deep thinking." Parris closed his eyes. "Give me a hint."

"I'll give you several. What folds up in a small package but can get big as a house in ten minutes? Is invisible in the dark, then wakes up spitting fire and roaring like a locomotive—"

"Aha—a portable dragon?"

"—and goes wherever the wind blows. Which, on the evening of April first, was from the south. Which, in case you forgot, is toward the north."

Parris sat straight up. "Shazam! I know what it was—"

Moon chuckled. "Sure. After I practically draw you a picture."

"A hot-air balloon? Fired by a propane flame?"

"But not just an ordinary hot-air rig. This was what balloonists call a 'special shape.' Had eight long legs dangling down."

Parris slammed his palm on the table. "Sure—a spider balloon."

Moon shook his head.

"If it wasn't a spider, then what?"

"Daniel Bignight told me what it looked like the morning after he'd found the abandoned trucks. I thought it was pretty funny—told Daniel he must've seen an octopus."

"Octopus?"

The Ute policeman nodded.

"What on earth would Mr. Tonompicket be doing with a hot-air balloon shaped like an octopus?"

"That's what we should have figured out, pardner. Tommy hauled stuff in his flatbed for Ozzie's Fine Seafood restaurants. Ozzie Octopus is their company logo. Trademark. Mascot. The whole shebang. Tommy had been up to Ozzie Corporation's Denver warehouse, got his truck loaded up for a run down to Albuquerque—where a new restaurant was about to have a grand opening."

"How'd you find all that out?"

"I have my scholarly side."

Parris snickered. "And I'm a concert pianist just back from a recital in Vienna."

"I'll be sure to make your next gig. Anyway, I went to the public library—did some serious research."

"I don't believe it—you actually got on the Internet?"

Moon would not even entertain such a question. "I had a look at the March issues of the *Albuquerque Journal*. There were some interesting advertisements. 'On April Third, Bring the Whole Family to the Grand Opening of Albuquerque's Newest Ozzie's Fine Seafood Restaurant.' There was a picture of the octopus balloon. I phoned the Albuquerque restaurant, asked a few questions. Turns out the balloon hadn't shown up for the grand opening and nobody seemed to know why. Then I rang up the Ozzie Corporation's franchise headquarters in Denver. Got stonewalled. Nobody had time to talk to me. Receptionist said she'd have somebody return my call. I'm still waiting."

"I am favorably impressed with your get-up-and-go."

"It got me where I am today."

"Even so. But I got to hand it to you, pal. The octopus balloon explains why Sarah Frank thought she saw Grandmother Spider dancing by your aunt Daisy's home. But wait a minute—how'd the hood come to be ripped off that truck?"

"Simple," Moon said. "The giant octopus tore it off."

"I've had a long, dreary day," Parris said. "Don't give me heartburn."

"It was supposed to be a tethered flight. Tommy Tonompicket was fairly drunk, but he wasn't an idiot. So he tied the anchor line to his truck. By the way, did I mention that the tie-down cable was made with a new and improved type of Kevlar fiber?"

"No. But do go on."

"Well, if he'd been sober, Tommy might have fastened the tie-line to the truck bumper, or maybe even to the frame. Being half looped, he looped the end of the cable around that steer-horn hood ornament. This was after he'd wrapped the slack around his body—so he could let the balloon up easylike. The inebriated Dr. Pizinski— who was in the gondola—his job was to light up the gas burner and fill the octopus' insides with hot air. Well, things go okay until here comes a big puff of wind off the lake—whooosh! Ozzie Octopus, he leaps off the ground like a scared jackrabbit—jerking poor Tommy right outta his boots."

"And rips the hood off his flatbed truck."

"That's the way it happened, pardner. There they go, Pizinski in the gondola, Tommy Tonompicket caught halfway down in the cable, the truck hood dangling somewhere below him, the octopus legs dancing along the ground. They go right by Danny Bignight's squad car with Tommy yelling bloody murder. Before Danny can get some shots off, they disappear into some low clouds. The hood eventually comes loose and gets dropped on a ridge top, amongst that bunch of sheep. Pizinski was still trying to haul ol' Tommy up and aboard when they come near Aunt Daisy's place. He saw a reflection off the trailer roof, figured this might be a good place to land. He let Tommy dangle long enough to shine a flashlight around some, looking for a nice, flat spot to set down. Daisy, she thought the beam of light was from some kinda alien spacecraft and fired off the old twelve-gauge."

Tough old lady. "Which was unfortunate for Mr. Tonompicket."

Moon thanked the hardworking waitress, who was sliding enchiladas onto their table, warning her customers that the double-stacked plates were very hot. He waited until her departure before continuing. "I expect bird shot in his butt sobered Tommy up pretty quick. It sure got Pizinski's attention. He hit the gas valve to get some altitude, then turned it off so's the balloon wouldn't make such an easy target for the antiaircraft fire. So the wind kept taking our bad boys to the north—toward Mining City. And First Finger Ridge."

"Where the patent attorney has his mountain cabin."

"Now think about it. It's the night of April first." Moon took time to taste the enchilada, which was several notches above merely good. "Weather's been unusually warm for ten days or so. Snow's melting fast. And the lawyer had showed up at his cabin that same day and turned on the gas furnace. Even had himself a nice blaze going in the fireplace. Later on that night, he's sitting at his desk by the front window—and here comes that ugly balloon." Moon moved a salt shaker just above the table-top. "The gondola's hanging low, the octopus' legs are bouncing along the ground . . . 'Well, goodness gracious,' he says, 'this looks like a fine photo opportunity.' "

Parris had forgotten about his enchilada. "So Armitage grabs his camera, rushes out the front door."

"A once-in-a-lifetime chance to catch a whatsit on film," Moon said. "He snaps off three shots. But now the eight-legged thing is stepping right over his cabin."

"So he runs back through the house, out the back door—to take another snapshot."

"But there's a big slab of ice on the back roof. And it's melted underneath from the heat in the house. Ready to slide down into the backyard . . ."

"The gondola hits the cabin roof hard enough to dislodge the big slab of ice. And down it comes. Right at Armitage."

"Takes off his head clean as a whistle."

Parris watched the Ute mount an attack on the enchilada. "But what about those round puncture marks in his chest?"

"I leave it to you."

"You better not tell me that Ozzie Octopus opened his enormous mouth and sank his fangs in the lawyer's torso."

"I'd never kid you, pardner."

"I am gratified to hear this." Parris applied a liberal dash of black pepper to a thick puddle of refried pinto beans. "Gimme a hint."

Fair enough. That's what I got from Sarah's geology lesson. "What hangs on cave ceilings?"

"I dunno . . . bats?"

"What *pointy* things hang on cave ceilings?"

"Unicorn-crested Transylvanian vampire bats?"

"Close. Try again."

"I got it—stalactites."

"That give you any notions?"

Parris stared across the table at his Ute friend. "You don't mean . . . icicles?"

"Pardner, if you ever decide to give up your cushy job as a manager, you might make a fair policeman."

"Your icicle theory is intriguing. In fact, you have a real flair for detection."

"I detect just a hint of doubt."

"Well . . . some proof would be nice."

"How about a highly scientific precision measurement?"

Parris had a taste of the refried beans. *For something that looks like it's been puked on my plate, not half bad.* "What sort of measurement?"

"Think high-energy neutron resonance absorption spectra for detecting trace amounts of rare meteoritic iridium isotopes in the meltwater in the lawyer's chest wounds." Moon had to catch his breath.

Parris didn't bother to look up from his plate. "Think how inadvisable it is to mess with a guy who reads *Scientific American* from cover to cover. And won first place three times running in his high-school science fair."

"Okay. Think . . . cubits, fathoms, and furlongs."

Now Parris did look up. "Your sophisticated instrument was a yardstick?"

"Stainless-steel tape measure. The kind that retracts when you push the plastic button."

"Well, that's entirely different."

"Remember how the medical examiner told us there were some extra, smaller holes in Armitage's chest . . . and all the penetrations were spaced the same distance apart—like teeth on a garden rake?"

"Seven centimeters," Parris said. Gratified that he had remembered the number.

"Which is about two and three-quarters of an inch." Moon drew an illustration on his napkin that looked like an inverted picket fence suspended from a wiggly line. "Icicles hanging off a corrugated metal roof tend to form at regular intervals. That's because the melting water drips off at the low places. So I went up to the lawyer's cabin with my trusty tape measure. Guess what the spacing is between corrugations."

"Two and three-quarter inches."

Moon nodded.

"So the sheet of ice slides off the roof, takes the guy's head off. And as if that wasn't bad enough—icicles bite him in the chest. Poor bastard."

"Some days a man might as well stay in bed."

"I hate to admit it, Charlie, but I am visibly impressed."

"Now how do you reckon Tommy Tonompicket got in the top of that spruce?"

"Well, it's pretty obvious. The balloon hit the treetop, he fell out of the gondola."

"Obvious," Moon agreed, "but that ain't quite the way it happened."

Parris thought about it for a moment. "You don't mean Pizinski *pushed* him out?"

"Oh no."

"What then?"

"He grabbed Tommy by the ankles and kinda flipped him over the side."

"But why would he do a thing like that?"

"The propane gauge was reading Empty. And them Finger Ridges get higher and higher as you head north. Situation was getting serious; Pizinski needed to lighten things up a bit."

"So Tonompicket had become just so much ballast." Parris felt a dark ripple run up his spine. "That was a damn cold thing to do."

"It was. But folks who think they're about to die tend to panic. If Tommy had thought of it first, I imagine he'd have given Pizinski the old heave-ho without batting an eyelash."

"So that's why, when he got his chance, Tonompicket dumped Pizinski into the river."

"Sure," Moon said. "Pizinski had pitched him out of the gondola into a tree."

"And all for nothing. Pizinski throws a man overboard to lighten the load, but he crashes the balloon anyway."

"In Hip Pocket Canyon—just beyond Third Finger Ridge."

"Where Pinky Packer saw the . . . ahh . . . commandos," Parris said.

"And where we found the burned tree."

"So the eight-legged balloon must've got snagged in that pine."

"That's the way Pizinski told it on the tape, pardner. And the next day, the new seafood restaurant in Albuquerque is expecting delivery of their Ozzie Octopus balloon for the grand opening."

"And Tommy Tonompicket—who was supposed to deliver the octopus on his flatbed—don't show."

Moon helped himself to a forkful of Mexican rice. "The chief executives of the Ozzie Corporation must've put things together. Not long after Tonompicket picks up the octopus balloon in Denver, he goes missing. At about the same time"—the Ute wriggled his fingers suggestively over the table—"weird stories started circulating about a giant spider creating havoc in southern Colorado. So whoever's in charge at Ozzie Corp considers the odds. And figures it's best to keep quiet about the firm's missing octopus balloon—maybe things will blow over."

"So to speak."

"It was a smart move. But Kenny Bright—who wanted to know what'd happened to his chief scientist and brother-in-law—shows up at Snyder Memorial to visit his relative by marriage. It turns out that Dr. Pizinski doesn't feel the least bit responsible for this mess. So he tells Bright the whole story, even the little detail about dumping Tommy Tonompicket overboard. It wasn't so much that he was trying to kill Tonompicket as save himself. And it was the Indian's balloon; Pizinski was just an innocent passenger. But Kenny Bright is no dummy. He knows about the dead lawyer and understands right away that Pizinski is up to his ears in wrongful death and maybe a few other odds and ends— all unseemly conduct for the chief scientist of Rocky Mountain Advanced Flight Systems. If the lawyer's survivors find out how he died, they'll not only go after Tonompicket and Ozzie Corporation, they'll also file suit against Pizinski, who—when he helped Tommy launch that ugly balloon—was on official travel for Rocky Mountain Advanced Flight Systems, on behalf of the U.S. Air Force."

"So Bright's high-tech firm is in jeopardy."

"Right. So Kenny Bright has to protect his company. It'd be fairly bad for his business plan if the United States Air Force learns that the contracting company's chief scientist is implicated in the death of the attorney. And worse yet, Pizinski had tried to dispose of a noble Native American truck driver by heavin' him out of the balloon gondola."

"Politically incorrect in the extreme," Parris muttered darkly.

"You said it. Us Indians got pretty popular after we stopped slaughtering land-grabbing settlers."

"So after Bright hears the tale, he orders Pizinski to keep his mouth shut."

"That's the way Pizinski told it on the tape. The amnesia ploy was Kenny Bright's idea. Also, he hopes Tonompicket don't come to his senses and start talking."

"Someone has to destroy the octopus-balloon evidence."

"That's right, pardner. By the time you and me showed up at the hospital and found Bright in Pizinski's room, he'd already learned the general location of the balloon crash site. Now, Kenny Bright is a mover and shaker who don't let any prickly pears grow under his toes. Right away, he contacts the chief executive at Ozzie Corporation. Tells him roughly where to locate the octopus carcass. Advises him to take decisive action to see that it is not found by casual passersby."

"How do you know this?"

"Bright told me."

"Just like that?"

"I have a certain native charm," the Ute said.

"Sure you do."

"Ozzie Corp—now knowing where to find their missing mascot—employs some mercenaries. The hired troopers hike into Hip Pocket Canyon and find the remains of the Ozzie Octopus balloon stuck in a pine tree. They incinerate most of it, carry out any pieces that won't burn. Like the gondola frame, the propane tank and burner. I'm kinda guessing about the details, but that's the way it looks."

Parris was visited by a sobering thought. "So what do we tell the FBI?"

Moon looked up from his plate. "Tell me you're joking."

"I'm serious, Charlie. Withholding evidence in a federal investigation is a criminal offense."

"Withholding what evidence? A telephone call in the night that I can't trace from a man who was already dead?"

"Yeah. I see what you mean. But Bright has confirmed at least some of—"

"Not officially he hasn't. Anyway, I kinda like Kenny Bright. I'd hate to see him get into trouble over something that wasn't his fault."

Parris was suffering an acute attack of conscience. It would pass. "I should at least send the Bureau a copy of those . . . ahh . . . octopus photographs from the lawyer's camera."

Moon thought it best to steer this circular conversation onto a new course. "Did I tell you Kenny Bright is getting married to a nice Ignacio lady—and wants me to be best man?"

"But you're supposed to be *my* best man!"

"Yeah." Moon tried not to look smug. "Looks like I'm very much in demand."

"When is Bright's wedding?"

"Some time in June."

"I hope you didn't make a firm commitment."

"Nah. Told him I've got a previous engagement with you and Anne." Moon winked at his worried friend. "And that you two still can't make up your minds about a date."

Parris snorted. "So Bright makes you his best man and you're protecting him."

"It wasn't Bright's balloon—he's a victim of circumstances."

Parris leaned back in the booth, folded his arms. "Charlie—you know what I'm thinking?"

Moon was looking for the waitress. "About some dessert?"

"I'm thinking you have a real knack for police work."

"I'm seriously thinking about finding another line of work." *Maybe they've got some pecan pie.*

Parris' merry blue eyes peeked out from under the brim of his hat. Charlie Moon was always threatening to quit his job at the Southern Ute Police Department. And he'd want his partner to ask him why he'd ever want to do that. "Why would you ever want to do that?"

"Gettin' tired of the politics." Moon drained the coffee cup. "If it ain't the tribal government yankin' my chain, it's the FBI. Or the BIA cops. And that old SUPD Blazer I'm drivin' is about ready to roll over in a ditch and give up the ghost." He waved at the waitress, who shot back a toothy smile. "Besides, the salary is pitiful."

"Things'll be lots better when you make chief." The Granite Creek chief of police reached for his wallet. "Take my word for it."

The acting SUPD chief nodded. Politics would be the same or worse once he made permanent chief. But the pay would be lots better. *And maybe they'll buy me a new squad car*. With income rolling in from the casino, it wasn't like the tribe was hurting for money.

LA PLATA COUNTY, SOUTHERN UTE RESERVATION

The SUPD Blazer's almost-bald tires hummed serenely along Route 151's black surface. Though the coolness of evening was emerging in the lengthening shadows, the road tar remained warm and sticky from the late-afternoon sun.

They had left Ignacio well behind, passing first over the rushing waters of the Pinos and then Ute Creek. Charlie Moon—like his ancestors—gauged his progress by the streams he crossed. Most were hardly noticeable in the twilight that was being pulled across the valley like a soft blanket . . . from toe to chin. Here and there, the shallow streams slithered under the pines like sinuous reptiles, muscles rippling under iridescent skin, dark scales flashing in the decaying sunlight. Descending the modest slope of Shellhammer Ridge, the SUPD Blazer crossed the Spring Creek bridge. Now the road elbowed south to intersect the smallest of the meandering streams, which was little more than a ditch. This trickle of muddy water was called Devil Creek. The reasons for this name were dark and obscure. And—as tribal elders hinted to curious youth—best not inquired about.

Now the road approached Tiffany and abruptly turned eastward toward Allison, paralleling the old railroad grade. As they crossed the "indefinite" boundary that divided La Plata and Archuleta counties, the blood-red sun settled lazily to its nightly rest. Minutes later, he slowed for Arboles, where hardy settlers had made their homes at the junction of the Piedra and the San Juan. Since the latter flow had been dammed far to the south in New Mexico, these broad river valleys were the northern and eastern tips of Navajo Lake. Where—Moon recalled glumly—barely a month ago, this tangled mess had started. The beginning of the troubles seemed much more distant, telescoped far into the past.

He glanced at his aunt. Her sharp black eyes—reflecting the glow of the dashboard lights—were peering anxiously through the windshield. As if by the strength of her will she could draw automobile and occupants more quickly to her home.

"We'll be there before long," he said.

Daisy Perika seemed not to hear him. Indeed, since they had left Ignacio, the old woman had said not a single word. Nor bothered to express herself with a disgruntled grunt. This in itself was not particularly unusual. Daisy Perika, like most of her people, was economical with words and grunts. It was the ominous character of the elder's silence that made her nephew uneasy. She was like one of those dark cloud banks that form far to the west. Inside, there are searing-hot flashes and grumbles and rumbles that a man can neither see nor hear. But the thing moves ever closer. And grows blacker. And finally comes the storm.

Charlie Moon slowed and made a left onto Fosset Gulch Road, crossing over the Piedra. This was the final rocky stream in the journey to the old woman's little trailer at the mouth of *Cañon del Espíritu*. The night was crystal-clear.

Nevertheless, the storm was gathering in its fury.

Finally, without looking at her nephew, the Ute elder spoke. "I don't see why Sarah has to stay with those town people for a whole week."

So that was it. He chose his words carefully. "It'll be good for her . . . a change."

It was—of course—the wrong thing to say.

"Change from what?" she snapped. "From living with a silly old woman?"

It was one of his aunt's more annoying characteristics—starting arguments by putting insulting words in her adversary's mouth. "Nobody said you were silly," he muttered. *Silly didn't half cover it.*

She wagged her head at him. "I know what you're thinking."

He hoped this was an idle boast.

"You took Sarah away from me because . . . because I *see* things."

"What've you seen lately?"

"Don't play dumb with me, Charlie Moon. You know what I'm talkin' about."

"Oh, yeah." The temptation was impossible to resist. "I remember now. Those little space cadets that passed by your place just after dark."

She held her tongue.

Charlie Moon should have let it go. But as Chief

Washakie of the Shoshone had said a century earlier, young men do foolish things. "Lemme see—that was on April Fool's Day, wasn't it?"

Daisy glared poisoned arrows at her nephew. "Some folks can be fooled just once in a dozen months. Others is yahoos the whole year 'round."

Intending to defuse the escalating situation, he chuckled amiably. Still another error.

Big jugheaded smart aleck.

He turned off the graveled road onto the rutted lane that led to the old woman's isolated trailer. It was not far to her home now, but the rough road compelled one to proceed slowly and with due caution. Otherwise, shocks and springs—even human vertebrae—might suffer injury.

"I took me a shot at them little bug-eyed bastards," she said smugly, "and one of 'em howled like a stuck pig." The old warrior cackled with pleasure at the memory of this successful skirmish. "I don't expect *they'll* be back to the reservation for a long time."

Moon was sobered by his recollection of the lead pellets the surgeon had dug out of Tommy Tonompicket's flesh. It was no wonder the poor man had howled. He was tempted to tell his aunt that she'd taken a potshot at Ozzie Octopus and come close to killing one of the People. But that mixture of comedy and felony remained confidential police information. He thought perhaps he could appeal to her common sense. The man could do nothing right. "That old twelve-gauge is pretty dangerous."

She understood where he was going with this. "It sure is—for anybody who messes with me."

He cleared his throat. "I was thinking more about . . . mistakes."

Her thin lips twisted into a nasty smile. "If somebody

comes sneakin' around my place after dark, that'll be a big mistake. But if I cut loose at 'em, it sure won't be no mistake. And I hit what I aim at." Both knew this was a great exaggeration. The old woman's eyes were . . . old woman's eyes.

"There might be an accident. There's a child living with you now. You have a responsibility for her safety."

Finally, he had got her attention. Daisy hesitated. "Sarah's safe enough. I keep it unloaded."

"Most firearms accidents happen with 'unloaded' weapons," the policeman pointed out grimly.

After a lengthy silence, she realized that his logic was inarguable. There was only one thing for a sensible person to do. Evade the issue with a counterattack. "I'll make you a deal."

He gave her a suspicious sideways look.

"You always wear that big horse pistol on your hip. When you hang it up, I'll give up my twelve-gauge."

"When I get so old and feeble that I'm a danger to society," he growled, "then I'll hang up my revolver."

Old and feeble? A danger to society? These were hurtful insults. She nursed this injury for some time before responding. "There was a time amongst the People when it was a good thing to be old. The young ones knew you'd gained lots of knowledge from all your years. And wisdom." She dabbed a handkerchief at her eyes. "Elders was respected then."

Not knowing how to respond, he grunted.

"Some of the young ones nowadays"—there was no mistaking whom she meant—"are like the *matukach*. Think all us old people are soft in the head. Ought to be locked up in one of them nursing homes, pushed around in wheelchairs, fed mashed-up baby food from plastic spoons. Strapped into our beds at night." She shook her finger at him. "Well, you'll never do that to me. And if anybody thinks they're gonna take my twelve-gauge away from me, mister—they better bring some help. And they'd better have bulletproof skins."

"Well," he said evenly, "what you've just said sure convinces me that you're a responsible citizen. Not a danger to anyone."

"Good. It's settled, then."

Moon groaned inwardly, wondering why he'd wanted to get her talking in the first place. A full minute of blessed silence passed as he maneuvered the big Blazer along the bone-jarring lane. It was not to last.

Daisy cleared her throat. "They say Tommy Tonompicket died accidentally—fell into the river and drowned. And that you was there when it happened."

"Is that what they say?"

Daisy nodded at her reflection in the windshield. "But I figure it was no accident."

Maybe she thinks I threw him into the river. "What do you think happened to Tommy?"

"Since I'm your aunt, I figured you'd tell me."

Gossip was butter for her bread. "Would if I could. But it's police business."

I knew it. "Then it wasn't no accident?"

"I'm not supposed to talk about it." That'd do it.

"Speak up. You know I can't hear too good with my left ear."

"I said—**I'm not supposed to talk about it.**"

She made a face. "You don't have to yell—I'm not stone-deaf. Anyway, I'm a friend of Tommy Tonompicket's wife. You can tell me what happened to him."

Temptation called once more. "You sure you could keep a secret?"

"What do you think I am—a tongue-flapper?"

You bet. He spoke barely above a whisper. "Well, not exactly, but . . ."

She cupped her hand by her left ear. "Speak up so's I can hear you!"

He leaned close to her. "What happened to Tommy Tonompicket—it wasn't entirely an accident."

She clasped her hands to her face in dismay. "I knew it! What happened?"

"Well, Tommy was standing there on the hospital balcony. And then *she* showed up . . ."

"Who showed up?"

Moon calibrated for just the right level. "It was . . . Grandmother Snyder."

She turned to frown at her nephew. "What'd you say?"

"Grandmother Snyder. Showed up right there on the balcony. Scared old Tommy so bad . . . he fell backward over the railing—into the river."

She eyed him suspiciously. "Are you telling me the truth?"

I will not laugh. He forced himself to think about an awful accident he'd investigated last February. Shattered bodies strewn across the asphalt. Great pools of blood. "I wouldn't lie to you. Especially about Grandmother *Snyder.*"

She watched his face for a sign that this was one of his jokes. Whenever he teased her, Charlie couldn't help grinning just a little bit. But his expression was deadly serious—filled with some unspoken dread. So it must be true. "Grandmother Spider," Daisy whispered, almost overcome by awe. "Well, I would've never thought *you'd* see her." The Ute elder was silent for some time, then: "What'd she look like—was it scary?"

He hesitated, took a deep breath. "Wasn't something I'd ever want to see again."

"There's some things best not seen by mortals."

Charlie Moon nodded solemnly.

"There's lots of awful things out there, creeping around in the dark. I can't always *see* 'em. But I feel 'em in my bones—I *know* they're there."

Charlie Moon could not see the satisfied smile on the old woman's face. But he felt it in his bones. Knew it was there.

THE SOUTHERN UTE tribal chairman tapped a plastic ballpoint pen against the polished surface of her oak desk. "I met with the council about an hour ago. They're all pretty unhappy about Tommy Tonompicket's death."

Charlie Moon shifted his weight in the uncomfortable chair.

Betty Flintcorn glared at the acting chief of police. "So how'd he die?"

"Accident."

"How'd this accident happen?"

"Tommy was on the balcony just outside his hospital room. Having a smoke. We were talking. He leaned backward, fell over the railing. Into the river."

Her brow furrowed into a puzzled frown. "I thought Tommy couldn't get out of bed."

"He'd gotten better."

"I guess there was no way to pull him out of the river."

Moon didn't respond.

"You talked to his wife?"

"Yeah." Bertha hadn't taken it too hard. She was already seeing an insurance salesman who had a nice home in Walsenburg.

The chairman sketched wavy lines on a ruled pad. "So what happened to those two men—Tommy and that *matukach*? How did they get all the way from Navajo Lake up to Mining City?"

Moon stared at the painting mounted on the wall behind her. It featured a bull buffalo, standing knee-deep in impossibly green grass. "FBI thinks they were kidnapped. Driven to the vicinity of Mining City. Where they either got away. Or were turned loose."

She drew two interlocking circles. "What do *you* think?"

"I think it's best to let the FBI deal with it."

She stared coldly at Moon. "You're our acting chief of police. It'd be nice if you'd figured out who'd kidnapped Tommy—and fired a shotgun at him—and chased him up a tree."

Moon could not tell the chairman that all these mysteries had been solved. Not without revealing that it was Aunt Daisy who'd shot at Tommy Tonompicket. Not without betraying several other confidences. And telling her what he knew wouldn't bring Tommy back.

She drew a stick figure on the yellow pad. It was lying on its back, all four legs pointing straight up. "Well, that's a dead horse we can't ride no more. Let's talk about something else."

Charlie Moon was grateful for a change of subject.

Betty Flintcorn scowled. "You've been acting chief of police for over six months now—while the council makes up its mind who to hire. I guess you know it's got down to you and another applicant."

"Yeah. The Northern Cheyenne, Wallace Whitehorse. Good man."

She nodded. "Whitehorse has got a fine record with the military police, managed lots of people. Knows how to handle budgets. But the council generally likes to hire one of our own people for a position as important as chief of police."

He appreciated Betty's way of not mincing words. Top jobs were virtually always given to Southern Utes— unless no tribal member was interested in the job. Or if the Ute applicants were judged unfit for the position. Moon had proved his competence over a period of years.

"At this morning's council meeting," Betty Flintcorn continued as she drew a grinning cartoon skull, "we made a decision."

"Well, I appreciate it. I'll do my best to—"

She raised her hand to silence him. "Hear me out."

Now he waited for the other shoe to drop. Maybe the council was going to put some conditions on the appointment. Like lower wages than Roy Severo had pulled down.

The chairman didn't speak until she had sketched a pair of crossed bones under the skull. Her heart was thumping hard. *This has to be said in just the right way.* "Charlie . . . I didn't say you'd got the job."

He sat there, staring at her wrinkled face. Unable to speak. Barely able to breathe.

The chairman licked her lips and chose each word carefully. "You've been a good policeman. But you know how tribal politics is." *Let Charlie figure it out for himself.*

He did. For one thing, the Cheyenne applicant had married a Ute woman whose sister was an influential member of the tribal council. For another, it was a small tribe. Almost everybody was somebody or other's relative or friend. And one time or another, Moon had arrested a relative or friend of every member of the council. Four years ago, he'd appeared as a witness when Betty Flintcorn's twenty-year-old daughter had gone on trial for reckless manslaughter. June Flintcorn had downed a six-pack, then dropped her heavy foot on the accelerator of a big Lincoln. Just a mile north of Ignacio, June had lost consciousness, crossed the center line, and run head-on into a compact car. The count in the smaller vehicle was three dead and one who would live out her years as a paraplegic. By chance, Moon had taken the call—and given June Flintcorn the Breathalyzer test. She had been carrying twice the legal limit of alcohol in her blood. Though not even scratched by the collision, she had been far too drunk to stand up, much less walk a straight line. His damning testimony had ensured that Betty's daughter would be in prison until at least her thirtieth birthday.

So he had never expected to have Betty Flintcorn's vote.

But there must be at least three or four additional members of the council who didn't want him to be chief of tribal police. There was no point in feeling bad about it; the thing was done.

The chairman waited for him to say something. He didn't.

"I hope you're not too disappointed." She had known Charlie would accept this quietly.

He shrugged. "The Cheyenne should make a fine chief of police."

This was going even better than she had expected. "Wallace Whitehorse gets discharged from the Army next week. You'll remain as acting chief till then."

Moon heard himself say: "Yeah. I imagine the new chief'll need to have someone help him out. I'll be glad to continue as his deputy." It was the right thing to do.

She stared at the skull and crossbones on her pad. "One of the Northern Cheyenne's conditions for accepting the job is that he appoints his own deputy. Effective on his hiring date next Friday, you'll go back to the rank and pay of sergeant."

It was one thing not to get the promotion. Another thing entirely to be demoted. Moon was unaware that he'd put his hat on. But he knew it was time to go.

"I know this is tough, Charlie. You want to take some leave with pay, I could set it up. Say thirty days."

He thought about pitching his gold shield onto her desk. But his fingers were numb and tingling—he was not sure he'd be able to unpin the damn thing from his shirt pocket. He couldn't afford to rip it off—this was an expensive new shirt and his income was about to shrink. Worse still, he could think of nothing to say. Nothing at all. He turned, walked woodenly toward the door.

Betty Flintcorn started to speak, then reconsidered. She waited a full minute after his departure. Then picked up the telephone and dialed three numbers to ring the extension in the council chamber. They were waiting to hear about her meeting with Charlie Moon.

Paul Begay, a long-term member of the council, answered.

"Hello. This is the chairman." This wasn't going to be easy.

"Hi, Betty. You can bring 'im in. We got the cake and punch ready for the big celebration."

"Paul—I got some bad news."

There was a frown in his voice. "I don't like to hear bad news."

She cleared her throat. "Charlie Moon isn't going to be our chief of police."

"What—he don't want the job?"

Betty Flintcorn sighed. "You know Charlie. He never did like to take on big responsibilities." *Except when he sent my daughter away to prison.* "He said that the Cheyenne would make us a fine chief of police."

Paul was yelling into the telephone. "But we want Charlie for the job—the Cheyenne only got one vote—and that was from his sister-in-law."

"I know. I tried to talk some sense into Charlie. But you know how stubborn he can be." The better to conceal her plan, Betty Flintcorn had voted for Moon. One of the few secrets the council managed to keep was the voting records on hiring and firing. There would be some peculiar rumors floating around for the next few weeks, but Charlie Moon wouldn't make any attempt to find out whether they were true. It wasn't in his character to pry into tribal politics. And even if he finally figured out that she'd duped him, he'd never say a word about it. It wasn't his way.

"Yeah," Paul muttered. "Charlie's pretty independent. Hardly ever comes to a council meeting when we call on him." *Maybe it's for the best.*

"Charlie's pretty upset. He wants me to authorize some leave. With full pay."

"With pay—how much?"

"Thirty days. I told him it'd be okay."

Paul whistled. "Thirty days *with pay*. You've been pretty damn generous with Charlie Moon."

"Well, he's served the tribe well." For the first time on this day, the tribal chairman smiled. "Now we're down to just one applicant. I guess we'd better make the Cheyenne an offer right away. Before he changes his mind."

Charlie Moon walked north, toward the new police station. At the SUPD parking lot, he got into the old Blazer.

And sat there, staring at the rain streaking down the windshield. The sun would be down in another hour. In his soul, darkness had already gathered.

The unexpected news from Betty Flintcorn had been a heavy kick in the gut. But in the long run, it might all be for the best. Maybe this Cheyenne would make a fine chief of police. Might even be a good guy to work for. Whatever the outcome, it must be accepted.

This small thought comforted him: There could not possibly be any more bad news today. He'd had his full quota and then some. He was turning the key in the ignition when the cellular telephone chirped. The offending instrument was in the pocket of his raincoat, which he'd left in the backseat of the squad car. Moon considered ignoring the call. The gadget chirped again. He couldn't recall ever getting any good news on the thing. Another chirp. He reached for the raincoat, pressed the black plastic instrument to his ear. "Yeah?"

It was Scott Parris. "Charlie?"

"Hi, pardner. Glad to hear your voice."

"You doing okay?"

"Just dandy. What's up?"

"I just got a phone call from an attorney in Durango—a Mr. Price. Says he's been trying to reach you through SUPD, but you haven't returned his calls. He wanted to know if I had any way of getting in touch with you. Fella seemed pretty agitated, so I didn't give him your cell-phone number."

"Thanks. Any idea what it's about?" Agitated lawyers were always bearers of bad news.

"Some bad news, I'm afraid."

Moon groaned. "Could it wait till tomorrow—or maybe next year?"

" 'Fraid not. You remember that eccentric old lady at the hospital—Matilda Snyder?"

"How could I forget her? One of my ancestors shot an arrow through her grandmother."

"That's the one," Parris said.

"What's happened?"

There was a pause as Scott Parris took a deep breath. "She passed away."

"Sorry to hear it." *Poor old soul.* "How'd it happen?"

"From what I hear, looks like natural causes. But this attorney has asked for an autopsy. I'll be talking to Doc Simpson in a few days—soon as he's finished with . . . the body."

Moon suddenly imagined Mattie's ghost was sitting beside him, wearing her enigmatic smile. A cold, dead hand reached out and touched his neck. Unconsciously, he leaned away from the shade. "If anything about Mrs. Snyder's death turns out to be police business, it's in your jurisdiction. Why does this lawyer want to talk to me?"

"Don't know. You have any ideas?"

"Not a one, pardner. So how do I get in touch with this friend of the court?"

Parris recited the attorney's telephone number and Durango address. "He wants to see you soon as possible. Asked if you would call his secretary and make an appointment. If you can't come to him, he'll pay you a visit at SUPD."

Moon didn't intend to be spending much time around the station. Except for moving his stuff out of the chief's office. "I'll head up to Durango first chance I get."

"After you've seen the lawyer, let's get together. You can tell me what this is all about."

"Okay. And I got some other stuff to tell you." *Like how I may be looking for another job.*

DURANGO,
9:30 A.M.

The attorney who stood up behind the desk wore a charcoal suit, a dark red tie with an opal clip. He was long and stringy and stoop-shouldered; looked to be in his early fifties. Beneath a carefully styled mane of dark hair was a pale face cast into an eternally suspicious expression. Iceberg-blue eyes, staring over a ridiculously small pair of round spectacles, appraised the big Ute. "Mr. Charles Moon, I presume. Acting chief of police for the Southern Utes."

Moon nodded, and accepted the attorney's outstretched hand.

"I am Wilbur Price. Good of you to stop by." He nodded to indicate a chair upholstered in dark red leather. "Please be seated."

The Ute policeman sat. It was a large chair. And comfortable.

The lawyer removed a letter opener from a thin leather sheath; it was a remarkable replica of a Byzantine dagger. "I assume you know why I requested this meeting."

To stab me in the heart? The Ute shook his head.

Frowning thoughtfully, Price ran his finger over the thin blade. "You are aware of the recent demise of Mrs. Matilda Snyder?"

"I am."

Though Wilbur Price's sallow face gave little away, his blue eyes betrayed a certain distaste for the task at hand. "I'll get right to the point, Mr. Moon. I know that you spent some time at Snyder Memorial Hospital—investigating that preposterous abduction report." He rolled the blue orbs. "Giant spiders. Great Godfrey—

what'll they think of next?" He pointed the dagger tip at the policeman. "I wish to learn more of your relationship with my client."

"Your client?"

"Matilda Snyder, of course. I also happen to be her grandson. Or, as the old dear delighted in describing me—'that pipsqueak Harvard lawyer.' But she trusted me for all that—I have Grandma's power of attorney." He tapped the letter-opener blade on his palm. "Do you know how she died?"

"No."

"Respiratory failure leading to cardiac arrest."

"Well, she was pretty old—"

The attorney's face flushed pink with anger. "Beta-pyridyl-alpha-methyl pyrrolidine."

"Beg your pardon?"

"I refer to that insidious molecule composed of ten carbons, fourteen hydrogens, two nitrogens."

"Oh. That one."

"A plant alkaloid, Mr. Moon. More commonly known as nicotine. Not only one of the most addictive substances known—also a deadly poison." Price turned to gaze out the window, oblivious to the rush of pedestrians and traffic below. "My grandmother was a heavy smoker for most of her life—it ruined her health. Later on, she had problems with her lungs. Moreover, she developed a sensitivity to nicotine. Nasty habit, cigarettes." He paused to cast a sideways glance at the policeman. "Are you a smoker, Mr. Moon?"

The Ute shook his head.

"I did my best to see that Grandmother Snyder had no access to tobacco products. But the old sneak was always plotting ways to get her hands on cigarettes." He opened a desk drawer. "Shortly after her death, the nurse found *this* under Grandma's pillow." Price produced a transparent plastic box for the policeman's inspection. Inside the sealed container was a crumpled package.

Moon stared in horror. *Juarez Gold.*

"Note that the package has been emptied. In her delicate condition, the nicotine dose—combined with the deleterious effect of smoke in her lungs—may have been enough to cause her demise."

Not from three cigarettes. But he couldn't tell the attorney.

Price peered quizzically through the tiny spectacles. "Do you have any idea where she may have gotten the cigarettes?"

So this is why he wanted to see me—I'm a suspect. He chose his words carefully and told the truth. But not the whole truth. "Tommy Tonompicket was in the next room to hers. He smoked that brand."

The attorney was silent for some time. "A pity that Mr. Tonompicket is no longer in the world of the living. It appears that he—or some unknown subject—provided these poisonous things to my grandmother."

Moon, now the sinister UNSUB, tried very hard to look innocent. His face felt like an image on a Ten Most Wanted poster.

"If this person was aware that Grandma was forbidden tobacco products because of the extremely frail state of her health—serious criminal charges might be made." Price continued to stare coldly at Moon. "It all depends upon . . . his motive."

"I can't imagine anyone having a reason for harming your grandmother."

"You know, old Mattie never much liked Indians of any stripe—particularly the Utes." The icy stare was replaced with a sharp-toothed smile.

Moon would have preferred the icy stare.

"Her grandmother—so Mattie said—was murdered by members of your tribe."

"Yeah. She told me about it."

"An eccentric old woman. Cranky at times. But I loved her dearly." Wilbur Price inserted the dagger into its sheath, and seated himself. The contrast with the massive desk made him seem smaller. But no less dangerous. "I feel obliged to tell you something."

Moon prepared himself for some ugly news.

"I have hired a private investigator. She has been conducting a discreet inquiry." He paused, making a tent of long, pale fingers. "The subject of the investigation, Mr. Moon . . . is yourself."

The Ute managed a tolerably good poker face. But the other fellow was holding all the cards.

The attorney opened a three-ring binder. "I have here the investigator's preliminary findings. Copy of your birth certificate. Transcripts of grades from junior high through college. Military records." Price flipped through several pages. "Before you joined the police force, you had a serious drinking problem. While intoxicated, you often got into brawls. Some years ago, you killed a man in Reno."

Almost in a daze, Moon nodded. *Just to watch him die.*

"The killing was ruled self-defense." The lawyer raised an eyebrow as if to express his doubt about this verdict.

"He had a butcher knife," Moon muttered. "I was unarmed." *And I never meant to kill him.*

"I naturally have considerable information on your performance as a member of the Southern Ute police force. You seem to have been quite effective. But in the course of carrying out your duties, you have killed four suspects. And the list of those injured covers a full two pages. Impressive." He slammed the folder shut. "Death and violence seem to accompany you."

"Why're you so interested in me?"

Price's face had all the expression of a beached carp. "Surely you've guessed."

Moon had guessed.

The lawyer patted the notebook fondly, as if it were the head of a favorite hound. "There is a brief report on interactions you had with my aunt . . . shortly before her death." He paused to frown at the pages before him. "Sir, we have some serious legal issues to address. If you have no objections, I will ask you a few questions. How you respond will affect a most solemn decision on my part . . . and your future."

Charlie Moon's mouth went powder-dry. *My prints must be on the cigarette package.* He opened his mouth to speak. No words came out.

Price aimed the glassy stare at him. "If you wish to have legal counsel present to represent you in this matter, you certainly may."

He's reading me my rights.

"If you cannot afford an attorney, I'm sure . . . suitable arrangements can be made."

The Ute was mute as a stone.

"Well?" Price grinned wolfishly.

Moon recalled Kenny Bright's warning. *"Some fine morning . . . staring you right in the eye is this great big hydrophobic wolf."*

The attorney licked his lips.

"He's lickin' his slobbering lips—about to put the bite on you . . . I expect you'd wish you was someplace else."

"Mr. Moon, if there is anything you wish to . . ."

I wish I was someplace else.

SOMEPLACE ELSE

MOON SAT ON the rusty tailgate of his pickup. His black Stetson was pushed back so the sun could warm his face. In this quiet place, there were no urgent problems to be solved. No troubles to gnaw away at a man's innards.

In the mossy shade of a basalt boulder, a cluster of columbines pretended to be white stars set in a pale blue sky. A red-winged blackbird fluttered to a landing on a fence post; she cocked her head and warbled at the Ute. The breeze also sang. *Sweet Lord . . . what a morning you have made for us.*

These extravagant gifts were offered . . . accepted . . . and spent like small change. He enjoyed them, every one.

And so time passed, uncounted by ticking clock.

It was a very perfect day.

Moon watched the serpentine strip of asphalt curl away to the horizon. He leaned forward, pulled the dark brim forward to shade his eyes. And saw it coming. Now, just a red speck. In another minute, he could hear the Volvo engine hum a throaty hymn.

The Granite Creek chief of police nosed the old sedan in behind Moon's pickup. Without a word, they shook hands. An odd ritual for these old friends. So formal. As if this were an exceedingly important occasion—unlike all others.

Moon leaned on the Volvo's roof. The paint was thin and powdery. "Glad you could make it, pardner."

"Me too, Charlie."

The Ute's gaze swept the distant valley. "You bring your gear?"

Parris nodded. "When I got your message about a great trout hole, I canceled some pretty important meetings."

"And just think—you got me to thank for it."

"You bet." Parris paused to help himself to a deep breath of immaculate mountain air. And treated his soul to a long look at the bowl-shaped valley where patches of tall pines stood in broad meadows. In a few low, marshy spots, the grass was already knee-deep. A herd of shaggy elk grazed not a quarter mile away. Forests of fir and freshly leafed aspens decorated the pleated skirts of the mountains. He looked up at the redwood sign. It was suspended from a massive log arch standing above a heavy steel gate. The letters had been burned deeply into the weathered plank.

COLUMBINE

RANCH

Paradise was spread out before them. But alas, the gate was locked. And this was not the sort of place a sensible man would care to be caught trespassing. Wealthy landowners tended to be fussy about such misdemeanors. "Charlie—you sure you got the right place?"

"Pretty sure."

"I guess you've been here before."

"Nope."

"You know the owner?"

The Ute nodded.

Parris frowned at a heavy padlock. "So how do we get in—ram the gate?"

"That'd be fun. But I got a better plan." Moon showed his friend a ring of keys.

Charlie Moon led the way in his big pickup.

So as not to eat so much dust, Scott Parris kept the Volvo a hundred yards behind the Ute's truck. The graveled road meandered around several wooded ridges, then approached a sturdy bridge over a sizable creek. It was roaring with snowmelt from the granite mountains towering protectively around the lush valley. Cottonwoods and willows shaded the banks.

Parris lifted his foot from the accelerator. *This must be the fishing place.*

But Moon's pickup passed over the bridge without slowing.

Parris followed for another mile, then slowed again as Moon coasted to a stop by a rambling log cabin that looked to be at least a century old. A thin wisp of gray smoke curled up from a sooty metal chimney set in a shingled roof. A mud-splattered Jeep CJ-5 was parked under a mushroom-shaped willow. Before the Ute had time to shut off the engine, an aged man dressed in faded jeans and a red shirt was limping across the porch, waving.

Moon shook the man's hard, knobby hand. It felt like a bag full of rocks.

"I'm Pete Bushman." He grinned through a fuzzy beard. "I'm foreman here at the Columbine. 'Course, there ain't much work goin' on, 'cept what little I do myself." He looked over the valley with a melancholy smile. "There's no reg'lar ranch hands no more, 'cause we don't have no stock to fuss with. It's just me and my old woman looks after the place. I patch up the bob-war fences and make sure all the tractors and trucks and machinery is kept in runnin' order. My Dolly, she looks in on the big house ever so often. Keeps it tolerably clean. Early this mornin', she got it all straightened up for you—'specially the kitchen. There's lotsa good grub in the Frigidaire. Steaks and bacon and pork sausage. And a couple dozen eggs."

A woman's round, rosy face appeared in the cabin window. It was quickly withdrawn behind a curtain when Moon glanced her way.

"She even started up the old grandfather clock for you."

"I appreciate what you've done," the Ute said. He nodded toward the approaching Volvo. "Me and my friend plan to do some fishing."

Parris slowed, watched Moon shake hands with the leathery-faced fellow. After a brief conversation, the old cowboy grinned at something the Ute said, then pointed down the road. Moon touched his hat and was back in the pickup before Parris had time to make up his mind about whether to get out or wait in the Volvo.

* * *

They parked under the largest of a dozen tall cotton-woods, near a black Ford Expedition. Like the gate, the automobile's door was emblazoned with COLUMBINE RANCH. The blue-and-white flower was expertly painted under the words.

The ranch headquarters—perched on a low knoll of layered basalt outcroppings—looked as solid as the bedrock under its foundations. Constructed of massive pine logs, it towered three stories under a blue steel roof that was sharply peaked to shed heavy winter snows. A man-sized porch wrapped around three sides of the massive structure. Near the front door, an old-fashioned swing was suspended from oiled chains. Someone had painted it bright blue, perhaps to match the roof. Or the sky.

Parris got out of the Volvo and stared.

From the west side of the knoll, the land sloped gently down to the shore of an honest-to-God river. Not some little mountain stream with ten-inch stock trout. This was the real McCoy. Deep and wide and running like it had somewhere important to go and was in a great big hurry to get there. On the east side of the house, a hundred yards away, was the rocky shore of a lake that had formed several millennia ago when a landslide slipped off the mountain to fill a deep crevasse. Its hue was a far deeper blue than the sky above. This was a respectable body of water; Parris estimated it as somewhere between fifty and sixty acres. While the men watched, a silvery trout broke the glassy surface to take a careless insect.

"That one's a good three pounds," Parris muttered.

Farther away to the south, there were two massive barns and three corrals. All around the ranch, the mountains towered up, their angular shoulders swathed in glistening, snowy shawls.

"Charlie—how big is this place?"

The Ute looked to the horizon. "Far as you can see in every direction."

Parris shook his head in awe. "My God." It was a piece of creation that moved one to commune with the Almighty. Or to partake of the sweet silence.

The Ute headed for the porch, the ring of keys jingling merrily in his hand. "Let's have a look inside."

Parris glanced uneasily toward the Ford Expedition. "Don't you think we'd better knock first?"

"There's nobody here but you and me, pardner."

Parris followed his friend into the house. This outfit obviously belonged to some very rich fella who lived in New York or Austin or Silicon Valley. Probably didn't spend one month in twelve here. But he'd loaned the place to Charlie Moon for a fishing holiday. Who did the Ute policeman know who had that kind of money?

They inspected the rooms on the ground floor; most of the furniture was covered by white linen sheets. The place had been furnished by someone with deep pockets indeed. The parlor, with a twenty-foot ceiling supported by huge polished logs, was magnificent. The fireplace—constructed from pinkish-white quartz—was big enough for a man to walk into. And somebody—it had to be the foreman—had laid in a big stack of split pine. There were huge windows on three sides. Scott Parris imagined himself living in a place like this. If a man got tired of looking at the reflection of the snowy mountains on the glassy surface of the lake, he could amble over to the other side of the room and gaze at the river as it rolled and crashed over glistening black boulders.

Predictably, Moon ended up in the kitchen. "Want a bite to eat, pardner?"

"I don't feel right—walking around some rich guy's house. Maybe we should lock this place up. Go do some fishing."

Moon stared out the window at the river. And liked what he saw. "There'll be plenty of time for fishing. I'll rustle up some lunch." He opened the refrigerator, then turned to smile at his friend. "How about I broil us some big steaks? Bake some Idaho spuds?"

Well, Charlie seems to feel all right about this. "Sure." Parris seated himself at the sturdy pine table. "Buddy, you must have a generous friend."

Moon lost the smile. "Yeah."

"So who is it—a Vanderbilt—a Rockefeller?"

The Ute set the oven on the propane range to Broil. "More like . . . a Snyder."

Parris frowned. "Matilda?"

Moon nodded. He plopped a matched pair of inch-thick T-bones onto the broiler tray.

Parris whistled. "I figured the Snyder clan had plenty, but I never suspected old Matilda owned anything like this." He grinned. "So how long do you get to stay?"

Charlie Moon sat down across the table. Gave his friend an enigmatic look. "Long as I want to."

Parris stared blankly back. "I don't get it."

"I did."

"What?"

"It's all mine, pardner. Land. River. Lake. Buildings. That big Ford parked out front. The whole shootin' match."

The white man's eyes widened. "Charlie—don't kid around."

The Ute's face was split by a fresh smile. "I never make jokes about real estate, pardner. It's true."

His mouth dry as talc, Parris managed a single word. "How?"

"I think that's my line," the Ute said.

"I still don't understand—"

"Matilda Snyder telephoned her grandson. He's a lawyer. Wilbur Price."

"That's the guy who called me, trying to get in touch with you."

"The very same. Mr. Price has Matilda's power of attorney. She instructed him to transfer the Columbine to me. Along with some cash—for taxes, operating expenses, buying some start-up stock. She wouldn't tell him why."

Parris shook his head. "That's incredible."

"That's pretty much what the lawyer thought. And when she died the next day, Mrs. Snyder's grandson was even more suspicious about the transaction, so he hired a private investigator to check me out. See if I was on the level. I passed the test." *Barely.*

"Why?"

"Why what?"

"Why did old Matilda give you"—Parris made a sweeping gesture—"all of this?"

"I guess she liked me."

Parris grinned. "Liked you? She must have *adored* you. But I can't imagine why."

Moon managed to look hurt. "You don't think I'm adorable?"

"Right at the moment, I think you're a sharp pain in the ass. But then I'm your buddy, so I'm biased. Now tell me—why did that old dame gave you a piece of paradise?"

"Pardner, can you keep a secret?"

"If it's a good one."

"She gave me this place because . . . I gave her some smokes."

Parris shook his head in utter bewilderment. "Smokes?"

"Three cigarettes. It was right after Matilda came out onto the balcony that night . . . when she scared Tommy Tonompicket so bad he stumbled and fell into the river. Poor old woman was naturally upset—said she needed a smoke. As luck would have it, Tommy had left some Juarez Golds behind."

"So you gave her three Mexican cigarettes . . ."

"And I guess she felt beholden to me." *Nice old lady.* "Must've forgiven me for shooting an arrow through her grandmother's heart."

"It's too wonderful." Scott Parris got up, stood stock-still, staring out the window. "I can't hardly believe it's true."

"Me neither," the Ute said. "It's like one of those sweet dreams. Where everything's going your way. And then you get suspicious that it's too good to be true—know you'll wake up and it'll all be gone."

There was a long silence before Parris spoke. "So what're your plans?"

"Guess I'll be busy making a paying operation out of this place. Start off with a couple hundred head of pure-bred Herefords. Dozen quarter horses. Get some alfalfa planted. I'll have to hire some experienced cowboys for my foreman to manage."

"So what about SUPD—how're you gonna have time to be chief of police?"

"Somebody else'll be doing that job." He clapped his friend on the shoulder. "Everything is A-number-one.

From now on, my life is going to be simple. Uncomplicated."

Parris cleared his throat. "Uh . . . maybe not."

The Ute frowned. "Pardner—please don't tell me no bad news."

The white man tried hard not to look guilty. "It's not *necessarily* bad news."

Moon stared at the ceiling.

Parris ran his thumb over the polished surface of the pine table. "Thing is—something has come up."

"What?"

Parris' expression was pained. "I can't exactly say."

"Run that by me again."

"Well . . . except to tell you that I got this telephone call."

"Who from?"

Parris avoided the Ute's suspicious gaze. "From . . . a person."

"That's who usually calls. What about?"

"This . . . person . . . has some serious business with you. Insisted on knowing where to find you. It seemed pretty urgent, so I . . ."

Moon shook his head in disbelief. "You told him we were going to meet at the Columbine spread?"

"Well, yes and no." *No and yes would be more accurate.*

"Pardner, what's this all about?"

Parris glanced anxiously at a door that opened onto the porch. "Tell you what—I'll go get my fishing gear all untangled whilst you burn us some beef." He bolted from the chair and was gone.

The Ute stared at the door. *Why won't he tell me?* But Time would tell. Always does.

The grandfather clock in the corner clicked the seconds away.

Moon left the kitchen for the spacious parlor. There was a slight chill in the dark room; he started up a snapping fire under the pine logs.

Scott Parris was at the lake. Casting feathery lures on the crystalline surface.

Moon stood at a window, watched his friend snag a fine-looking trout. *So far, this is the one completely perfect day of my life.* So far. He thought about calling the foreman, instructing Pete to turn away any potential troublemaker who showed up. *But sooner or later, Bad News will find me. Might as well get it over and done with.*

The Ute wandered around the vast space, inspecting the furnishings. He examined bronze statuary and ancient Mimbres pottery. Leafed through leather-bound books of history and other romance. Moon opened a drawer under a small mahogany lamp table and found a deck of cards. He sat down at the table and shuffled the deck. Began to deal a hand of solitaire. All went well until a card slid too far on the polished surface. Fluttering like a falling autumn leaf, it dropped to the floor, landing facedown. Instinctively, he started to reach for it—then hesitated. There is an old Leadville gambler's superstition about such a misfortune. If a fallen card is hiding its face, leave it be till the morrow. Turn it over today, your life will change forever.

Moon let it lie.

Not because he believed such foolishness. But he did play the odds. *Some superstitions—even if you don't believe in 'em—will still rear up and fang you.* So he ignored the sinister pasteboard. Only a fool would invite trouble in when life was finally perfect.

Well . . . *almost* perfect.

The sly rectangle tugged at the corner of his eye. *Go on. Have a look.*

He reached down . . . turned it over.

Queen of Hearts.

The hinges were well oiled; the Ute didn't hear the big door swing open behind him. He did feel the slight draft. And hear her voice.

"Hello, big man."

He turned. There she was. Snugly sheathed in a black cotton dress. A single pearl suspended from her neck on an invisible cord. Waves of golden hair falling to her slender waist. He didn't know what to say.

She did. "You sent me roses."

Charlie Moon tried to come up with a sensible reply. But his tongue did cleave unto the roof of his mouth.

A tear coursed its tender way down her cheek. "No man ever sent me roses."

The Ute's tongue uncleaved. "I thought maybe you'd like 'em."

Another tear joined the first. "Or wrote me such a sweet note."

All I said was Thank You. But he'd let that dog lie.

Camilla had not taken a direct route. She had driven a thousand miles and more. "You're a hard man to track down."

"Sorry. Been lookin' for me a long time?"

She nodded. *All my life.*

"If I'd known you were coming, I'd have been easy to find."

She gave the Ute a long, thoughtful look. "I haven't quite made up my mind about you."

He waited.

"It's not like you're perfect."

There was no sensible answer to this.

"You're kind of . . . well . . . extremely tall."

Moon managed a grin. "Saw me off at the knees."

"Charlie Moon . . . are you looking for a real woman?"

"Not now that you're here."

She bit her lip. "If you ever lie to me—or cheat on me . . ."

"I'd never, ever do that . . ."

". . . I'll slit your throat while you sleep."

"Sounds fair to me."

"I'm not kidding."

"I know."

"Come close to me."

He did.

"Lean over, big man."

He did.

She wrapped her arms around his neck. "Now kiss me."

He did.

And that was that.

Turn the page for a glimpse at another
Charlie Moon Mystery by James D. Doss

WHITE SHELL WOMAN

Available wherever books are sold

*All of a sudden she heard something behind her.
Looking around she saw a great white horse with
black eyes. He had a long white mane, and he
pranced above the ground—not on the earth itself. . . . And there was a young man sitting on the
horse. The young man's moccasins and leggings
and clothing were all white. All was as for a bride.*
— Sandoval, Hastin Tlo'tsi hee

THE SHAMAN

An excellent breakfast of refried beans, pork sausage,
and eggs (fried in the popping sausage grease) was finished. When the sun got a smidgen higher, Daisy
Perika's nephew would drive her to Ignacio for Sunday-
morning mass at St. Ignatius Catholic Church. The Ute
elder stood at the window, her thin forearms folded
over a purple woolen shawl. Squinting at the gaping
mouth of *Cañon del Espíritu*, she licked her lips in
preparation for what must be said. And said it. "I won't
be in Middle World much longer." The grim pronouncement was directed at the visitor in her trailer home.

Charlie Moon, his seven-foot frame folded over the
small kitchen table, was engrossed in a copy of the
Southern Ute Drum.

She waited.

Nothing.

"Did you hear what I said?" *Big jughead.*

The former tribal policeman—now a cattle rancher—did not look up from the article about falling beef prices. "Yeah." Aunt Daisy had been predicting her imminent death for two decades. *She'll likely live to bury me.*

She knew what he was thinking. "Won't be long till you'll be at my funeral."

He looked up to smile affectionately at the aged woman's bowed form. "You not feeling well?"

Daisy put a hand to the small of her back and groaned. "Haven't had a good day since that peanut farmer was president."

Charlie Moon folded the tribal newspaper, downed the last dregs of an extraordinarily strong cup of coffee. "So what's the matter?" He knew the answer. Too many years.

"Too many years," she said.

"It'll take more than old age to do you in."

He always says that. The tribal elder shook her head and sighed. Charlie was too young to understand. "When you get really old, things start to stop workin'. That's when you know the end isn't far off. And," she added with a knowing wag of her head, "the signs are plain enough."

He was obligated to ask. "What signs?" *It'll be pains in her chest.*

"Toenails," she muttered.

He wondered whether he'd heard her correctly.

The aged woman looked down, wiggled her toes. "I generally have to clip 'em at least once a month. So they won't poke holes in my stockings."

Charlie Moon wondered where this was going.

So that gaunt Rider on the Pale Horse would not hear the grim news and come a-galloping her way, Daisy whispered. "My toenails . . . they've stopped growing."

He stared at her feet. "That's bad?"

She gave him the pitying look reserved for the terminally ignorant.

Moon, who had never really understood his aunt, thought she wanted reassurance. "It's probably just some kind of dietary problem. A little more calcium, you'll be right as rain."

This uncalled-for optimism earned him a venomous stare.

He understood his error, and added in a conciliatory tone: "Or maybe you *are* about to fall off the saddle."

Pleased to have browbeaten her nephew into submission, Daisy treated herself to a deeply melancholy sigh. "It won't be long now. Some dark night, that snow-white owl will swoop down. He'll perch on that old piñon snag by my bedroom window . . . and call my name."

He looked at the pot on the stove. "You got any more coffee?"

ST. IGNATIUS CATHOLIC CHURCH

Daisy Perika was mildly annoyed that Charlie Moon was not sitting beside her. Her nephew had been lured away by April Tavishuts, who was sitting across the aisle. Moon was smiling at something the young woman had whispered in his ear. Daisy scowled. *Hah. I bet you'd wipe that silly grin off your face if your yella-haired matukach sweetheart was to walk into church right now.* But the old woman was pleased that her nephew was paying some attention to a nice Ute girl. As far as Daisy knew, April didn't have herself a man. Or anything you could call a real family. Her father had died during the flu epidemic. And not long after marrying a Navajo last year, April's mother had left Middle World. Daisy said a brief prayer for the unfortunate soul. But Misfortune visits those who are foolish. *She should've known better than to get into bed with one of them Navajos. But I guess she must've been awfully lonely.* Daisy Perika closed her eyes. And wished that someone would come and sit beside her.

As he delivered his carefully crafted sermon on those twin sins of Pride and Envy, Father Raes Delfino tried not to notice the elderly woman in a pew near the rear of the church. But her form—hunched forward in an odd, froggish manner—tugged at his gaze as the gravity of a black hole bends a beam of rainbow light. The Ute elder was an enigma to the scholarly little Jesuit. He had no doubt that Daisy Perika's faith was firmly anchored in Christ. But like other traditional Utes, she was the creature of a complex culture shaped in darkest prehistory. He knew from several unsettling experiences that Daisy was haunted by it. As he was.

Daisy was, in fact, dozing. This was primarily because she was old and tired to the marrow. Only partly because in the back of the church she could not quite make out the priest's words. The syllables fluttered softly about her ears like little yucca moths. Lulling her sweetly to sleep.

But presently, something disturbed her nap. An urgent tugging at her sleeve.

Believing another member of the flock was awakening her for Holy Communion, she cleared her throat and whispered hoarsely: " 'S all right—I was just resting my eyes."

Daisy glanced across her shoulder. There was no one there.

Almost.

Another tugging at her sleeve. *Must be a child.* She looked down. And almost swallowed her tongue. *I must be dreaming.* She closed her eyes ever so tightly. Counted toward ten. At seven, she cracked the lid on one eye. The little man was still beside her. Right here in church, like a regular Sunday-go-to-meeting Christian. This was outrageous. "What are you doing *here*?" she rasped.

He scratched his belly and yawned.

She tried to speak without moving her lips. "Go 'way—before somebody sees you!"

No response from the dwarf.

Daisy stared in horror at the priest. Though he had not missed a beat in his sermon, Father Raes seemed to be looking in her direction—as if she were the chief of all sinners. But the Ute shaman remembered—to her enormous relief—that only a Ute could see the *pitukupf*. Well, that wasn't necessarily always the case. There were occasional exceptions. That *matukach* chief of police up in Granite Creek had seen the dwarf. But Scott Parris—Charlie Moon's best friend—was a very special white man. With gifts not unlike her own. Father Raes was of another sort entirely. She was certain the priest could not see the tiny fellow who sat by her side. And so she stared boldly at the man of the cloth.

Without turning her head, Daisy Perika spoke from the corner of her mouth. "Take off your hat." Still unnerved by his unexpected appearance, she had spoken in English.

The *pitukupf* did not respond.

She repeated the command in the Ute tongue.

The dwarf ignored her.

Daisy snatched the floppy green hat from his head, slammed it down on the pew between them.

The little man aimed an outraged look at the shaman. And muttered something best not heard by an old woman's ears. Especially not in church.

In the choppy Ute dialect, Daisy tersely inquired what the *pitukupf* was doing here. He knew very well that his sort had no business in God's house. He belonged in *Cañon del Espíritu*. Under the ground. In his badger hole.

Apparently unmoved, the *pitukupf* said not a word. But he did reach out to touch the Ute elder's wrist. And point upward with a crooked little finger.

Following his gesture, the shaman tilted her head. She was astonished to see flames—the church roof melting away like wax. And far above—in a sky that was unnaturally dark for late on a Sunday morning—Daisy Perika saw something like stars. Falling from the heavens.

At the door, Farther Raes had already exchanged pleasantries with April Tavishuts and Charlie Moon, who were waiting a few paces ahead of the old woman. The priest took Daisy Perika's wrinkled hand in his. The tribal elder had a peculiar look in her eye. "And how are you this morning?"

She responded with a shrug, punctuated with a grunt.

"During the sermon," he said with a wry grin, "you seemed somewhat distracted."

Confident that the *matukach* priest could not have seen her diminutive visitor, the shaman returned the crooked smile in kind. "Well, if I told you what I saw, you wouldn't believe me." *Or maybe you would.* But Father Raes strongly disapproved of her association with the *pitukupf*. He had told her so on several occasions.

"Try me."

To Daisy, a half-truth was quite as good as the whole thing. "While you was talking, I had this vision. It was very strange." She squinted up at a pale turquoise heaven. "There was something like little specks of fire—and they was falling down from the sky like—" She wriggled her fingers to illustrate the poetry of motion. "Like . . . like . . ." The aged woman seemed unable to find the word.

The kindly priest tried to help. "You saw something falling—like rain?"

She shook her head. "It was like . . . mañana."

He did not respond to this nonsensical statement. *Poor old soul must still be half-asleep.*

Daisy Perika waved her hand impatiently. "You know—that food that fell from heaven."

The Jesuit scholar smiled. "I believe you mean manna."

She nodded. "That's what I said—that stuff God fed to Moses. And them Philippines."

"Philistines," he said automatically.

She stared at the priest as if he'd lost his mind. "So you're sayin' it was the *Philistines* that Moses led outta slavery in Egypt?"

"Well, of course not. I was merely—"

The Ute elder cackled a raspy laugh. Right in his face.

It was hardly the first time Father Raes had been taken in by the sly old creature. This troublesome woman delighted in teasing him. But he could play the game as well. "How fascinating that you've had this revelation. And such a remarkable coincidence." The cleric clasped his hands and raised his gaze to the heavens. "On this very morning, I also had a strange vision."

Daisy's dark eyes were still sparkling with the flame of her small victory.

Father Raes wondered what the vision should be. "During my sermon, I noticed that you were talking. Though at first, I could not see with whom you were conversing." This much was true enough. "And then— for just a moment—I thought I saw someone sitting beside you." He was about to suggest that it must have been her guardian angel when he noticed an expression of alarm pass over Daisy's face. The priest—who suspected that the elder still occasionally talked to the dwarf—seized the opportunity. "Someone small it was—a most peculiar-looking little creature." His brow furrowed in feigned puzzlement. "I only saw it for a moment, and then—whatever it was—it was gone." He flicked his fingers. "Poof!" Father Raes smiled. "Now what do you think of that?"

Daisy Perika met the priest's penetrating gaze with the most brazen expression she could muster. "I think it must be something you ate." But her old legs were trembling as she hurried away.

For once, the long-suffering priest had the last laugh.